THE FIRES OF PASSION

The door of the private apartment closed behind the landlord of the inn, and at last Eugénia and André were alone. Eugénie found that she was trembling, so conscious was she of his nearness and his maleness.

"Eugénie!" André's voice was trembling with desire. "I love you and I need you. Eugénie, my darling, I want you so much!"

"Oh, André." She was blushing, but her eyes shone like a thousand stars.

"I won't force you, you know that. I believe, though, that you feel as I do. I promise I shall be gentle, my darling," he said, slipping an arm around her shoulders and drawing her close to him.

For a fleeting instant, Eugénie's conscience told her that it was wrong to giver herself without marriage, but, overwhelmed by her love and desire, she whispered, "My darling, I love you so very much! When there is love like ours, nothing can be wrong."

Every nerve in her body tingled at the magic touch of his hands. He buried his face in her breast, then slowly unbuttoned her dress. At last she stood before him, her beautiful body glowing in the firelight. They clung together, caressing each other passionately. Their desire became an all-consuming flame in which the last vestige of Eugénie's fear was burned away. . . .

AUTHOR'S NOTE: This is a work of fiction, and any resemblance to persons living or dead is purely coincidental, other than references to actual historical figures.

I have taken some liberties in Part 3. Parramatta was known as Rose Hill until June 2, 1791. The Hawkesbury River was named by Governor Arthur Phillip on June 28, 1789. There were few settlers outside of Sydney until around 1794. Other than the above, I have attempted to depict the colony as accurately as possible.

DARK DESTINY

Alexandra Lang-Carlin

LEISURE BOOKS NEW YORK CITY

I dedicate this book to the memory of my grandmother Sarah J. Costello, with all my love.

I wish to thank Toby Levin for her warm friendship and encouragement, and Gail and Betty for theirs.

I also thank my husband and children for putting up with me throughout the writing of this book.

A LEISURE BOOK

Published by

Dorchester Publishing Co., Inc.
6 East 39th Street
New York, NY 10016

Copyright © 1984 by Alexandra Lang-Carlin

Printed in the United States of America

Prologue

I gaze in the mirror and I see a rather plain, intelligent looking girl whose only outstanding feature, I suppose, are deep blue eyes, which I have been told I inherited from my Great-Grandmother Eugénie. My name is Victoria Eugénie Dewhurst, the only daughter and youngest child of Colin and Margaret Dewhurst. My dear papa comes from a long line of stiff-upper-lip, heroic, military Dewhursts and my four brothers are obviously following in our ancestors' gallant tradition. Oh, I am so sick of the emphasis they put on war and heroics! How can any war be glorious? Our home is a museum for trophies that one or the other oh so gallant Dewhurst has brought triumphantly home. I hate them all. Where is humanity, love and feeling? All these souvenirs mean to me is that people died on some cold, grey day, on some nameless battlefield, alone and uncared for.

I have tried to communicate my feelings to my family but my Aunt Regina Dewhurst constantly exclaims in exasperation, I really don't know who you take after, Victoria! Indeed, you are like no one in the family I can remember.'' Well, to be honest I don't know either. Even my mother, who of course is not a Dewhurst by birth, seems to have become completely one of them . . .

I have always detested Sundays. The quiet and the dreariness irritate me so. This particular Sunday was no exception, even though were were visiting my Grand-mère Paulette at her home in Sussex. My grandmère is really quite marvellous and wonderfully full of life; that is the French half of her nature, I suppose. However, on Sundays even she becomes very, very British.

It was a particularly dreary Sunday, chilly and depressing. November is such a gloomy month, I've always thought. When we came home from church we ate an early dinner after which, as usual, everyone retired to their beds or favorite chairs and either read the various newspapers or napped. And as usual, I thought I should go quietly mad. Instead I wandered around the old house and my footsteps led me to the attic, although I knew the door would be locked. Surprisingly I found the door ajar, and feeling very much like an interloper, I tiptoed in. It was a veritable treasure-trove of old pictures, broken toys, discarded furniture and ancient, weather-beaten trunks.

Having nothing better to do, I went through the old trunks, discovering wonderful old-fashioned clothes and old books. In one trunk I found a boomerang, of all things, and the most beautiful white lace dress which was covered in tiny pearls. I couldn't resist trying it on. Amazingly it fitted quite well, though the waist was a little tight. I felt like a princess as I paraded in front of the tall cracked mirror that stood in one corner of the attic. At last, I reluctantly removed it and was about to place it back in the trunk when I spotted four leather-bound diaries tucked away in one of the trays of the trunk. Feeling rather daring and at the same time quite guilty, I picked them up, closed the trunk and hurried away to my room.

The discovery of my Great-Grandmother's precious

diaries was the turning point of my life. From them I got the inspiration to write this book. I read and re-read those intimate thoughts and secrets until I felt I knew her better than I knew myself. I pestered my grandmère to tell me all she remembered about my Great-Grandmother Eugénie, and willingly she complied. I listened enraptured and she seemed so happy that I should want to hear about her wonderful, exciting mother and her great love. (I didn't tell her I had borrowed the diaries because I doubt if she would have approved of my reading them.)

When my family returned to London, I spent the next six months beseeching my Great-Aunt Marie for her memories. I wrote to Australia (New South Wales) and begged by Great-Uncle David McCallum for his memories, and to France where my Great-Aunt Joséphine, now ninety-five years old, resides. When I had gathered all the memories I could, I began this book.

No longer were my Sundays dreary, for I spent them reliving my Great-Grandmother's life. I have attempted to follow the paths that my Great-Grandmother Eugénie took through life. In Part One and Part Two, I used a great deal of my own imagination—based on facts, of course—but Part Three was much easier, since it was then that my great-grandmother first began keeping a diary. The first one was given to her by the man my grandmère loved and respected like a father, though he was not related to her. Obviously he was a wonderful man, adored by my grandmère and my great-aunt Marie. I wish I had known all her friends. I wish I had known her and my great-grandfather, for I truly feel they would have understood me very well . . .

Part One

FRANCE

It was a time of great unrest. France was like a mighty volcano ready to erupt after endless suffering and injustice. After centuries of being ground under by the brilliantly bejewelled heels of the aristocracy, the peasants were coming to the end of their endurance. Their blood had been drained, drop by precious drop, until they were no more than walking corpses. Louis XVI and his Austrian Queen, Marie Antoinette, were on the throne of France, oblivious to the fact that the wild and untamed seeds of revolution were already sown and that the angel of doom and the grim reaper, Madame la Guillotine, were biding their time.

The elusive moon saw all the suffering and the gaiety, the immorality and the goodness that embraced France on this spring night of 1785. Inquisitively it continued on its way and cheekily peeked through an upstairs window of a cottage not far from the little village of Poissy. This great peeping Tom looked in and Luisa Fabré, lying restless beside her husband Antoine, gazed back. Tired of tossing and turning, she arose quietly and tiptoed to the window where she perched herself on the sill. It was a glorious night. The stars filled the sky and the wonderful moon was inexpressibly brilliant and dazzling.

Luisa sat on the window sill, a beautiful tall, slim silhouette. Her smooth olive skin proclaimed her Italian origin. Her dark hair cascaded down her back like a shimmering cloak of silk. She looked fondly at her beloved Antoine who was snoring peacefully and she smiled as she noticed how the moonlight lit up the few remaining strands of hair which lay upon his shiny bald dome.

After about twenty minutes, she went downstairs to the kitchen and made herself some warm milk. She was sitting at the table sipping it when a little figure appeared in the doorway.

"Eugénie! Whatever are you doing up?"

"I woke up, Maman. I was very thirsty."

Luisa smiled. "Would you like some warm milk?"

Eugénie nodded sleepily. Luisa poured her daughter a small cupful and Eugénie sat on her knee contentedly.

"Why were you up, Maman?"

"I couldn't sleep darling. My mind was restless."

"What were you thinking of? Do tell me."

Luisa told her daughter then about her own childhood in the beautiful city of Florence and of her wonderful mother and brilliant father, Francesca and Carlo Bartoli. She told Eugénie that her mother belonged to the great de Medici family but when she married Carlo Bartoli, a mere physician in their eyes, they had shunned her.

"That wasn't very nice of them, Maman. Was Grandmère very sad?"

"I'm sure it caused her some heartache, darling, but she loved my father so much it didn't matter. They were very much in love and very happy."

Luisa told her daughter how she had been tutored in her own language, German, English, French and a little

Russian. She told her about the dancing lessons and the music and art lessons and about the wonderful world of the stars.

"I don't think I'd like to have to learn quite so much."

Luisa laughed. "Darling, I loved every minute of it!" She was quiet for a moment thinking about her mother's death, and Eugénie felt her sorrow.

"Maman, why are you so sad?"

"I was thinking about my mother. She died when I was fifteen and your grandfather was never quite able to get over her death. His grief helped me because I knew he needed me more than ever and I spent my days with him, trying to fill the void. I even began to take an interest in medicine and when he would permit me I accompanied him on his visits to the sick. But Eugénie, love, my efforts were in vain. My poor father's spirit had been shattered when my mother died and it simply could not be healed. Three years later, my darling, death knocked on our door and this time it was my father who answered the call."

"Oh, Maman, if anything happened to you or Papa I shouldn't want to live. I'd die! I would."

"Darling, don't worry. Your Papa and I are very strong. We wouldn't leave you."

"Promise?"

"Promise. Now are you ready for bed?"

"Please tell me more, Maman. What happened to you then?"

"There wasn't much money left after father died and I refused help from my mother's family. I was too proud, I suppose. At any rate, I sought help from an old friend and obtained the position of governess to the Comte de Montalembert's two daughters. They returned to France just six months after I joined them, but I didn't mind. Italy held too many painful memories for me.

"The years that followed were exciting ones. The French nobility certainly know how to enjoy life! There were parties and balls constantly. Of course I didn't attend the balls, but the girls and I would peer down through the bannisters and watch. We travelled a great deal to other countries and on weekends we would either go to the Montalembert's country estate or visit that of a friend. Well, darling, as you very well know, one weekend when we were here at the Marquis de Varney's estate I was horseback riding with the girls and my horse bolted. Your father, who was head groom then, saved me and I suppose I fell in love with him right then and there. The Comte wasn't too pleased and called me stupid. He was only thinking of me, though. But I didn't care what he said. I loved your father with all my heart. I loved him then, as I do now, for his strength, his goodness, his gentle nature and his hearty laughter. I'm very proud of him, darling. He has been a wonderful husband to me and a marvellous father to you three girls."

Luisa looked at her daughter and laughed. "But you are a little rogue, Eugénie! You have heard this story at least a dozen times. You'll listen to anything that will allow you to stay up later. But enough is enough. Come up to bed now."

Luisa carried Eugénie up the stairs and tucked her into bed. She worried about this second child of hers. Eugénie was given to such extreme moods. She should have been a boy by rights. Luisa sighed. The child wanted too much from life.

She brushed a strand of hair from her eldest child's eyes. Marie was so steady. At fourteen she was as

14

dependable as a woman of twenty. She had a sunny disposition and level head like her father and was quite round like him in shape as well. Marie would do very well in life, Luisa thought. She would settle down and make some lucky young man an excellent wife.

Then she turned to her baby, Joséphine, lying peacefully in her crib with her fingers in her mouth. Little Joséphine, so soft and cuddly, was spoiled by all the family.

Luisa looked at each of them again and smiled contentedly. Then murmuring gently, "Sleep well, my darlings. Sleep well," she returned to the warmth of her own bed where she couldn't resist giving Antoine's bald head a final goodnight kiss.

The tantalizing aroma of ham and eggs and fresh baked bread wafted upstairs, beckoning three sleepyheads to get up and face the glorious spring morning. Sure enough, it wasn't very long before Luisa heard their cheery voices.

"Maman, why didn't you wake me? You knew I wanted to go with Papa to see the new foal this morning!"

"My goodness, Eugénie, you know Papa leaves much too early for you. When you finish breakfast and your chores you may go. Now please eat."

"But, Maman. . ."

"Eugénie, no more chit-chat! I told you you may go to the stables after you eat and finish your chores."

The Fabrés were a happy family and one only had to look at them to know it. They had a pleasant home on the de Varney estate, plenty to eat, and Antoine, as caretaker of the de Varney estates, was well respected. Luisa was beloved by all the villagers. They had no doctor and because of her knowledge of medicine, she was

15

the nearest thing to one. She did what she could, but it broke her heart when her skill proved to be hopelessly inadequate and she longed for the benefit of a real doctor for the people of Poissy. Eugénie loved to go with her mother on her "sick visits." She had a knack for soothing the poor sick souls and comforting the family. However, Luisa shielded Eugénie from the trauma of witnessing a death or someone in the throes of excruciating agony. She felt that her child was far too young for such heartrending experiences.

Though busy with her home, Luisa found time to pass on her learning to her children. She had taught them to read at an early age and both Marie and Eugénie could write beautifully. She was teaching her girls Italian, English, history, geography and much to Marie's dread, mathematics. Poor Marie, try though she would, could not grasp the mysterious science of numbers.

The girls also had their share of housework to do, even little Joséphine, whose special job was to feed the chickens and collect the eggs. Marie loved housework but Eugénie hated anything to do with it. Luisa despaired that Eugénie would ever be able to darn a stocking without having lumps in it. Such was their life, busy and happy. At that time not a hint clouded their days of the horrors that would follow.

Leaving the clatter of dishes and the excited chatter of her daughters, Luisa walked outside and sat down on the bench in front of the house. She beamed with pleasure at her garden which was a rainbow of color. The grass was soft beneath her feet and smelled so sweet. The sunshine sprayed gold on the leaves of the vines that climbed up the walls to the roof. It seemed to Luisa that there was an extraordinary sense of vitality and joy that day that made one very much aware of the glory of almighty God.

Eugénie broke into her reverie by rushing from the house and quickly kissing her mother.

"Don't dilly-dally, darling. Come straight home when you have seen the foal."

"Oui, Mama."

Eugénie ran but when she had gone a little way she turned and waved to her mother.

"How lovely she is," thought Eugénie.

It was a scene that was to stay in her memory forever, a memory that would lighten many a dark day in her life to come.

Antoine was giving instructions to the stable boys about the care of the new foal when he heard his daughter shouting, "Papa! Papa! Where is the little foal? *Montrez moi!* Show him to me quickly! Please Papa, I can hardly wait!"

Father and daughter smiled at each other tenderly. Antoine held out his arms and she raced toward him. He hoisted her up on to his shoulders. The men chuckled with pleasure at the sight of the rather portly man with his round, cheerful face, twinkling blue eyes and shiny bald head and the pretty little girl, with her long chestnut braids flying in the breeze, a little girl with twinkling blue eyes just like her father's.

"Make way, men, my little dove is very impatient this morning!" Antoine always called her his little dove, except on the rare occasions when he was really angry with her which, thankfully, was not often. He carried her into the stables and set her down outside the stall where Victoire, the foal's mother, cast an anxious look in their direction.

"Easy now, Victoire, we are only admiring your son," Antoine soothed.

Eugénie's eyes had grown wide in awe at the miracle

before her. The little black foal with the white stripe on his forehead was bravely trying to walk gracefully on his spindly legs. Her eyes glowed.

"Oh, Papa, he is beautiful, *n'est-ce-pas?*"

"I agree, my lamb, he's the best looking foal we have had around here in years. Now, little *colombe,* off you go. Tell your mother I shall be home at noon."

"Oui, Papa." She kissed him and clung to him for a moment.

But as soon as she was out of sight of the stables she took off her shoes and socks and ran blithely into the woods. The sunshine beamed down through the trees and the grass felt soft beneath her bare feet. This was her magic kingdom. Here in these woods she could be anything she wished—a beautiful princess or a brave knight. Here she could forget all about the nasty humdrum things of life such as baking, laundry, housecleaning and, worst of all, mending! In these woods all alone she could dream beautiful dreams.

She came to her favorite stream and, sitting down on the sweet smelling grass with her dress pulled up around her thighs, she dangled her brown legs in the clear water. At last, contented, she lay back on the ground and watched the small soft clouds dancing in the blue sky above. Then, lulled by the symphony of nature and the slow movement of the clouds, she soon fell fast asleep.

Chapter 2

While Eugénie was sleeping and dreaming, Catherine and Phillipe, the Marquise and Marquis de Varney, were in the morning room eagerly waiting for their son to appear. It was André's fourteenth birthday and the tables were piled high with brightly wrapped gifts hidden under a damaske cloth.

"Philippe, you are quite sure that he is capable of handling a horse so big?" asked the Marquise anxiously.

"Hush, darling. He might hear you." Then, seeing the worried look in his wife's eyes the Marquis added, "Don't worry Catherine. He's a strong lad and it's time he had a man-sized horse." He put his finger to his lips. "I hear him coming. Let's pretend we have forgotten all about his birthday."

André rushed into the room expectantly.

"Bonjour, Maman. Bonjour, Papa!"

"Good morning, my son, and I may add, is that any way to enter a room?" The Marquis tried very hard to stifle a smile at the sight of his son's disconcerted face.

"Sorry Papa, Maman. It's only that I'm so excited." He hesitated a moment. "Don't you know what day this is?"

"Why yes, darling. It's Saturday, I believe."

André's face was the picture of gloom. He looked at them accusingly. "You forgot! It's my birthday and you forgot."

Catherine de Varney couldn't bear to see the hurt in his face any longer. She rushed to her son and enveloped him in a warm embrace. "Oh, my precious! Of course we haven't forgotten! Happy birthday, my darling. Look around you, André. You have so many presents we could hardly find room for them." As she spoke, she pulled the cloth away.

It was exciting for the de Varneys to watch their son opening gifts and exclaiming over each—but the best was yet to come. When the last package had been opened and admired, Philippe de Varney spoke to his child with a twinkle in his eyes.

"André, Jean-Paul has been waiting for you outside for quite a long time. I'm afraid I quite forgot about him. The poor lad must be tired of waiting."

Jean-Paul was André's special groom. He was standing at the bottom of the steps with his cap in one hand and holding the reins of a beautiful mare in the other. André exclaimed, "Jean-Paul, she is gorgeous!"

"She is yours my son, with all our love."

André turned to his parents and his smile was radiant. He hugged them and then jumped up into the saddle.

"She is magnificent! I shall name her Valiant."

The mare was indeed magnificent, sixteen hands high and every inch a thoroughbred.

"May I ride her now, Papa?" André pleaded.

Catherine protested, "Darling, you haven't even eaten breakfast yet!"

Phillipe de Varney looked at his son and winked. Then he turned to his wife. "Let him go. I'm afraid he is far too excited to eat. The food would stick in his throat."

Jean-Paul mounted his own horse in order to accompany André but the lad protested. "Papa, I must go alone today. I'm a man now and a man does not need a nursemaid!"

His father hesitated for an instant then cautioned the lad, "Go, young man, but stay on our estate."

André nodded and they watched him until he had ridden out of sight.

Young de Varney was deleriously happy. It was thrilling to be free, to wander wherever he chose without the company of Jean-Paul. Oh, he liked Jean-Paul well enough but . . . His active imagination took full rein the further away from the chateau he rode. He was no longer André de Varney, but a gallant knight on his way to slay a dragon and rescue a beautiful princess. So completely absorbed was he in his daydreams that he failed to realize that he was entering the woods. Suddenly he felt a stabbing pain as a branch whipped across his face and he was falling; falling into a great velvet darkness.

Eugénie was abruptly awakened by a terrible cry. She sat up, her eyes wide open in fright. She was frozen with fear. Then she heard a groan and a horse whinnying. Her first instinct was to run for her life but the thought that someone might be in need of help forced her to stay. Cautiously she walked in the direction she thought the sounds had come from, and found a horse standing, reins dragging, nuzzling the motionless figure of the most beautiful boy she had ever seen. His eyes were closed and he lay so very still. Her heart thumped. What if he were dead! She was too frightened to find out. Instead she climbed into the saddle and while speaking softly to the mare and gently stroking her neck, she headed for home and help.

The Fabrés were sitting down to lunch and Luisa was very angry. "I told that girl to come straight home!" She glared at Antoine.

"I sent her home hours ago, dear. I can't imagine where she has gone."

"It's all your fault, Antoine Fabré. If you didn't spoil her so . . ."

She was interrupted by the sound of galloping hooves.

"What on earth!" she cried.

Marie ran to the window.

"It's Eugénie, Papa!"

Antoine bounded to the door in one long stride.

"Papa, come quickly! A boy is hurt in the woods. I'm so afraid he's dead." Antoine recognized the mare and immediately knew that the boy must be from the de Varney estate. He mounted his own horse and followed Eugénie back towards the woods and André. When he saw the boy's face, his own turned ashen. *"Mon Dieu!* Tis young Monsieur André!"

He examined the boy and realized that he was not too badly hurt. There were no bones broken but there was a nasty bump on his head. Young André was a good-looking boy, Antoine thought. He had the de Varney nose but he looked more like his mother with his fair skin, golden hair and long, thick lashes.

"Will he die, Papa?" Eugénie asked in a whisper.

"No, little one. But we must get him home to your mother. She'll take care of him."

Tenderly he lifted the boy up on to his saddle and held him there as he climbed up behind. When they reached the house, Luisa and Marie were waiting for them. Antoine laid the boy on the sofa and Marie covered him with a blanket. Luisa bathed his forehead and moistened his lips with some wine and André soon regained consciousness, but his head hurt so terribly that he fell back into a faint again. When he opened his eyes again, he saw the sweetest face before him. Her eyes were closed and her hair, the color of a ripe chestnut, was framing the pale face. She was praying.

"Oh, dear God, have compassion! Don't let him die. Please, I beg you, don't let him die. He is so beautiful!"

Suddenly Eugénie became aware of André's earnest gaze. Their eyes met and for a moment they were alone in the whole world.

Antoine rode to the chateau when he saw that André had regained his senses. He assured the de Varneys that their son was not too badly hurt. Nevertheless the Marquis called for his carriage and headed for the Fabrés cottage. André was sleeping when the two men arrived. Phillipe de Varney looked at his son anxiously and lovingly then turned to Luisa.

"Madame Fabré, how can I ever thank you?"

"Monseigneur, *c'est tres bien*. Your son is a strong lad. He's had a bad fall but rest will take care of that. By tomorrow he will be as good as new. It was our daughter Eugénie who found him and rode for help."

The Marquis looked at the long, flushed faces of the three girls who were staring in awe at his resplendent figure. They thought his dark green velvet coat and breeches, with the pale green waistcoat and his snowy white shirt and cravat were magnificent. But never in their wildest dreams had they ever imagined anything as gorgeous as his shoes which were studded with what looked like emeralds.

"Which one of you is Eugénie?" asked the Marquis.

"It is I, m'Lord." Eugénie stepped forward shyly.

"Young lady, I shall send my carriage for you tomorrow. The Marquise, I am sure, would like to thank you in person for saving our son's life."

Before she could reply, he made a motion with his hand and Antoine called the two footmen who had accompanied the carriage. They carried the sleeping André to the carriage and the Marquis de Varney bade the Fabrés adieu.

That night Eugénie could not sleep. She tossed and turned, but remained wide awake. Her mother had laundered her best dress and she couldn't take her eyes off it as it lay across her chair. She was wildly excited and impatiently waited for night to pass. She strained her eyes, watching for the first streaks of dawn. At last the sun arose and she jumped out of bed, dressed with great care in the white muslin dress and adjusted the pink satin sash around her tiny waist. She brushed her hair until it shone and hung down her back in rippling waves. Then she rushed downstairs and paced up and down the kitchen all morning, eating nothing and driving everyone mad with her constant sighs.

"Perhaps no one will come for me. The Marquis must have forgotten," she moaned.

"It's early yet, child. Besides, no time was specified."

"Mama, I shall just *die* if they have forgotten!"

Scarcely had the words left her lips when the carriage arrived and André came running to the door with a huge basket of sweets and pastries which he presented to Luisa.

"For you, Madame Fabré. Thank you for your kindness. Mademoiselle Eugénie, are you ready?"

Eugénie started to shout, "I've been ready for *hours!*" and rushed out the door. However, she noticed her mother's stern eyes fixed upon her so she proceeded in a more dignified manner and allowed André to assist her into the carriage as though this were an everyday occurrence.

The drive from the Fabrés' cottage to the chateau was

at least three miles. The driveway was lined with poplar trees and divided into two curving arcs in front of the chateau, which stood proud and impressive admist its enchanting surroundings of lush green lawn and majestic trees.

Eugénie's heart fluttered as she looked up at the immense chateau. Her mother had often described it to her and yet she still wasn't prepared for the magnificent reality. They stepped down from the carriage and climbed the twenty marble steps to the front door. She stared at the massive carved oak portal with the de Varney coat of arms emblazoned above it in gold and blue. It seemed to overpower her.

They hadn't even rung the bell when, like magic, the door was opened by two footmen in powdered wigs and dressed in the pale blue and gold livery of the de Varneys. When they entered the great hall, Eugénie's eyes were drawn like a magnet to the splendid staircase covered in deep blue velvet carpet with gold fleur-de-lis embroidered on it.

"This place is unbelievable, Monsieur André," she whispered in awe.

André was amused at Eugénie's look of rapture. She stood transfixed, her eyes taking in the beauty of the scene depicted on the walls and ceiling of the great hall and stairway.

"Mademoiselle, come," he said gently at last. "My parents are waiting."

He led her into the drawing room and Eugénie's feet sank into the soft pile of the pink and gold Persian carpet. She gasped at the beauty of the gracefully carved furniture which was gilded with gold-leaf and whose seats and backs were covered with rose brocade. A great black marble fireplace dominated the end of the room, above which a portrait of the family captured the eye of all who entered.

André's parents sat close to the fireplace. The Marquise was a plump woman of thirty-five, with a rather pouting mouth. Her bosom threatened to overflow her low-necked gown. However, her grey eyes held a gentle expression. The Marquis, a man of fifty, was indeed a distinguished-looking personage, more than six feet tall. His skin was swarthy, his eyes almost black and his nose slightly arched. On the whole he had rather an austere face and yet, in spite of this, Eugénie sensed a radiant charm which put her very much at ease. She curtsied and the Marquise beckoned her to sit beside her, then took Eugénie's hand. "My dear child, thank you for saving my son's life."

"Madame, I did nothing."

The Marquise de Varney smiled. "You are a dear, sweet little thing."

"Would you like some chocolate and cake, Mademoiselle Eugénie?" asked the Marquis.

"Thank you, m'Lord. I truly would," Eugénie said primly.

The Marquis rang a bell and almost immediately a servant entered bearing a tray. The chocolate and cake were served on gold-rimmed dishes. Eugénie thought she had never tasted anything so delicious.

After they had eaten the Marquis turned to her. "Mademoiselle, I have spoken to your father and he has agreed to allow you to come here and play with my son every day during our stay in Poissy. That is, of course, if you are willing."

Eugénie forgot her ladylike poise and clapped her hands. "Oh, Monseigneur, I would be so happy!"

Everyone laughed at her youthful exuberance and the Marquis told the two young people to run along and have fun.

As soon as the drawing-room doors had closed behind them Eugénie seized André's hand. "André, could we please just wander around this marvellous, exquisite place?" she pleaded.

"I'd much rather go to the woods. Besides, the chateau isn't very interesting. Why, it's nothing compared to our home in Paris."

But Eugénie insisted and André reluctantly gave in.

They spent the remainder of the day exploring the house. To Eugénie, each room seemed more beautiful than the one before. All the ceilings were high and adorned with marvellous frescoes—hunting scenes, religious scenes of The Last Judgment, Adam and Eve in the garden of Eden, Moses and the Red Sea, and the walls were covered with battle scenes where ancient de Varneys had distinguished themselves and covered themselves with glory. The floors of the rooms were covered with Oriental carpets, and in the resplendent ballroom the most exquisite of Carrara marble seemed to stretch to infinity. She decided that perhaps the ballroom was her favorite room of all. The ceiling was painted with marvellous forest scene. Trees, flowers, deer, rabbits, streams and the most beautiful birds covered every inch of the immense dome. The walls were painted pale green and were heavily ornamented with gold-framed mirrors. A platform of marble encircled by a gold railing separated the musicians from the dancers. The chairs were delicate and fine, with exquisite giltwork showing through the pale green paint, and the seats and backs were covered with green and gold striped silk. Overhead hung twelve splendid chandeliers. Their countless crystal droplets caught the sunlight illuminating the room with their brilliance. Eugénie closed her eyes and heard wondrous music. She could see the chandeliers lit and sparkling on the jewels and fine clothes of the lords and ladies dancing beneath them.

"Eugénie! What's the matter with you. Are you dreaming?" fussed André.

"Yes—it was such a lovely dream. But I don't think a mere boy would understand."

André led her through the peaceful chapel where candles cast a mystical glow on the mosaics and stained glass windows. He was getting tired of the tour.

"Haven't you seen enough? How about something to eat? All this trudging around has made me hungry."

"Oh, André, the kitchen! I do so want to see that."

André sighed but took her hand and led her to the basement. Eugénie couldn't quite believe her eyes. Dozens of rooms had been set aside just for the preparation of food!

"All these rooms just to cook a meal! Why, André, my mother just has one small kitchen with a fireplace, a table and some chairs. It's incredible!" Incredible it was. There was a great big kitchen, a larder, a pantry, a wine cellar, a smaller kitchen, a buttery, a scullery, a kitchen for the preparation of fish, and a kitchen for the preparation of pastry and confectionery. Her eyes grew wide in wonder, and their stomachs grew even wider as they sampled goodies from all the delectable dishes put before them by the proud chefs.

"I think I have died and gone to heaven," Eugénie sighed.

André laughed. "Have some more, Eugénie."

They were sampling a cream-filled pastry when a footman came in search of them.

"Master André, it is time for the young lady to go home. Jean-Paul is waiting to escort her."

Reluctantly they said goodbye.

"Shall I see you tomorrow, André?" Eugénie asked wistfully.

"Yes, indeed. Why don't you meet me in the woods where you found me yesterday? I'll bring a picnic lunch."

"Oh, André, I can hardly wait! I'm so happy, so very happy!"

Chapter 3 ————————————

The golden summer sunshine beamed through the open window of the hayloft. It shone on Eugénie and André as they lay on their backs on the sweet smelling hay.

"André, just think! We have three whole months together. Oh, what fun we shall have! I've got so much to show you."

"Eugénie, I'm really glad we met last Spring. I just hated to come to Poissy before that. I was so terribly bored. Sometimes my good friend Jean-Emile was allowed to come with me but not very often and then he wasn't allowed to stay very long. You'll probably meet him this summer. He's great fun."

Eugénie felt a pang of jealousy but she said nothing. André continued jabbering about Jean-Emile and then suddenly asked, "Eugénie, what do you want to do when you grow up?"

Without a moment's hesitation she answered, "I want to be a great lady and see the world. I want to sail on a big ship and discover new lands." André doubled up laughing. He laughed so much the tears rolled down his cheeks. Eugénie, quite indignant, threw a big bundle of hay at him. "I don't think it's so funny!"

"Girls can't do things like that. You'll have to get

married and have babies."

"Never! I shall do what I want. Just wait and see."

In the days and months that followed they rode together in the woods, watched the animals and fished. Eugénie opened up a whole new world for André. Sometimes they wandered around the beautiful gardens of the Chateau or filled their stomachs with fruit from the abundant trees in the orchard. She loved to play around the fountain in the rose garden. The base of the fountain was delicately sculptured with statues of Pan and Orpheus. Rising from the center was a statue of Diana, Goddess of the Chase.

"Do you think I shall be as beautiful as that when I am a woman?" she asked one day.

"I doubt it," André said wickedly, and then the chase began, ending in a tussle until, overcome with laughter, they were too weak to wrestle anymore.

She had names for all the animals and a feeling of oneness with nature. She could imitate bird calls and animal cries. All this she shared with André. He had never known such freedom before. They were well suited—two funloving young people. Mischief sparkled in their beautiful eyes, the grey pair and the deep blue. André was very spoiled and Eugénie gave into him as much as his parents did.

Of course, Eugénie still had her chores to do and André had to practice fencing every afternoon for two hours with Monsieur Domet. Even at the age of fourteen he as on the way to being an expert swordsman. In fact, André was an excellent athlete and a superb horseman. Eugénie loved to watch his fencing lessons. She would sit quietly in a corner, never taking her eyes from André, those eyes which shone with devotion. However, one day as she sat watching, she suddenly got an idea and interrupted the lesson.

"I wish to learn to fence. Monsieur Domet, will you please teach me?"

"Mademoiselle!" Monsieur Domet's face was a study of shock.

André simply laughed. "What will you say next? You really are the most amusing girl I've ever met, Eugénie Fabré!"

"Don't laugh at me. I'm serious."

"Eugénie, ma chère, it's simply not the thing for a girl to fence," André explained patiently.

"Zut!" She stamped her foot in anger. "Are you afraid that I shall be better than you?"

That did it. André looked at Monsieur Domet, who simply shrugged his shoulders in resignation. "Mademoiselle, you cannot fence in those clothes. It would be impossible," he told her.

"*Je comprends*. André will find something for me to wear, won't you André?"

"If you insist. But I really don't want to do this, Eugénie."

She made a face at him and made him laugh until he finally gave in and beckoned her to follow him.

A short while later they returned. André had provided her with a fine silk shirt and velvet breeches. Poor Monsieur Domet wiped his brow. "Monsieur André, what will the Marquis say?" he protested.

"The Marquis will not know, I assure you."

In the days that followed, Eugénie threw herself wholeheartedly into learning everything Monsieur Domet taught her. After a time even André and the reluctant Monsieur Domet became so impressed with her skill that they quite forgot about her being a girl and became enthusiastic teachers. Eugénie was beautifully coordinated and since successful fencing demands perfect coordination, she showed more and more promise as the weeks went by. Little did they know that they would have cause to thank Le Bon Dieu for the inspiration that she should learn to fence, but in that year of 1785 not a trouble loomed on their horizon. Life was beautiful and wonderfully exciting.

The years passed quietly and joyfully for the two friends. They were inseparable companions when the de Varney family came to Poissy and when they did not come, Eugénie devoted herself to her studies and continued to perfect her fencing skills in secret. André had given her a sword of her own as a gift on her fourteenth birthday and in the absence of André and Monsieur Domet she attacked every tree and branch. Every shadow in the woods became her adversary.

By the time she was fourteen and a half, the child in Eugénie had almost vanished. Physically she had become a woman. She had grown tall and slender like her mother. Her breasts were full and her chestnut hair cascaded down her back in thick waves. Her nose was straight, her lips full and seductive. Her deep blue eyes, which usually held a merry twinkle, were framed by thick dark lashes. Her forehead showed strength and pride and her heart belonged to André de Varney. She worshipped him and was becoming increasingly saddened by the fact that he was spending more and more time in Paris. When he came to Poissy he was as friendly and gentle as ever, but Eugénie couldn't help noticing that he was drawing away from her. His speech and manners were now more suited to the Court at Versailles than to quiet, carefree Poissy. But he was seventeen and who could blame him if Paris held more attractions? He had a man's feelings and desires now. He was well aware the Eugénie was feeling left out but he told himself that she would just have to get used to his way of life. He was a man now and had no time for children's games.

Exactly one month before Eugénie's fifteenth birthday, much to the joy of the Fabré family, they welcomed M. Fabré's sister Louise and her husband Pierre to their home. The girls loved their Aunt and Uncle very much and would have dearly loved to see more of them, but the Brogards owned a wine shop in Paris and seldom took too much time away from their business.

Eugénie couldn't help noticing that they seemed to be unusually tense and Uncle Pierre kept drawing her father into what seemed to be very serious conversations. However, as soon as one of the girls would approach, their conversation would abruptly cease and Uncle Pierre would once more become the funloving Uncle they loved so much, laughing and teasing them.

In their honor, Luisa prepared a sumptuous dinner and they feasted and laughed and sang until finally the girls became so exhausted that Luisa shooed them upstairs to bed and lovingly tucked them in for the night. Marie and Joséphine were asleep as soon as their heads hit their pillows but Eugénie, in spite of her exhaustion, was strangely restless. She decided to go down to the kitchen and get a cup of milk. She tiptoed downstairs and heard the murmur of voices coming from the parlor. She didn't pay much heed until she heard her Uncle's voice raised in anger.

"Mon Dieu, Antoine, what can I say to get through to you? What can I say to make you wake up to the danger which surrounds you?"

Eugénie stood riveted to the spot where she stood.

"I think you are making too much of this, Pierre. Surely you exaggerate?"

"I tell you Antoine, France is on the verge of a revolution, and a bloody one at that. How much longer do you think the people of France can continue to endure the indignities and torture inflicted upon them by the damned aristos? I tell you the poor of France are tired of being stepped on. You, my dear Antoine—and you too Luisa—feel so safe in your little corner, but I tell you the day is not far off when no one will be safe. The people of France are suffering, I tell you, and the souls of those who died in misery are crying out for vengeance!"

Eugénie could bear to hear no more. She marched into the parlor and confronted them, her face pale and her voice shaking with emotion.

"Stop it! Stop it! I won't believe it. I *can't* believe it. Uncle Pierre, say it's not true!"

Antoine started to say something to soothe his daughter but Pierre stopped him. "It's true, my lamb. Would to God it were not so."

Eugénie appealed to her father. "But Papa, surely the King can do something to help his people?"

Louise Brogard answered for her brother. "Alas, chèrie, the King can do nothing. He is a mere puppet on a throne and a fat one at that."

Eugénie looked to her father for confirmation. He nodded. "I'm afraid your Aunt is right, even I have to admit that. The real rulers of France are the nobles and certain esteemed members of the clergy."

"But we won't have any trouble here in Poissy. Our Marquis is good and kind. He will help and there must be others like him."

"Unfortunately, not enough," Pierre Brogard said bitterly. "Eugénie, my precious, beyond this safe little haven of yours there are millions of people who are groaning, shedding their blood, crying out from hunger and pain. These people are tired of being stepped on. The cry for equality and justice echoes through the streets of Paris and those cries will soon turn into a mighty roar that will sweep throughout the land. God help us all!''

Eugénie's brow furrowed in deep thought and when she spoke it was slowly and with a great gravity. ''Uncle Pierre, how can everyone be equal? Surely that is impossible! Even if everyone started out equal, it would not end up so. The clever and the strong would surely climb to the top and everything would become as before.''

Antoine looked at his daughter with pride and amazement. This child of his had wisdom far beyond her years. Seeing the look of worry on her daughter's face, Luisa took her gently by the hand. ''Come, darling, I'll tuck you into bed again. There is nothing for you to worry about. God will protect us,'' she said.

It was July 14th and Eugénie was full of happy anticipation on this, the eve of her fifteenth birthday. She was happy because she knew that tomorrow André would come to see her. They would meet at their own special place in the woods.

Since Pierre and Louise Brogard's visit, it had become the habit for Antoine, Luisa, Marie and Eugénie to sit up for an hour or so and talk after little Joséphine had gone to bed. The girls looked forward to these evening chats, and tonight was no exception. They were sitting outside in the garden and the night was bright and warm. Eugénie smiled in sheer contentment.

''Isn't it a marvelous evening? France must be the most beautiful country on earth,'' sighed Marie.

Antoine was puffing on his pipe contentedly but at Marie's words he sighed. ''Yes, Marie, France is the most beautiful country on earth but, alas, also the most unhappy.''

Marie looked at her father in disbelief.

"Your sister found out the truth when your Aunt and Uncle came to visit and I suppose it's time we stopped sheltering you,'' Antoine continued.

"What truth, Papa?''

"My poor child, the truth is that in this beautiful country of ours there are a handful of people who think they *are* France. To them, the remainder of its inhabitants are mere nothings. To those privileged beings, the other poor souls in this troubled land are of no worth whatsoever except as chattels to be used or discarded at will. The nobles wallow in luxury while the peasants have to watch their children die from lack of food.''

Marie broke into floods of trears. "Can't something be done? Can't someone make the nobles see what they are doing? Surely they can't possibly know how the poor people are suffering.''

Eugénie broke in. "Stop crying, Marie. Tears won't help. What we need is power to make them see what they are doing to France.''

"Ah, Eugénie, power is a terrible burden and where there is power there are always far too many who will use it for the worst possible motives,'' said Antoine solemnly.

"Papa, couldn't you make the Marquis de Varney see? He could use his influence at Court,'' Marie suggested.

"Marie, even if he would listen I doubt if he could help. It took Pierre a long time to make me see how bad things really are and I think our dear Marquis would laugh at me and think I had gone quite mad.''

Not wishing to burden his daughters with worry beyond their years, he laughed.

"Come on you two, let me see you smile. I don't think things will be half as bad as Uncle Pierre's dire prophecy."

"Are you sure you really mean that, Papa? You aren't just trying to make us feel better?"

"Why, you young scamp, Eugénie Fabré! Don't you trust your old Papa after all these years?"

"Of course I do, Papa, and you aren't old one little bit."

Antoine laughed again. The tension was broken and the worry erased from their young faces. He tapped out his pipe and glanced at Luisa. "It's getting late, darling. If we sit up talking any longer it will be Eugénie's birthday."

"I bet she won't sleep anyway," Marie said mischievously. "She'll be too excited about seeing André tomorrow."

"I couldn't care less," Eugénie said nonchalantly, then said her goodnights quickly and rushed off to bed so she could be alone with her thoughts.

Eugénie was up at the crack of dawn and, seeing that Marie was still fast asleep, she threw her pillow at her and then proceeded to tickle little Joséphine. At last, with much laughter, they dressed and raced down to breakfast. Her family wished her every happiness and gave her their presents. Marie and Joséphine gave her some pretty hair ribbons and Marie grinned when she handed them over. "I know these aren't much, so we decided to do all your chores today as part of our gift."

Eugénie hugged them. "What a marvellous present! And these hair ribbons are just what I needed. Thank you both so much."

Luisa and Antoine gave her a locket on a black velvet ribbon. Luisa clasped it around her neck and Eugénie ran to look at herself in the mirror. "It is beautiful. I *do* love you so!" She was close to tears of happiness and she kissed them tenderly. "Thank you so much, all of you."

She looked anxiously towards the door and Luisa said teasingly, "Yes, precious, you may go. André will be bored waiting for you and that would never do."

Eugénie picked up her skirts and ran. She was filled with vitality and her happiness and eagerness to see André lent wings to her feet. She looked like a beautiful nymph as she raced towards the woods, her hair streaming around her shoulders. The day was gloriously beautiful and she felt delirious with excitement. She was fifteen and she knew she had grown quite pretty in the past six months. André hadn't seen her since Christmas and she was eager for him to see the change in her. But André was nowhere in sight. Where was he, she wondered. He had always been waiting for her on her birthday. It had become a tradition with them. She waited for over an hour and finally set off for the chateau in search of him. Only the servants were there, and they did not expect the de Varneys at all that summer. Sadly she headed for home with a lump in her throat and an ache in her heart that would not go away. She loved him and he didn't seem to care for her at all.

That night when she heard her mother come up to bed she crept to her parents' room. Luisa was kneeling by her bed saying her prayers so Eugénie kicked off her slippers and jumped up on the high feather bed. She sank right down in its comforting softness. Luisa finished her prayers and looked at her daughter's sad face.

"Well, my love, what's on your mind at such a late hour?"

"Maman, I must talk to you now. Say yes."

"Well, darling, what do you want to talk about?"

Eugénie hesitated a moment. "About . . . about André. Maman, he didn't come today. He isn't going to come at all this summer, and I think my heart is broken. Maman, I think I love him."

"Of course you do child. He is your very dear friend."

"No, Maman, I don't love him just as a friend. I love him, I am quite sure, in the way you love Papa."

Luisa's heart was deeply troubled. Why hadn't she seen the possibility of this happening? What an imbecile she had been! Yet, she consoled herself, Eugénie is just a child and at her age all girls are in love with love.

"My precious, I believe you, but you must not allow yourself to love André in this way. We are of different classes and between his class and ours there is a barrier that cannot be crossed. As children your friendship was not objected to but now since you feel you are falling in love with him it is best that you put André out of your mind and your heart at once." Seeing the look of acute sadness in her daughter's eyes she added, "You are young, Eugénie, you will get over him in time and one day you will find a love greater than you ever dreamt possible."

"Thank you for listening, Maman, but you are wrong. I shall find a way to cross that barrier, just wait and see. I'll never love anyone but André. Never!"

She looked so serious that Luisa couldn't help smiling. This daughter of hers was so impulsive and so ardent . . .

"What nonsense you talk, but it is wonderful to have dreams. Now run along to bed. I love you, chérie."

André didn't come back to Poissy until the following Christmas. He didn't even apologize for missing her birthday. All he could talk about was Versailles and Marie Antoinette. Eugénie thought for a fleeting second, that he sounded pompous and was immediately sorry for such disloyalty.

She listened to him in rapture. When he finally stopped to catch his breath, she whispered.

"Oh André, I missed you so much."

"And I missed you too, Eugénie." He didn't really mean those words. He had been having too good a time in Paris to miss her, and if the truth were known, he had only thought of her in fleeting moments. He felt sorry for her and quickly changed the subject.

"I brought you a present. I hope you'll like it. I had it specially made for you in Paris."

Eagerly she opened the package and her eyes sparkled when she saw a deep sapphire blue velvet cloak with an emerald satin lining nestling in the soft paper.

"Oh, André, thank you so much! It is the most exquisite thing I have ever seen!"

He placed the cloak around her shoulders and she looked so lovely that he felt an irresistible urge to hold her. Eugénie noticed the look in his eyes and found herself blushing. Suddenly she was in his arms and his throbbing lips were touching hers. It was like nothing she had ever experienced before. She felt lighter than air and it seemed as if she were floating through space and didn't want to stop. On and on she floated—and then he released her.

"I hate to leave you now but, Eugénie, I must. There are over one hundred guests expected today and I must be at home to greet them. *Chérie—chérie,* you look so enticing!"

Eugénie was breathless and she couldn't quite bring herself to meet his gaze. Her voice trembled as she asked, "Shall I see you soon?"

"But of course. We shall spend lots of time together. Have a merry Christmas. I'll get in touch with you as soon as our guests leave."

She watched him ride away with eyes aglow with love. She touched her lips and felt her body quiver when she thought of his burning kisses. She was sure she looked quite different now. Such feelings just had to change one enormously. But when she went home and looked in the mirror, except for a slight flush and brighter eyes, she was still the same Eugénie Fabré.

But André left without seeing Eugénie, and when he didn't return at Easter, she began to mope. Luisa and Antoine watched her with great concern, and after much deliberation decided that for Eugénie's sake, the girls should pay a visit to their aunt and uncle in Paris. The other reason, though they were reluctant to admit it, was that they were very worried about the growing unrest throughout the country. News had reached them that the peasants were burning chateaux, looting and killing. True, so far it was confined to the more isolated areas of the countryside. They were still not convinced that they had anything to fear in Poissy and it was more because of Eugénie's state of mind that they decided to let their daughters leave. They knew that Louise and Pierre Brogard, though they were ardent proponents of revolution, were devoted to the Fabré girls. Louise worshipped her brother Antoine and would see that no harm came to his children.

On the eve of their departure for Paris, the girls were packing their belongings and little Joséphine was bubbling with excitement when their parents came into the bedroom.

"Oh Maman, Papa, I'm so excited! Imagine me going to Paris!"

Antoine smiled at his youngest daughter. "I know, my little one. You'll have a superb time. But calm down now, for your mother has something wonderful to show you."

The girls looked at their mother. Luisa held a square gold box in her hands and when she opened it they gasped. There on the black velvet lining lay an array of the most exquisite jewels—earrings, necklaces and rings encrusted in rubies, diamonds, sapphires and emeralds. The girls stared at them in utter astonishment. Never had they seen anything so dazzlingly beautiful.

"Maman, where did you get them? They are so gorgeous."

"Most of them belonged to my mother. Some were gifts from the Montalemberts. They are quite valuable and we have put them aside so that each of you will have a dowry. We wanted you to know about them before you leave for Paris. In these troubled times one never knows if . . ." She couldn't continue.

Antoine took up the conversation. "Girls, don't look so worried. We aren't expecting trouble but if it should come we want you to know that you are not destitute. Now come with us." He led them downstairs to the kitchen and showed them how a stone could be removed from the fireplace. Then he placed the box in the aperture and replaced the stone.

"Promise me that you will tell no one of this," he said sternly. "These are trying times and the temptation might be just too much. Tell no one, not even your uncle and aunt." The girls nodded in agreement.

Antoine grinned. "Good girls. We know we can rely on you. Now be off to bed, you'll have an early start in the morning. Old René will be here with the wagon at six o'clock."

The following morning, they awoke to their favorite

smells of ham and eggs and fresh baked bread. Antoine had stayed late to have breakfast with them. Usually he was out on the estate by five o'clock. Marie and Joséphine were chattering excitedly but Eugénie was unusually quiet. When René arrived and they had said their goodbyes, she was overcome with such an ominous sense of foreboding that she ran back to give Luisa and Antoine one last kiss. She clung to them as though she didn't want to ever let them go. As she turned away from her parents and climbed into the wagon, she didn't notice her mother wipe the tears from her eyes and see the sadness in her father's face. Old René took up the reins and thus began Eugénie's journey to sorrow and, sometimes, even despair.

Chapter 4

The wheels of the cart turned steadily, drawing them closer to the city of their dreams. As they neared their destination, the girls grew more excited. Even Eugénie had thrown off her gloom and was filled with eager anticipation. André had talked so much about the wonders of Paris, and their Aunt Louise, when she had visited them in Poissy had spun marvellous tales of that great city for her darling nieces.

Alas, when they entered the gates of Paris they found that things were not as they had imagined they would be. They wept at the sights that met their eyes. Somehow, in spite of what they had learned from Louise and Pierre Brogard and the rumors that had filtered through to them in Poissy, they had not quite believed that conditions could be so bad. They had been told about the miseries many people suffered and the inhumane treatment meted out by the aristocracy, but, as with most people, unless confronted face to face with misery and upheaval, it had no reality for them. When they were told that millions of people were starving and that the threat of famine hung over the land as a result of the terrible hailstorm in July 1788, they had put the thought out of their young minds as being too terrible to be real.

Now they looked at one another as if to say, "How could we not have realized?"

Their sad eyes gazed upon long, narrow, winding streets filled with dirt and garbage, streets where the houses leaned against each other as though their lives depended on it. Poverty was apparent everywhere they looked. It stared from the faces of ragged urchins fighting over a crust of bread and from the emaciated faces of the men and women who stood in lines hoping for a crust of bread from the bakers. Hatred filled those eyes, and dark despair. Beauty and youth were seldom seen in Paris this year of 1789.

On the cart trundled towards St. Jacques, where Louise and Pierre Brogard lived. They were better off than most of the citizens in their district for they owned a wine shop and, though bread was scarce, wine was available for all and the price was comparatively low. In fact, sad to say, there was more drinking going on than eating. The poor people didn't have much choice. The Brogards were ardent revolutionaries, very different from the Fabrés. Their wine shop was the meeting place of the district for the leaders of St. Jacques. There, plans were laid and progress made in other parts of the country was reported on. The Brogards were highly respected and Pierre was considered to be the most intelligent of St. Jacques' revolutionary leaders.

At last the cart pulled up in front of the wine shop and the girls said goodbye to old René. Pierre Brogard was wiping tankards and his thoughts appeared gloomy for he had a terrible frown on his face. But when he looked up and saw the girls, he beamed and let out a bellow of joyful greeting. "Welcome! Welcome to Paris, girls!"

He called out, "Louise, come in here! Our nieces have come to visit us at last."

Louise rushed in and hugged the girls to her expansive bosom. She looked so much like Antoine except for her dark, thick hair, and her eyes shone with love. The Brogards had no children of their own and had always looked upon their dear nieces as their own, especially the little one, Joséphine. But Marie and Eugénie couldn't help noticing that their beloved aunt and uncle seemed more preoccupied and somehow harder since they had seen them last. Still, from what they had just seen on the way, it was small wonder.

"Girls, we'll try very hard to give you a good time, but I only wish you had been able to see Paris even a few years ago. Since last July things have gone from bad to worse."

"Don't worry about us, Uncle Pierre. We are just happy to be here with you. We want to help you both as much as we can," said Marie.

Pierre smiled. "You are good girls. We shall do our best for you."

Life in St. Jacques was not easy. The Fabré girls were happy with their aunt and uncle but life in the district appalled them. Marie and Joséphine had settled in to the daily routine of helping Aunt Louise in the house, but Eugénie couldn't stand it. Finally with a great deal of coaxing she managed to persuade them to let her help in the wine shop. At first they were aghast at the suggestion.

"Whatever would your parents say, Eugénie! They would be furious with us."

"Oh please, Uncle Pierre! They will never know. I have to do something and there just isn't enough for all four of us to do in the house. Besides, I hate housework, and you will be in the shop to keep an eye on me. Please?"

"Well, we can try, I suppose. But if it doesn't work out, back you go to the housework and no arguments."

Eugénie really enjoyed working in the wine shop. She listened in fascination to the conversation of the customers and though some of these patrons were rather free with their curses, she learned to ignore them. It seemed to her that all the most sinister and evil-looking men in Paris must gather here. The tension hung thick around them and throughout Paris there was a strange, eerie calm. Eugénie once again felt threatened by a sense of impending doom. The threat haunted her night and day though she tried desperately to shrug it away. Then one night she had the most horrifying dream. She saw her parents lying bleeding in the mud and she could hear people shouting and jeering at them. They bled so much that the blood blotted out their faces and she woke up screaming. Louise and Pierre rushed in to the girls' room. Eugénie was sitting up in bed, screaming, and Marie and little Joséphine were trying desperately to calm her. Louise took her in her arms and soothed her. "There, there, Eugénie, it was only a bad dream. You are here with us and everything is fine."

She clung to her Aunt, trembling. "It was so real! I'm so scared. I've got to go home. Please take me home. I'm so afraid something terrible is going to happen to Maman and Papa!"

Pierre felt his heart respond to her fear. "Very well, dear. I'll take you home tomorrow. Aunt Louise can take care of the shop."

As they journeyed towards Poissy the following morning both Eugénie and Pierre were silent. Eugénie was filled with dread and Pierre himself was full of anxiety. He knew that the uprisings in the surrounding countryside were becoming more numerous and more violent. He remembered the last time he had talked with

Antoine and his brother-in-law had scoffed at his fears.

"Pierre, the people of Poissy would never turn on the de Varneys. They have too well treated over the years."

Antoine's words echoed in his ears. He had tried to tell him about the outside agitators who could stir up even the most contented communities, but Antoine simply would not believe it. Nevertheless he had agreed to allow the girls to go to Paris if the need arose. The fact that he had kept his word worried Pierre more for if Antoine had realized that there could be trouble, he must have had good reason to believe that even Poissy was not immune to upheaval.

The old horse plodded along. It was almost dark by the time they reached the de Varney estate. When they arrived at the Fabré cottage, lights were burning and everything seemed quiet and serene. Eugénie's legs felt like lead as they walked up to the door and the feeling of dread became stronger and stronger at every approaching step. When the Curé appeared at the door in answer to their knock, Eugénie fainted. Pierre picked her up and carried her into the house.

"The poor child!" Father Renoir exclaimed. "She must have known. I always suspected that child had the second sight."

Pierre had grown very pale. "Father Renoir, what's wrong? Where are Luisa and Antoine?"

Father Renoir looked at him with tears in his old eyes. "My son, they are both dead. I had their bodies brought back here and my faithful Hélène is laying them out in the parlor."

Pierre trembled with emotion. *"Mon Dieu!* How did it happen?"

"A terrible madness took possession of this town early this morning. Some strangers, ruffians they were, had been trying to stir up the people here for several days. They were drunk with wine and the spirit of revolution. I tried to reason with our people but could do nothing. This morning they marched on the chateau in a frenzy, killing the Marquis and Marquise de Varney. They cut off their heads and stuck them on pikes for all to see. They killed those servants who refused to wear the cockade and join the *'canaille'*."

"But my mother and father? Father Renoir, tell me!"

Startled, both men turned to Eugénie, who had regained consciousness and was staring at them in horror.

"My dear, they were very brave. They heard the mob coming and when they met them at the gates they tried to plead with them to turn back. The mob turned on them. All their kindness towards these people was forgotten. The mob, as mobs usually are, were no longer rational people, but a conglomeration of everything evil that man is capable of."

"I want to see them," Eugénie insisted.

Pierre looked at Father Renoir. The good old priest shook his head, but Eugénie pushed past the two men.

"I must see them," she cried. She rushed into the parlor. There on the floor lay two crude coffins. Father Renoir's housekeeper, Hélène, was kneeling by one of them. She tried to stop Eugénie from looking but it was too late. She recoiled in horror. Her parents were unrecognizable. Poor Hélène had done her best to make them more presentable but those butchers had done their worst.

Eugénie screamed, "No! No!" and ran out of the house.

She ran from the horror but it pursued her. She wanted to scream and scream. Her body was consumed with sorrow and agony. She kept on running until she had reached the chateau—or what remained of it. A mist hung over everything in ghostly veils. The trees were forbidding silhouettes. Seeing the chateau a mass of still smoldering ruins shattered her last link with self control. She screamed loud and shrill like a wounded animal, until she sank to the ground exhausted. For hours she lay there thinking about her kind, loving parents, and once again their wise advice echoed in her mind. She remembered the picnics they had and the smell of her mother's bread baking. All these things passed before her mind and her grief was renewed. She gave way to the terrible, heartrending sorrow that wracked her soul.

Then anger took the place of grief and gentle Eugénie became strong and determined. Right there and then she made a vow that she would find André and keep him out of the clutches of the mob. He would be one that would not die at the hand of the fiends who had butchered his parents and her own beloved mother and father. She would find him and keep him safe at all costs. Yes, that would be one precious life those cursed people would not get! When she returned to the cottage Pierre and Father Renoir were amazed at the change that had come over her.

They buried Luisa and Antoine a few hours later in the de Varney family's graveyard. When the coffins were lowered, Eugénie ran back to the cottage. She couldn't bear to hear the sound of the dirt falling on the bare wood of the coffins. While she waited for her uncle, she remembered the jewels. She removed them from their hiding place and concealed the box on her person. They spent the rest of the night at the cottage and early next morning set out on the return journey to Paris.

Upon her return to Paris, Eugénie's first concern was

to comfort her sisters. She was so glad Aunt Louise was there. She could handle her own sorrow but watching her sisters' was more than she could bear. Their tears tore her apart. When their grief subsided somewhat, she turned her thoughts to André de Varney. She knew that he would be caught sooner or later. She decided that if she was ever to learn of his whereabouts it would be necessary to gain the trust of the leaders in St. Jacques. This would be no easy task. In those days people were suspicious of their own shadow. They trusted few and with good reason.

A new Eugénie returned to her duties in the wine shop —a Eugénie who seemed vivacious, flirtatious and full of fun. She lifted the spirits of the citizens who frequented the wine shop. She even went so far as to stick a cockade in her hair and sing the songs André and his friend Jean-Emile had taught her. The rousing drinking songs gave her courage and even in these troubled times they struck a chord in even the most unresponsive breast. Marie and Joséphine were appalled and looked at her as though she had betrayed them, but Eugénie pretended not to care. She longed to share her plan with them and tell them that her shocking behavior was just an act, but she knew it would be too dangerous. If the plan should fail, only she would be involved. She shrugged her shoulders and gaily flirted with the customers. She teased the men and sang the rousing songs. The ragged lot loved her. Uncle Pierre was astonished at the change. He couldn't understand it. "I don't know what has come over the child," he would say, shaking his head. The customers laughed and clapped him on the back. "Leave her alone, Pierre. She has the spirit of the revolution!"

St. Jacques was busy. The smiths and the other men

were hammering pikes and gathering up anything that would serve as a weapon. The women were sewing cockades—red, white, and blue. Everyone was muttering, *"A bas les aristocrates!"* All over the country, chateaux were being attacked. Hatred for the nobility was at fever pitch. The peasants continued to be bombarded with taxes—King's taxes, rents and church taxes. They had to pay a tax on livestock to one lord and a tax on grain to another. The clergy were disliked almost as much as the nobles because in addition to being supported by the taxes the peasants had to pay, they themselves were exempted from paying many of them and were granted special favors.

The people of France suffered and cried out in anguish in many ways. They might have cried out, "We were hungry but you would not feed us, thirsty but you would not give us drink, naked but you would not clothe us; sick and in prison but you would not take care of us." Out of their misery and despair the Revolution was born. On the 13th of July, 1789, the debtor's prison, La Force, was broken into and the wretches in bondage set free. The nobles began hastily packing for departure. They saw the handwriting on the wall. However, they didn't get far. The "canaille" had seized the barricades—all who entered or sought to leave through the gates of Paris were stopped and dragged to the Hotel-de-Ville.

All eyes then focused on the dread Bastille which had become the symbol of despotism in the minds of the downtrodden. It dominated Paris with its eight towers which were one hundred feet in height and joined by thick walls equally high. With the fury of the bougeoisie upon it, there was no doubt—the Bastille was doomed.

On the morning of July 14th, Eugénie and Uncle Pierre joined the crowds in the Rue Saint-Antoine. All eyes were focused on the grim Bastille. Some of the people were firing towards the towers but no fire was returned. "The imbeciles!" Uncle Pierre exclaimed. "They can't take the Bastille with muskets."

Noon came and not much had happened. The governor had still not permitted his men to shoot back. A delegation of commoners was sent into the fortress but Governor de Launay refused to surrender or give them arms and ammunition. "I shall blow up myself, the garrison and the prisoners if you persist in this madness," was his answer to the delegation. As they were leaving he called after them, "If I do so, rest assured, we won't be alone."

The delegation returned to the streets with those words ringing in their ears. Then the crowd attacked the drawbridge, spanning the eighty-foot-wide moat, and this time de Launay gave the order to fire back. But only his Swiss soldiers fired; the Invalides had taken an oath not to fire upon the people of Paris. The mob was cut down but they kept on coming. They piled carts with straw which they set on fire and pushed towards the drawbridge in an attempt to smoke de Launay and his garrison out, but only succeeded in almost suffocating themselves. Uncle Pierre, was was standing to one side watching their foolish actions, suddenly shouted, "The Gardes Francais have arrived! They have cannon. The Bastille is ours!"

Eugénie echoed his words and the news spread throughout the mob. Cheering went up as the Gardes Francais set up the cannon. It wasn't long before blood turned the streets red. Eugénie listened in horror to the screams of pain. When at last the Bastille was taken, the mob went berserk. They seized Governor de Launay. The Gardes Francais were helpless to stop them. The mob pulled de Launay's hair, spat at him and kicked him without mercy.

Eugénie watched in horror. "Uncle Pierre, stop them! This is wrong! He is a brave man."

"Hush, child. I cannot," Pierre said sadly. He was all for the revolution but not for needless torture.

De Launay screamed, "For God's sake, have done, kill me!"

Their faces distorted with hate, the maddened throng plunged bayonets and pikes through his torn body. Eugénie watched in helpless horror as one man reached for a saber and started hacking at de Launay's neck. Only Pierre's firm grip on her arm prevented her from fainting. Then the frenzied mob, by mistake, turned on the Invalides instead of the Swiss and more blood flowed. Eugénie and Uncle Pierre heard shouts— *"Voila!* There they are!" They found themselves being lifted onto broad shoulders along with other leaders of St. Jacques and cheers went up from the happy crowd. Emotions ran wild. Men, women and children were singing, dancing and laughing in the midst of the horror. Parents held little children up to look at what had become of the dread fortress—the Bastille, the shame of France. The men carrying Pierre and his pretty niece finally put them down at the entrance to the Bastille. The seven poor wretches who had been incarcerated there were being released and the poor things cried in pain when the sunlight struck their eyes. Some of them had been sealed away in that tomb of a prison for twenty years or more.

Hand in hand Eugénie and Pierre walked, passing endless rows of dungeons. The place was freezing cold and damp. They saw skeletons still chained to the walls and long forgotten. Eugénie kept asking herself, "How

55

is it possible that men could inflict such torture on their fellow men?" At last she cried, "Uncle, I can't bear it. I must go home."

"*Oui,* my little one. It is not a pleasant place to visit. Come, I shall go with you."

They made their way home past grisly bodies swinging from the lampposts. The faces of these tortured corpses, bloated and wracked with pain, were hideous to behold. She clutched at her uncle's arm and whispered, "I never dreamt that our people could become such murderous fiends. We wanted to put an end to injustice and torture. Instead, I fear we have unleashed Satan himself in our precious land!"

"There, there, child. It may not be as bad as all that," Pierre soothed. He spoke those words for Eugénie's sake but deep in his heart he didn't believe them.

The people of France were out for blood and revenge. The Tribunal of the Seventeenth went into session at the Hotel-de-Ville. The aristocracy were dragged from their hiding places and after a mock trial were either thrown in prison or taken out and hanged. Heads were cut off and paraded around the streets for all to see. The sight was sickening. Screams of terrified men and women filled the air. Yet all this was just a small taste of what was to come. Before the Revolution ended, it would seem that the gates of Hell had opened and demons had taken possession of the souls of the people of France. It was a time of suspicion and distrust and hate.

People trembled in their beds at night and listened in suffocating fear to the tramp of the feet of members of the Revolutionary Tribunal. Behind locked doors and closed windows, men and women waited in terror for the knock and the order to open up. No one was safe. Anyone bearing a grudge against an enemy could at the slightest provocation see to it that the dread knock would be heard. If the footsteps went past a certain door the inhabitants would breathe a sigh of relief—for an hour or so. Such was the state of Paris.

The Revolution picked up momentum like a great avalanche. In spite of her horror, Eugénie realized that the peasants could do nothing else but revolt when the burdens they carried became too much for their aching backs to carry. It wasn't possible that they could watch their families eating the bark of trees during bad winters so that they could give the fodder they scraped together to their emaciated animals. How could they be expected to go on accepting in dumb misery the deaths of their children from a multitude of illnesses stemming from hunger? But still, deep within her heart, her disgust grew.

The weeks went by and the strain of keeping up a brave, revolutionary front was making her most disagreeable. She snapped at her sisters and they just couldn't understand what had changed their gentle sister into this ardent citizeness of the revolution. Eugénie knew they were deeply troubled but she was afraid to take them into her confidence, afraid one of them might let something slip. Marie and Joséphine tried to talk to her but she ignored them. The Brogards, however, were very proud of their niece—she was a true, brave daughter of the Republic. The horrors she continued to witness almost made her lose her mind. Only her vow to save André gave her the strength to endure the nightmare. But how was she to find him in the vast *abbatoire* that Paris had become?

It was towards the end of August when her search for André finally neared its end. She walked into the wine shop one morning in time to see her uncle embrace a rather shifty looking character dressed in black with a tricolor sash around his waist and wearing a tri-cornered hat. They greeted each other like long-lost brothers.

"Pierre, you old rogue, how are things?"

"Gustave! Where did you escape from? It must be ten years! Sit down and have a drink. Eugénie, bring wine."

Gustave Tisant eyed her up and down. She felt that he was stripping her naked with his eyes.

"I come from Marseille, Pierre. They have put me in charge of La Force," the man said.

On hearing this, Eugénie felt the first stirrings of hope. If anyone could find news of André, this disreputable-appearing fellow certainly could if he were indeed in charge of that prison where the aristocrats were being held. She made up her mind to be as friendly as she could to him, though he was one of the most repulsive men she had ever seen. He had oily black hair, high cheekbones, a large, bulbous nose and huge, protruding, dark brown eyes. His face glistened with sweat and his teeth were a sickly yellow. He looked as strong as a bull and cruel—very cruel. He eyed Eugénie up and down with a lecherous look, and she knew with revulsion that his thoughts were as horrible as his looks. Still, if he could find André, she would endure anything.

Tisant became a regular visitor at the Brogard's wine shop. Eugénie made herself as agreeable and charming to him as she possibly could, concealing her disgust. The gleam in his eyes grew brighter but his behavior was above reproach, thanks to Uncle Pierre's watchful eyes. Eugénie's hope that Tisant might want her favors and possibly help her find André were not in vain. One hot murky afternoon when she was resting on her bed, Uncle Pierre came in search of her.

"*Chérie,* would you take this small keg of wine over to La Force? Citoyen Tisant is waiting for it."

Her heart missed a beat—here, at last, was her chance.

She walked past the hovels and the squalor, over the cobbled, winding streets, with keg of wine clutched in her arms. At every street corner there was a gathering of men and women. These people were starving and their clothes seemed more ragged than when she first arrived in Paris. The smells which arose from the sewers and gutters were still nauseating, but one thing had changed. The faces of the people were no longer the characterless faces of the walking dead. Their faces now were animated. The people of Paris at last had a purpose to their existence.

When she reached the prison of La Force the wicket was opened by a loud-mouthed turnkey.

"What do you there, citizeness? Speak up!" he bawled.

"I've come with a keg of wine for Citizen Tisant, you clod! Let me through!"

The turnkey laughed, taking a closer look. "Why, if it isn't the little song-bird. Welcome! Sing something for me and I'll let you pass."

"Cochon!" Eugénie spat. "Stand back and let me pass. I have no songs for *canaille* such as you!"

The turnkey at last led her over a stinking courtyard, past the guards' room and finally to Tisant's office. Citizen Gustave Tisant was sitting with his feet propped up on a long, heavy oak table, surrounded by a disreputable crew of ruffians. At Eugénie's entrance he stood up and bowed.

"Why, if it isn't little Citizeness Fabré. Come to visit your old friend Tisant, have you?"

Eugénie felt like slapping him but instead she smiled beguilingly, saying nothing. Tisant took the keg of wine from her hands and lifted it high in the air. "Come, men, let us drink. Perhaps the little Citizeness will sing for us."

One of the men poured the wine into tankards and Tisant lifted Eugénie up onto the table.

"Sing, Citizeness, while we partake of this nectar of the devil," he commanded.

Eugénie did not have a powerful voice but she sang with such spirit and feeling that their evil hearts responded and they sang and cheered with her. Before she left she turned to them and smiled, saying, *"Bonjour, mes amis."* Then she wrote the words *"Liberté, Egalité, Fraternité"* in the dust that lay thick on Tisant's desk. All of them cheered and Tisant leered at her in admiration, and much to Eugénie's disgust, lust.

After that visit to La Force, Tisant contrived for her to come quite often to deliver wine, using the excuse that he couldn't get away from the prison. She teased him and tantalized him and very soon he was drooling at the very sight of her. She was careful not to show too much interest in the prisoners at first. However, on her sixth visit to La Force, opportunity knocked. She was alone with Tisant in his office and he was watching her intently.

"What has made you such an ardent revolutionary?" he asked. "I'm surprised. You didn't live in poverty. *Au contraire,* my dear, you had it pretty easy on the de Varney estate, *n'est-ce-pas?*"

"How did you know that?"

"I make it my business to know everything, my dear. But you haven't answered my question."

Eugénie's eyes blazed. "Citizen Tisant, if it hadn't been for my parents' misguided loyalty to those cursed de Varneys, they would still be alive. If they had only listened to Uncle Pierre! How could they have been such fools! Oh, if only those cursed de Varneys had not all been killed! I'd give anything to get my hands on just one of them!''

Tisant laughed and there was a strange glint in his eyes which caused her to feel very apprehensive, and also hopeful.

"Perhaps you'll get your wish, my dear."

"Why do you say that Gustave?" she asked sweetly.

"There was a son, wasn't there? I believe he was not numbered among the dead."

"Are you sure? Is it possible that you could find him?"

"I have influence, my dear. If he is not already dead I shall find him."

Eugénie felt the first stirrings of real hope and she grabbed Tisant's big, ugly, hairy hand and kissed it, concealing her disgust.

"Oh Gustave, if you could I would be forever in your debt!"

"I'll remember you said that, Eugénie Fabré. Now go on home. I have much to do if I'm going to find that damned aristo. And when I do, I'll expect to be suitably rewarded!''

Chapter 5

How long had they been here? André didn't know. He felt so weak. He knew that if it wasn't for the shackles which encircled his wrists and held him upright, he would have pitched forward on to his face. Trickles of filthy water, which the guards had thrown in his face, dripped from his once beautiful clothes to the dirty floor beneath. He heard a groan and very painfully he forced open his bruised and swollen eyelids and stared at his poor friend Jean-Émile. Jean-Émile was hanging by shackles from the wall a short distance from André. He seemed to be unconscious and his clothes were torn and bloody. Suddenly a flicker of memory came to him and then more and more . . .

They had been touring Austria and having a marvellous time when word had reached them of the trouble in France. Without hesitation they had ridden for home. André didn't remember much about the journey to Poissy. He remembered knocking at Father Renoir's door and seeing the look of terror on Hélène's face when she saw who was there.

"Mon Dieu! Mon Dieu! Quickly, get in here!"* She had ushered them frantically into the house and led them to the back room where Father Renois was pacing up and down reading his breviary. His face had turned

pale when he looked up and saw the two boys.

"Father Renoir, what's happening? Hélène looks as if she had seen a ghost."

"My poor child, it has been like a nightmare here. We have had a dreadful uprising. The brutes came from other towns and incited many of our own villagers to join their fiendish band. Oh my poor, poor boy!"

"Father, please! What are you trying to tell me?"

"Flee, my children! Flee for your lives. Your father and mother and the good Fabrés have all been murdered. Your beautiful home has been burned to the ground."

"Mon Dieu! Mon Dieu!" André staggered and would have collapsed had Jean-Émile not held him up. Father Renoir handed him a glass of wine.

"Here—drink this, child, and then you must get on your way. Get out of France. You too, Jean-Émile."

"I must go to the Chateau," André whispered.

"Non, Monsieur André. It would do no good. We gave them a decent burial. No more can be done."

Father Renoir turned to Jean-Émile. "Take him. Ride like the wind and be careful. Trust no one. The devil has taken over this land. God help us all!"

He remembered getting on his horse but after that everything was hazy. He had ridden by Jean-Émile's side like a man of ice.

His thoughts were interrupted by the heavy door being dragged open. Two guards marched in and kicked at Jean-Émile. When he didn't respond they threw a bucket of water at him and the poor boy was taken down from the wall and dragged away. All through the night André kept listening and hoping for the return of his friend.

Early next morning the guards returned and dragged a protesting André outside the prison. A dozen soldiers were mounted and surrounding a cart with two skinny horses standing between the shafts.

"Up, dog. You are going to Paris. It's a crime that the good people of Marseille are to be cheated of your head!"

He was thrown into the cart and then he saw his friend's head, with an agony that was more than mortal depicted on that ghastly face. André trembled with fear. Then something was thrown at his feet—a bloody mess —Jean-Émile's manhood. All at once every sensation in André's body seemed to be swallowed up in a frenzied, whirling descent as of the soul into Hell.

Two of the soldiers climbed in. One gave him a kick which brought him back to his senses and forced him to face the crowd of avid faces that stared up at him, faces crazed with blood-lust and hunger. The procession of soldiers and their prisoner headed for Paris followed by shouts of obscenities and threats from the citizens of Marseille. They journeyed past village after village filled with screaming citizens. Every street and every window was crowded with faces howling obscenities.

"A la lanterne!" *"A la lanterne!"* André wanted to cover his ears to drown out their shouts. The soldiers who guarded him were either unable or unwilling to control the crowds completely and once in a while some of those cadaverous creatures reached the cart and tugged at the helpless André's clothes and hair, pushing their evil faces close to his so that their wine-laden breath almost suffocated him. His face and hair were covered with their slimy spit. He was filthy and hungry, and worse, he was nauseated by the stench of Jean-Émile's putrefying head.

At long last Paris was sighted. By this time André was numb with fear. The cart stopped in front of the prison of La Force and he was pulled roughly to the ground and pushed through the wicket. His poor, weak legs couldn't hold him up. They buckled beneath him.

"Up, *cochon!* Citizen Tisant wishes to see you."

Rough hands pulled him to his feet and led him to Tisant. Tisant threw back his head and laughed.

"Well, well, surely this can't be the *ci-devant* de Varney! Welcome to our humble abode. Enjoy it while you can, for I doubt your stay will be a lengthy one. Take him away."

Tisant's head jailor, Tuvache, a repulsively ugly man with purple veins bulging beneath his skin, yelled at André, "Out, scum." He planted a kick on André's rear and sent him sprawling on the dirty floor outside Tisant's office.

Tuvache led him through corridor after corridor past cells where pale faces surrounded by dirty, greasy hair and eyes filled with despair haunted him as he passed by. At length they reached a cell with a large iron, barred gate.

"In you go. Have fun with your friends." Tuvache pushed him; the gate slammed shut and the key clicked.

He was too weak to stand so he crawled to a corner and fell asleep, oblivious to the curious stares of the other prisoners.

"Eugénie!" Marie came running up the stairs two at a time. She was out of breath by the time she reached their bedroom in the attic. "Eugénie, Monsieur Tisant sent a messenger for you. He wants you to come to La Force as quickly as you can."

Eugénie's heart leaped with joy and fear, both at the same time. She gripped Marie's hand. "Marie, if you love me, ask no questions now but please pray for me, *please!* Pray harder than you have ever prayed before."

She sat down and wrote a quick note to André. She

knew that Tisant must have found him or he wouldn't have sent for her like this. She kissed Marie and then quickly ran to La Force.

Tisant was pacing up and down in his office, impatiently waiting for her. When he saw her, he beamed. "Well, Citizeness, what did you say you would give for a chance to see a de Varney hang?" He looked at her slyly.

She forced herself to remain calm. "Don't tease me, Gustave. It's impossible."

He handed her a sheet of paper. "Feast your eyes on that list of prisoners."

Eugénie attempted to control herself. Tisant was watching her like a hawk. She took the list and scanned it. There, about two-thirds from the top was the name— "*ci-devant* André Phillipe Sebastian de Varney, captured—Marseilles—1789."

"Where is he? Take me to him!"

"Not so fast, my dear. Not so fast. Remember what you said—anything?"

"Yes, yes, Gustave. *Je me rapelle.*"

"My price, my little cabbage, is marriage."

"*What?* Gustave, you are joking. *C'est impossible!*"

Tisant grew red in the face with anger. "Then it is impossible for you to see de Varney."

"But Gustave, my uncle would never permit it."

"Ah, but Pierre has already given us his blessing. I thought you liked me. Were you making a fool of me?"

Eugénie noticed the angry flush on his face and since she couldn't afford to have him turn against her now, she smiled sweetly. "Oh, Gustave, I *do* like you, but it's only that I never thought of you in that way before. Why, you were like another dear uncle to me!"

The thought of marrying Tisant nauseated her and she was afraid he would see the revulsion in her face.

Then she thought, "But it won't happen," so she looked him straight in the eyes and said, *"C'est bien soit.* If that's what you really wish—but, Gustave, you will give me a little time to get used to the idea? After all, a girl doesn't get married every day and I do want things to be perfect."

Tisant couldn't believe his ears. "Oh, *chèrie,* you make me very happy! Come, give me a kiss to seal our bargain."

She shuddered but she gave a little laugh and raised her face to his. If she had been an actress she would have deserved a standing ovation for her performance. Tisant's fat hand caressed her arm. "My dear, I can hardly wait. But let us go and take a look at that son of Satan. His proud head won't be on his shoulders much longer."

The prison of La Force was gloomy, damp, filthy and evil smelling. She followed Tisant down the long, low-ceilinged corridors past rooms crowded with prisoners, both men and women, and even children. Her heart was beating madly. Soon, soon, she would come face to face with her dear love, her beloved André. On and on they went, her heart pounding desparately. She knew she had to be cautious. Tisant was watching her carefully, his black eyes penetrating, it seemed, to the very depths of her soul. At last they came to a winding staircase which led down to the dungeons. The smell and the damp were nauseating. Rats scampered here and there. She was almost afraid to breath, so foul was the air. Finally they came to a gate guarded by a dirty, scarfaced individual whose breath and clothes reeked of stale wine. At a signal from Tisant, he unlocked the gate and they stepped into a room that one could only imagine in Hades.

Men, women and children were thrown together in

that rat-infested hole. The room was lit only by some sputtering tallow candles. Tisant never once took his eyes off Eugénie's face. She was conscious of his penetrating gaze all the time. Her eyes swept over the poor miserable creatures in the cell and she swore at them, "Damned aristos!"

This made him laugh and he swung her around, giving her a kiss and exclaiming joyfully, "Spoken like a true daughter of France, *citoyenne!*"

Tears burned her eyes as she looked around. It wasn't the dirt or the smells that tore her apart but the quiet dignity and resignation of the faces of the men and women in their once beautiful clothes which, like them, were now dirty and torn. Some of the children even played games as though they were in their own homes, oblivious to their horrendous surroundings. The women mended torn clothes with hands that had never done anything more strenuous than work on a piece of embroidery. They chatted and worked as though there was no dirty prison and no tomorrow with its inevitable ending, calling them or their loved ones to a mock trial and death.

Tisant called out, *"Ci-devant* de Varney, step forward!"

Out of the gloom stepped André. He was pale and haggard and his once fine clothes were in tatters. As he stepped forward, Eugénie felt her knees buckling under her and she thought, *"Mon Dieu,* I must not faint— I must hold on!" André's eyes lit up when he saw her and he was about to speak. She had to stop him at all costs.

"Curse you, de Varney!" She flew at him, beating her fists on his chest like a wildcat. "Damn your soul, aristo!"

Tisant pulled her away. Eugénie kicked, screaming,

"Let me at him!" She spat at André—"*Cochon!*"

Tisant laughed. "Little vixen, don't cheat La Lanterne of its lunch!"

At this interchange, André's eyes regained their hopeless look of despair. Seeing the beautiful girl who had been so dear to him turn into the evil, foul-mouthed wretch standing before him drained away his last shred of hope. Now he wished for death.

Since Eugénie had been prepared for the possibility that she would not be able to speak to André alone, she had written the note and contrived to stick it in his shirt front as she struck at him. André was, of course, not aware of this until much later, and so at Eugénie's attack and vitriolic language his face went pale and he trembled with emotion. It didn't seem possible that his Eugénie could have turned into this daughter of Satan, but his eyes and ears couldn't be deceived.

"Come, *citoyenne,* you can watch his head roll in a few days. Now I need some wine. *Allons!*"

Hours later, André discovered the letter. It was so wrinkled that at first glance he wasn't sure what it was. He read it by the feeble glow of a candle. As he read, his light came back into his eyes and his heart seemed to beat with renewed strength.

My heart overflows with sorrow at the thought of your danger. Would that I could exchange my miserable life for yours! Do not despair, I have a plan to free you. Be prepared, rest and gather your strength. The plan must be carried out tomorrow night because we dare not wait any longer. My precious darling, have faith in me and God willing we shall soon be together and safe. Destroy this letter, my love.

Until tomorrow night, adieu.
Eugénie

He pressed his lips to the crumpled page and then tore

it into a thousand pieces.

When Eugénie had written the letter she didn't really have any plan at all. She only knew that she must do something to save him or die in the attempt. However, as they made their way back to Tisant's office her mind was at work, and by the time they arrived she had already conceived a plan to free André. With all the enthusiasm she could muster, she grasped Tisant's rough hands and danced around with him.

"Oh, Gustave, do let us have a party! I am so happy! Now my parents' murder will be avenged. The last of the de Varneys will die and justice will have been served."

"Is that the only reason you are happy?"

"Now Gustave, don't you think we should celebrate our betrothal?" she said coyly. "We should have a party. Oh, Gustave, we would have a marvellous time singing and dancing! Say yes. Please do say yes."

"How can I refuse you anything?" he sighed. Her face was flushed with excitement and she looked remarkably beautiful. Tisant looked at her with longing. She was so beguiling and he thought how lucky he was to have won such a creature for a wife. He would be the envy of his friends and rivals. He couldn't resist her pleading.

"Eugénie, ask your Uncle Pierre to give us some of his best wine and bring your sisters along. It just might be fun, my little vixen. It just might be fun."

She gave him her most provocative look and forced herself to sit on his knee and give him a kiss. But as he bent down to embrace her again she laughed and pulled away.

"Patience, my Gustave! Patience. There will be plenty of time for that." She winked at him tantalizingly. Oh, she thought, if her parents could see her now! How horrified they would be to see their daughter behaving like a harlot. But if they knew her reason, they would have to approve.

"I really must go now, Gustave. There is so much to prepare," she said, sliding off his lap.

"Eugénie, you know the *ci-devant* de Varney will be tried in the morning. Will you be there?"

"You know very well I wouldn't miss that trial for anything in the world."

Her heart was heavy as she trudged through the dirty streets. She had a sick feeling of dread in the pit of her stomach, but when she entered the wine shop not a trace of unhappiness or fear showed. She beamed at her uncle and then called out excitedly for Aunt Louise, Marie and Joséphine. "I have wonderful news for you! I am going to marry Gustave Tisant," she cried. Uncle Pierre, Aunt Louise and Joséphine were thrilled.

"That's marvellous, *chèrie*. Tisant is a powerful man and will go far in his career. You are a lucky young lady indeed," said Pierre.

"Thank you, Uncle Pierre. Tisant is a fine man and he can give me the things I have always wanted. We are to have a party tomorrow night, Uncle Pierre, and Gustave says we must have the best wine to celebrate. I am so excited! We shall have an absolutely marvellous time!"

"Yes, my little one, we know you must be very happy. It will be the best party ever. I wish your aunt and I could be there, but as you know, it is impossible. I don't think Joséphine should go either. She is much too young."

Joséphine made a face but said nothing. Eugénie went to her uncle and aunt and hugged each of them in turn.

71

"I understand. You two have been so wonderful. Please remember, no matter what happens, that I love you dearly."

She went to her room and was surprised to see Marie there. She hadn't noticed her leaving. Poor Marie was stunned by the announcement. Eugénie saw the hurt and puzzlement on her sister's face. Marie's soft brown eyes filled with tears and her voice broke as she said, "Eugénie Fabré, how could you? I just can't understand what has changed you so much! I don't even know you anymore. You are like a stranger!"

Eugénie decided that since she was going to need Marie's help tomorrow night she had no choice but to tell her everything. She motioned for Marie to sit on the bed with her.

"Marie, dearest, forgive me for the way I have been treating you lately. Forgive me for letting you believe that I had changed so drastically. It was all an act."

Marie looked at her in amazement. "But why, Eugénie? Why?"

"I wanted to save André. I made up my mind at Poissy that that was one life those monsters would be cheated of. I hated the killing and the misery but I had to pretend that the Revolution meant more to me than life itself. I was just beginning to despair of ever finding him when Tistant walked into our lives."

"But André might be dead already."

"No, Marie. Tisant found him! He was captured in Marseille and Tisant had him brought to La Force. I . . . saw him today. Oh, Marie, he looked so wretched! He must have suffered so very much."

"Eugénie, how can you possibly free André?" Marie gasped. "It would be too dangerous. If you are caught, Tisant will murder you!"

"I know that very well, and that is why I hesitated to

ask you to help me. I shall understand if you refuse. The risk will be great indeed."

Marie blanched. "You need my help?"

"Believe me, if there was any other way I would not ask."

Marie was silent for a long time. She was happy to discover that her beloved sister had not really changed but she was afraid. It was sheer madness to attempt to free André. She looked at Eugénie's anxious face and then made up her mind.

"You shall have my help, and gladly. What do you plan to do? Where do you plan to go?"

"I think we must try and get to England."

"What about Joséphine?"

"We can't possibly take her. She could never endure the hardships and misery we shall most certainly have to face before we find peace and happiness again. I know she will be safe here and you know that Aunt Louise and Uncle Pierre simply adore her. I shall write to both Uncle and Tisant explaining my actions and making it quite clear that it was all my doing and that Aunt and Uncle were in no way involved. Now Marie, this is what I have planned . . ."

All through that night she tossed and turned. Marie did not sleep well either. Eugénie was afraid, more afraid than she had ever been in her whole life, more afraid even than when she was eight and had fallen off a horse and everyone thought that she would never be able to walk again. She was always more afraid when others were involved. When she was just responsible for herself it wasn't so bad.

She lay there rehearsing the plan in her mind, over and over. Pray God nothing would go wrong! Her heart smote her when she remembered how thin and pale André looked. He had been half dead with fatigue and his eyes, those wonderful grey eyes, had lost their lustre. He had a terrible despairing look on his face. Suddenly overcome by emotion, she left her bed and stood by the tiny window. If she failed—if indeed it was God's will that she should fail—at least she would be by his side at the end. Then, impatient with herself, and with a sudden urge of firm resolve, she put all thought of failure out of her mind. Her eyes glowed with the determination to succeed and she lay down on the bed once again.

"Eugénie are you asleep?" The whisper came from out of the darkness.

"No, Marie."

"I am so scared, really scared!"

"Marie, I promise you we shall escape. If there is a God in Heaven, we shall escape. Sleep now, you will need to be at your best tomorrow night."

Even as she reassured Marie, fear tugged at her heart with a cold, clammy hand. The moon cast cold beams that made the shadows in the room even more dark and menacing. She pushed Monsieur Fear away with a violent effort of her will. Nothing, she vowed, not even fear, was going to stand in the way of rescuing André!

Chapter 6

With the first streaks of dawn, Eugénie dressed in haste and with much trepidation made her way to the Hotel de Ville where André's fate would be sealed. Though it was hours before the Tribunal would be in session, there was a large crowd of fiendish wretches already gathered outside—the lowest and most cruel dregs of humanity, shouting obscenities and thirsty for blood, all of them eagerly waiting to feast their eyes on the human misery that would appear before the Tribunal that day. Eugénie shoved her way through so that when the doors were opened she was one of the first to get in.

It seemed to her that an eternity passed before the judges finally took their places. They were a grim, dirty lot of men. The signal was given and the prisoners were brought before them. Eugénie's compassion went out to all those poor souls. It was obvious to her that most of the prisoners were innocent of any crime save that they were aristocrats. One young girl couldn't have been more than thirteen years old.

Twenty prisoners were called and twenty condemned without mercy before André's name was announced. He stood before the judges, pale but proud.

"Your name?"

"André Phillipe Sebastian de Varney."

"An aristocrat?"

"Yes."

"Ci-devant de Varney, you are accused by the people of France of plotting against the Republic. Do you confess your crime?"

"Hang him! Hang him!" yelled the crowd in a sudden burst of enthusiasm. "Off with the traitor's head!"

Among that corrupt Tribunal, justice was a stranger, and as Eugénie cast an anxious look around her at the crowd, it was obvious that every heart there was beating the death knell. There was no trace of pity or feeling for those poor souls on trial. At last . . .

"André Phillipe Sebastian de Varney, you have been found guilty of your crime. You are an enemy of the Republic and therefore, you are condemned to death. Sentence will be carried out tomorrow morning. Have you anything to say?"

André's voice shook but he looked at the judges without flinching. "I am innocent. Before God, I have never done anyone any harm."

Eugénie felt tears prick her eyes. She quickly forced them back as the crowd went into a frenzy of booing and cheering.

"Take him away," said the judge.

She watched with an aching heart as André was led away, then hurried home. All had gone as she had expected. More evidence of man's inhumanity to man.

Eugénie worked in the wine shop with her Uncle Pierre all afternoon. Tisant had supplied Aunt Louise with a gift of flour and she and Marie were busy baking bread for the party. The wonderful smell permeated the entire house. Eugénie seemed strangly exhilarated but the Brogards thought it was due to the excitement of her betrothal to "good old Tisant." To Eugénie, the hours seemed endless. It was a great effort for her to respond to the usual banter of the customers, but respond she did. Her eyes glowed and her face was unusually flushed, which caused many a man to catch his breath at her loveliness. All afternoon she had tried to have a word with Marie who she suspected must be dreadfully nervous and upset, but it hadn't been possible. At long last Pierre, with a grin, told them it was about time for them to get ready for the party.

"I'll go and hitch up the old horse and load the wagon. Hurry now girls, you mustn't keep Gustave waiting."

Thirty minutes later they said their goodbyes and were wished an enjoyable evening. Both girls were desolate at leaving little Joséphine and saddened at the thought of leaving their new home. The Brogards had shown them nothing but love. They wanted to cry and kiss Joséphine and tell her how much they loved her, but this they could not do. It would have caused too much comment and perhaps arouse suspicion. With leaden legs they climbed up onto the cart where Eugénie had already hidden their clothes and her precious sword. Marie held a basket of bread and cheese and a small bottle—a mixture of laudanum and herbs Eugénie had prepared. Her mother used to give this mixture to the girls when they were ill and needed sleep, but Eugénie had increased the amount of landanum. Around her waist, under her underclothes, Marie had tied a small sack which held their share of the jewels.

Eugénie took the reins and the old horse ambled along the dirty, cobbled streets. When they were well out of sight of the wine shop they stopped and poured the drug into one of the barrels. This barrel they marked with a piece of chalk.

"It won't kill them, will it?" Marie asked, worried.

"Oh, Marie, you know I couldn't do that! Mother showed me how to make it up. It should make them sleep for hours. Long enough, I hope for us to get far away from this wretched city."

They continued on their way in silence, both girls praying that the plan would be successful. If it failed, it meant certain death. Eugénie knew there would be no mercy for her. Tisant, she knew, without a doubt would hate her with an uncontrollable hatred and she could not blame him. She only hoped that in the event they were discovered, she could convince him that Marie was innocent and knew nothing about her plan. She had simply come along, believing in good faith that she was about to celebrate her sister's betrothal.

"Are you scared, Eugénie?" Marie persisted.

"Yes, Marie, but my mind is made up. If André dies I shall have nothing to live for. I love him so much. Without him, life would be without meaning."

"How can you say such a thing? Don't Joséphine and I matter? We love you, doesn't that mean anything?"

Marie sounded very upset but before Eugénie could answer, the gloomy facade of La Force loomed before them.

The wicket-keeper came out to meet them and Eugénie grinned at him. "Citizen, that barrel must be brought in first—the one with the chalk mark. After all, the best wine must be drunk first while it can still be appreciated, *n'est-ce-pas?*"

He gave her a toothless grin and called for some of his cronies to carry the big barrel into the guards' room where the party was to take place. Eugénie and Marie followed them and when Tisant saw his "little vixen" he picked her up and swung her around. The party had begun. The guards had invited their wives or sweethearts so there were about thirty people in all, ready to make merry and dance their cares away. Tankards were filled and toasts were made. They danced, sang and greedily ate the bread and cheese. Tisant was congratulated by all, and many a lewd comment reached the ears of Eugénie.

Marie's task was difficult, for Tisant wouldn't let Eugénie leave his side. It fell on her to run back and forth filling the tankards of the guards on duty and the wicket-keeper, while at the same time dancing with the few men who had no women to entertain them. When she thought back on it, she wondered how on earth she had managed to do it.

Eugénie had never appeared more desirable to Tisant. Her face was flushed with what he assumed was happiness. He had tried since the first moment she had arrived to make love to her, but she had artfully avoided his embraces. Her attitude aroused him all the more.

"Eugénie, don't turn away from me again," he begged.

She saw that he was beginning to get irritable and she didn't wish to stir his anger or his suspicions. Desperately she wondered what had gone wrong. The drugged wine should have taken effect by this time.

"Come here, my beautiful citizeness. Come to your love," he commanded now.

Suppressing her revulsion, she moved closer to him and he pulled her down on the dirty floor. His face came closer and his breath, reeking of garlic and a thousand ugly smells, filled her nostrils. He pressed his fat, wet lips against hers and his tongue forced her lips apart and flicked and explored every crevice of her mouth. His breathing became labored and he pawed at her breasts. She could feel his sweat soaking through her dress. Panic took possession of her and just as she was about to pull away from him he yawned and then yawned again.

"Diable! I must have had too much wine. Snuggle up with me, my love, and we'll take up where we left off later . . ."

Soon he was snoring and one by one the merrymakers yawned and slumped against the walls and each other, joining their snores with his.

Marie, coming back from her latest jaunt around the prison, filling tankards, discovered that the drug had finally taken effect. She glanced around for Eugénie and was about to say something when she saw her snuggled beside Tisant. Eugénie put her finger to her lips and signalled her to be quiet. They waited for about fifteen minutes in silence, listening to the stertorous breathing and the snores. Then slowly and gently Eugénie removed Tisant's heavy arm from around her and slipped away.

"How about the wicket-keeper and the other guards, Marie?" she asked anxiously.

"Don't worry about them. They're feeling no pain," said Marie with a nervous giggle.

The time for action had come at last.

They searched for passes that might fit their appearance. Marie took one that belonged to one of the women, one that was close to her own description. She smudged the name because she was not going to be in disguise and was afraid someone might recognize her. Then, as planned, she went out to the wagon and emptied the remaining barrel of wine which flowed between the cobbles in the courtyard like freshly shed blood. Then she climbed up on to the wagon and waited with a heart that had suddenly gone berserk inside her trembling body.

Eugénie meanwhile glanced around the room and

sighed with relief when she discovered that one of the men was about her height. With trembling fingers she managed to strip him of the uniform which she quickly donned. Then very stealthily she made her way down the long, dank corridors. The silence was appalling. She scarcely breathed. Suddenly she heard a noise.

"Oh God! One of the guards must be awake," she thought, terrified.

But no, it was a scrawny, grey rat visiting his neighbors. Still her body remained motionless for a minute, then she pressed on. Each time she passed a sleeping guard, her heart seemed to beat so loudly that surely even the dead couldn't help but wake up. At length she found herself outside the dungeon where André was incarcerated. Her heart seemed to stop beating for an instant; then she grabbed the key from the hook on the wall and opened the heavy gate. It creaked and groaned in protest. The guard stirred in his sleep, mumbling to himself.

André had been watching for her and he went to her immediately and took her in his arms.

"Oh, *chérie,* my dearest love, you're here!"

She looked at him tenderly and gently withdrew from his arms. "We must make haste. There is no time to lose."

He gave her a tender kiss on the forehead and sprang into action. He grabbed the sleeping guard's sword, stripped him and donned the uniform. In the meantime Eugénie was looking around at the other prisoners and her heart was filled with pity. Most of them were sleeping. The others didn't even seem to be aware of her presence.

"Come on, Eugénie, let's go!"

"What about them, André? We just can't leave them here," she whispered.

"Eugénie, don't be a fool! If we let them all loose, it will lessen our chances of escape."

"Wait, André—I must think of something." She was silent for a few minutes and André was getting nervous. "André, is there anyone here who could be depended upon to carry out an orderly escape? Anyone who could control the others enough so that they would not rush madly out of here?"

"Well, I suppose Monsieur Cabanes could do it. He seems to be a very calm, controlled type of person and the others seem to respect him," André said reluctantly.

"André, please ask him to come here."

He left unwillingly and was back in a few minutes with a rather round, grey-haired man. Monsieur Cabanes bowed when he saw Eugénie, though he was quite taken aback by her attire.

"Monsieur Cabanes, listen carefully, please. You must give us twenty minutes' start before waking the others. Wake them a few at a time—that way there will be less confusion. We shall leave the wicket open. I don't know if all of you will escape, but God willing, many will," Eugénie said breathlessly.

"Mademoiselle, what can I say?' the man mumbled.

"Nothing, Monsieur. Good luck, and don't worry about time. Tisant and the others should sleep until morning."

He kissed her hand with such respect and emotion that Eugénie was moved to touch his grey head in response. Then she and André fled to the waiting Marie.

They made a silent departure. The old horse wasn't able to go very fast which was perhaps just as well, since though they were filled with the great desire to leave the gates of Paris far behind as quickly as possible, they didn't want to attract undue attention to themselves. Eugénie took over the reins from Marie and pulled her tricorne hat down over her eyes. André had stolen one of the horses from the courtyard and rode alongside in silence. They knew they had a long journey ahead of them filled with danger, and they had not even got out of Paris. The thought sent shivers down their spines. The wheels of the cart thumped against the rough cobblestones and Eugénie's heart thumped along with them. Added to her fears was the terrible thought that perhaps she had jeopardized Marie's life for nothing. At that moment she honestly didn't feel they had the slightest chance of getting away.

It was about two o'clock in the morning when they reached the barrier at the North Gate. Even so, there were many carts already lined up for inspection. Most were heading for the nearby countryside to fetch produce for the morning's market. The carts were being checked very carefully. The sergeants in charge of the gates of Paris feared for their lives lest any aristos escape. Eugénie, Marie and André waited with baited breath and by the time their turn came they were sweating for fear. The guard yelled at them, "Passes! Passes!"

They handed them over. He scrutinized them carefully, and their breath caught in their throats. Then he walked over to the Sergeant of the Guard. The wine barrels were inspected and they were told to move on. Sighing with relief, Eugénie took the reins, when a gruff voice shouted, "Hold there!"

They became frozen with fear—was it all over? Had Tisant recovered already? Surely not! The sergeant strolled up to them in his ill-fitting uniform and his ugly face seemed to swim before their eyes.

"You forgot your passes. You would never get back in without them. Hey, there!" He looked at Marie. "Aren't you from the wine shop in St. Jacques? When is your sister going to marry the old rogue Tisant? I'm ready for some merrymaking!" Then he gave her a suspicious look. "Say, what are you doing here? Why aren't you at the big party?"

Marie wasn't the most quick-thinking girl in the world, but fear and perhaps God inspired her and she answered promptly, "Why, *Citoyen*, I *was* at the party and it is still going strong. Alas, I have to take these barrels to Argenteuil to replenish our supplies. The party left us a little short. You ought to know how the good soldiers and citizens of St. Jacques like their wine. It would never do to deprive them, now would it? Besides, I just do what I'm told. It seems I always get the dirty work to do. But at least Citizen Tisant gave me an escort. Oh, it was a greaty party and I hated to leave! Everyone is singing and dancing and having a marvellous time. Now, sir, it is eight weary miles to Argenteuil, so will you please let my cart pass."

The Sergeant laughed heartily at this sally. "Pass on your royal way, pussycat. When you get back, have a drink with me, *non?*"

With relief they continued on their way. Once again they were grateful that the old horse moved slowly because their every instinct told them to run like the wind. They kept a steady pace, afraid to look back, every muscle tense, every nerve on edge.

They had only covered a couple of miles when suddenly the heavens opened and driving rain descended upon them. Soon they were soaked to the skin, and cold. The going got rougher and the road became a sea of mud. The cart got stuck more than once and it was difficult to keep going. They left the main road and unhitched the old horse, leaving the cart behind a hedge. Then they continued the first lap of their journey and headed for Argenteuil. Eugénie rode the old horse and

Marie rode behind André. On and on they rode, over muddy roads, past small villages and country mansions. There was scarcely a soul to be seen. The rain, fortunately, kept the people from their work in the fields.

Many hours later they came within sight of Argenteuil. They were weary and dirty but decided they had better avoid the town and move on. For another terrible hour, sore and wet, they rode until they could go no further. They saw an old barn in the distance and headed for it. The sky was dark with rain clouds. Everything looked mournful and dreary. There was such weariness in their bodies and minds that no prodding of the imagination could make them think of beauty or freedom. Nothing but desolation seemed to stretch before them. They were wet, hungry and ached in every portion of their bodies, yet they couldn't dark risk stopping for food.

"Girls, I'd better keep watch. I doubt if anyone will find us here in this storm, but one never can tell," Andre said at last as they stopped by the side of the field. "You lie down and rest." The girls were too weary to protest. They lay down on the dirty straw in the shelter of a tree and immediately fell fast asleep. They slept so soundly even the rats didn't bother them.

Eugénie awoke after about three hours' sleep. She lay there for a while, listening to Marie's quiet breathing and the occasional squeak of a rat. Then she walked outside to where André was standing guard.

"Eugénie! Why aren't you asleep?" he asked.

"I slept long enough. Why don't you get some rest now? I'll stand guard."

He looked at her very intently and took her hand in his. "Eugénie! Eugénie! I owe you my life. How can I ever hope to repay you? How brave you are, my darling!"

Eugénie blushed with pleasure. "André, dearest, say no more, please. I just couldn't let you die. I . . . I love you. I always have."

"Eugénie!" He pulled her gently into his arms and held her for one heavenly moment, a moment when time seemed to stand still. Eugénie knew a wondrous excitement and a stirring within her. His eyes filled with desire and what she saw in them made her blood race. Their lips met, trembling, and then he savored her forehead, her eyelids, and her cheeks with burning kisses filled with passion.

"My beautiful Eugénie, have you any idea what torture this is for me? What torture to tease myself with your touch and your kisses! Those wonderful kisses that tell me you desire me as much as I desire you, my love. I need you, darling, and I want you. Oh, how I want you!"

He loosened the guard's tunic she wore and tenderly fondled her breasts. Then he bent and touched each nipple with his lips. She cried out from the desperation of her great need. Suddenly they heard a noise, and painfully and hastily drew apart—just in time. Marie had awakened and stood there, rubbing her sleepy eyes.

"Is it time to leave yet?" she murmured drowsily.

"No, Marie. I just thought I'd let André get some rest. Go on back to sleep, dear," said Eugénie gently.

"Eugénie, I hope you'll let me take my turn, too. You know, dear sister, I can see just as well as you," Marie said.

Eugénie smiled. "Marie, you have been wonderful—just wonderful!"

Throughout the long rainy night they took turns standing guard and as the ran beat down on the branches above them, so their hearts beat a tattoo inside their frozen bodies.

The rain was still coming down in torrents when they started their long journey toward Calais, where they hoped they might be able to escape to England. They kept to the back roads and the fields, going as fast as the mud and the old horse would permit. They passed the town of Pontoise and went some miles before camping for the night. There was no protection that night. They tried to shelter under the trees but the rain seemed to come down with increased vigor. They huddled close together for warmth and Marie, in spite of it, soon fell into an exhausted sleep.

"Eugénie, I'm going to come back to France some-day. There are thousands of émigrés and we shall join together so that we can restore France to its former glory. You'll see, things will be as they were before!" André whispered into her ear.

Eugénie was suddenly very quiet. She didn't want to spoil this moment with André, but yet she felt she had to try and make him see that France could never be the same again.

"André, can't you see that our country will never be as it was before? I don't think it should be."

"What! How can you say that when the rabble that is now in power murdered our parents?"

"The rabble didn't murder them André—poverty, injustice and above all hunger did that. Oh, André, we lived in a dream world all these years! How could we not have realized the misfortune of so many others?"

"I don't understand you. How can you say such a thing? My parents treated their workers fairly and with kindness," he said stiffly.

"I know that, *mon amour*. I know that. They were good, wonderful people, but there were not enough like them. These past few months really opened my eyes. I have seen people actually starving. Children foraging in garbage heaps, desperate to find one scrap of food. André, the peasants for the most part were treated worse than animals. They had no dignity, no sense of pride and no purpose to their life. Now, at least, they have a purpose and some sense of worth."

"I can't quite believe it was as bad as that. The lazy are always griping about everything. They want everything handed to them on a platter. Eugénie, do let's change this depressing subject!"

Eugénie looked at him sadly. "Oh, my love, someday you will know the truth!"

André made no comment and before long he was sleeping as peacefully as Marie. But Eugénie felt feverish and it seemed to her that she could still feel the movement of the old horse beneath her. Their stomachs were growling in protest at the lack of food. All they had with them were a few scraps of bread and cheese they had salvaged from the party. Yet she thought, how spoiled they were to complain of hunger when they should be thanking God for keeping them safe thus far.

Their journey continued and after three long weary days they saw the spires of St. Pierre standing stark against the sky. They knew they had reached Beauvais. So far they had seen no sign of pursuit and for the first time since leaving Paris they were beginning to feel secure. Then distinctly they heard the sound of galloping hooves. They glanced back and saw the outlines of horses and men. Terror laid icy fingers on their hearts and for a short space of time they were frozen in their tracks.

They urged their horses on but the old horse didn't have the strength. He faltered and gallantly tried to go on, but in vain. He fell to his knees. Eugénie picked herself up and ran as fast as she could in pursuit of André and Marie, who were unaware that she was not close behind them. The sound of hooves grew louder and they could hear the soldiers shouting. They came relentlessly closer to Eugénie. Then there was a shot and she felt an incredible pain which was swallowed up in the dark black velvet of the unconsciousness which mercifully enveloped her. At the sound of the shot, Marie looked over her shoulder.

"No! Dear God, Eugénie has been shot!"

"Marie, get down," André commanded. "Run as fast as you can and hide in the town."

She did as he asked without question and André spurred his horse in a frenzy back towards the inert body of Eugénie. He sprang down and picked her up in his arms. How he got back on the horse with Eugénie was a miracle, for he felt dizzy from fear when he saw the soldiers coming relentlessly nearer. They were firing at the fugitives and André prayed for the first time in years.

At last they reached the town and he dismounted and ran down a side street hoping to find a place to hide, carrying Eugénie tenderly in his arms. He hoped that the soldiers would be confused and follow his horse, giving them time to hide. He scarcely knew where he was going. He felt sick, sick to death with the terrible agony of fear. Suddenly he heard a small voice. "Monsieur. Quickly, follow me!"

André was aware that a small, slender boy with a crop of dark, curly hair was tugging frantically at his sleeve.

"Please, Monsieur. We don't have much time."

André followed the boy through narrow streets until at last they came to a stop in front of a modest house in the middle of town. The boy knocked three times and the door was opened at once by a plump, rosy-cheeked woman.

"Thank God you are safe, my son. Quickly, come in."

She bustled them through the house to the kitchen where a big, brawny man was raising one of the stone slabs of the kitchen floor. He motioned for André to climb down at the same time taking Eugénie from his aching arms. Then very carefully he lowered Eugénie through the hole.

"I will talk to you later when it is safe. Trust us, please."

The slab fell with an ominous thud before André could say one word. "We don't have very much choice, it seems," he thought. "We have to trust them."

It was dark in the cellar. He heard a noise and then a little, nervous voice saying, "André, is that you?"

"Marie? Thank God you are safe! Is there any light in this place? We must take care of Eugénie. I am afraid she has been badly wounded."

Marie lit a candle and looked at André. "I was so afraid down here in the dark but I didn't want to waste the only candle," she explained. She gasped in horror and cried out when she noticed the jagged wound in her sister's shoulder. The blood was flowing steadily and at the sight Marie burst into tears. André laid Eugénie on the small cot that stood in one corner of the tiny room and turned impatiently to Marie.

"Oh, for God's sake, Marie, hush up! Here—see if you can clean the wound." That was no easy task. The blood was flowing in a steady stream from where the bullet was lodged in Eugénie's shoulder.

"André, I can't stop the bleeding," Marie whimpered. André steeled himself for what was to come. "I'm going to have to get that bullet out somehow," he said.

There wasn't much light given off by that single

candle but he had no choice. There was a little wooden table in the middle of the room with a plate of bread and cheese, a jug of wine and a knife. He took the knife and held the blade in the flame from a few minutes. Then while Marie held the candle he pried the bullet out of the soft flesh of Eugénie's shoulder. It was indeed merciful that Eugénie, unconscious as she was, was oblivious to pain. Marie washed the wound and bandaged it with a strip she had torn from her chemise. Some time later, Eugénie regained her senses. She looked from one anxious face to the other, wincing in pain.

"Where are we?"

"We don't really know," Adreé admitted. "But we seem to be safe from the soldiers for the time being. Here, drink this." He held the jug of wine to her lips and she closed her eyes in sleep at last.

Marie and André sat with their backs propped against the wall and waited anxiously for some signal from their rescuers. The floor above them was so thick it was impossible to hear a single sound. The waiting and the silence became unbearable to their ragged nerves and when André put out the candle in order to save it, a blackness so intense enveloped them that it seemed to stifle their breath. But within a few hours, merciful sleep took over and soothed their exhausted minds and bodies.

All through the following day and night they watched for a word from their rescuers. Eugénie was too weak to be concerned about her surroundings. She slept most of the time but André and poor Marie were sick with worry. A hundred questions were tumbling around in their tortured minds. Who were these people? Why had they risked their lives to help them? They couldn't shake off fear and suspicion. In this day and time in France, brother turned against brother and sons turned against their fathers. The wise man trusted no one, so why should they trust complete strangers?

On the following night they heard the stone slab being pulled up. The man of the house climbed down into the little room, and André lit the candle.

"Don't be afraid. You are safe," the man told them. "The soldiers are still searching the town so I'm afraid you'll have to stay here until they leave. They came here yesterday but, of course, found nothing. I don't think they'll come back."

"How can we ever thank you, Monsieur?" cried Marie.

"My name is Dupons—Louis Dupons. I don't require your thanks, Mademoiselle. I am simply doing my duty."

"I don't understand, Monsieur Dupons. Your duty?"

"*Oui,* Mademoiselle. I have the honor of being a member of an organization, headed by an Englishman, whose members have sworn to devote themselves to freeing as many of the victims of this dreadful revolution as they possibly can. There are a great many of us who care and are willing to die for our cause. Our leader is brave and compassionate and has our undying loyalty. God bless him!"

"God bless you all, sir. But we can't stay hidden here forever."

"Oh, my dear, I know that. As soon as it is reasonably safe we shall make arrangements for you to get to England," Monsieur Dupons assured them.

Noticing that Eugénie was awake he said cheerily, "How is our little wounded lamb tonight?"

"Fine, thank you, sir," said Eugénie weakly. "I'm afraid I don't remember too much about these past few days, though I believe we are in your debt."

"Young lady, with God's help your troubles will soon be over. I am going to set plans in motion that, if all goes well, will see you all safely in England before the month is over."

Eugénie clasped Louis Dupons' hand. "How wonderful you are! We shall pay our way, thought. Marie, give him some of our jewels and please, Monsieur, do what you can for us."

Louis Dupons shook his head. "That's not necessary. We have our own funds."

"Please take them, Monsieur. If not for us, perhaps they will help others."

He saw that it was useless to argue. "Thank you, my dear. Now get some rest."

He called up to his son, "Jean! Come here, son."

"*Oui,* Papa?"

"Here—take this and fetch me a clean bucket."

Dupons handed the bucket they had used for a chamber pot to his son. In a few minutes the boy returned and handed a clean bucket down to his father. Madame Dupons appeared right behind him and gave a plate of bread and cheese to Monsieur Dupons.

"Do they need more wine, dear?" she asked.

"Yes, indeed. Wine restores the body as well as the spirit, and our guests are in need of both." The wine was brought to them and Monsieur Dupons bid them goodnight.

Eugénie began to feel much better in the days that followed. She often spoke to the others about the new life ahead of them. "God has protected us so far and I just know we are going to succeed. When we get to England, we can sell more of the jewels to help us live until we can find work."

"Work?" André echoed, astonished.

"Yes, André, don't look so shocked. Your life is

93

going to be very different from now on. We must all find work as soon as possible. We must make a new life for ourselves. But, I think we should keep some of the jewels in memory of our mother . . ."

They talked for hours making plans for the future. Hope filled their breasts and the following days and nights seemed to pass much more quickly.

It was exactly one week from the day they had escaped from the soldiers when Madame Dupons' cheery face appeared in the opening and her plump body descended the narrow ladder.

"My dears, the soldiers have been gone for two days now, so perhaps we can risk having you come upstairs tonight for a wash and a decent meal."

"Oh, Madame, that would be so nice! How can we ever thank you?" said Marie.

Madame Dupons smiled at her. "Just eat hearty tonight, my dear." Then she added, "I'm afraid you'll have to wait until late tonight because of the neighbors. We don't know who to trust so it is better to trust no one. *Au revoir, mes enfants.*"

Eagerly they waited for the signal to come up and finally at about ten o'clock little Jean came down and helped them climb up to the kitchen. Madame Dupons had filled a big wooden tub with hot water and they took turns washing the dirt from their bodies. Madame Dupons also gave them some clean clothes to change into after they had bathed—their own were so filthy and torn that she had simply burned them. It certainly hadn't been easy living in that cramped, dark, little room. The three were dirty, cramped and smelly. It was sheer rapture to bathe in the warm, soothing water and to be beautifully clean once more. How fortunate we are, Eugénie thought as she basked in the soothing water.

After they had bathed, Madame called them to eat. She had prepared a meal of chicken and potatoes. They couldn't believe their eyes—it seemed like a royal feast. They laughed hysterically when they tasted that good food and savored every mouthful. The hysteria was the result of so many weeks of fear and anguish.

"I never thought that I would find the taste of chicken and potatoes exquisite, but I do," André said with a laugh.

It was a cheerful little group that sat around the table that night. Their cares were forgotten for a few peaceful hours. Eugénie felt much better. Her wound was healing quite well though it was still a little sore and the muscles in her shoulders were a trifle stiff. Before they said goodnight, Louis Dupons told them that he would set out in the morning to make his contacts and arrange for their escape.

True to his word, Monsieur Dupons left Beauvais the next morning. Among other things, he had to arrange for new travel passes for the *emigrés*. While he was gone the hours seemed interminable. But three days later he was home again and very pleased with the plans he had made. Turning to André, he said, "Young man, you and I shall leave tomorrow on foot. I hope you feel like walking. We shall wait for the others at Amiens. From now on, your name is Dr. Lupin from Paris, and I shall be your humble assistant. If you'll excuse me for saying so, it's the best I could come up with. You could never pass as a farmer or any kind of workman, not with your hands. As for you, Mademoiselle Marie, you and Madame Dupons will leave two days later. You are to be mother and daughter, Claire and Louise Dubois. Don't worry, you won't have to walk to Amiens, you can go by cart."

Marie laughed in relief. "Thank goodness, walking

was never my favorite pastime. I doubt if I'd last very long."

"What about me Monsieur? When do I leave?" asked Eugénie.

"You, Mademoiselle Eugénie, will leave three days after your sister. My little Jean will accompany you. If you are stopped, your passes will show that you are brother and sister. You will say that you are travelling to Amiens to stay with relatives because your parents have too many mouths to feed. I'm afraid you will have to walk as far as Noyon. I hope *you* don't mind walking?"

"Eugénie loves to walk, Monsieur. You don't have to worry about her," Marie assured him. "Well, Mademoiselle Eugénie, you'll be met by a friend of mine at Noyon who will take you to Amiens. My son will know the way so you have nothing to worry about. Now, I suggest you all get some rest. Monsieur de Varney and I must be off at daybreak."

When the time came for Eugénie to say goodbye to André he held her close for a moment and then gazed tenderly into her eyes.

"Eugénie, I will never forget what you have done for me since the day we met so long ago. Not only have you saved my life twice, but more important, you have given me courage when mine had deserted me. Someday I shall make it up to you in some small measure, for I could never repay in full. Be careful, *chérie,* and God speed."

She watched him leave with tears in her eyes. Then a few days later she and little Jean said goodbye to Marie and Madame Dupons.

"Jean, *mon fils,* take care of Mademoiselle Eugénie," Madame Dupons ordered.

"Maman, I shall guard her with my life. *Adieu."*

Little Jean and Eugénie felt very much alone as they watched Madame and Marie drive away. They had three more days of waiting before they too would set off on their journey to Amiens.

"Don't cry, Mademoiselle," said Jean, touching her hand. "We shall all see each other again. I just know it. My father is a clever man and you are not the first he has saved."

Eugénie smiled through her tears. "Yes, Jean, I'm sure you're right." Looking down at his solemn little face she felt ashamed of her weakness, and said merrily, "Enough of this crying! Let us be happy, for it will be a gerat adventure. You shall be my brave knight and I shall be your princess."

Little Jean smiled with pleasure and admiration.

"You are the most beautiful princess in the world, Mademoiselle Eugénie!"

Chapter 7 _____

It was a damp, misty morning when Eugénie and little Jean Dupons prepared to leave for Noyon. Madame had provided Eugénie with a red dress, muslin kerchief and heavy shoes and coarse stockings. She wore a mob cap over her hair. When she took her sword and fastened it around her waist with a sash, little Jean's eyes grew wide in astonishment.

"Mademoiselle, you might hurt yourself with that!"

Eugénie laughed. "Don't worry, Jean, I know how to use it very well!"

She put on a dark brown cloak which covered the sword effectively. Then she put out her hand to the young boy. "Shall we go, Sir Knight?"

Gallently he took her arm and smiled. "Yes, m'lady, before anyone stirs from their bed."

They locked up the house and set out on their way. All went well until they reached the little hamlet of Noyon. It was dark by this time and they were footsore and weary. They heard shouting and raucous laughter coming from two soldiers who were lurching drunkenly down the street toward them.

"Jean, pay no attention. Perhaps they won't even see us," Eugénie whispered.

But the two drunkards saw them and blocked their

way. "Here, wench, let us see your pretty face," said the first.

The two young people tried to pass on their way but the other foul-smelling rogue caught hold of Eugénie's arm.

"My friend said let us look at your pretty face, girl. You, brat—get out of the way!"

He pushed Jean out of his path and the boy fell. He was up again in an instant, kicking at the big, burly fellow. The other knave moved towards Eugénie. He turned for an instant to glance at his companion and Eugénie saw her chance. She threw off her cloak and drew her sword. The scoundrel stared at her in utter disbelief, then grinned, thinking it a great joke. He drew his own weapon. His beady eyes flashed and the wicked blades clashed and gleamed in the moonlight, faster and faster until it was difficult for little Jean to distinguish one from the other. Eugénie had the advantage of surprise but in spite of the soldier's drunken state, he had superior strength. Her wound was aching and her long skirt hampered her movements. Still her technique was perfect. Little Jean tried to run and help Eugénie but the ruffian who had been guarding him knocked him down. This time the lad hit his head hard and lost consciousness. The other lout then joined his friend, but Eugénie was fighting for their lives. Her strength seemed to be superhuman. All at once she saw an opening and thrust with all her strength at her opponent. He fell backwards with a loud cry and lay still. She didn't have time to exult because the other was attacking, but since he was even more inebriated than his companion, he wasn't too steady on his feet and tripped, just when she was beginning to feel as though she couldn't hold out much longer. His sword went flying from his hand and Eugénie stood over him with her sword point at his throat. She was raging inside with a terrible turmoil. "Will you leave us in peace, rogue? Swear it or I shall run you through!"

"Yes, yes, for God's sake let me go!" The man was sweating with fear. His eyes were staring right out of his head.

"Get out of here or I shall show no mercy the next time we meet," she snarled.

The ruffian fled, his heart pounding as he ran down the street. He was convinced that Eugénie was a witch.

Little Jean opened his eyes. His head hurt terribly. He looked for Eugénie and saw her, standing very still, looking at the motionless body of one of the soldiers. There was dismay on her face. In fact, Eugénie was numb with shock and horror at what she had done. The soldier was dead. She had destroyed a man's life. It didn't matter one bit to her that it had been in self-defense. She felt she had committed murder, the worst possible sin.

Jean tugged at her arm frantically. "Let us go, Mademoiselle. Let us go from this dreadful place!"

At last she allowed him to lead her away. The little boy was frightened. They had three miles to go beyond Noyon to meet his father's friend, and Eugénie's lack of response worried him. At last she allowed herself to be led away. They were both exhausted and Eugénie followed little Jean's lead mindlessly.

Monsieur Ragon was anxiously waiting for them when they arrived at the meeting place. He bundled them into a cart and piled hay on top of them. It didn't smell very good at all. In fact, it smelled strongly of manure. Still, it was quite comfortable and the lumbering motion of the cart lulled little Jean to sleep. When they reached the valley of the Somme they stopped for the night. Eugénie lay staring at the sky, yet she didn't really see it. Her eyes saw nothing but the body of the man she had killed. Little Jean was awakened by their escort's not so gentle nudge.

"Wake up, young fellow. We must be off."

The little boy looked anxiously towards Eugénie, hoping that she would have recovered her senses—but no. He tried desperately to draw her out of her stupor. It was useless. He looked beseechingly at Monsieur Ragon, pleading for help, but that worthy yeoman simply shrugged his shoulders in Gallic fashion and pointed to his head.

"Come on, up you go." He tossed Jean up into the hay and then he helped Eugénie. Little Jean thought the journey would never end. He wanted his father desparately.

The journey finally ended as all journeys must. Monsieur Ragon stopped the cart just outside the Amiens and allowed Jean and Eugénie to sit beside him on the seat. When they saw the tall spires of Notre Dame Cathedral standing stark against the moonlit sky, Jean breathed a sigh of relief. They had reached Amiens in safety. Monsieur Ragon dropped them off a short distance away from the cathedral and then left quickly, not wanting to risk drawing attention to them. Jean led Eugénie as quickly as he could towards the cathedral and his relief knew no bounds when he saw his father. Monsieur Dupons had been waiting there an hour. Jean rushed into his father's arms, weeping.

"My son, why are you crying? A man doesn't cry."

"Oh, Papa, Mademoiselle Eugénie has lost her mind! We were attacked by two hor . . . horrible soldiers in Noyon and—oh, Papa, she was so brave! She killed one and chased the other one away. Oh Papa, she was so wonderful! But when it was all over she realized she had killed one of them and she has just stared vacantly like that ever since," Jean sobbed.

Monsieur Dupons looked at Eugénie. "Don't worry, *mon fils,* I shall see to her in a little while. She will be fine. We must hurry now. There is no time to lose."

They followed Monsieur Dupons to the river where a boat was waiting to take them to St. Valery. It was a long, hard night's rowing on the part of Monsieur Dupons and the two men who were helping them, but they reached St. Valery in one piece. A two-masted ship was anchored offshore waiting for their signal. When the signal had been flashed and an answer received, they rowed out to the waiting brig. They were helped on board by willing hands. André, Marie and Madame Dupons were smiling through tears of joy. But then they noticed the state Eugénie was in.

Monsier Dupons put his finger to his lips, indicating that they should say nothing. Then he took Eugénie by the shoulders and shook her very hard. No response. She was like a person in a trance. Finally, he raised his hand and slapped her hard across the face a couple of times. She gasped and then recognition dawned. She threw herself into his arms and began to cry, heartrending cries like a wounded animal. He held her until her cries had subsided.

"There now, girl, you are all right. Your journey is almost over."

"Where are we, Monsieur?" Eugénie asked tremulously.

"St. Valery, my dear. This ship will take you to England." Then he turned to his wife and son. "Come, we must say goodbye to these good people. Perhaps someday, in better times, we may meet again."

The three fugitives watched sadly as the Dupons rowed away towards shore. The captain gave the signal to cast off and then appointed one of the sailors to show the passengers to their cabins. Eugénie was completely drained after her experiences of the past few weeks, indeed, the past months of scheming and pretense. In spite of her cramped quarters she soon fell fast asleep on the narrow bunk.

She awoke a few hours later and lay there listening to the waves churning. Then she became aware of the smell of the water in the bilges which permeated the cabin. Suddenly she was overcome by nausea and ran up on deck. Marie and André were there already, hanging over the side. Both had acquired an unbecoming greenish hue to their complexions. They three remained on deck until at last they sailed into the harbour of Dover. It was a bright October day and their hearts filled with happiness and a marvellous sense of peace as they gazed at the famous white cliffs which guarded England. The harbor was crowded with vessels of all shapes and sizes. As the seagulls winged overhead uttering their shrill cry, the three weary adventurers fell to their knees and offered up a prayer of thanks to the good God who had guided them safely out of the darkness of danger and despair into the light of peace and safety.

Part Two

ENGLAND

The ship docked and amidst all the activity, Captain Rogers bellowed in their ears, "Well, 'ere we are at last, all safe and sound."

"I can't quite believe it's true," Eugénie whispered.

"Aye, lassie, 'tis true enough. 'Ere—you'll be needing this." He handed Eugénie a bag of English coins. She shook her head.

"Sir, we cannot accept charity. But bless you for your kind heart."

"Nonsense, girl! 'Tis *your* money. Our mutual friend exchanged certain gems ye gave 'im for the coins. Take the bag, girl. 'Tis no time for false pride. Now if ye will follow me, I 'ave arranged rooms for ye at the inn."

They followed the captain through the streets to the "Squire George" amidst a buzz of curiosity and stares from passersby.

When they arrived at the inn, Captain Rogers turned them over to the care of the jovial landlord, Mr. Marble.

"Why, ye poor creatures, ye must be exhausted, and 'ungry too, Oi'll wager!"

He bade them follow him and, having shown André to his room, took the girls further down the hall to a cozy little room overlooking the harbor. He lit a fire in the grate and soon their frozen limbs began to thaw. After they had washed the grime of the journey off their tired bodies and brushed the dust from their clothes, they joined André downstairs for supper. The landlord saw to it that they were well fed. After supper they went into the parlor and sat before the roaring fire, feeling very content.

"We shall get along famously. We've got enough money to see us through until we can find work," Marie said enthusiastically.

"Did I happen to mention, girls, that a very old friend of my father's lives in England?" asked André. "It's been some time since we heard from her, but I'm sure she'll help if we can find her. I believe she's very well off."

"André, that's wonderful! Things are beginning to look better and better," cried Eugénie.

"On that happy note, I shall say goodnight. The landlord told me that there's a coach leaving for London in the morning."

"Goodnight, André." Eugénie looked at him lovingly. He blew her a kiss and left.

"Eugénie, I do hope André's friend helps him because I honestly can't imagine him working for a living," sighed Marie.

"*Zut!* Marie, you underestimate him. Why are you always against him? I am sure he won't let us down. If he has to work he will. You always think the worst of him. It is just not fair." Eugénie stalked off to bed in a huff. Marie said no more. She didn't want to upset Eugénie but she felt that, as always, Eugénie saw André through a golden veil.

The next morning they were awakened by a loud knock on the door. It was André. He called, "Girls, get dressed quickly and come down to breakfast. The mail coach is leaving for London within the hour!"

One hour later they were seated in the coach and on their way to the big city. The passengers were silent—each heart was beating with its own secrets, each soul alone with its own fears and hopes. How little we really know of what goes on in our fellow man's brain! Even those we know and love have a world all their own in which no one may intrude. At the very least, we can hardly share more than a glimpse from time to time. So we shall leave the three young exiles now and take a look at the England they had come to, the England of the French *emigrés*.

Pitt was Prime Minister at the time and England opened its arms to the unfortunate fugitives from France. Many of the *emigrés* had friends and relatives already living in England and those who were related by ties of blood or friendship to English families were secure in their welcome. But those who arrived without friends or acquaintances were confused and full of anxiety. When they got off the ship they found themselves the object of good-natured curiosity and stares that made them feel even more strange and anxious.

The English people, to their great credit, rallied to the aid of these wretched people, despite the fact that France and England had never had much love for one another. To their credit also, no national prejudice and no religious bigotry interferred with their sense of compassion. Later, when on January 21, 1793, King Louis climbed the stairs to eternity, whatever sympathy the English common people might have had for the Revolution vanished. England was a country that had witnessed the execution of many kings and queens, but times had changed and they were not at heart a violent race. To cap it all, ten days after the execution, France declared war on England.

Once the French *emigrés* settled and realized that they were safe, their natural gay spirits returned, though, they found England very strange. The climate was never really hot, and never really cold. Heavy fog hung over London a great deal of the time. The English people matched their climate—neither outgoing or gay. Worst of all were those dreadful English Sundays, quiet and sombre as the grave—no amusements. To the funloving French, this was extremely bewildering and melancholy. The comparison between the French and the English people could be described as the difference between the sun and the moon. The French were very effusive and sparkling with gaiety. The English were more reserved, hiding their warmth until they were sure of the other person, but like the moon, nonetheless beautiful in the glow of their acceptance, though at first glance they seemed cold and distant.

The coach rumbled along the bumpy roads until at last it reached its final destination—London. Church-bells were clanging and chiming from every direction. The three weary travelers soon found themselves trudging along streets that twisted and turned. Buildings seemed to blot out of the sky. Wrought-iron shop signs creaked and groaned overhead. Drainage canals ran down the center of most of the narrow cobbled streets. They quickly discovered that it was best to keep close to the walls of the houses so as to avoid being hit by the garbage and human excrement that was nonchalantly dumped from the windows above. Brightly emblazoned coaches and crude wagons rolled along the streets. Amidst the press of traffic, young boys sold newspapers and bellowed the fact through tin horns. Ragpickers rang handbells to announce their presence and cries of "Fresh 'erring, fresh 'erring" resounded from the lips of fishmongers. The great city was a melange of brick and wood buildings of every imaginable shape and size. The buildings bordered the great river Thames upstream and down for at least two or three miles. Magnificent, majestic church domes gleamed in the light of day, in spite of the curtain of smoke that arose from thousands of chimney pots all over the city.

Wearily they trudged the streets, confused by the unbelievable press of traffic and startled by the raucous shouts of the barrowers and other hawkers. They walked and walked, not knowing where they were going, and at last they spotted a sign in a window— "Rooms to Let." The house looked neat and clean, so they knocked. The door was opened by a round-faced little woman with brown hair slightly peppered with grey. She looked at them suspiciously.

" 'Ello then. Wot can Oi do fer ye?"

"Pardon, Madame, we are looking for a room to rent. In fact, two rooms," said André.

She stood with her hands on her hips, eyeing them up and down. "Ye'll 'ave to pay a week in advance. Mind ye, Oi want no goings on and Oi expect ye to be on time fer meals. Oi'll feed ye breakfast and supper."

They followed her up a flight of rickety stairs to their rooms. The girls' room had a bed, a washstand and two comfortable looking chairs. The wallpaper was faded but there was a rug on the floor and bright curtains at the windows. Everything was spotlessly clean.

"By the way, me name is Mag Boles. Oi 'opes ye'll be comfortable," their landlady said as she departed.

The girls were so happy to have a roof over their heads that they failed to notice André's look of disdain. He said nothing, but already his mind was at work figuring out a way to get out of this dreadful place. He followed Mrs. Boles to his room, and the girls undressed and washed up after their long, dusty journey from Dover. After they had brushed the dust from the only clothes they had, they climbed into the soft, comfortable bed and fell fast asleep. They slept right through to the next morning. No one disturbed them.

As soon as she had shown her new boarders to their rooms, Mag ran across the alley to her good friend and neighbor Moll Finn.

"Moll, Oi've got new boarders! They just arrived. Frenchies! They look right enough, but ye never can tell."

"If Oi were ye, Mag, Oi'd really keep me eyes peeled. These furriners 'ave strange ways, Oi've 'eard."

"Aye. Oi want no 'anky-panky under me roof. Oi keeps a respec'able 'ouse, Oi do. Come over and meet them when ye get a chance."

"Aye, Oi'll do that, luv."

The trio were awakened the next morning by the joyous clanging of churchbells. The streets were quiet— no shouting, no barrows. It was their first Sunday in England. The music of the bells reverberated through all the streets, calling people to prayer. They dressed quickly and hurried downstairs for breakfast. André was there before them. Mrs. Boles looked at them with approval. She set great store by punctuality.

"Oi expect ye'll want to go to Church. Well, Oi suggest ye go to St. Pancras. Ye'll likely meet many of yer countrymen there. Oi've 'eard tis a favorite meeting place of the Frenchies."

Marie beamed. "That would be nice. Perhaps someone could help us find work."

"Oui, Marie. Let us hurry and go there. It would be so wonderful to meet some people from our beloved France. Will you go with us, André?"

André frowned. "I couldn't possibly go dressed like

112

this. I would bring shame to my family. Just look at us —why, we are practically in rags!"

It was true. André looked much worse than the girls. The clothes Monsieur Dupons had supplied were clean and sturdy, but did not fit well, having been made for a much shorter man. He did look rather pathetic.

"Perhaps you are right. It must be distressing for you to be dressed like this. But I feel like doing something," sighed Eugénie.

Marie pushed them both in the direction of the stairs. "Let's at least go for a walk. It's a glorious day. Do hurry up! Eugénie, would you bring my shawl, please? I'll help Mrs. Boles with the dishes, then we'll set out."

It was a perfect day for walking, bright, cold and sunny. They wandered here and there until they found themselves in St. James' Park. It reminded them all of the de Varney estate and suddenly they were overcome by loneliness and sorrow. But they were young, and their gloomy mood didn't last. They became completely absorbed in watching the passersby. People from all walks of life strolled here on Sunday, some beautifully attired, others a little threadbare, like themselves. It was six o'clock when Mrs. Boles opened her front door to three hungry young people ready to do justice to her well-cooked supper. After they had eaten their fill, they sat by the fire in the parlor and relaxed.

"André, tell us about your friend," Eugénie suggested, taking his hand.

"Lady Jerningham? Well, I know she is very rich. She knew my father long before he married my mother. I think there may have been a romance between them. I really don't know too much about it. She did keep in touch with my parents over the years, though. The last address we had was Bolton Row, Piccadilly. I am sure she won't be too difficult to find if she is still alive."

André paused, obviously uncomfortable. "Girls, I've a really embarrassing request to make of you—could you lend me enough money to buy some new clothes? I can't possibly appear before her ladyship looking like this."

"I'm sure she would understand if she's as good a friend as you say," Marie put in. "We must be careful not to spend too much money for it might be some time before we find suitable employment. André, you must not depend on your father's friend so much. She might disappoint you."

André said nothing. Marie thought she saw him frown but he covered it up quickly. Then Eugénie spoke up. "Marie, I think we should *all* buy some new clothes. We certainly can't apply for work looking like beggars. Why don't we go and buy some nice things tomorrow? Let us have at least one day of fun, we deserve it. Who knows, perhaps André is right and Lady Jerningham will help us all." André smiled, but Marie didn't like his expression. He looked so smug.

"Magnifique! It's a marvellous idea! We shall have one glorious, frivolous day to remember for a long time to come," said André, his good spirits restored. They sat talking excitedly about the future until the fire in the parlor had faded to a few dying embers, signalling that it was time to go to bed.

It was a glorious morning, the sort that can lift the spirits of even the most depressed. The birds were singing with joy. Even Mag sang as she prepared breakfast for her lodgers.

"Good morning then," she greated them. "Oi'll 'ave yer breakfast in 'alf a mo'."

"*Bonjour,* Madame Boles," chorused her three cheerful guests.

"Are you goin' shoppin' then?"

"*Oui,* Madame. Perhaps you could tell us the very best place to go," said André.

"Well, Bond Street is where the quality shop, but Oi do think it's a mite expensive fer yer pockets. Now if Oi were ye . . ."

André broke in, "That's quite all right, Madame. This Bond Street is where we shall undoubtedly go. Now if you will excuse me, ladies . . ." André rose from his place at the table and left the room to see to his appearance.

"That one is too big for 'is own boots, if yer arsk me," said Mrs. Boles. The girls laughed. "Oh, Madame Boles!"

"Now girls, why don't ye call me Mag? Oi just can't get used to this 'Madame! Wot were ye sayin'?"

"Well . . . Mag. Don't be too hard on André. He has had a dreadful time. He's the son of a Marquis. Both his parents were brutally murdered and . . ." The girls unburdened themselves to the sympathetic ears of Mag Boles, telling her all that had happened to them in the past six months. Mag wiped the tears from her eyes with the corner of her apron when they had finished.

"Why, me poor darlin's, yer safe 'ere with old Mag Boles!" She hugged them both to her ample bosom.

"Thank you, Mag dear, but we must find work," said Eugénie. "I know André expects his friend Lady Jerningham to help us, but I don't like to depend on that. Do you know of anyone who might need help? We are not afraid of hard work."

Mag opened the kitchen window and screamed, " 'Ey Moll—Moll, do ye 'ear me?"

"Oi, 'ear ye, Mag! The whole neighborhood 'ears ye. In fact 'alf London can 'ear ye," bellowed another voice.

"Come 'ere 'alf a mo'."

"Wot ye want then, Mag? Gotta cuppa tea?"

"Get over 'ere, luv."

The girls listened in complete fascination at this interchange, barely able to understand the peculiar words.

Moll bustled in. She was a big roly-poly woman with a booming voice. Her sleeves were rolled up, showing powerful forearms. Moll was a washerwoman by trade and a good one, much in demand even if she did like a nip more often than was good for her.

"Moll, this 'eres Marie and Eugénie. They need work and Oi'll vouch fer them. There's ought wrong with these lassies. Moll, ye know right well ye need 'elp, now don't ye?"

Mag went on and on, finally convincing Moll that she needed help more than anyone else in London. At last

116

Moll said, "Oh, very well then. Ye don't 'ave to go on. Oi'm convinced. Oi'll take *that* one since yer twisting me arm. Oi don' want that skinny one, though." So Marie got the job. Mag poured tea and they celebrated the event with much good humor, though Eugénie was a little miffed at being described as "that skinny one."

" 'Ere's to ye, ducks. Oi only wish it were a mite stronger," said Moll cheerfully. Mag frowned at her friend. "Oi was only joking Mag, only joking," she added hastily.

About an hour later the three young exiles set out on their shopping spree.

"Don't let anybody cheat ye now," Mag warned.

"We won't. We'll be back in time for supper. *Au revoir,*" called Eugénie.

Bond Street, with its elegantly arrayed patrons, was vibrantly exciting. They mingled with the shoppers unnoticed but when they attempted to enter the very exclusive shops, eyebrows were raised and many a dainty handkerchief was raised hastily to many an aristocratic nose. It was quite apparent that Bond Street was not the place for them, but André protested, "This is the *only* place to shop. We cannot settle for inferior merchandise."

"André, we can't afford those prices," said Marie patiently. "But if you insist on shopping here, go right ahead. Eugénie and I will go elsewhere."

Eugénie was reluctant to leave André but Marie was insistent.

"You don't mind, André? We can meet back at the house later," Eugénie said anxiously. Marie, however, thought he seemed eager to get rid of them.

The two sisters wandered around enjoying the crowds and gazing in rapture at the brightly decorated windows. They finally came to a shopping area just off the Strand that was more suited to their modest wants. With much laughter and delight they bought two serviceable day dresses, a dress for Sunday, two pairs of shoes, various undergarments and then, feeling very frivolous, they eached selected what they called a party dress.

"We shouldn't really buy them, should we, Marie?" said Eugénie wistfully.

"Well, one never can tell. Perhaps André's Lady what's-her-name will invite us to dinner or something."

"Wouldn't that be marvelous! We wouldn't want André to be ashamed of us."

"Stuff!" Marie exclaimed. "Let's go back. I'm getting terribly hungry."

Eugénie had an idea. "Let's get something for Mag and Moll," she suggested.

"What a good idea! They *will* be surprised."

At last they hurried home with their bundles. Mag's kitchen felt warm and cozy. Mag beamed when she saw them. "Well, Oi can tell ye enjoyed yourselves," she said. A moment later, the door opened.

"Well, look 'ose 'ere! Mrs. Nosy from across the alley!"

The girls laughed and displayed their treasures. "We bought something for you both. It's not much but it might keep you warm," said Eugénie shyly.

Mag and Moll were touched by the girls' thoughtful gifts.

"The scarves are just what we need for winter. It's already getting pretty chilly. But where is the bold Monsure André?" asked Mag.

Eugénie giggled at Mag's pronunciation of "Monsieur" and she couldn't help giving Mag a hug. Marie however, said acidly, "It is hard to say where he might be. We left him in Bond Street. Perhaps he got thrown in jail!''

"Oh, Marie, how can you say a thing like that!'' cried Eugénie, turning pale.

"I was only joking. Really, Eugénie, you have no sense of humor whatever when it comes to André.''

Mag was busily putting supper on the table when André sauntered in. What a vision! Mag almost dropped the platter she was holding. They stared at him in amazement. His hat breeches and coat were of bright blue velvet. His stockings were yellow silk and matched the lining of his coat. Both the coat and hat were trimmed in silver. Silver buckles glittered on his shoes, and he carried a cane with a silver head. Marie was the first to find her voice.

"Where did you get the money to buy all that? I know they cost much more than you had with you.''

André shrugged his shoulders. "Oh, no problem, m'dear. I simply told them who I was and that I was Lady Jerningham's *protégé*. The shop assistants couldn't do enough for me. They wouldn't even take what money I had. Said there was no hurry. By the way, I sent a messenger to her ladyship, so I am sure she will come very soon and take us away from this dingy place.''

Mag exploded. "Hoity toity! If ye don't like it 'ere, ye knows where the door is!'' Eugénie quickly stepped into the fray. "Oh, dear Mag, I am sure André didn't mean it like that. It's just that he has always been used to the most magnificent of everything. André, tell her you didn't mean to insult her home.''

"Of course not, Madame,'' said André, with an elaborate bow. "My humblest apologies. I certainly did not mean to offend.''

119

Mag sniffed, tossed her head and marched out of the kitchen. She was not convinced one whit of his sincerity but for Eugénie's sake she would hold her tongue. It was apparent that the poor child was head over heels in love with the foolish youth.

The next week passed quickly for Marie who was busy washing clothes for Moll. André, however, was miserable. He had expected to hear from Lady Jerningham as soon as his message had been delivered. He moped around the house, getting in Mag's way, looking completely dejected. Mag was convinced he'd never hear from his high and mighty friend. As for Eugénie, she was trudging around London looking for work and at the same time observing and absorbing the life of that great city.

One half a million people, rich, poor and middle class, formed the pyramid of London society. The Royal Family, of course, crowned the pyramid. Not far below them were such notable families as the Devonshires, the Newcastles and the Bedfords. The rich were receiving more than 20,000 pounds a year from their estates while the laborer made twenty pounds. But all in all, it was a free society and those with talent and enterprise could make their mark. Land was the most secure form of investment then and successful merchants, lawyers and politicians and others of the middle classes were buying out those of the gentry who had failed on hard times.

Eugénie longed to be part of the "ton" who flocked to the clubs—White's, Boodle's or Almack's. She gazed wistfully at the magnificent coaches that rattled along the streets filled with merry, dashing young blades and their beautiful ladies. She made up her mind that this was the life for her. She would not allow herself to fall to the bottom of the pyramid where the yeomen, cottagers, artisans and factory hands, together with the chimney sweeps, builders, drovers, scavengers, odd-job-men and shop assistants were forced by fate to belong. She refused to join the fish-mongers, ballad sellers, rag pickers, sailors, porters, coal-heavers and chairmen, and looked askance at the cut-throats and burglars and the gentlemen-of-the-road and, of course, the princesses of the streets. She did not belong to this group of citizens, oh no, not Eugénie Fabré. All of them were only too familiar with overwork, disease, sudden death or destitute old age. Eugénie saw babies left exposed on the streets or their bodies dumped on dung heaps to save the cost of a funeral. Hunger and hardship was the lot of many. Those who were lucky enough to find jobs worked long hours for low wages. Children were hired rather than adults because they were cheaper. They worked twelve hours a day, seven days a week. There were many murders and equally many executions. One could be hanged just as high for picking a pocket as for setting fire to a town. Penalties were severe and the prisons were horrible beyond description. Eugénie's compassion overflowed at some of the sad sights and many a tear she shed as she trod the streets of London. Still and all, conditions were, even at their worst, only half as bad as those in France.

It became her custom to regale Marie, Mag and Moll with the adventures of her day as soon as the dishes had been cleared away after supper each evening. As for André, he was becoming a complete recluse and Mag was getting more and more irritated with him. She would glare at him and bite her tongue, so as to keep from telling him to "get orf 'is duff and find some gainful employment." She had no time for sluggards.

Eugénie was also becoming discouraged. Another week had sped by and still she couldn't find work. She was afraid she never would. Mag was worried about her too and finally, against her better judgment, asked an old friend to help. Eugénie was overjoyed at the chance and hoped that Harry Boggs would like her enough to hire her.

"Oi can't say as 'ow Oi'm 'appy to 'ave ye workin' in such a place, but Oi don't want to see ye mopin' like that one over there," said Mag, giving André a nasty glance.

Eugénie had just left for her interview with Harry Boggs when Mag heard a commotion in the street. She peeked out the parlor window and saw the little waifs of the alley staring goggle-eyed at a magnifcent coach and four splendidly dressed footmen. One of the footmen scattered coins and the children scampered like little squirrels foraging for nuts. When a tall, elegant looking lady emerged from the carriage Mag exclaimed, "It must be 'er nibs—Lor' love a duck!"

Lady Jerningham held a delicate lace handkerchief to her noble nose. The smells were not to be endured. It had been sheer madness for her to venture into this neighborhood. How could she have let her emotions carry her away like that? The little ragamuffins stared at her. They had never seen such gorgeous clothes or such a glittering array of jewels, not even in their wildest dreams.

Lady Jerningham sailed into Mag's house with her head held high, looking neither to the right or to the left. Mag bobbed a curtsy and ushered her fine guest into the parlor. She dusted a chair with her apron and Lady Jerningham with some trepidation sat down.

"My good woman, be so kind as to inform the Marquis de Varney that I wish to see him," she ordered.

"Yes'm, to be sure." Mag climbed the stairs as fast as she could, and tapped on André's door.

"Monsure André!" she hissed.

André came to the door. "What is it, Mrs. Boles? I am in no mood for a lecture today," he said irritably.

"It's 'er ladyship! She's 'ere—downstairs in me parlor!"

André turned pale with excitement. He had no time to change into his elegant new clothes, but ran eagerly downstairs. As soon as he entered the parlor, Lady Jerningham's eyes filled with tears and she gestured for him to come close. He knelt at her feet.

"My little one! How like your dear father you look. Your poor, dear father—what a terrible way to die. You poor child, how you must have suffered."

André kissed her hand as Lady Jerningham caressed his face. She had been madly in love with André's father long, long, ago, when they were just sixteen. Their families had been good friends, but as the years went by, the friendship was dissipated by the many miles that separated France from England. Although Lady Jerningham had married a fine man, she had never ceased to love Phillipe de Varney, and she now transferred that love to his only son.

"Come—sit down and tell me what you can about your escape from France," she said. She noticed a shadow across his face and hastily added, "If it is too painful, my dear, pray don't, I shall understand."

"*Oui,* Madame, it is painful but I must tell you."

André unburdened himself, speaking slowly and painfully, of the terror of his last months in France. He spoke to her of Eugénie and Marie and how it was thanks to them that he was alive today. Lady Jerningham listened in horrified silence until he had poured out the whole terrible story.

"You poor, poor darling," she sighed.

"You must meet Eugénie and Marie, dear Aunt. I

owe them so much.''

"Yes, my dear, and so I shall. They must be rewarded for their gallant efforts on your behalf. Such loyalty in servants is to be highly commended, and so rare. I shall send a carriage for them this evening. You must come with me now." Her ladyship looked around the room. "How you could bear to live in this terrible establishment, if one could call it an establishment, I really can't imagine!"

André hesitated. "Aunt, if you don't mind, perhaps I should wait for them. They might feel less nervous about meeting you if I were with them."

"Very well, André, but *do* get rid of those dreadful clothes! Do you need any money?"

"Thank you Aunt, but no. I promise I shall be suitably dressed this evening. But are you sure that I shall not be a burden to you?"

Lady Jerningham dabbed at her eyes. "My poor child, how can you think such a thing? For your father I would have walked to the ends of the earth and through fire. How can I do less for his son!"

Lady Jerningham began to cry and it was all André could do to comfort her. Finally she pulled herself together and when André escorted her to her carriage, her face was once again set in its familiar haughty expression.

Meanwhile, Eugénie was sitting in "The Black Bear," a tavern run by Mag's good friend Harry Boggs. She watched him serving the few customers that had strayed by at this early hour. He looked kindly enough, rather tall and very rotund, with a full, wide face, grey wavy hair and a beautifully trimmed beard. He looked very distinguished, she thought.

She listened to the loud laughter and the mutter of

conversation and was impressed by the feeling of warm friendliness that pervaded. Through clouds of tobacco smoke, she saw the same warmth reflected on the faces of Mr. Harry Boggs and his jolly customers. When she saw the friendly landlord of the "Black Bear" come towards her, she prayed fervently that he would give her a job. She knew she would like him—he had such a kindly twinkle in his eyes.

"Well now, young lady, what can I do for you?"

"I . . . I believe Mrs. Boles spoke to you about me, sir," Eugénie faltered.

He grinned at her. "Why, you must be that little French Mademoiselle Eugénie. Welcome!"

Eugénie thought she had never heard a more beautiful voice. It filled the air with sonorous sounds. His eyes twinkled and his lips twitched in a smile.

"I must say I am astounded that dear Margaret would send you to me. Do you know that I am very much enamored of that dear lady? Have been for quite some time. Alas, she will have nothing to do with me. She hates, as she sees fit to call it, 'Devil's brew,' but perhaps there's hope for me yet."

Eugénie smiled at him. "I didn't know that. Mag just said you were old friends."

"I'm not surprised. I think she would like to forget my feelings for her." He sat down beside Eugénie and patted her hand.

"Will you give me a job, Monsieur? Please, I am quite desperate. I have had experience working in my uncle's wine shop in Paris. Really I have," she pleaded.

Harry looked at the eager, anxious young face before him. "Well, I tell you what, Mademoiselle Eugénie. If you put in a good word for me with Margaret, the job is yours."

Eugénie clasped his hand, ecstatic with joy.

"You are so kind, Monsieur. So very kind!"

Marie was up to her elbows in suds when Mag rushed over in a dither. Marie felt a twinge of fear—what could be wrong to make Mag dash over in such an excited state? Marie shoved a chair under her and Mag sank down and tried to catch her breath.

"Mag, whatever is the matter? Has something happened to Eugénie?"

Mag could hardly speak, she was so excited. Marie wiped her hands on her apron and handed her a cup of tea.

"Thank ye, child," Mag gasped.

"Mag, do tell me! Is something wrong?"

Mag noticed the look of anxiety on Marie's face. "Bless ye child, no. Oi didn't mean to worry ye like that. But 'er ladyship came and André said that yer both to dine with 'er tonight. But Marie, Oi don't know about that one. Oi wouldn't put too much stock in 'er 'elp if Oi were ye. She's a proud peacock if Oi ever sawr one. Oi also think that that André is a weak sort of bloke. Oh, 'e 'as charm enough, but ye won't get fat on charm. Oi 'opes Eugénie don't 'ave 'er 'opes built too 'igh. But Oi'm afraid that girl is blind where 'is nibs is concerned."

"Mag, I am so afraid you're right. Eugénie can see no wrong where André is concerned," sighed Marie.

They were still sitting there a half hour later when Eugénie came home. Not finding Mag in the house, she ran across the alley to Moll's.

"I got the job! I got the job!" she cried. "Mag, darling, Mr. Boggs is wonderful! He's such a kind man and so handsome. He asked about you."

Mag tried to act unconcerned but Eugénie could tell she was pleased.

"Aye, luv, Oi suppose ye could find worse," she admitted.

"Eugénie, sit down," Marie commanded. "We have wonderful news for you! Lady Jerningham came to see André just after you left. Mag says she wants us to dine with her tonight!"

"Aye and 'is nibs 'as been gettin' ready ever since she left," said Mag dryly.

Eugénie's eyes shone. "How marvellous! Isn't life astounding? Marie has a job and now I have a job and Lady Jerningham will take care of André and we shall all be so very happy!"

Marie and Mag looked at each other. No words were needed. They understood each other perfectly.

Chapter 10

The girls were dressed in their party dresses long before Lady Jergingham's carriage was supposed to pick them up. They chatted excitedly until Mag finally had to beg them to stop.

"Me 'ead is spinning! Go on upstairs and try and calm down. Ye'll be too excited to eat and Oi warrant there'll be a fine table set at yon place."

Reluctantly they went to their room and admired themselves in the little mirror. They really looked quite lovely. Marie was clad in green and Eugénie in blue. The color made her eyes look even more blue and bright. André was dazzling, of course, in the magnificent clothes he had bought in Bond Street. By the time the carriage arrived the two girls had worked themselves up into quite a state of nerves. André tried to calm them.

"I know you will love Lady Jerningham. She's a marvellous person and I have told her how much you've done for me. She said you must be rewarded."

"We don't want to be rewarded, André. We did it because we cared," said Eugénie softly.

Suddenly Mag's scream reached their ears. "The carriage is 'ere. Come down quickly! Don't keep them waiting." Mag was in as bad a state of nerves now as the two girls.

They hurried downstairs and there was Moll waiting at the foor of the stairs.

" 'Urry, me loves," she urged. They kissed Mag and Moll goodbye and were handed into the carriage by one of the footmen, followed by André. It was so exciting. Eugénie sat back in the luxurious seat and closed her eyes. She was all at once transported into a dream world. No longer was she in Lady Jerningham's coach but in her own and she was going to a marvellous soirée with her beloved André.

She was still deep in her reverie when the carriage pulled up at Lady Jerningham's town house. The footmen helped them descend from the carriage and a carpet was rolled from the carriage to the door so that they wouldn't get their shoes soiled. A moment later they were ushered into the grand drawing-room. Lady Jerningham was seated by the fire and she looked at them through a lorgnette as they made their curtseys. She was surprised at their grace and beauty. They didn't look like peasants, that connection for dear André was not to be borne. Though André was now impoverished, he must move in the right circles, and be seen with only the best people. None of these thoughts showed on her well-bred face or in her well-bred manner, however. She was most gracious to her young guests.

They spoke of insignificant things until, to Eugénie's great relief, a servant announced that dinner was served. They followed Lady Jerningham, who was escorted by André, to the dining-room. This room was aglow with the dancing lights of what seemed to be hundreds of candles. The sparkling light was reflected in the magnificent chandeliers, as well as in the exquisite china and crystal. Bouquets of flowers filled the room with delicate fragrance. The atmosphere was somewhat strained, however, and the girls were very glad when the sumptuous meal was over.

They returned to the drawing-room and after a polite interval Lady Jerningham rang for the carriage. As they waited for its arrival, she said, "I am sure you must realize that André will now be staying here with me. I imagine you will agree that it is the proper place for him. I shall be in touch with you in the next few days. Goodnight."

"Goodnight, Lady Jerningham and thank you for letting us come. It was most kind of you," said Marie, as she and Eugénie curtsied again.

André escorted them to the carriage. "Girls, give me time to establish myself here, and then I shall do all I can to set you up comfortably," he promised.

Eugénie looked at him adoringly. "André, darling, don't worry about us. Be happy. All we ask is that you keep in touch with us. Don't forget us, André."

"Eugénie, how could you ever think I would forget you? Never!" He kissed her hand tenderly and blew a kiss to Marie. *"Au revoir."*

He found Lady Jerningham waiting for him when he returned to the drawing-room.

"Come, sit down, my darling André. We must talk at once," she began. "I know how you feel about those two young ladies and I quite understand that you feel obligated to them. Nevertheless, for your own sake you must have nothing more to do with them." Seeing that André was about to protest she added, "I mean, of course, until you are firmly established. We know that you cannot hope to regain your estates in France and so I strongly urge you to think about a good marriage. I, of course, shall see you have adequate funds for your daily requirements, but a wealthy wife would be a distinct asset. You must take your place in society—the honor of your family demands it. I shall help you to find such

130

a wife. London is bursting with eligible young ladies of the first 'ton'."

"But Aunt, I can not abandon Marie and Eugénie just like that. I owe them my life," he protested.

"My dear André, I never for one moment suggested that you abandon them. I shall see that they are justly repaid for their service to you."

"But I must continue to see them. They just wouldn't understand if I don't. In all honor, I must."

"My dear, I am in full sympathy with your noble sentiments. But don't you see that if you persist in continuing this relationship, not even my patronage will save you from social ruin? Society frowns on such lowly connections. It is just not permitted—at least it is not permitted for one in your circumstances—to have such inferior friends. Now protest no more. Look on the bright side. Once you are established, you may do as you please. There will be no end to the good that you may accomplish for them. However, if you insist on pursuing this unsuitable friendship, then for your own sake I shall cut you off without a penny, and then what could you possibly do for them? For your dear father's sake I would even do that. You, André, have no training and no money. Think about what I have said. And now we shall say goodnight, my little love." She took André's arm and he led her to her room, his head spinning.

"Goodnight, Madame, and thank you so much . . ."

André couldn't sleep. He paced the floor, thinking about all Lady Jerningham had said. He knew in his heart she was right. André was not a cruel young man, only weak and spoiled. He knew he couldn't bear to go back to Mag Boles and live that kind of life. He just wasn't cut out to live like a peasant. As he looked about the magnificent room and felt the silken sheets on the bed and sniffed at the colognes on his dressing table, he tried to rationalize his desire to remain with Lady Jerningham. He told himself that everything she had said was true and he vowed that when he became wealthy and established in London society, when he was accepted in the highest circles, he would buy a cottage for Eugénie and Marie, perhaps set them up in some kind of business—dressmaking or something like that. French dressmakers were all the rage. As for Eugénie, he loved her and certainly something could be arranged. No doubt everything would work out for the best. With that last thought he went to sleep without a care in the world for the first time in months.

Mag and Moll were eagerly awaiting the girls. They were not surprised that André had stayed with Lady Jerningham and were secretly glad.

"Now sit ye down and 'ave a cuppa tea and tell us about 'er ladyship's big 'ouse. Was it gorgeous?" Mag asked eagerly the minute Eugénie and Marie walked in the door.

They drank tea and talked until the wee hours of the morning. Then the yawns became contagious and they said reluctant goodnights.

Eugénie lay in bed thinking about André for a long time. She basked in her love for him and was confident that he loved her. Her love for him was so great that he had to love her just as much. She knew with absolute certainty that as soon as he was able to arrange it, they would be together forever. In the meantime, she was so lucky. She had a job, and Marie, Mag and Moll with their warm love and friendship. She went to sleep with a smile of contentment on her face . . .

It was a dark morning and very chilly but Eugénie

awoke with a marvellous feeling of anticipation. She was going to belong to the working world today, and that was enough to gladden any girl's heart—that is, any girl like Eugénie. She noticed that Marie had already made her bed and was preparing to go down to breakfast.

"Isn't it a lovely, wonderful morning, Marie?" she chirped, bounding out of bed. Marie looked at the sky and then back to her sister as though she thought Eugénie had taken leave of her senses. "You'd better hurry up, Eugénie, or you will be late for breakfast."

After Marie had left for work and the kitchen had been cleaned up, Eugénie and Mag sat drinking another cup of soothing tea.

"Well, luv, this is yer big day. Oi do 'ope Oi didn't make a mistake in tellin' ye about that job. God knows Oi'd rather ye worked at somethin' else," sighed Mag.

"Now don't worry, Mag. Harry is a wonderful man and he, I am sure, runs an orderly place. Surely you must know what a fine person he is. He's your friend isn't he?"

A faraway look appeared in Mag's eyes. "Aye," she said wistfully. "That 'e is."

Eugénie decided to go to the tavern and learn what she could of the layout of "The Black Bear." She was excited and anxious to do her very best. The rain held off although the sun hadn't appeared. That didn't quench her spirits, for as she walked towards "The Black Bear," Eugénie had the sun in her heart.

A fire crackled cheerfully in the hearth, filling Eugénie with a sense of peace and security as she listened to Harry's instructions. It was still quite early and the evening rush had not yet begun.

"Harry, how did you and Mag become friends? I

133

noticed she looked a little sad when we talked about you this morning. Why does she dislike 'The Black Bear' so much?'' Eugénie asked boldly.

Harry sighed. "It's a sad story, little one. You see, Margaret's father was as big a drunkard as ever trod this earth. Her mother, poor soul, was a sickly woman and poor Margaret, being the eldest child, from about the age of six was obliged to struggle and even steal to feed the family. She told me how she used to cringe in her bed at night, waiting for her father to come home and dreading it. Often as not when he did come in, he would pull her poor mother out of bed and Margaret would hear him berating her and calling her all sorts of names. Sometimes he would come into her room, which she shared with her three little sisters and her baby brother, roaring drunk. On those nights he would cry over her and hold her close with his rotten whiskey breath choking her. She told me she used to cringe when he touched her. It was a horrible life for a child.''

Eugénie had tears in her eyes. "Poor Mag! Poor dear sweet Mag. How brave she must have been!''

"Margaret was a brave child no doubt, but my dear young lady, her story is far from unique, sad to say.''

"What happened to her parents and her brother and sisters? She never speaks of them.''

"Her mother died when she was about eight and a few years later her father's body was pulled out of the Thames. She kept the family together until eventually the girls married and her brother ran off. She never hears from them and I say just as well. She was pushing a barrow full of vegetables when I saw her for the first time,'' Harry said, his face softening at the memory. "She looked so tired and alone. Some young scamps came running around the corner and knocked poor Margaret's barrow over. All the vegetables were ruined and she sat down and cried. She looked so pathetic that my heart went out to her. I went over to her and handed her a handkerchief. Then I bought her a cup of tea and she told me the whole story. I think I loved her then but didn't know it. Anyway, to make a long story short, I lent her the money to buy the house she now lives in. Needless to say she paid me back, every brass farthing. We remained good friends but she would have nothing to do with me, romantically speaking, because I ran a tavern. Well, I wasn't about to give up my livelihood and we had some hard words. From then on she stayed away from me as much as possible, but I have never ceased to love her."

"Oh, Harry, that is a shame! I know she must be lonely, though she does have Moll."

"Yes, Eugénie, she has a very good friend in Moll, though it breaks her heart that she drinks so much. She has tried everything to make her give up drinking. Moll, to give her her due, does try to do her drinking quietly and goes to great lengths not to let Margaret see her in her cups."

Their conversation was interrupted by the first of a long string of revellers, and from then on Eugénie was constantly busy. She was enthralled with her work and thought that "The Black Bear" was an attractive place. It had many dark wood tables, cushioned seats and some tables with snow white cloths were set aside in the ladies' parlor. A bright fire warmed the toes of the customers and the glowing flames were reflected in the pewter tankards and trenchers. The food being prepared in the kitchen sent out inviting smells to stimulate any appetite. "The Black Bear" was patronized by an affluent segment of society. It was certainly very different from her Uncle Pierre's place in Paris. Moll came in once to pick up a bottle, wished Eugénie luck, and went home. Moll was quite well off since her customers were from the gentry and paid a high price for her services.

Eugénie's experience in the wine shop helped her now and it wasn't long before she was ble to mix any of the drinks so popular here. She was pretty and pleasing and the customers loved her. Many of them jokingly said to Harry, "About time, Boggs. About time we had a pretty face around here. We're sick of looking at your ugly mug."

Harry took the ribbing with a good grace. When they closed up shop that night, Harry walked Eugénie to her door and, of course, Mag invited him in to give him a good talking-to.

" 'Arry Boggs, ye'd better take care of this child or ye'll answer to me, do ye 'ear? Oi'll not 'ave 'er run off 'er feet. Mind yer language, too. Do ye 'ear me, 'Arry Boggs, ye great lump?"

"Aye, Margaret, don't worry about Eugénie. I shall take care of her as if she were my own daughter." He winked at Eugénie and then turned to Mag. "Margaret, if you are so worried, why don't you come over tomorrow night and see for yourself?"

Mag looked at him for a long time. Dear Harry—she really did care a lot for him, but as long as he was selling that devil's brew, he'd never know it. She disliked Eugénie having to work in such a place but she knew that Harry would look after her and there was simply nothing else for the girl to do.

"Well, Oi just might, 'Arry Boggs, but don't go gettin' any ideas. If Oi go, it would only be to see with me own eyes 'ow that child is really gettin' along. But Oi won't be eatin' in that den of iniquity and don't ye go offerin' me anythin'. Oi'll sit in that little back room behind the bar and stay out of the way. Why, Oi'd choke if Oi 'ad to watch people guzzlin' that wicked stuff! And another thing, 'Arry Boggs, me name is *Mag* and Oi'd thank ye to stop callin' me Margaret!''

After that speech she poured tea for them all and Harry stayed about a half hour longer. When he finally left, Mag turned to Eugénie. ''Luv, this 'ere letter was delivered after ye left for work this afternoon. Oh, and this bag of money with it. Is it from André, do ye think?''

Eugénie opened it, trembling with excitement. It must be from André. Such beautiful stationery and such exquisite writing—strange that through the years they had known one another, she had never seen his handwriting. Mag saw Eugénie's face grow very pale as she read the letter. The words swam in front of Eugénie's eyes and seemed to penetrate to her brain like burning coals:

> *My Dear Mademoiselle,*
> *I feel it is my painful duty to inform you that it would be in the best interests of one whom I know you care a great deal for, namely André de Varney, if you would avoid seeing him in the future. Society will not tolerate a person in his precarious position mixing with someone of your class. While I have seen for myself that you and your sister are both fine, well-mannered young women, I am quite sure you will agree that you are far below the station of the de Varneys. If he should attempt to see you, please try to dissuade him from further contact. He is an honorable man, as his father was, and I know he feels greatly indebted to you both and will therefore feel honor-bound to continue the friendship. I know that you felt it your duty to the family to try to help him and looked for no reward; still, such loyalty is to be commended. I hope you will accept this reimbursement for your services. I send this letter to you, Mademoiselle Eugénie, since it is to you that André seems to have the greatest attachment. I have confidence in your loyalty*

and good sense to see that what I have said is for the good of all concerned.

Charlotte Jerningham

Eugénie was furious and desolate at the same time. How dare Lady Jerningham insult them like this. There was no way that they would accept the money! They didn't want payment, and she felt sure that André would not cut himself off from her. She couldn't bear that and was positive that André felt the same way. Of course, they would be discreet—she wouldn't want to ruin André's chance to take his place in English society. There wasn't no reason why anyone should know of their continuing relationship. He could visit them secretly. Once he was well established, they could meet openly again.

Marie walked in and saw the letter in Eugénie's hand.

"Well, what did André have to say?" she asked.

"It's not from André," said Eugénie grimly, holding it out to her sister.

Marie took the letter and read it aloud. She was furious by the time she had read the last line. "Why, the old windbag!" she cried.

"Marie, such language!"

Marie had picked up quite a few of Moll's colorful phrases and she repeated, "Eugénie, that's just what she is—an old windbag! How dare she! We'll keep the money and let them both go hang."

"No, Marie. I shall take it back to her tomorrow. I want to see her face when I throw it at her feet."

"Eugénie, you are such a little fool. André *owes* us the money and I doubt very much if you will ever see him again. He'll forget about us as soon as he takes up with his fine feathered friends."

"Marie, you are wrong. You are very wrong. Please don't say anything more or else we shall quarrel and I

138

don't want to do that," said Eugénie, trying to swallow her tears.

Next morning Eugénie was up and dressed in her Sunday best long before Marie was awake. She went down to the kitchen, fixed breakfast for herself and then walked around to Sutton Place. She raised the heavy brass knocker and a butler came to the door.

"Kindly go to the service entrance," he said coldly. "How dare you come to the front door?"

"I wish to see Lady Jerningham or Monsieur de Varney. I am Mademoiselle Fabré—I was a guest of Lady Jerningham the other evening."

"I beg your pardon, Miss, I didn't recognize you," the butler said. He gave her a rather disdainful look and told her to wait in the hall for a moment. He was back in a few minutes and ushered up to Lady Jerningham's boudoir. Lady Jerningham was sitting up in bed drinking her morning chocolate. She smiled frostily at Eugénie. "You received my letter, I take it. But you need not have troubled to come here—I do not expect you to thank me. I was very pleased to reward you."

Eugénie's eyes blazed in anger. "Lady Jerningham, I came to return your bribe. My sister and I may not be of your class, but we have our pride. How *dare* you assume that we would accept payment for what we did out of our great affection for André?"

Lady Jerningham almost chocked on her chocolate. "Really, my dear, don't be foolish. I am sure you can use the money. You can't afford to be proud. Pride is not becoming to one of your class." Eugénie smarted under that slight but she forced herself to remain calm. She had learned long ago that anger only made one lose control.

"Lady Jerningham, you do not have to worry. We

shall not inflict our company of you or André. But if he wishes to see us, I shall not turn him away. We are friends regardless of our class. But you wouldn't understand that." She placed the pouch of coins on the bed.

Lady Jerningham's face turned purple. "How dare you! You ungrateful young slut! Get out of my sight!" she cried.

Eugénie dropped a disdainful curtsy and took her leave without a backward glance. She was so angry that she felt close to tears, but consoled herself with the thought that André would be sure to visit her soon. But weeks went by and André did not appear. Neither did he write. Eugénie longed to see him. She made excuses for his absence but they did nothing to alleviate her pain.

A month passed and then one evening when Eugénie was busy setting up the glasses for the evening rush at "The Black Bear," André walked in. Eugénie's heart skipped a beat. She felt embarrassed that he should see her doing such menial tasks and for the first time felt how truly inferior her position was compared to his. In spite of this, she tossed her head and greeted him cheerfully.

"André, how wonderful to see you! We have missed you so much."

Eugénie noticed that André felt ill at ease though he tried very hard to hide it. "Mag told me where to find you," he began. "You have no idea how busy I have been. Lady Jerningham took me on a whirlwind shopping spree, then packed everything up, including me, and went to her country estate in Kent. We had a marvellous time. I wish you could have been there. It was one exciting party after another. I've met so many people, my head is swimming trying to keep their names and titles straight. Eugénie, I never knew how much I missed that life until I found it again!"

"I'm so glad. You're really happy, aren't you?" she said wistfully. Eugénie's face glowed with love as she gazed at his dear face. André felt a lump from in his throat—she was so lovely—but he had to go.

"Eugénie, *cherie,* I must leave now but I promise I shall call on Sunday and spend the afternoon with you. I have so much to tell you. *Au revoir.*" "*Au revoir,* darling," she called after him.

Eugénie was bubbling with excitement when she came home that night. She danced into the kitchen where her three companions sat over their nightly cup of tea.

"André is coming on Sunday, isn't it just wonderful?" There was no comment from the trio at the table but Eugénie didn't seem to notice.

"Mag, love, could we cook something special and perhaps have a small party? We could invite Harry."

Mag was certainly not full of enthusiasm at the prospect of entertaining André, but nevertheless she agreed.

All of them pitched in to prepare a splendid dinner for Sunday. Mag baked and cleaned and Eugénie worked with her, urging her on to great efforts. Mag grumbled from time to time. "A body would think we were expectin' the King 'imself!"

A last the long awaited day was heralded in by the usual Sunday chorus of church bells. Eugénie sprang from her bed, and Marie pulled the covers over her head.

"Marie, it's Sunday! André is coming today! Aren't you excited?"

"I'm glad he's coming for your sake, but right now I want to sleep. If it will please you, I'll get excited later," Marie mumbled.

Eugénie pulled the covers off. "Do let us go to chapel right away. I don't want to miss one moment of his visit

141

and he might come early." Reluctantly, Marie bathed and dressed and they went off to mass.

It was almost noon by the time they got home. Eugénie rushed in eagerly, to find Harry and Moll but not André. By the time he arrived at two o'clock, Eugénie was a bundle of nerves. Mag took one look at him and glared. "Humph! At least ye got 'ere in time fer dinner!"

André had no desire to eat with them but he couldn't very well refuse gracefully. He wished he could see Eugénie alone. He despised himself for his attitude towards her friends. They were good people no doubt, but definitely inferior. Mag ushered them into the parlor and with great relief took herself off to the kitchen to put the finishing touches to dinner.

Harry settled back in the chair with his pipe and urged André to tell them about life with Lady Jerningham. He didn't need much encouragement. He spoke enthusiastically about the interesting people he had met and described in detail the beauty of Lady Jerningham's estate in Kent.

"Of course it isn't quite as beautiful as my home in France," he added.

Eugénie sat at his feet and listened, enraptured, to every word that fell from his lips. Harry noticed the look of worship on her face and his thoughts became very troubled indeed. Mag interrupted by yelling for them to come to dinner. She had prepared a sumptuous meal. She had wanted everything to be perfect and had spared no expense.

Eugénie felt proud and oh, so very, very happy!

After they had eaten their fill, they returned to the parlor and Harry lit the fire. The fact that the fire smoked a little didn't bother them at all, though Mag noticed that André stayed as far from it as he could. He stayed for a few hours after dinner but didn't say much. Harry, who loved to talk, monopolized most of the conversation, eloquently regaling them with amusing stories about his customers. Finally, André interrupted and apologized, "I really hate to leave so soon, but Lady Jerningham expects me to accompany her to the Devonshires'. Thank you for your hospitality. I shall certainly see you all soon again." In truth he could scarcely wait to get out of there.

After that, his visits were few and grew shorter and shorter. Mag and Marie couldn't have cared less, except for the fact that it was so very upsetting to Eugénie. She grew more quiet and withdrawn and spent more and more time alone in her room. After one of his visits one wet Sunday, she was despondent. André had been charming as usual, but he seemed so detached. His conversation was very stilted and he had paid no special attention to her. After he had gone, she didn't feel like being around the others so went directly to her room. She sat and listened to the wind whistling and the rain beating against the window panes. She felt so alone. It struck her how strange it was that those sounds could evoke such contrasting emotions depending on one's state of mind. When one is happy, the sound is welcome, accentuating the coziness of being indoors, warm and safe. When one is sad, as Eugénie was, it seems to increase one's loneliness and sadness one-hundred fold.

She sat there making excuses for André. He had to do what he could to establish his position in society. It wasn't that he didn't love her. He did. Even if his visits were short and few, at least he did come, and she knew it couldn't be easy for him. But oh, how she longed for him! How she longed to be close to him and feel the warmth of his love! She must have loved him from the first moment she saw him so long ago in the woods. She cried out to the night, "Oh André, my love, please love me!"

When Marie came up to bed later, she found Eugénie asleep in the chair with tears on her face. Marie put a blanket over her and stormed back downstairs where Mag, Moll and Harry were still sitting chatting.

"I could *kill* André!" she fumed.

"Calm down now, luv, calm down," soothed Mag.

"What is bothering you, my dear?"

"Oh, Harry, it's Eugénie. She's breaking her heart over that *cochon!*" Marie raged.

"That *wot?*" Moll asked.

"That *pig*. That *pig*, Moll."

"Oi likes that word—cochon. Oi must add it to me list of choice expressions," mused Moll.

"Well." Mag said. "It seems to me that there's nought we can do. Maybe Eugénie is right about 'im and we are wrong. Oi certainly 'ope so."

"Ladies, if I may say so, he *does* come by and that can't be very easy to manage. I'm sure Lady Jerningham keeps a sharp eye on him. Let's just bide a while before we judge him."

"Aye, ye be right 'Arry. Marie, lass, there's nought else we can do," sighed Mag.

Chapter 11

Lady Jerningham had taken André deeply into her heart. He was the son she had never had. She saw to it that excitement filled his every waking moment. He was dressed in the latest, most magnificent of fashions. She saw to it that he was invited to the best parties and associated with the very best people. It wasn't long before the invitations came for his sake, because of his good looks and endearing manners, as much as for Lady Jerningham's. Indeed, he had become quite a favorite of the Devonshires, the Bessboroughs, the Spencers and the Greenvilles and the other notable families of the "ton." He had also renewed his acquaintance with the Comte d'Artois and others of the French aristocracy who had been fortunate enough to escape to England. His life had become an exhilarating social whirl. He was happy. Nothing more had been mentioned about his finding a wealthy wife and he hoped that Lady Jerningham had put it out of her mind.

It had become André's habit to take an early morning ride. Upon his return one morning, he was informed that her ladyship wished to speak with him at once. He bounded up the stairs and presented himself to Lady Jerningham who was, as was her habit at this time of day, sitting up in bed drinking her chocolate and looking extremely pleased with life in general. Her eyes lit up with pride and love when André strode into her boudoir.

"My love, I am so proud of you, so very proud! You are a great success and so I have decided it is time for us to give a magnificent ball in your honor. The Prince of Wales and only the most distinguished families shall be invited. This house, my precious, I assure you, will be buzzing with females of the highest eligibility vying for your attention."

"Aunt Charlotte, I am deeply touched. You have done so much for me already," he said, kissing the hand she extented to him. "Is there anything I can do to help?"

"Yes, my darling André. I want you to go out and order the most expensive, the most dazzling attire. Spare no expense. For your grand debut as a host, you must look like a prince out of a fairy tale."

"I shall try to make you proud."

"You already do, dear heart. Now run along. I have much to do."

The ball was set for the following month. Invitations were sent and accepted. Flowers and food were carried in at every hour for weeks before the big event. Servants were busy setting up tables in the grand dining-room and festooning the halls with greenery. The maids were frantically cleaning every nook and cranny and the great crystal chandeliers were polished until they shone like a million stars. Lady Jerningham's ball was the most anticipated event of the year. Everyone had accepted, including the Prince of Wales.

On the evening of the long awaited ball, Lady Jerningham, looking very regal in grey silk, knocked on André's door. She looked him up and down and was entirely satisfied. He looked especially handsome in his blue satin coat and breeches. A sapphire gleamed in the lace at his throat and his stockings and waistcoat were embroidered in silver thread. The fit of his coat proclaimed that it had been created by the most fashionable tailor of the day. She smiled with pleasure at the sight of his high, blue heeled shoes with their dazzling sapphire-studded buckles.

"Those shoes, my love, are really too ridiculous for words. They are magnificent!"

"Do I meet with your approval, Madame?" André asked with a smile.

"Indeed you do. If I were thirty years younger, I'd vye for your attentions myself."

"Madame if you were thirty years younger, no one else would stand a chance," he replied gallantly.

He kissed her hand and she patted his head fondly.

"Come—let us go downstairs, André. Your guests will be arriving shortly."

They walked downstairs arm in arm and she cast her critical eye on the magnificence which had been created solely for this one night. She nodded. All was well. Outside, the windows of the house glowed with the reflections of the lights within. At the brightly lit, red-carpeted entrance stood footmen in gold-trimmed livery awaiting the arrival of the guests. At about eight o'clock, a steady steam of elegant carriages began to arrive, disgorging beautifully gowned and bejewelled ladies and their equally dazzlingly clad escorts.

In the entrance hall just off the grand ballroom, Lady Jerningham and André stood ready to receive their illustrious guests. The elite of England filed past, exchanging the elaborate bows and curtsies that eitquette demanded. By nine o'clock the ballroom and card rooms were filled, but the Prince of Wales had not yet arrived. From the ballroom the strains of a delightful minuet floated in to the reception chamber, accompanied by merry chatter and gay laughter. André's head was whirling.

"Well, my love, have you got your eye on one of the beauties that are now adorning our ballroom?" Lady Jerningham asked behind her fan.

André laughed. "Aunt Charlotte, to tell the truth I am in such a state of excitement that I can hardly distinguish one face from another. Shall we join our guests, since it appears that His Royal Highness is not coming?"

Scarcely were the words out of his mouth when the major-domo's voice was heard:

"His Royal Highness, the Prince of Wales and party."

The Prince of Wales, dressed in burgundy velvet lavishly embroidered in silver, kissed Lady Jerningham's white hand.

"Will Your Highness permit me to introduce my ward, the Marquis de Varney?"

"A pleasure, Marquis. We are always pleased to welcome those of you who have been driven from your homeland," said the prince.

André bowed low. "Your Royal Highness is most gracious." The Prince of Wales then took Lady Jerningham's arm and they proceeded to the ballroom.

Lady Angela Shrewsbury, one of the most eligible of the heiresses present, had felt her heart flutter when André had greeted her in the reception chamber. It was fluttering again when she noticed that he had just walked into the ballroom. She turned to her mother.

"Mama, I *must* dance with him. He is absolutely heavenly! Please, Mama, do arrange it. It annoys me to think I wasted all that time in Switzerland while this gorgeous creature was running loose in London!"

"My dear Angela, are you quite sure? You know he is quite penniless except for what Charlotte Jerningham graciously bestows on him. But I must say you are right, he *is* a gorgeous creature," her mother agreed.

She glided off to find Lady Jerningham and within a few minutes returned with her ladyship and André in tow. Angela was sitting by the French doors looking delicate and lovely. Dark curls framed her face, showing off her enormous dark brown eyes. She looked more like a Spanish Señorita than a member of one of the most notable English families, and was one of the most sought-after beauties of the day. Besides being beautiful, she had a yearly income in excess of 10,000 pounds.

"Why Angela, how lovely you look this evening—of course you always do. Did you have a marvellous time in Switzerland?" asked Lady Jerningham. Then, seeing the look that Angela was giving André, she hastened to introduce the young people.

"Angela, may I present André, the Marquis de Varney? André, my love, this delightful creature is Lady Angela Shrewsbury. I am sure you two will become firm friends."

André bowed and, taking Angela's dainty hand, kissed it with that particular grace and charm that only the French seem to have in abundance. He thought he had never seen anyone more exquisite.

"Mademoiselle, may I have the honor of this dance?" he asked.

He led her to the floor and they danced, or rather floated, in each other's arms. Her dainty feet and graceful body moved to the music with perfect ease. André could not take his eyes off her beautiful face. He could have danced with her all night, but etiquette demanded that, as host, he circulate among the other guests.

In the weeks that followed Angela and André

contrived to see a great deal of each other. Lady Jerningham was highly enthusiastic about their friendship and encouraged André in every way. André was definitely attracted to Angela and basked in her obvious adoration. Angela's mother and Lady Jerningham put theirs heads together and decided that the match would be perfect. A house party was arranged at the Jerningham estate in Kent, where the good ladies hoped that an engagement would come about.

"My dear Charlotte, we shall see to it that André and Angela spend every possible moment together. Our plan cannot fail. They make such a handsome couple," sighed Lady Shrewsbury.

"Their children will be the most gorgeous combination. Oh, my dear Elizabeth, they will be so happy."

About sixty young people were invited under the watchful eyes, of course, of the anxious mothers and maiden aunts who accompanied them. As planned, Angela and André were thrown together at every opportunity and they found that they had a great deal in common. By the end of the first week, they announced their engagement. Lady Jerningham and Angela's mother congratulated themselves. Angela was radiantly happy and André felt proud that he had captured the heart of the most beautiful girl in London.

But his happiness was clouded somewhat, in spite of his excitement, by thoughts of Eugénie. She cast a pall over his otherwise perfect happiness. Was it guilt? He knew he loved Eugénie more than Angela, but he was unprepared to give up everything for her. Angela and he would get along beautifully even if he didn't love her. Perhaps Eugénie would agree to some arrangement. He knew that she adored him. Why not? Arrangements were made every day. Wives understood and so did husbands, for that matter. Of course, he would wait a reasonable time after he was married before engaging in such a venture. Having once reconciled himself to his weakness, he sat down and wrote to Eugénie.

The letter was delivered to her the next day before she left for work. Marie was out and Mag and Eugénie were having a last cup of tea before clearing the breakfast dishes. She broke open the seal and Mag saw her face drain of its color. She read the letter in silence then threw it down and ran out of the house without a word. Mag picked up and managed to puzzle out the words with great difficulty:

> *Dearest Eugénie:*
>
> *I know that what you are about to read will pain you deeply. Forgive me. There was no other way. As you well know, I am completely dependent on the kind generosity of Lady Jerningham and so I must comply with her wishes as much as possible. So I have agreed to marry the Lady Angela Shrewsbury, the heiress to a large fortune. But my dearest Eugénie, my marriage should not make the slightest difference to our love for each other. You know that I love you deeply, as I know you also love me. Hold this thought until we can arrange to be together. We shall speak more about our love and our future when I see you.*
>
> *I remain your ever loving and devoted,*
>
> > *André*

Mag was purple with rage and disgust. "Now wot does 'e mean by that? Oi don' like it one little bit, Oi don't! Wher can that child be?"

Poor Mag was beside herself with worry. She looked up and down the alley, asking the children if they had seen Eugénie. After an hour had gone by, in sheer desperation, she ran to "The Black Bear."

" 'Arry, 'Arry, for God's sake come 'elp me look for me darlin'. That blighter 'as broken 'er poor 'eart, 'e 'as!" she wailed.

"Now calm down, old girl. Calm yourself. Tell Harry all about it."

Mag told him the contents of the letter and then began to cry. "The poor child read it and than ran off. Oi can't find 'er anywhere. 'Arry, 'elp me look for 'er. You go one way and Oi'll go the other."

Two hours later, it was Harry who found Eugénie in St. Pancras Church. She had wandered around in a daze of misery and somehow her footsteps had led her to the church. Desolate, she was kneeling, pouring out her heart to God, when Harry walked in. He was anguished as he saw such deep sorrow on the face of the young woman he had grown to love. He went up to her and held out his arms.

"Come, Eugénie. Come with me," he urged.

"Leave me alone, Harry, please. I am no good for anyone. Just go away and leave me alone," Eugénie sobbed.

Harry wanted to comfort her, tell her everything would be worked out, but he knew it wouldn't, not as long as she persisted in her attachment to André. Instead he spoke sternly and with a great deal of feeling.

"Now listen to me, child. If you wish to indulge in self-pity and misery, that is your privilege, but at least stop and think of what you are doing to those who love you. That boy is not worth your tears. He is, I grant you, charming and amiable enough, but he is not for you. How you could ever have fallen in love with him is a mystery to me. Eugénie, it is about time you learned that a person must stand on his own two feet in this life. Don't ever depend on other people to fulfill your expectations. If one expects too much from people, one will usually be disappointed. Now that doesn't mean we must not love. By all means, love, but don't expect others to hold you up. Be strong in yourself, Eugénie my dear, as I am quite sure you can be. A weak person could not have accomplished all that you have done in the past few months. Apart from anything else, Eugénie, Mag, Moll and your dear sister do not deserve to be afflicted with the agony of watching your suffering. If you must have a broken heart, don't wear it on your sleeve for all to see. Have some dignity. Now, Eugénie Fabré, you have a choice between wallowing in your own sorrow or trying to achieve happiness and peace of mind of those who care about you. What is it going to be?"

Eugénie didn't answer. She turned her back on Harry. He took her by the chin and turned her face towards him. "Am I getting through to you or must I go on?" he demanded.

He saw a spark of anger in her eyes and she straightened her shoulders and stood up.

"You have made yourself perfectly clear, sir." Her voice was like ice. They walked home in silence. He could feel Eugénie seething with rage. However, when they reached the house, she kissed him on the cheek and smiled sadly. "I'll be fine now, Harry. Thank you for making me take a good look at myself. I love you dearly."

In the days that followed Eugénie seemed once more to be her old self, but at night she lay and imagined all sorts of impossible things. She saw herself being very gay and irresistible, easily luring André away from Angela even with all her money. He came to her in her dream with eyes full of love and admiration, wanting only her and telling her that he belonged to her completely. In another beautiful scene she saw herself very aloof and very mysterious and André was drawn to her like a magnet, his desire for her rekindled by her disdain. These fantasies soothed her aching heart and helped to mute the reality of losing André. She hadn't given up hope. She told herself that nothing was impossible and she knew André's love for her could not possibly have died so soon. He truly loved her and she was sure he would be unable to go through with his mercenary marriage. It was as well that neither her friends nor Marie knew what was going on in her head or they would have been sick with worry. As it was, they were happy to see her smile again and congratulated Harry on making her come to her senses.

Chapter 12

Laughter and merriment, the clink of glasses, music and chitchat reverberated around the rooms of the famous clubs. Every night thousands of pounds changed hands as lords and ladies gathered around the gaming tables with bated breath and anxious looks, watching the roll of the dice. André was caught up in this whirl. Between soirees in town, parties in the country and the thrill of gambling, his life was full. He and Angela were the toast of London. He had made some very good friends in Lord Langley, Sir Harry Farthingale and Sir Peter Mayhew. The four had become quite inseparable. These scions of noble families were wealthy, gay blades who vied with each other in leading the fashion and who constantly dared and wagered each other to see who could accomplish the most outrageous exploits. Their escapades were discussed at every party and applauded with much mirth. But while the others had enough money to indulge their every whim, André did not. He only had the pocket money Lady Jerningham chose to give him. While she was most generous in seeing that he was dressed in the height of fashion and that his horses were the finest, she was not so foolish as to entrust a frivolous young man with any great sums of money. His companions, to give them their due, did not urge him to gamble heavily, knowing his circumstances. However, once his engagement to Lady Angela had been announced they urged him to try his luck more often. Their persuasion fell on fertile soil and André determined to do so the next time they were all together at White's.

About one week later the four young men wandered into that sanctum sanctorum. They partook of champagne and idly watched some men dicing. Growing tired of watching, Lord Langley and Sir Peter started a game of piquet. Lord Langley lost heavily and Sir Harry sat down opposite Peter Mayhew. "Well, Pete, old boy, see what you can fleece me of. I promise you I shan't be so easy." But it was soon apparent that he too was no match for Sir Peter.

"Egad, Peter, you have the devil's own luck tonight! You ought to play Brewster and clip his wings."

"Aye, you're right. Go, Gerald, and extend my invitation to Lord Brewster." Gerald Langley did as he was bid and returned forthwith with Gordon Brewster. Brewster was a wily sort. It was said he had his hand in many a shady deal but no one could prove it. He bowed to the other three men and sat down opposite Peter.

The stakes were low at first and Peter won the first three hands. Meanwhile the champagne was flowing freely. They raised the stakes and Peter found himself losing quite steadily. At last he pushed back his chair and grinned. "Gentlemen, Lord Brewster is much too good for me. How about one of you taking him on?"

Gerald Langley turned to André and clapped him on the back. "Go on, de Varney. Have a shot at it."

By this time André was quite in his cups so with a laugh he took Peter's place at the table, thinking to himself, "Why not? I used to be quite lucky at cards." Even so, a little nagging voice deep within him added, "Yes, but in those days you didn't care whether you won or lost.''

Brewster graciously gestured towards the cards. "You deal, sir.''

André dealt and bid. His luck seemed to be in, and always his glass seemed to be full, no matter how much he drank. They played and drank for over an hour. André seemed to have an extraordinary run of luck. Brewster was losing heavily. But he didn't seem to mind. "What say you de Varney, shall we double the bet?" he suggested.

"Mais oui, Monsieur, but why not triple it?" André said recklessly, winking at his three friends. Gerald, Harry and Peter roared in intoxicated delight. "Let's drink to it!" They yelled at a waiter, "Bring more champagne!" They drank to each other's health and pounded each other on the back. By this time André swore that the table was moving and at times he believed Brewster had a twin who was helping him play cards. In the end, Brewster won the pot and, in addition, held André's note for 3,000 pounds. As he handed his note to Brewster, André shrugged his shoulders in that typically French fashion, saying, "Zut! It's only money, and besides *je me suis trés bien amusé.*" With a last farewell to Brewster, the four merry companions, their arms around each other, sang at the top of their voices and finally hours later staggered home to their separate beds.

André awoke with a terrible pounding in his head. It seemed as if a thousand little men were inside his brain beating a thousand little drums and stamping their feet. The pounding grew louder and he heard Harry Farthingale calling his name. He groaned, *"Allez-vous-en!"* and pulled the covers over his head.

"Get up, André, get up! Peter, throw some cold

water on him," said his friend.

Hearing this, André sat up and painfully opened his eyes. Harry was sitting on the edge of his bed and Peter and Gerald were standing at the foot.

"André, for God's sake wake up. We just realized you owe that devil Brewster quite a lot of money," said Gerald.

André suddenly felt quite ill. He had forgotten completely. What a pickle he was in! What ever was he going to do?

"Mon Dieu! I had forgotten about it. 3,000 pounds is a fortune to me. Perhaps he'll give me an extension on the debt."

Gerald shook his head mournfully. "He wouldn't give his own mother an extension."

Harry clucked sympathetically. "Sorry, old chap. I'm afraid you'll have to spring for the money somehow." Then the three friends left Andé to his misery, promising to check back with him later.

He could have borrowed the money from any of these young men, but one simply did not sponge on one's friends. He groaned—last night had seemed such a lark but alas, in the cold light of day it became all too clear what a mess he had got himself into. Where was he to find 3,000 pounds by next week? He certainly could not ask Lady Jerningham—she would be furious. Angela certainly could afford it, but it was unthinkable that he should shame himself in front of her. There was only one hope—Eugénie.

He dressed and made his way quickly to Islington. Mag opened the door to his knock. Seeing who it was she said curtly, "Wot do ye want then?"

"I should like to speak to Eugénie, Madame."

Mag barred his way. "She's not 'ere."

But just then Eugénie came down the stairs and saw

him at the door. Her eyes lit up and she ran to him with open arms.

"Oh, André, what a marvellous surprise! Do come in," she cried.

"Eugénie, come walk with me in the park, please. There's something I must talk to you about," said André nervously.

She put on her bonnet and shawl and went with him to St. James Park. They walked for some time talking about trivialities. Then he drew her to a bench in a secluded area and proceeded to acqauint her with the facts. "Eugénie, you are my dearest friend and I love you. So to whom could I possibly turn but to you, dearest, when I am in such dire need? Last night, I am ashamed to say, I made a complete idiot of myself. I lost 3,000 pounds to the worst bounder in England."

"Andé, how *could* you lose 3,000 pounds? That's a small fortune!" Eugénie gasped.

"Oh, a few of us went to Whites and like a complete fool, I played cards. I won at first, but in the end lost everything, including 3,000 pounds I don't have," he confessed.

"But, André, how can I help you? I don't have any money."

"Eugénie, you have the jewels. They are worth much more than 3,000 pounds. Please let me have them. I promise I shall pay back every penny and more. Please Eugénie."

Stunned, Eugénie hesitated. "I don't believe they are worth that much. Besides, the jewels are not only mine but Marie's as well. I shall have to get her permission. They are all we have in the world."

André pouted. "I know Marie will say no. She hates me."

"No, André, no! She just doesn't understand you.

Leave her to me. Why don't you meet me here tomorrow at the same time, and I'll let you know."

He took her hand and pressed it to his lips. "Bless you, darling! I promise you won't regret it." She looked at him adoringly and gently took his hand. "Don't worry my love, I'll find a way."

All the way home she asked herself how on earth she was going to convince Marie to give up the jewels. It would certainly not be easy. It wasn't until she had come home from work that night that she managed to bring up the subject. Marie seemed to be in a particularly good mood, so Eugénie plunged right to the point.

"Marie, do you love me?"

Marie looked surprised. "Of course, silly. What brought that on?"

"I need your help, Marie. Please say you will help me."

"What is it? Of course I'll help if I can."

"Dear Marie, what would I ever do without you! André came to see me today. He's in terrible trouble. I promised I'd give him our jewels to pay off a gambling debt." Seeing the look on her sister's face, she pleaded. "He's desperate, Marie, and he will repay us. He promised. As soon as possible."

Marie snapped, "For André, absolutely nothing. *Nothing,* do you hear?"

"Marie, I beg of you, please do it for me, if not for him. Please. I love him so and I need to help him."

Marie looked at her sister. There were tears in Eugénie's eyes, and at last she relented. "Very well then. Oh, Eugénie, you fool, you *fool!* I wish to God we had never laid eyes on André de Varney!"

Eugénie hugged her sister. "Thank you, Marie! Thank you with all my heart!"

Marie lay awake all night. She had the most awful feeling that disaster was about to strike. Somehow those

160

jewels were like a good luck charm. It seemed to her that as long as they had them everything would be all right. Now they were to be lost to them, most likely forever . . .

Eugénie was up at the crack of dawn. She carefully wrapped the jewels in a piece of cloth and hurried downstairs for a quick breakfast, then went directly to the park. André was already there, sitting on a bench with his head in his hands, looking very dejected. At her approach he looked up. "My love, have you got them?" he asked eagerly.

"Yes, André, I have." She sat down beside him on the bench and with a smile handed over the precious package. He kissed her hand over and over. Then he stood up, drawing her with him, and clasped her close to him. "Oh, my precious love, if only I could tell you how much you mean to me!" he sighed. There were tears in his eyes and Eugénie's heart ached for him. He might have added, "If only I were not so weak," but that was too much to admit to himself, much less to Eugénie. Instead, carried away by emotion and the longing to possess her, he said, "Eugénie, come away with me to the country next Sunday. I can't bear to be away from you any longer. I need you so much!"

Eugénie could hardly believe what she was hearing. All her dreams were coming true! André was telling her that he needed her. She would spend her life trying to make him happy! He was kissing her hand again and then she realized that he was leaving.

"*Adieu,* my precious. Until Sunday. Eugénie, will you meet me at Hampstead Heath about seven in the morning?"

"Oh, André, I can't believe it! Sunday cannot come too soon for me. *Adieu,* my love."

She returned home with a glow on her face and her heart seemed to beat out the words that were music to her ears—"He loves me. We are going to spend the day in the country on Sunday. On Sunday we shall be alone with our love."

The days seemed to crawl by but eventually Sunday arrived, bathed in a golden glow. Eugénie took a hackney to the Heath where she saw André sitting astride his horse. Both man and beast seemed to have been molded as one. How handsome he looked! André's fair hair gleamed in the morning sunlight. His brown velvet coat fitted him like a second skin and his brown riding boots shone like dark satin. He looked anxious, but when he saw Eugénie standing there looking at him with such love in her eyes, his face lit up like the sun.

"You have come, *chérie!* I was in utter torment all night, fearing you would not."

"Oh, André, nothing could keep me from you!" she breathed.

He jumped down from his horse and clasped her in his arms. "My darling, Eugénie, *je t'aime,"* he whispered.

Shyly she answered, "I love you too, my darling. I always have."

Their lips met with all the urgent sweetness of a tender kiss and they clung to one another, their hearts pounding.

He lifted her into the saddle, then mounted behind her. "Come my dear. I have arranged for a room at a nearby inn." As the horse trotted off, Eugénie's heart seemed to keep saying over and over, "He loves me. He loves me!"

Evidently the landlord was expecting them, for when they entered the warmth of the inn, he greeted them jovially and ushered them upstairs to a private sitting room. It was a comfortable room with thick carpet, a table and chairs, an enormous sofa and a wonderfully warm fire with dancing flames. The walls were panelled and the windows were hung with red velvet draperie. The landlord bowed to them and announced that luncheon would be served at their convenience.

"Bring it in about thirty minutes, my good fellow." André winked at him and passed him a sovereign. The innkeeper bowed and with a smile at Eugénie, left.

The door closed and at last they were alone. Eugénie felt strangely shy. André gently took her cloak and bonnet and they sat before the fire talking quietly and enjoying being together. Their lunch was brought and they sat at opposite ends of the table. Neither was hungry, but to satisfy the curious eyes of the young serving girl, they ate sparingly. At last the food had been cleared away and they were alone once more. Eugénie wandered back towards the warmth of the fire and André brought her a glass of wine. They sat side by side. She found that she was trembling, so conscious was she of his nearness and his maleness.

"Eugénie!" André's voice was trembling with desire. "I love you and I need you. Eugénie, my darling, I want you so much!"

"Oh, André." She was blushing but her eyes shone like a thousand stars.

"I won't force you, you know that. I believe, though, that you feel as I do. I promise I shall be gentle, my darling," he said, slipping an arm around her shoulders and drawing her close to him.

For a fleeting instant, Eugénie's conscience told her that it was wrong to give herself without marriage, but, overwhelmed by her love and desire, she whispered, "My darling, I love you so very much! When there is love like ours, nothing can be wrong."

Every nerve in her body tingled at the magic touch of

his hands. He buried his face in her breast, then slowly unbuttoned her dress. At last she stood naked before him, her beautiful body glowing in the firelight. He caught his breath at the sight. Very gently his hands touched her face in a tender caress, then moved slowly down to her breasts which he tenderly kissed as one kisses a statue one worships. Then slowly and still gently he touched the smooth skin of her stomach and thighs. Desire was overwhelming him and he could feel an answering response emanating from Eugénie. Feverishly he undressed and a moment later he was standing before her, proud of his manhood. She shyly turned her head away.

"Look at me Eugénie. Look at me," he commanded.

She raised her eyes and with a gasp reached out for him. They clung together, caressing each other passionately. Their desire became an all-consuming flame in which the last vestige of Eugénie's fear was burned away. At last with a moan he pulled her down on the carpet in front of the fire.

"Now my darling? Now?" he whispered, his lips against her throat.

"Yes André, oh yes! I am not afraid."

She closed her eyes and with a cry of sheer rapture he thrust himself into her, plunging deeply into the soft, moist flesh. She cried out but then clasped him to her with the fierceness of her own desire. Together they reached the heights of passion, as he kissed her parted lips and murmured his love for her. They lay back, exhausted but deliriously happy. When he fell asleep, Eugénie held him in her arms and thanked God for giving her such a supreme love.

When they awoke hours later and had dressed, André poured both of them another glass of wine and, raising his glass in a toast, he said, "To you, my precious love. To you, *ma chére petite.*"

"André, I wish we could remain here together always, but I am afraid we cannot stay here much longer," Eugénie said with a sigh.

"Darling, promise me you'll always be mine," begged André.

"Need you ask, my love? I have always belonged to you and I always will."

"Eugénie, after I am married a reasonable length of time, I shall find us a wonderful house where our love will be sheltered and nurtured. We shall have a marvellous life, my precious," André continued happily.

His words suddenly penetrated through the rosy glow of Eugénie's love. She felt her body grow icy cold and a hard knot formed inside her stomach. She was afraid she might faint from shock, but some strength within her came to her aid. She stood up tall and proud, and in a voice she herself hardly recognized, cold, determined and dignified, answered, "No, André. No."

"What do you mean? I love you," he repeated, taken aback.

She looked at him sadly. "André, I suppose you do, in your own way, but I refuse to be your mistress. I thought you loved me and wished me to be your wife. That is why I gave myself to you."

He was about to speak but she cut him off. "Say nothing, André." Then she ran down the stairs, out of the inn, and made her way home.

Without a word to Mag, she raced upstairs and flung herself on her bed. She felt numb. She had given herself to him completely and it had felt so right! Surely he couldn't go through with his proposed marriage, no matter what he had said. He couldn't do this to her. He wouldn't!

But a few days later the announcement of the forthcoming marriage appeared in the papers. André did not send a message to Eugénie nor did he come to see her. Her face lost its tint of pink and dark shadows appeared beneath her eyes, those beautiful blue eyes which now held such a depth of sorrow that the heartstrings of Marie and her three dear friends were torn asunder.

As André's wedding date of November 19th crept steadily nearer, the days and the hours seemed to fly past Eugénie at the speed of light. With the passing days, her faint hopes that André would come for her and call off his marriage began to fade away.

On the eve of November 19th, she was sitting in the kitchen looking very forlorn and paying no attention to the chatter of her sister and friends. Suddenly breaking into the conversation she turned to Marie.

"Will you come with me to St. Paul's tomorrow, Marie? I must see him one last time."

Marie shook her head vehemently. "Are you mad? Absolutely not! Eugénie, why do you want to torture yourself so? Leave him alone, he's not worth the anguish he has caused you!"

"I shall go alone, then. Don't look so cross, Marie. Can't you understand that I have to go?"

She looked so sad tht Mag took pity on her. "Eugénie child, ye'll not go alone. Oi'll go with ye. Oi don't think it's wise, mind ye, but Oi'll go. Ye know ye'll only cause yerself more pain. Forget about 'im, child."

"I'll try, Mag, but I've got to see him just this one last time."

All night Eugénie cried silent tears of despair. Her

dreams were shattered and life would never be the same. She wished fervently that morning would not come, but in vain.

November 19th dawned golden and crispy cold. Eugénie and Mag ate breakfast early and by seven o'clock were at the steps of St. Paul's Cathedral. The wedding was not scheduled until ten o'clock but even at that early hour there was a crowd of gawkers already gathered. It was bitterly cold, but Eugénie felt nothing. She was aware of nothing but the numbness of her heart. She wanted to cry and scream in protest against her feeling of impotence, to make time stand still so that she might have a chance to stop this farce of a marriage. She was consumed with jealousy.

At nine o'clock, the first carriage arrived and from then a steady stream of elegant guests climbed the steps to the cathedral. The Prince of Wales arrived, clad in rich, gold velvet, causing a stir in the crowd. He waved to the crowd graciously from the top step and then hurried inside out of the cold.

"Well, love, 'is nibs won't be long now," said Mag with forced cheerfulness.

Eugénie sighed and waited. Mag was right. Within fifteen minutes Lady Jerningham's carriage arrived and André stepped out, followed by Lord Langley, Sir Harry Farthingale and Sir Peter Mayhew, who held Lady Jerningham's arm and led her up the steps.

Eugénie's heart pounded violently and she felt slightly faint. Mag put a protective arm around her. "Are ye well, lass? Ye look so pale."

Eugénie's eyes were riveted on André. He looked like a prince, clad in silver from head to toe. Diamonds sparkled on his shoes, on his hat and in the magnificent pin in his cravat. Her eyes, filled with pain and longing, remained fixed on him until he disappeared through the portals.

A few minutes later she heard the crowd gasp. Lady Angela had arrived. She was escorted up the steps by her father and was breathtakingly beautiful. She was clad in white. Diamonds sparkled on the bodice of her dress and also shone brilliantly from the magnificent tiara that held her long veil in place. A cloak of ermine was wrapped around her and fastened at her slender neck by a huge diamond clasp. She was followed up the steps by eight bridesmaids, two flower girls and a ring bearer, all clad in red velvet trimmed with white fur. Mag was goggle-eyed at all the splendor. Then she noticed that Eugénie was shivering and begged her to leave.

"You've seen him now, lass. Don't wait for them to come out. It'll be too much for ye to bear."

"Please, Mag. I've got to stay," Eugénie whispered through chattering teeth.

So they stood there in the bitter November cold for another hour, waiting for the bride and groom to come out.

At last the bells began to peal joyfully and André and Angela appeared arm in arm. Angela was radiant and André couldn't have looked more handsome. Truly they were a magnificently matched couple. Eugénie watched them and felt a terrible lump in her throat. She wanted to cry but couldn't. She watched with an aching heart until they had stepped into their carriage and vanished from sight amid cheers from the crowd. Mag sighed with relief when they left.

"Now, love, let's go 'ome. There's no more to see. Oi do 'ope now, Eugénie, that ye'll put 'im out of yer mind once and for all."

Eugénie answered cheerfully—a little too cheerfully,

Mag thought. "Mag darling, you are absolutely right. I can do nothing now. He's married and that's that. But would you mind going home alone? I'd like to walk for awhile."

"Oi don't like to leave ye, love, but Oi must get back. Ye won't do anythin' foolish now, will ye?"

Eugénie forced a laugh. "Please don't worry about me. I shall be home in time for dinner. I've a job to go to and I can't afford to lose it."

Eugénie wandered around in a daze of misery. For hours she walked and when she finally became aware of the world around her she found that she was in the Strand. This was one of her favorite places. She loved to watch the magnificent carriages and the lords and ladies who frequently strolled here. She envied the diners in the many luxurious restaurants that she passed. But today none of these things gave her pleasure. She was deeply disturbed. When she thought about André and his bride honeymooning in Italy, it was almost too much for her to bear. Jealousy again reared its ugly head and she railed against God for the unfairness of it all. It should be *she* who was with André. It should have been *she* who had been so beautifully gowned being joined to André in marriage at St. Paul's Cathedral. It should be *she* who was now the Marquise de Varney, the envy of all the girls in London.

While she was engrossed in her unhappy thoughts, the Earl of St. Swithins left his club in a very bad humor.

"Take me home, George. There's nothing but a pack of nincompoops in there today and me gout is killing me," he growled. He leaned against the plush uphol-stery of his carriage and sighed with relief. The carriage made its way through the crowded streets and had reached the Strand when he sat up with a jerk.

"Well, I'll be damned! The young blighter."

He had just happened to glance out the window at the time a young pickpocket was nimbly plucking a purse from a rather ill-tempered looking individual. "Oh, probably serves the chap right. He looks like he can afford it. Anyway, it's none of my business if the fellow is dumb enough to have his pocket picked." So thought the earl, soothing his conscience.

All at once his eyes grew wide in astonishment. A rather attractive young lady, seeing what had happened, stuck out her foot and the pickpocket fell headlong. Quickly he got to his feet and took off like a rocket, leaving the gentleman's purse behind. The girl picked up the purse and had just turned towards the gentleman, obviously intending to hand it to him.

"Well, I'll be damned, there's some honest folk left in the world after all," thought the earl. All at once he yelled, "What's this?"

The ill-tempered gentleman, having discovered the loss of his purse and assuming that the girl had stolen it, was holding her in a vice-like grip and shouting at the top of his lungs, "Police! Police!"

The earl saw that the girl was shaking her head and obviously trying desperately to explain. He pounded on the carriage ceiling with his cane. George stopped the carriage and peered down through the hatch.

"You called, sir?"

"Yes, dammit! Turn this confounded contraption around! Did you see what happened back there?"

"Yes, sir. Dreadful situation, sir. What shall we do?"

"Do, George?" bellowed the earl. "Do as I tell you and turn this damned thing around! Quickly, do you hear?"

George did as he was bid, which was no easy task in the extremely crowded street. By the time they had made their way back to the scene of the robbery, none of the participants were in sight.

"Drat! Here, boy. Yes, you boy! Come here," the earl bellowed at a scrawny urchin who was leaning against a doorway.

"Here, boy, I say. Did you see what happened to that girl?"

The cheeky fellow grinned. He saw his chance of making a shilling sure enough. "Wot's it worth to ye guv'nor?" he asked.

"Here, you young scallywag!" The earl tossed him a coin.

The boy picked up the coin and bit it. He seemed satisfied. "It's orf to jail fer 'er. She'll probably be 'anged fer sure. Serves 'er right, Oi say, interferin' where it's not 'er business!"

"Do you know where they took her?"

"Oi'm sure Oi don' know, Guv. Wot's it to ye anyways?"

The earl asked himself the same question—what was it to him? A mere chit of a girl disturbing his day like this. Unthinkable!

"George, take me home," he sighed. "I'll search for her later. A few hours in jail won't hurt her. I'm beastly tired and hungry and what's more, I'm in pain." He sank back against the soft cushions and promptly went to sleep.

Meanwhile Eugénie, numb with shock, was being carted off to Newgate Prison, frantically protesting her innocence.

"That's wot they all say, luvey. Oi'd keep me gob shut if ye know wot's good fer ye," said someone.

"Aw, leave 'er alone. She's frightened," said another.

"She's a blasted furriner. Comin' over 'ere thievin'! Tis a cryin' shame, that's wot Oi says," said a third.

Eugénie gave the policeman who was dragging her along a beseeching look. "Please help me. Please take a message for me to Harry Boggs at "The Black Bear" tavern in Holborn. Tell him what has happened. Here is a shilling for your trouble. Will you help me?"

He was stirred with pity for the pretty girl. The other policeman argued with him. "Wot ye goin' to 'elp the likes o' 'er fer? Ye'll get yerself in trouble and see if Oi care."

"Nonsense, it won't 'urt to take a message to 'er friend. Come with me and Oi'll stand ye a drink."

Eugénie waited anxiously for the other's reaction and when he shrugged his shoulders in agreement she sighed with relief.

"Will you help me, Monsieur?"

"Aye, lass, Oi'll do that fer ye. Do ye 'ave any more money?" he asked hopefully.

"Yes, a little."

"Good. For when ye get in yon excuse fer a prison they'll make ye strip lessen ye can pay up."

"What do you mean?" Eugénie was horrified. What was she getting into? She felt fear clutching at her heart and trying to stangle her with long, cold fingers.

"Well, it's like this, see. The ladies—ha, ha, that's a good one that is—well, Oi should say, the 'old lodgers' makes the new lodgers pay up or they take all their clothes. 'Tis as simple as that. Ye'll 'ave to pay fer other services as well. But don't let them rob ye. It's not worth more than a shillin' to keep yer clothes. They'll try and 'assle ye fer more but stand firm. Remember wot Oi says, fer 'ere we are."

The clang of the huge gates behind them sent a cold chill through her. What was to become of her in this place? But surely André would rescue her as soon as he heard. Now that he was married to Angela, money would be no object. Her thoughts were interrupted by a woman of amazing height with mean, little eyes and the most dazzling yellow hair that one could imagine. It just couldn't be real, Eugénie thought. She was dressed in a dirty woolen skirt and an even dirtier sweater. A bunch of keys hung from a ring at her waist. She took one look at Eugénie and smiled, but the smile was not pleasant. She looked Eugénie up and down. "Well, well, wot 'ave we 'ere? A bloomin' ladyship. Wot *she* 'ere fer?"

"Thievin'. She stole a sack of money from some nob in the Strand," said the policeman.

"I am innocent. Oh, *why* won't you believe me?" cried Eugénie.

"That's wot they all say, dearie. Why, Oi 'ave a whole prison full of innocent lambs."

"But I really am! I just tripped the thief and he dropped the sack and I picked it up to give to the gentleman . . ."

"Take 'er away. Oi've listened to enough of this drivel," snarled the woman.

"Where'll we put 'er?"

"Throw 'er into the common cell for the condemned. It might take 'er down a peg or two."

The policeman who had promised to take a message to Harry protested. "But she can pay for better quarters."

"Oh she can, can she? We'll see about that later." Then she cackled and nudged the friendly policeman with her elbow. "Wot's up, ducks? You fancy this little piece fer yourself, do ye?"

There was nothing more Eugénie could say. She was taken to the Condemned Cell. As the door closed behind her, she became aware first of the horrible stench that filled her nostrils, then of at least a hundred pairs of eyes staring at her. She remembered what she had been told about the demands that would be made of her and she stood as straight as she could and waited for one of those miserable wretches to make the first move.

A big slovenly woman came forward. She was even taller than the amazon with the keys and had equally unbelievable red hair. This harridan had piercing blue eyes and a head of hair that stood straight up in all directions. She looked Eugénie straight in the eyes. "Pay or strip, me foine lady."

"I beg your pardon, Madame?" Eugénie said coolly.

"Oh, she begs me pardon. 'Oity toity, she begs me pardon, she does! Oi said, pay yer shilling and sixpense or strip! That's the lawr 'ere. Those whose 'ere first gets yer clothes lessen ye pays up."

They were eyeing her greedily. A few even came up and felt her shawl and her skirt and some started arguing about who was to get what.

"Quiet, you lot!" yelled the big woman, whose name was Nan Coward. "Quiet, ye scum! Well, wot's it to be? Pay or strip? We're waitin'."

"How much did you say, Madame?"

"One shilling and sixpence, yer ladyship," sneered Nan.

"I am not a ladyship and here is a shilling. Not a penny more will you get." Eugénie spoke calmly but she was feeling completely terrified. Nan Coward looked at her in amazement, then grabbed the money. The rest of the dirty lot left her mercifully alone.

She sat down on the filthy straw and looked around at this hodge-podge of humanity. She saw that some poor wretches were chained to the walls and there were other chains inbedded in the walls waiting for other unfortunate souls. Slime covered the walls and the cell was so damp that she shivered and drew her shawl more tightly around her shoulders. Rats were scurrying around searching for scraps of food, or perhaps a bite of human flesh. Eugénie had never seen such a conglomeration of women in one place. Some looked quite decent, though many were quite obviously prostitutes, while others like Nan Coward—God only knew what they were! Eugénie thought that she had never seen more menacing-looking women nor heard such foul language coming from a woman's mouth. Not even in St. Jacques had she seen such horrors.

She was sitting against the slimy wall feeling very sorry for herself when she happened to notice a young woman who was propped against the damp wall on the opposite side of the room. The poor girl was deathly pale except for two bright spots of color on her cheeks. She was coughing constantly, a harsh, wracking cough that shook her entire body. The poor lass was clad in a dress of thin material and she was shivering. Eugénie's tender heart went out to the poor girl and she got up and walked over to her.

"Bonjour, Mademoiselle. My name is Eugénie Fabré. Here, take my shawl—it will keep you warm," she said.

There was no response. It was almost as though the girl were in a trance. It was obvious to Eugénie that she was completely unaware of what was going on around her. Eugénie took off her shawl and put it around the girl's skinny shoulders. Then she noticed that her feet were bare and blue from the cold. Eugénie found tears blinding her eyes. She took off her shoes and stockings and gently put the stockings on the girl's feet. Suddenly a voice she recognized boomed at her side.

"Wot ye wastin' yer stuff on 'er for? She's 'ad it, she 'as."

Eugénie looked up—sure enough, it was Nan Coward. "She needs a doctor. Don't they have a doctor here?"

Nan Coward laughed. "That's a good one, that is! Doctors cost money. A lot of money. They fished 'er out of the river and she ain't got no money. If ye arsk me, they should 'ave let 'er drown."

"Surely you don't mean that! Do you know who she is?" Eugénie asked.

"Aye. When she first came 'ere, she told us 'er name was Katy Miller. She's nobody, so wot yer worryin' about, Oi don't know."

"What could this poor soul have done to be thrown in here?"

"Oi must say, ye arsk a lot of questions, but fer yer information she stole a loaf of bread and when the baker chased 'er, she jumped in the river," said Nan cheerfully.

"Poor soul!" Eugénie gasped.

"Aw, yer a fool! Quit yer worrin', 'er time 'as come, Oi'd say."

Eugénie felt the girl's forehead. Poor Katy! Her face was burning with fever. Seeing those bright, flushed cheeks Eugénie guessed that Katy had consumption. There was nothing she could do but try and comfort her. It was quite dark in the cell, which was lit only by a few tallow candles. Poor Katy had another attack of coughing. Eugénie helped her sit up so it would be easier on her and noticed that the girl's phlegm was bloody.

Hours dragged by. Finally Nan Coward came back and sat down beside Eugénie. She sat there in silence for a while, catching lice and crushing them between her dirty fingernails. "Wot ye in fer?" she asked.

"They thought I stole a purse from a gentleman in the Strand. But I just tripped the thief and when he dropped the purse, I picked it up and was just about to give it to the gentleman when he started calling 'thief, thief' and grabbed me. I am quite sure my friends will help me. I

177

have one special friend who is married to Lady Angela Shrewsbury. I'm sure he will come to my aid," said Eugénie.

"Well, Oi 'ope so fer yer sake. Yer alright fer a 'oity toity," Nan admitted.

"Is there more to this prison than this cell, Madame?"

"Me name is Nan Coward, and in answer to yer question, the truth is, this 'ere place is the worst spot of all fer us women. If ye got money ye can get better than this pigsty. The old crow ought to be along anytime now to collect. That one, she'd bleed ye dry if she could."

Sure enough, about twenty minutes later they heard a key in the lock and in walked the amazon Eugénie had met earlier.

"Alright then, you lot, who wants out of 'ere?" she bawled.

Nan snarled, "We all do, ye big bag of wind! 'Ow much this time?"

"Not so fast, and mind yer tongue, or Oi'll 'ave ye chained to the wall!"

"Who is she?" Eugénie whispered.

"She's the jailor's wife, and a proper thief she be. The magic word around 'ere is 'garnish.' Why, ye practically 'ave to pay garnish to breathe this stinkin' air! It's either that, or ye can sell yerself to the 'ighest bidder. Y'er a goodlookin' lass. There's a lot o' men upstairs would give a lot fer ye."

"I'm sorry, but I don't think that I could do that. I do have some money left and I know I won't be here long."

"Well, good luck to ye, that's wot Oi sez," grumbled Nan.

"Silence, ye scum! Alright, then. Three shillings to

get out of 'ere. Who wants out of 'ere?'' The jailor's wife roared again.

Nan stepped forward and Eugénie followed her with about twenty others who were lucky enough to have three shillings.

The jailor's wife collected the money. "Now there'll be nine shillings charge if ye want blankets, coal and candles. Eight shillings and sixpence for sheets and for the turnkey's services. Three shillings for a bed, plus five shillings to the steward for carrying the coal and bringing ye yer candles. The whole sum comes to one pound, eight shillings and sixpence. That's fer starters."

Most of the women sighed and took their three shillings back. They had no more money so what was the point in leaving for just a while. If they couldn't buy a bed, there wasn't much use in leaving. A fortunate few gathered up their meager belongings if they had any. Just as she was about to go out the door, Eugénie looked back at pathetic Katy. "Wait, please. I want to take her with me," she said.

"Wot?"

"I want to pay for Katy Miller. Here is the money. Will somebody please help me to carry her?"

"Oi think yer a bloody fool," whispered Nan, "but Oi'll help ye."

Between them they carried poor Katy. She was as light as a feather, nothing but skin and bone. They were led down a narrow hall and up a flight of winding steps. When they reached the stairs Nan said, "Oi'll carry 'er meself. She's like a drop in the ocean."

Mrs. Sparks (for that was the name of the jailor's wife) stopped at a door at the head of the stairs and proceeded to unlock it with a huge key. They followed her down a hallway with about seventy rooms leading off it. About two-thirds of the way down the hall she stopped and jerked her head at Eugénie, Nan and her burden.

"You turds in 'ere."

The room had about a dozen beds set close to the walls, tables, chairs and a big fireplace. It was so good to see a warm fire burning, almost welcoming, Eugénie thought. Six other women were already there and they eyed the newcomers warily. Mrs. Sparks pointed to a group of beds furthest away from the fireplace. "Fight over 'em. The steward will be along later with the sheets and blankets and the other things ye paid for. Ye'll all share the expense of the coal."

Nan laid Katy on one of the beds. Eugénie got some water and held it to the poor girl's lips, but Nan shook her head. "Oi doubt she'll last the night. Ye wasted yer money."

"I couldn't leave her there. I just couldn't."

The cheerful sound of singing filtered through to them from somewhere. Eugénie looked at Nan in amazement.

"That's comin' from the tap-room. This old place can be quite merry at times. If yer wealthy—and there's many 'ere wot is—ye can 'ave anythin' yer greedy 'earts desires. Why, some even 'as their families come stay with them. Sometimes we 'ave grand parties."

"You've been here before, Mrs. Coward?"

Nan chuckled. "Dozens of times, though Oi expect this 'ere will be me last."

At last the day came to an end. Eugénie felt that she had been weeks in the prison instead of just one horrible day. Night brought a certain kind of peace for a short time. Some of the other women had gone to a party, but when they came back hours later, they were loud-mouthed and bad tempered. When they heard Katy

180

coughing they yelled, "Keep that slime quiet over there or we'll do it for ye!"

Eugénie was so afraid they would hurt the poor creature that she immediately climbed out of bed and sat beside Katy. She bathed the girl's head and moistened her lips. Towards morning she must have dozed off for she awoke to find Nan shaking her.

"Wake up. She be a goner."

Katy's hand was clutched in Eugénie's and it was cold and stiff. Eugénie gasped in horror as Nan wrenched it out of her grasp.

"She's out of 'er misery now. Oi'll yell fer the turn-key."

Later that morning some men came and hauled Katy's body away. Eugénie was in tears.

"Cheer up then, ducks," said Nan. "She's better orf than she's probably ever been in 'er whole wretched life."

Nan and Eugénie bought food and wine but they had to wait their turn to use the pots and pans hanging from the fireplace. Though a most unlikely pair, they had somehow become drawn to each other, the tall, ugly woman with her pock-marked face and the pretty young French mademoiselle. Their situation could have been much worse, in spite of the fact that they had to take turns emptying the stinking chamber pots and perform other dirty work around the place. The rule was that the newcomers had to take care of all this. But at least they had a bed and food and wine and each other's company.

Several days passed and there was no word from Harry. Eugénie wondered if the policeman hadn't bothered to take her message after all. She wondered if it would be possible to get a letter out. But on the fourth day a message came for her to come to the visitors' hall.

"Nan! Nan!" she cried. "Someone has come to see

181

me! I'm sure it's Harry. Say a prayer for me, please."

"Well, lovely, Oi don' suppose Oi'm much in favor with the Bloke up above, but fer whatever it's worth, Oi'll give it a try."

Eugénie had tried to clean herself up a bit and fix her hair, but when she entered the visitors' hall, Harry Boggs' stout heart sank within him to see his poor darling girl so dirty and bedraggled and her beautiful eyes lit up with hope at the sight of him. How was he going to tell her?

"Oh, Harry, it is so wonderful to see you! I was so afraid you didn't get my message," she said happily.

"Eugénie, love, I wish I could take you away from here right now. If it was only money that was needed I would, but I'm afraid that won't do it. We need someone with influence."

"André?"

"We sent a message, dear. In fact, I took it to Sutton Place myself. But Lady Jerningham's house was closed up."

Tears started to trickle down Eugénie's face. "Mon Dieu, what am I to do?"

"There, there, dear heart, don't fret. I took another message to Shrewsbury House. I told the butler it was imperative that André get the message without delay. I'm afraid, though, it will be at least a few days more before we hear anything."

"Oh, Harry, thank you for all you've done!" Eugénie sighed.

"My little love, how did you ever get in such a predicament?" Harry asked.

"I was only trying to help. I was walking around the Strand when I spotted someone stealing a purse from a gentleman's pocket. I . . . tripped the thief up and retrieved the purse but the gentleman thought . . . I stole it and wouldn't listen to my explanation. Harry, it's been like a dreadful dream! When André got married, I thought I would never care about anything again, but I do. I'm afraid, so very much afraid! Harry, I might hang for something I haven't done!"

"Precious, keep your chin up. Here—I've brought you some money and a basket of food Mag sent. Marie packed some clothes she thought you might need. Eugénie, we love you very much and you are very much in our thoughts and prayers."

A guard came over to them and growled, "Time's up."

Harry took Eugénie in his strong arms and smoothed her dirty, tangled hair. "God be with you, love. It won't be long before you are back home."

Eugénie clung to him. He had become like a father to her. But she remembered all that he had said that day in St. Pancras church, so she straightened up and held her chin high. He smiled at her. "That's my brave lass."

Eugénie walked slowly back to her room. Nan saw her downcast face but didn't say anything. All at once Eugénie turned to her and smiled sadly. "Nan, it'll be a while yet. Can you put up with me, do you think? Look, Nan, my friends sent some food. Why don't we have a party, you and I? Is there any wine left?"

When the other 'ladies' had departed for the carousing in the tap-room, Eugénie and Nan spread out the food and poured the wine.

" 'Ere's to ye, ducks," Nan said cheerfully.

The long, weary days rolled by into long, weary weeks. There was still no word from André. Harry visited often. Marie, Mag and Moll came less often because it was too painful for them, seeing Eugénie in that dreadful prison. At night the four of them would sit

183

over their tea and the three women would curse André de Varney.

"Oi just don't know 'ow 'e could be so cruel! After all she's done for 'im!" growled Mag.

" 'E's one swine, that one. 'Ow can he be so unfeelin'?" Moll put in.

Only Harry said a good word for him. "Now, now, you know he is on his honeymoon. Perhaps they couldn't get in touch with him. I don't think the young fellow could be as bad a all that."

"Humph!" Mag exploded. "That blighter could do *anythin'!*"

Chapter 14

Three terrible weeks passed by and one day the prisoners received word that they would be tried at the next Quarter Sessions. Despair set in. Eugénie's mind went into a state of panic. Would she not see Christmas? Was she going to be hanged for something she hadn't done? Dear God, it just couldn't be possible!

"Cheer up, ducks." Nan didn't seem at all troubled by the news of their impending trial. "Ye won't be 'anged, love. Oi expecs they'll give us both 'Transportation'."

"Oh, Nan, what is 'Transportation'? It sounds terrible."

"Where 'ave ye been all yer life? 'Aven't ye 'eard o' New South Wales? They used to send us convicts to America but now Oi 'ear tell we are to be sent out to this new land. It's a far piece orf. Oi 'ear they need convicts to work the land. Oi 'eard tell it's an enormous land. Oi won't mind goin'. Oi also 'eard they be a-goin' to give married couples land o' their own once their sentence is up if they'll stay out there. Even the likes o' me will get a 'usband out there. They must be a might 'ard up fer women though. But you, ducks, you'll 'ave yer pick o' the bunch! Who knows—ye might even catch a freeman. They're not all convicts out there. Anyway,

Oi've none 'ere to mourn fer me goin' and it's a sight better than 'angin', that's wot Oi say!''

When Marie came to see Eugénie a few days later she told her about the trial. "Marie, I shall be tried next week. Please don't come to see me anymore. Any of you. I just can't bear it."

Marie began to cry. "Oh, Eugénie, I can't lose you like this! I'll find André. He has got to help you."

"Marie, don't cry. If God wills it, I shall be all right."

"Would you mind if we come to the trial? Please let us be there, at least," Marie begged.

"Yes, Marie, I'd like to know I had someone there in case the worst happens. But cheer up—there's still hope."

"Oh, Eugénie, you always were so brave!" Poor Marie was heartbroken.

"Now don't make me sad. Please go on home and tell the others not to worry. Nan tells me that it's unlikely we shall be hanged. She feels that we will, more than likely, be sent to a place called New South Wales. Now go on, dear, go on home," said Eugénie firmly.

The week flashed past all too quickly and Eugénie, Nan and fifty other women from Newgate found themselves in a crowded courtroom. There must have been eleven hundred prisoners besides the group from Newgate. The Judge looked very stern and very impressive in his wig and robes of office. Each prisoner was given a number—Nan was number forty-eight and Eugénie was number sixty-three. She sat on the bench numb with fright and scarcely aware of the sentences being passed on her unfortunate companions. Then it was Nan's turn. As her name was called she exclaimed, "Present ducks! 'Ere Oi am." Then she turned and gave Eugénie a broad wink. The people in the courtroom laughed.

"Silence!" yelled the clerk.

The Judge looked at Nan with a withering glare. "Nan Coward, it is the judgment of His Majesty's Court that you are guilty of the crime as charged. This is not the first time you have appeared before this Court and so your punishment shall be hanging by the neck until you are dead."

Nan almost fainted. Eugénie gasped in horror. "Oh, Nan!"

The Judge continued, "However, in the Court's mercy, sentence has been commuted to Transportation to New South Wales for a period of seven years."

Nan sank to her knees and wiped the sweat from her brow. Then she stood up and whispered to Eugénie, "Oi thought Oi was a goner fer sure!"

At long last Eugénie's name was called. She listened in horror as the gentleman whose money had been stolen gave his testimony. She had just about resigned herself to her fate when suddenly there was a commotion in the back of the courtroom. She looked back and saw a tall, distinguished looking elderly gentleman approaching the judge.

"Just one moment, your Honor. One moment, please. I am the Earl of St. Swithins and I have something important to say with regard to this case."

There was a stirring in the courtroom and a din of whispering and excited chatter.

"Silence in the court!" The Judge was furious, but he turned to the earl with courtesy. "Your Lordship, this is an honor indeed. Please feel free to speak, sir."

"If it pleases the Court, I have been searching for this young woman ever since the day the incident took place. I was a witness to the whole scene and this young lady is completely innocent. She tripped the thief and was about to return the money to that nincompoop in the witness box when he turned and saw her with the sack. Of course the idiot assumed that she was the thief.''

There was a great murmur of astonishment in the room. Nothing so dramatic as this had ever happened before. The convicts who knew Eugénie cheered. As for Marie, Mag and Moll, they were crying with happiness and even Harry had to wipe away a tear.

The Judge banged his gravel. "Case dismissed."

Eugénie ran over to Nan and hugged her. Then she walked over to the Earl of St. Swithins with tears in her eyes. She took his hand in hers and, much to that gentleman's great consternation, showered it with kisses.

"Thank you, sir! Thank you a million times! I shall remember you all my life," she vowed.

The earl was quite flustered. He had never had any time for female "hysterics." He was quite at a loss as to how to deal with the situation.

"There, there my dear. Come and see me tomorrow and you can thank the person who found you for me. I shall expect to see you tomorrow at noon. Goodbye until then." There was something about this child, even under all that dirt, that touched him deeply. He had never been close to young people, except perhaps for the nephew who was his heir and god-child. It was rather strange but this young girl stirred memories of a long forgotten love. He watched as she made her way towards some people who were obviously her friends. They hugged and kissed her and carried on as they left the courtroom arm in arm.

Harry led his little group of women to Mag's house where the five of them celebrated Eugénie's release. Only the thought of Nan cast a shadow on Eugénie's joy.

"Poor Nan! I wish I could have done something for

her. I must go back and see her before she is shipped out."

Mag patted her hand. "Now Eugénie love, ye can't go worryin' yer 'ead about everyone ye meet."

"Eugénie, you look exhausted, why don't you go on upstairs? Mag will bring hot water so you can bathe, and then you must rest. I'm sure you haven't had a decent night's sleep in weeks."

"Harry, I hate to leave you all but I feel exhausted all of a sudden. Goodnight everyone." Eugénie kissed each dear face in turn, then started up the stairs. After her bath, she felt so weary that she thought she could sleep for a week but once she lay down in bed, sleep evaded her. She thought about Nan and was obsessed with what she had said about New South Wales. That far-off land intrigued her. She made up her mind to ask the earl about the country, and with that decision made she fell asleep at last.

It was wonderful to wake up in her own bed and to get up and have breakfast in the warm kitchen with Mag. Marie had already left for work. With Christmas around the corner, Moll was busier than ever and was really glad of Marie's help.

"Did ye sleep well, love?" asked Mag solicitously.

"No, Mag. I lay awake for a long time. I had so much on my mind, so much to think about," Eugénie confessed.

"Lord love ye, whatever about? Ye should be restin' and relaxin' after all ye've been through, not thinkin'," chided Mag.

"Mag darling, I shall tell you all about it later. It's just an idea that caught my imagination. My mind is not quite made up about it yet though."

After she had eaten and helped Mag with the dishes, Eugénie went upstairs to change into her Sunday best dress. She put on her bonnet with the cherries which she thought would distract attention from her pale face.

"Mag, I'm going to Newgate now to see Nan Coward, then I shall go on from there to visit the Earl of St. Swithins. I expect I shall be home for dinner, though," she told her friend.

" 'Ave a good time, lovey, and ye can give that old geezer a big hug for me! If it 'adn't been for 'im, ye'd still be in yon hell of a place and almost on yer way to that God forsaken land, whatever they call it," said Mag.

As she stood before the gates of Newgate, cold shivers went through Eugénie when she thought about all that went on behind those grim doors. How she would love to see the whole place burned to the ground! It reminded her in many ways of the Bastille. While she waited for Nan in the visitors' hall, she thought how strange it was that of all people she should have made friends with her. Trouble certainly made strange bed-fellows!

Nan came into the hall and her face lit up when she saw Eugénie. "Why, Oi th ought ye would have forgotten me already. Ow are ye, ducks? My, but ye look grand!"

"Nan, how do you feel about my going to New South Wales with you?" Eugénie asked breathlessly.

"Wot? Are ye mad? Why, ye are as free as a seagull now! Wot would the loikes o' ye want to do a crazy thing like that for?"

"I've thought about it all night. There's nothing for me here. Oh, I know I've wonderful friends, the dearest sister a person could have, and a job, and I suppose I should be very content. But Nan, I want something more out of life and I know I won't find it here. I have a strange compulsion to go to New South Wales. It seems as if the land is calling me."

"Ye are a rum 'un, Eugénie, no doubt about it. Oi don't understand all ye said, but Oi wish ye luck. But will the authorities let ye? They'll be convict ships, ye know. The only other women on board will be the wives of the officers who are going to be stationed out there. And even if they let ye, can ye afford it?"

"I don't know," Eugénie admitted, "but I am going to see the Earl of Swithins—you know, the kind gentleman who saved me. Perhaps he can help me get passage on one of the ships. Do you know the name of the ship you'll be put on?"

"Oh ducks, Oi don't really know. Oi did 'ear the 'Duke of York' mentioned. Eugénie, if ye don't mind me sayin' so and even if ye do, Oi think ye are stark, ravin' bonkers!"

Eugénie laughed. "I expect that's what everyone will say. I shan't try to convince them I'm not. My mind is made up and somehow I shall get there."

She left Nan with the promise that she would see her before Christmas and took a hackney to Sutton Place. The earl lived just a few houses away from Lady Jerningham. She felt a sudden pang when she saw Lady Jerningham's house but didn't have time to dwell on it before the hackney pulled up in front of the earl's house.

" 'Ere we are, Miss," the driver said. She handed him the fare and a tip. "Thank ye kindly, Miss."

The door was opened by a butler who greeted her warmly. "We have been expecting you, Mademoiselle. His lordship is waiting in the library. If you will please follow me, Mademoiselle."

She followed him to the library where he opened the

doors for her and announced her name as if she were a grand duchess.

"Mademoiselle Fabré, your lordship."

The earl's eyes twinkled, even though his foot was propped up on a cushion and hurt like the devil. "Thank you, Giles. Come in, my dear girl. Forgive me for not getting up, my damned foot you know. Now let me look at you."

He studied her carefully for a moment. Kindness was etched in every line of his face. "Yes, my dear, you look decidedly better. By the way, the gentleman whose money you restored so gallantly asked me to give you this."

He handed Eugénie a purse. It felt heavy.

"I couldn't accept this. It looks like a lot of money," she said.

"One hundred pounds, and it's little enough after all you have been through, my girl. Won't you sit down, my dear? I'm forgetting my manners."

She took a seat on a gold and green striped chair and looked around the magnificently furnished room. The library was Sir Charles' favorite room in the house. A cheerful fire illuminated the rich paneling and the Oriental rugs glowed in the noonday sun.

"My dear, there is someone I want you to meet. He should be here shortly. Do you remember my telling you that there was someone else you owed your thanks to, not I?"

"But your Lordship, you saved my life."

"Oh yes, my dear, I arrived very dramatically at the eleventh hour, as it were but I'm too old and grouchy to go traipsing around London searching for a lost girl. No, if it had been left up to me, I'd never have got to you in time. My nephew was the one who found you.

Now would you like a glass of sherry, Mademoiselle Eugénie?"

She was about to reply when all at once the doors opened and a man of medium height strode into the room. He moved towards them with all the grace of a panther, easy and unhurried. His hair was almost black, his mouth firm yet sensuous, his nose straight and thin.

"Mademoiselle Fabré, allow me to present my nephew, Paul Bruce Gordon," said the earl. "Paul, Mademoiselle Eugénie Fabré."

"*Enchanté,* Mademoiselle." He took her hand and kissed it. His eyes seemed to bore right through her, almost hypnotizing her. They were almost yellow. His body was magnificent, strong and seemingly bursting with suppressed energy. His legs were superbly muscled, and his tight breeches showed them to advantage. His skin was tanned and rugged looking in a way that was quite unusual in an Englishman. Eugénie wondered where he could have got such a tan. She realized that she had been staring at him and at once became aware that those steady, serious eyes were making her feel very uncomfortable. She felt herself blush and was relieved when he moved over to stand by the fireplace.

Sir Charles couldn't help noticing the look that had passed between the two young people. He thought that Eugénie looked tired—and no wonder. Newgate had broken many a stronger spirit. The girl intrigued him. He sighed. What a pity he wasn't twenty years younger! Aloud he said, "Come sit by me, my dear." She moved to the sofa and sat down beside him. He nodded towards Paul. "He's my sister's boy, you know, of all things, he's a doctor. He could have everything he wants in this world but he couldn't be content to be a gentleman of leisure or even join the Navy or some such. No,

he has some grand idea of helping suffering humanity!''
He added sadly, ''He can't seem to do much for my
gout, though. But my dear, don't tell him I told you, I
have to say I'm really quite proud of him. There isn't a
lazy bone in his body.''

Eugénie was surprised. She looked at Paul Gordon
with renewed interest. ''Oh, your lordship, I think
that's wonderful! I would never have guessed. I thought
perhaps he was a soldier or something like that. Do you
know, my grandfather was a Doctor. I never knew him
but my mother said he was the best. She must have inherited his gift for healing. I often went with her on her
visits to the sick of our village. Everyone called on her
for help. She was the closest thing to a doctor Poissy
had. She nursed the sick and helped the poor. She was a
friend to all—and they killed her!'' Eugénie began to
weep uncontrollably. During the long month in
Newgate she had remained strong and in control of her
feelings, but just now as she spoke of her darling
mother, all her pent-up emotions became too strong and
the dam that held back the tears for so long finally
broke. The Earl gasped in consternation, ''Paul, for
pity's sake don't just stand there! *Do* something!''

''Why, Uncle, I thought you were doing just beautifully. Besides, a good cry never hurt anyone,'' said Paul
coolly.

''Damn you, boy, I can't cope with something like
this!'' roared his uncle.

Paul moved towards Eugénie and knelt on one knee
at her feet. ''Mademoiselle, go right ahead and cry all
you want. It's not good to keep one's emotions locked
up inside as I can see you must have done for a long
time. You, Mademoiselle Fabré, have been through a
great deal of unpleasantness of late, so cry all you
want.''

"Merci, Monsieur. I am so ashamed of carrying on like this. You are very kind," Eugénie said through her tears.

"Nonsense, Mademoiselle. You are definitely entitled to a moment of weakness, you who have been so strong." Paul poured a glass of brandy and handed it to her. "Here—drink this. It will make you feel much better."

She noticed his hands then. Such delicate hands and yet they seemed so strong. Eugénie sipped the brandy and looked into his strange yellow eyes. For some extraordinary reason she felt very shy and very moved.

Sir Charles, seeing she had pulled herself together, was anxious to help. "Is there anything I can do for you, my dear young lady?" he asked with a smile.

"Your lordship has been so kind to me already—and yet, yes, there is one thing . . ."

"Ask, my dear."

"Could you tell me how I can get passage on the next ship leaving for New South Wales?" she asked eagerly.

The earl almost choked on his brandy. "Did I hear you correctly?" he spluttered.

Eugénie nodded. "I really do wish to go to New South Wales. In fact, I must go. I long to go."

Paul looked at the girl intently. How strange! So delicate looking, yet obviously her heart was filled with the courage of a lion. What on earth would make her want to go to a country she probably knew very little about? When he spoke, his voice sounded stern to Eugénie's ears. "Why do you want to go out there? How much do you know about New South Wales, Mademoiselle?"

"I first heard about the country when I was in New-gate. If Sir Charles hadn't come to rescue me when he did, I should have probably bent sent out there as a

195

convict. To be honest, I hardly know a thing about the place. I do know that they need people and—this may sound rather peculiar, but I strongly believe my destiny lies in that far-off country. It's almost as though that land is calling me. Many years ago I made a promise to myself that my life would be meaningful and somehow I feel that my best chance to fulfill those dreams lies beyond the sea in that vast continent.''

Paul was deeply stirred by her words. Never had he met such a girl. Yes, as far as he was concerned she belonged to New South Wales and it to her.

Sir Charles looked at Eugénie with eyes filled with anxiety. ''You are determined to do? Don't you realize, girl, that it is a wild, uncultivated country? It's a tough place for a man, let alone a young, refined girl.''

''Nevertheless, your lordship, I shall go whether or not you help me. Somehow I shall find a way,'' said Eugénie, her head held high.

''Mademoiselle Fabré, my uncle is right. I have been to New South Wales and I assure you it is no place for a lady. The country is, at the moment, intended as a prison, one might say, for convicts. It has no amenities whatsoever. What the country *does* need is farmers and people with a good knowledge of the land, not snips of girls. You don't look as though you have ever worked the land. I ask you, Mademoiselle, how do you think you will possibly survive out there? What you will do I simply can't imagine.''

''Lord Gordon, if I survived Newgate, I assure you that there isn't anything on earth that could possibly be too harsh for me to take!'' said Eugénie with spirit.

''Hear! Hear!'' the earl cheered. He was thoroughly enjoying the interchange between the two young people. ''If Mademoiselle Fabré wants to go, I say let her go and good luck to her! Young lady, you can count on my support. Something you said reminds me of a verse by Thomas Tickell which helps me to understand exactly what it is you are feeling. It goes like this—

> *I hear a voice you cannot hear,*
> *Which says you must not stay.*
> *I see a hand you cannot see,*
> *Which beckons me away."*

"That was wonderful! It describes exactly how I feel about New South Wales. How very understanding you are, Sir Charles!" She turned to Paul beseechingly. "Will you help me, too?"

Paul shrugged his shoulders. "Mademoiselle, I shall be leaving for New South Wales myself on 'The Duke of York.' It is due to sail around the end of January and I shall endeavor to arrange a passage for you. I suggest you be on board ship at least four hours before she sails. It would be better if you were in your cabin when they load the convicts. Mademoiselle, the voyage will be long and unpleasant, so be prepared. Convict ships are not noted for their luxurious accomodations."

"Thank you, sir. May I ask why you are going back there if it is as bad as you say?" Eugénie asked.

"Mademoiselle, need I remind you that I am a doctor? I have found that there is a great need for doctors there. I intend to make my home there. My Aunt Aggie Gordon is already out there and by now my house should be completed. I came back to England for medical supplies and other equipment I need. It will be a long time before New South Wales ever becomes civilized to the point where it will be self-supporting so for now, everything had to be brought from England or Capetown. I'll have all the information you will need as to the exact sailing date by December 22 or 23. And now Mademoiselle, and dear Uncle Charles, if you will excuse me, I must take my leave.''

Eugénie watched as he left with a frown on her pretty face, then turned to Sir Charles. ''Does he never smile?'' she asked.

''My dear, even as a child he was slow to smile, but when he does, it is like the moon coming out on a dark, bleary night, or as if the brightest sun suddenly peeked from behind the darkest clouds. He takes life too seriously, I'm afraid. Always has. Don't let him fool you, though, he loves that blasted country over there. His Aung Aggie Gordon brought him up ever since his mother died and she wouldn't leave him for the world. One thing I have to say about the old girl, she's got courage. There's not many her age would venture to such a place. You'll probably meet her when you get out there. Don't let her scare you. She can be extremely formidable. Don't really go for these strong-minded women too much meself. Still, I have to admire her. At any rate, you can probably learn a lot from Miss Aggie Gordon.''

''Your Lordship, I don't intend to take advantage of our acquaintance. I do need your help now, but I shall repay you for the expenses of the voyage. I am owed quite a bit of money, 3,000 pounds to be exact, which I am sure I shall collect any day now. Your nephew need not fear that I shall be a burden to him. I shall not need him and I intend to make it on my own every step of the way.''

''My dear, you are a stubborn as he is! Pride is all very well, but remember this, young lady, advice from an old man, sometimes we have too much pride. But, by jove, I wish you all the best.''

Having said goodbye to Sir Charles, Eugénie decided to walk home. He had offered her the use of his carriage but she declined. Her mind was in a quandary—how was she going to break the news of her decision to go to New South Wales to Mag, Moll and Harry and above all, Marie? She told herself, "Nothing they could say could change my mind. I will just have to shut my ears to their arguments."

By the time she reached home, she had made up her mind not to tell them anything just yet. It was so close to Christmas and there was no need to spoil it for them. She would wait until after the New Year. This would be the most wonderfully happy Christmas, one that they could all remember, a consolation for Christmas to come when they would no longer be together. Memories were so important, especially the happy ones . . .

Chapter 15

Mag was sitting in the kitchen kneading dough when Eugénie got home. " 'Ow did it go, love? Did ye 'ave a good time?"

"Oh, yes, Mag. The earl is an old darling. I met his nephew, too. It was he who found me. He's a doctor and he's got these strange, yellow eyes . . . And he never smiles. It's so sad."

"It seems like ye rather fancy 'im love."

"Nonsense, Mag! From the little I've seen of him, I think I would rub him the wrong way. He's far too serious and I, for my part, would rather stay away from him."

"Well, me little love, since they be nobs Oi doubt ye'll see 'em much. Oi must say they were good to 'elp ye, though."

"Mag, there's something else. You know the man who said I was a thief . . .?"

"Aow, if Oi could only get me 'ands on that bloke, Oi'd tear 'im apart!" Mag growled.

"Now Mag, listen! He gave the Earl one hundred pounds and told him to say he wished me to have it for all that he had put me through. Mag darling, we are going to have a marvellous Christmas!"

Mag beamed at Eugénie with love and pleasure.

"Thank God, child! We were so afraid ye wouldn't be with us, and if it wasn't for that old earl ye wouldn't, bless 'is 'eart. Do ye want somethin' to eat, Eugénie? Ye must be 'ungry."

"I am. I'm starved, in fact. But let me go change for work."

"Ye're not goin' to work! Don't be daft, child! Ye just got out of Newgate. Ye must get yer strength back before ye go traipsin' orf to that pub."

"Now, Mag, I want to go, and besides, Harry needs me. I promise if I get too tired I'll come home early," Eugénie said, and, giving Mag a hug, went up to change her clothes.

Harry's eyes almost popped out of his head when he saw Eugénie coming in to "The Black Bear." "Lass, are you crazy? Why aren't you resting?" he shouted.

"Don't fuss, Harry dear. I've heard enough fussing from Mag. I feel fine and I do so enjoy being here," she told him. She waved to the regular customers who were always the first to arrive in the late afternoon. They cheered when they saw her. "Welcome back, lass! It's good to see ye back."

Eugénie looked lovingly around her at "The Black Bear" and then suddenly she exclaimed, "Harry! What's the matter with you? Don't you realize that it's only ten days to Christmas and you haven't put up one decoration? We're going to have to get busy in the morning and make this place more festive-looking." She swung him around. "Don't forget, this is the season to be merry, and merry it shall be!" Harry hugged her and the patrons laughed. "Lass, I didn't feel much like celebrating with you in that infernal place. You're right though, now we *do* have something to celebrate." She gave him a kiss. "I do love you, Harry!" Several

201

customers came in then clamoring for attention, and for the rest of the evening they were so busy they didn't have another chance to talk.

It was seven days before Christmas. The weather was cold and bleak and to make matters worse, terribly foggy. People went about their business, however, with happy hearts. Secrets abounded everywhere as gifts were bought and hidden from families and friends. In Mag's little household, preparations were underway for the great Christmas feast. Mag and Marie were busy in the kitchen baking all sorts of pies and cookies. Eugénie was quite useless in the kitchen and so she just stayed out of the way and spent her time shopping. She not only bought presents for everyone but also some things she thought she might need for her journey to New South Wales. These she hid so that no one would get suspicious. At night she worked for Harry and "The Black Bear" was filled with the merry spirits that prevailed in this season of joy. Everywhere people greeted each other with warm shouts of, "Merry Christmas. God bless you!" Hearts were filled with love. Even those whose hearts were closed most of the year opened them a crack now in honor of Christmas.

Eugénie had left for work on December 22nd and Mag and Marie were in the kitchen when they heard an urgent knocking on the door. Marie went to answer it. She was shocked and angered when she saw it was André. "It's you, is it? We've no wish to see you! You're a coward and the most ungrateful wretch that ever walked this earth!" she spat.

"Let me in, Marie. I just got back from Italy. I assure you I came as soon as I got the note." Just then Mag came out of the kitchen. She glared at him but said,

"Let 'im come in—we don't want all the neighbors knowin' our business."

When he was seated at the kitchen table, Mag gave vent to her fury. "So ye came back at last! Fer yer information, ye're a little late! Eugénie doesn't need ye anymore. That child suffered, God how she's suffered, but she's safe now, no thanks to ye. Let me tell ye, if ye care fer 'er at all, stay out 'er life. Ye keep sayin' ye love 'er but all ye do is bring 'er pain. Yer married now so why don't ye live yer life and let Eugénie live 'ers?"

André was close to tears. If only he had got that damn note in time! But they had been travelling so much no one could catch up with them. He pleaded with them to understand. "I would have helped if I had known. Please believe me!"

"Maybe you would and maybe you wouldn't. I just don't know about you, André. I don't think you even know yourself. At any rate, pay her back for the jewels you took and leave us all alone. Don't come with it—just send it. I'm not even sure we'll tell her you were here," said Marie furiously.

"Marie, don't be cruel. I promise I shall stay away from her—but please, I beg of you, let her know I came. Let her know I tried," André begged.

Mag nodded. "Marie, love, we must. We 'ave no right to keep it from 'er. But as far as Oi'm concerned, Oi don't want to see ye 'ere again. Is that clear?" She scowled at him, and André wilted.

He left with a very heavy heart, but by the time he had reached home, he was ashamed to admit that he was relieved. He was living the life he had been born to live, the life he loved. He had money, position and a wife who was the envy of all. She was beautiful and sweet, a wife any man would be proud of. So André eased his conscience by sending a messanger to Eugénie with

3,000 pounds and a note which read:

Eugénie dearest,
    Thank you for everything. I cannot find the words to express the sorrow I feel that I was unable to come to your rescue. I owe you so much and when you needed me I wasn't able to help. At any rate, here is the money you lent me which I hope will repay you in part for the suffering you have endured. I shall not be seeing you again, Eugénie, as I feel it is better for you that I don't. Be happy, Eugénie. You deserve everything good that life has to offer. Think of me sometimes.
                                        Affectionately yours,
                                                André

Mag took the letter and the bag of money and put them on the sideboard. She stared at them with a worried frown on her face. She was filled with dread. She just didn't trust André.

When Eugénie came home that night, Mag handed her the letter and the bag. She was worried sick. "Eugénie, love, before ye open that letter, Oi must tell ye 'e came 'ere this afternoon. 'E said 'e just got our message when 'e came 'ome from Italy. Much as it pains me to say any good about 'im, Oi 'ave to say Oi believe 'im."

Eugénie opened the letter and read it aloud. Mag held her breath as she watched and listened. Eugénie was pale but calm as she read.

"Aye ye all right, lass?" Mag asked at last.

"Yes, Mag. I suppose it's better this way. Perhaps it will be easier if I don't ever see him again. At any rate, it makes it easier to do what I plan to do."

"Whatever do ye mean, love?" Mag asked anxiously.

"Nothing dear, only that it may all be for the best." What Mag didn't know was that since Eugénie had already made up her mind to go to New South Wales, even André had no place in her life. She hadn't expected to see him again anyway. At least now she had some money so she would be able to pay her own fare and still have enough left over to put to good use when she arrived in that far distant land. She would, of course, give Marie her share of the money.

"Well," said Mag. "Ye don't know 'ow relieved me poor 'eart is to 'ear ye say that! Let's 'ave a spot of tea."

The following day Eugénie walked around to the earl's house. The butler recognized her and smiled at her quite cheerfully.

"Good-day, ma'am."

"*Bonjour,* Monsieur Giles, how are you today?"

"Very well, thank you, Mademoiselle, and you may call me Giles."

"Giles, I know I am not expected, but would it be possible to see his lordship for just a few minutes? I have something to give him."

"His lordship is in the library. If you would wait here for a moment, I'll see if he wishes to be disturbed."

"Thank you, Giles, you are very kind."

He was back in an instant. "Come with me, Mademoiselle, his lordship will be pleased to see you."

The Earl of St. Swithins was sitting with his foot propped up as usual, and looking extremely dejected. "Come in, my dear. Do forgive me for not getting up, but me gout is killing me again. It's a pleasure to see you."

"I'm sorry for coming uninvited, your lordship, but I have the money that was owed to me, and so if you will tell me how much my expenses will be, I shall give you the money now."

"Now my dear, that is not necessary. I am only too glad to be of help. But I can see you have your mind set, so I'll accept 200 pounds and not a penny more. You know, my dear, you remind me of me nephew. Stubborn as a mule!" he said with a huge sigh.

Eugénie handed him the money and a prettily decorated package. "I made something for you. I'm afraid it's not very well made, but perhaps it will remind you of me from time to time," she said, blushing.

Sir Charles opened the package with all the eagerness of a schoolboy.

"It's lovely m'dear, just what I need." It was a blue velvet pillow filled with down from the elder duck, soft and oh, so comfortable. "Here, my dear—would you place it under my foot?"

Eugénie gently placed the cushion under his pain-wracked foot and Sir Charles sat back in sheer contentment. He looked at Eugénie in silence for a few minutes. "So you are still determined to go, Mademoiselle Eugénie?"

"Oui, Sir Charles, more than ever. I must admit, though, I get frightened thinking about it sometimes. I suppose the unknown is always scary."

"My dear girl, if it doesn't meet all your expectations, you can always come back to England. Remember that. There is no shame in failure, young lady, only in not trying. You will write to me, won't you? I shall always be interested in your well-being."

"Of course I shall write, if you really wish it. It will help to fill the lonely hours," she said, taking his hand.

"Mademoiselle, never allow the word 'impossible' to enter your thoughts. You have the intelligence to think your way through the most difficult problems if you draw upon your mind to its full capacity. Keep the discouraging thought of defeat out of your thinking. As long as you do that, defeat can never conquer you."

"I'll try to remember all you have said, dear Sir Charles."

Eugénie stayed for another hour and they chatted about New South Wales. Sir Charles also told her about his childhood and early life. Then Eugénie sighed, "Dear Sir Charles, I'm afraid I must leave now. If I never see you again, remember I shall think of you always with deep affection. And I shall write, I promise."

Impulsively she placed a gentle, tender kiss on his cheek. The old earl choked back a tear and patted her hand. "My dear child, my prayers will be with you. You have courage, my dear, and I am quite sure you will succeed in whatever you undertake."

Eugénie was close to tears herself and couldn't speak. He understood, and rang for Giles. "Giles, will you see that Mademoiselle Fabré gets safely home, there's a good fellow."

Eugénie followed Giles from the room and had just reached the library door when Sir Charles called out, "Oh, and Mademoiselle Eugénie, 'never' is a word that I seldom tolerate in my vocabulary. I am sure we shall meet again. God speed, my dear."

She blew him a kiss. "With all my heart, I do hope so! *Au revoir* then, your lordship. *Au revoir!*"

Chapter 16

Christmas, the season of cheerfulness, hospitality and loving hearts, watched the old year pack and prepare to say farewell. At Mag's house, and indeed everywhere in London and in the country, there was a great deal of laughter and merrymaking. People were coming home from work or shopping sprees with flushed faces that had been nipped by the ever playful Jack Frost. Last-minute shopping was an excitement that Marie and Eugénie had never known before. The shops were a joy to behold. One store was filled with turkeys, geese, game and poultry and long strings of sausages hanging from nails and rows of barrels filled to the brim with oysters. Another store was filled with fruit from all over the world, while here and there a chestnut seller cried out temptingly, " 'Ot chestnuts! 'Ot chestnuts!"

Christmas in England was unlike any Christmas they had ever known in France. The sisters loved every exciting moment of the preparations. If only it would snow, they thought, their joy would be complete.

On Christmas Eve they got their wish. They awoke to the soft hush of falling snow. The ground was covered and the rooftops sparkled. "Isn't it beautiful, Marie?" whispered Eugénie as they looked out their bedroom window.

"Yes, dear. How I wish I didn't have to work today! I'd simply love to take a long walk."

"Marie, I do hate to tantalize you, but since I *don't* have to work until this afternoon, I'll just take a walk to Newgate and see Nan Coward. I shall take her a basket of food so that she can celebrate Christmas in style."

Shortly after Marie left for work, Eugénie, carrying her basket, merrily set out for the gloomy prison. Nan was overjoyed to see her though she protested, "Eugénie, ye shouldn't come 'ere anymore! Tis no place for the likes of ye."

"Now, Nan, you befriended me when I most needed a friend and we shall continue to be friends in New South Wales."

"Don't tell me ye still 'ave the notion to go to that God forsaken land! 'Tis madness."

"Nan, it's all arranged. I shall be sailing with you, perhaps even on the same ship. Now, are we friends and are we still going to be in our new land?" Eugénie persisted.

Nan shook her head. "It wouldn't be wise, luv."

"Don't be foolish, Nan! Having a friend is always wise. Now here's a basket of food, and there's a little surprise at the bottom. So try and have a good Christmas, Nan, and goodbye for now. I may not be able to see you before we sail, but I'll look for you in New South Wales."

"God bless ye, Eugénie Fabré. Ye're a good sort an' that's a fact," said Nan, blinking tears from her eyes.

"God bless *you,* Nan Coward. You aren't so bad yourself," Eugénie laughed.

Eugénie left Nan and danced her way home with a light heart. She loved snow and she thought of a little verse she had made up when she was a child:

Oh beautiful, beautiful snow
Which only God can make,
You leave the earth like Paradise
When you drop each fragile flake.

To her, at this moment in time, London *did* look like Paradise and she felt completely happy for the first time in many months. She was so filled with joy of life that she joined the alley urchins in a snowball fight. There was a great deal of laughter as they ducked the flying white missiles.

Mag, happening to look out her kitchen window, saw the happy crew and as she watched with love in her heart, she thought what a blessed day it was when the two girls came into her life. She watched the children with their twinkling eyes and cherry noses and the older folk wheezing along with their mufflers up to their ears, but even they had a twinkle in their eyes.

At last the greatest day of the year arrived, the greatest day to millions and millions of people all over the world. The girls awoke to the sound of church bells chiming and clanging all over the city, calling the people to church and chapel. Men, women and children flocked through the streets in their Sunday best with bright, merry faces, light hearts and a 'Merry Christmas" on their lips. Eugénie and Marie attended St. Pancras while Mag and Harry went to St. Paul's as a special treat. Moll wasn't much for churchgoing so she stayed home and watched the turkey and had her little nip of brandy in peace away from Mag's disapproving eyes.

When the services were over and people came pouring out of the churches all over London, the bells pealed gloriously, oh how gloriously, proclaiming the great joy at the birth of Christ. It was a clear, bright day. Crisp snow covered the ground and crunched under foot. Joy was in everyone's heart. A glorious day indeed!

The two girls were the first to arrive home, but Mag and Harry were close behind. Since Eugénie had started to work for Harry, Mag had grown closer to him, much to his great joy and the delight of their friends. The five of them hugged and kissed and danced about. Moll had prepared breakfast in the kitchen but they were too excited to do it justice. The smells of the cooking turkey and the pies baking in the over were too much for them. They toyed with their food for a while. Then, almost with one accord, the five of them looked at each other, dashed into the parlor as eager as a bunch of children, and exchanged their gifts. It was a happy, memorable morning.

Harry left for a few hours and while Mag and Moll were busy in the kitchen, Eugénie and Marie set out the best dishes on the dining-room table. The dining-room was only used for really special occasions.

"Eugénie, doesn't it seem to you as though we have been here for ever?" asked Marie.

"Yes, it really does. So much has happened to us in the past year—terrible things—and yet we have been happy, too. We have our wonderful friends to thank for that," said Eugénie.

When Harry came back a few hours later, he carried with him a few bottles of sherry and shortly thereafter it was time for the long awaited Christmas feast. The dishes shone. The table groaned under the weight of the food piled on it. There was a huge turkey, a large roast, platters of vegetables, bowls of fruit and plates of cakes. In the center was a steaming bowl of punch.

" 'Arry, luv, will ye say the blessin'?" asked Mag.

"It will be my pleasure, Mag."

They bowed their heads and joined hands. Harry's prayer came from his heart. "Oh, Heavenly Father, we thank you for the love around his table this day and for the food we have to eat. But most of all, we thank you for bringing our Eugénie home safely so that she can share in this day with those of us who love her. Amen.''

Four pairs of eyes watched him eagerly as he picked up the carving knife and fork. He looked at each of them in turn.

"Get on with it, 'Arry! We've waited long enough. Yer just one big tease!'' joked Mag.

At last he plunged the knife into that great bird with its sage and onion stuffing. The feast had begun. Eugénie couldn't help thinking that even if it was a time to be happy, people all over the world sitting at their Christmas dinners would be remembering other Christmasses, as she was, when others they had loved were with them, others whose hearts would beat no more. She thought about her parents and about Joséphine and the wonderful Christmasses they had spent together. She knew the others would have their memories too.

But though this little group had indeed their own sad moments of memory, they didn't share them that day. They ate and ate until they thought their stomachs would burst. Then they collapsed in their chairs for an hour until the supreme moment came when Mag drew the curtains to shut out the cold and the darkness and Moll, beaming with pride, carried in the plump plum pudding blazing with dancing flames.

Late in the night they sat by the fire in the parlor and roasted chestnuts by the shovelfull. The chestnuts crackled on the fire and outside in the streets the carolers were singing.

They put on their shawls and hurried to the door. Harry ladled out hot punch to the merry singers and they all stood at the door listening to the bells tinkling in the icy air of night, while the stars above twinkled and they felt a glory and a peace that should be felt all year —but, alas, is not. When the carol singers left, the little group returned to the parlor where toasts were drunk (Mag made hers with tea). They toasted each other, their countries and the future. It was a fitting climax to a perfect day.

The following week flew by and then the Old Year was gone. What a nightmare of a year it had been for the girls, especially Eugénie! New Year's Eve was one of the busiest nights at "The Black Bear" and since Eugénie and Harry had to work, Moll and Marie decided to join them there to see the Old Year out. Mag not wishing to be left alone, reluctantly agreed to accompany them. They had a gay old time. Everyone was singing at the top of their lungs and the drink was flowing. Mag kept a sharp eye on poor Moll all evening, much to Moll's chagrin. At midnight, the bells pealed and everyone sang and held hands. For Eugénie, it symbolized the end of her old life and the beginning of a completely new one.

On New Year's Day, they relaxed after the hectic carousing of the night before. It was a lazy, peaceful day. Harry came over for dinner and when the dishes had been cleared and they sat by the fire, Eugénie decided it was time to tell them about her plans for emigrating to New South Wales.

"I have something to tell all of you, and please don't be sad or upset," she began. "I realize there is no easy way to tell you, so I shall just have to say it right out— I am going to go to New South Wales—to Australia."

There was dead silence. They were at a loss for words. Marie began to cry.

"Harry, stop her!" she wailed. "She doesn't know what she's saying! She *can't* go there."

213

"Ay, 'Arry, tell 'er she can't go to that 'eathen country with naked savages runnin' around," added Mag.

Eugénie looked at their dear faces and sighed. "Please, there's nothing you can say. I've thought it over very carefully and everything has been arranged. I sail in three weeks on the convict ship 'The Duke of York'."

Harry puffed thoughtfully on his pipe for a moment, then spoke very calmly. "Eugénie, just answer me one thing—has it anything to do with André? He's not worth it, lass."

"No, Harry, I made my decision the day I left Newgate. Please don't make it harder for me."

Tears were streaming down Marie's face. "Eugénie, if you love us, don't leave. I couldn't bear it! You are the only family I have."

"Marie, please, please don't cry. You have Mag and Moll and Harry. I love you all, but I've had a dream all my life to do something exciting and to *be* somebody. Don't you understand that I feel I can fulfill that dream in that far-off land? I beg of you all, say no more," Eugénie pleaded.

Though their hearts were heavy, they spent the next two weeks helping Eugénie pack her trunks with everything they thought she might need, things like threads and needles, ribbons and odds and ends, things that Eugénie would never had thought of. They wanted to go to Woolwich to see her off but she wouldn't hear of it.

A few days before she left, Paul Gordon arrived unexpectedly at Mag's. Eugénie was upstairs in her room getting ready for work, when Mag came dashing up the stairs.

"Lovey, ye got a visitor. Oi think it's the one with the

strange eyes ye told me about. A proper gent 'e is, though. Oi must say Oi like 'im.''

"Lord Gordon here! Oh, I do hope nothing has gone wrong!" cried Eugenie.

She gasped when she walked into the parlor, for truly it was a very different Paul Gordon that met her eyes than the one she had seen at Sir Charles'. He was elegantly dressed in the latest of fashion. He looked like the most frivolous dandy in town.

"Is it really you?" she whispered, astonished.

"Mademoiselle Fabré, I do assure you that it is indeed I, Paul Gordon, who stands before you. I am on my way to the Prince of Wales' soiree and I scarcely can appear in the sober attire in which you evidently think, and indeed you are right, I belong.''

"Why are you here, m'Lord? Has something gone wrong?''

"No, Mademoiselle, nothing has gone wrong. There's been a slight change in plan. You are to sail on the 'Scarboro,' Mademoiselle, and since I shall be among the passengers, you may call on me for any assistance. And, (his voice softened) I do wish you well, Mademoiselle Fabré.''

Mag was waiting in the hall when they came out of the parlor. "M'Lord, if ye'll excuse me arskin' this, would ye do me a favor?" she asked.

"Anything, Madame." Paul smiled at Mag, who was twisting her apron into knots with embarrassment. His smile was everything Sir Charles had said it would be, a smile that came from the heart.

"Would ye keep an eye on me little love and keep 'er safe from those 'eathens out there? Me 'eart fails me when Oi think of 'er all the way out there and no one to look after 'er.''

Eugénie stood there, blushing at Mag's words.

"Madame I give you my word Mademoiselle Fabré shall be well looked after," Paul promised.

"Aow, yer a proper gent, ye are! Oi'll always be obliged to ye, me Lord."

The day Marie dreaded came at last. After tearful farewells, Harry took Eugénie to the coach which was to take her to Woolwich where the *Scarboro* was docked.

"Eugénie, we'll all be thinking about you," he said solemnly. "I know you won't change your mind now, so I won't even try to dissuade you. You're a strong-minded girl and you'll be all right if you remember to stand up to the harshness of life that comes your way. Don't back away from trouble, but look it square in the face and deal with it with imagination and forthrightness. Remember what I said about keeping your chin up, and write to us often so that we'll know how you're doing and not worry quite so much. Eugénie, we love you dearly and if you ever need us, please let us know."

Eugénie was choking back tears and couldn't speak. She threw her arms around him and hugged him close. God only knew when she would ever seem him again! Her heart felt as if it was breaking.

"Lass, I've got something for you that might help to fill the lonely hours. Don't open it until you're on board, because that might be your worst moment," he said hoarsely.

Clutching the little package, Eugénie climbed into the coach and Harry waved until it was out of sight. He wiped the tears from his eyes and silently prayed, "God be with you, our Eugénie. God guide you and bring you peace!"

Part Three

NEW SOUTH WALES

Eugénie stepped down from the coach sleepy and stiff after the long, uncomfortable ride. It was early evening and a cold, penetrating wind blew in from the sea. She shivered and clutched her cloak, wrapped it more securely around her. She was feeling very much alone and wondering where she would spend the night when she noticed a very, round, bald-headed man approaching her.

"Good evening, Miss. Be ye Miss Fabré?" he asked.

Eugénie nodded.

"Well, Miss, me name is Bottom. Oi'm the landlord of the 'Grey Kettle'. 'Is Lordship, that is Lord Gordon, said Oi was to see ye were comfortable." Mr. Botton was a jovial soul and soon Eugénie felt her fears subside.

"It is kind of Lord Gordon to bother about my welfare," she said.

"Well, 'is Lordship is like that—thoughtful. Oi've known 'im many a year and Oi do think the world of 'im."

He picked up her luggage and they walked to the "Grey Kettle."

"Now don't ye worry, Miss. Oi'll see to it that this 'ere luggage gets on board the *Scarboro,* aye and ye too, first thing in the mornin'," he assured her.

When they arrived at the Inn, Mr. Bottom insisted that Eugénie have a bite to eat, even though she told him that she had very little appetite. He sat with her until he was satisifed that she had eaten enough and the whole time his tongue didn't cease.

"All right, Miss, Oi suppose ye've 'ad yer fill," he said at last. "Now 'ow about gettin' some rest? Oi doubt that ye'll be too comfortable on board yon ship. Oi must say it's odd fer a snip of a girl to go traipsin' orf to no man's land, but Oi suppose it's none of me business and Oi always say, each to 'is own." Then he yelled, "Polly! Come 'ere girl!"

A young girl with merry eyes came in answer to his summons. She had rosy red cheeks and looked the picture of health.

"Aye, Sir?"

"Show the young Miss 'ere to 'er room an' 'urry back. No dawdlin', mind." Polly curtsied to Eugénie. "Will ye follow me, Miss?"

Polly pulled back the bedspread and having seen to Eugénie's comfort, left. With Polly's departure, Eugénie all at once was overwhelmed with the realization that she was far from dear Marie and her wonderful friends. She was consumed with an aching loneliness and the incessant ticking of the clock on the mantle only seemed to mock her.

Lightning lit up the room and she drew close to the fire for comfort. A raging storm had sprung up and the wind rattled the windows and gusted down the chimney, causing the fire to smoke. She wondered if the journey to New South Wales would be delayed and, though she was loathe to admit it, hoped it might. It was long past midnight when at last she succumbed to fatigue and fell asleep in the chair by the fireside.

About five o'clock the next morning young Polly brought her a cup of chocolate. "Tis a dreadful mornin', Miss. The fog be that thick. Mr. Bottom said fer me to wake ye. 'E said it were best ye get on board early-like. Would you be wantin' somethin' to eat, Miss?"

"Thank you Polly, perhaps some toast," Eugénie said faintly.

Polly was back ten minutes later with toast, tea and a boiled egg. "Oi know ye didn't ask fer all this, Miss. But ye'd best eat it or ye might be seasick. Mr. Bottom told me to tell ye that when yer ready 'e'll 'ave someone take ye to the dock. 'Ave a good journey, Miss. If ye don't mine me sayin' so, Miss, Oi think ye be that brave. Oi'd be scared witless to go orf like that, Oi would!"

Eugénie thought, "Oh Polly, if you only knew just how scared I am!"

When she came downstairs, she found Mr. Bottom waiting for her. "Oi thought Oi'd better take ye to the ship meself, Miss. Those docks are crawlin' with vermin, two-legged as well as four, and wot with the fog an' all, Oi daren't trust ye to anyone else. Why, if anythin' 'appened to ye, 'is Lordship would 'ave my life!"

When they opened the door, the fog hit them like a great, grey blanket. Eugénie was afraid she'd smother. She clutched Mr. Bottom by his sleeve and marvelled how he was able to see where he was going. She only knew they had reached the docks when she heard the waves slapping against the ships. Even at this early hour the families and friends of the convicts, who were being kept under lock and key at nearby warehouses, had gathered to catch a last glimpse of their loved ones. Eugénie could just make out their blurred shapes and hear their muffled voices. On and on Mr. Bottom led her. Eugénie followed like a sightless person, trusting him and yet fearing that at any moment they would find themselves in the ocean. How on earth would he be able to tell which of the large, dark shapes was the *Scarboro?*

Finally they came to a stop.

" 'Ere we are, Miss. Yer luggage is already on board." Then he yelled out, "Ahoy, there! Oi got one o' yer passengers 'ere. Come and 'elp 'er on board!"

An answer came out of the blanket of grey. "Be right there, mate."

Mr. Bottom turned to Eugénie. "Ye'll be taken care of now. Best of luck to ye."

A tall shaped emerged out of the fog and a strong hand gripped hers. "Follow me, Miss."

She groped her way up the gangplank clutching the hand that held hers in desperation. Then someone lifted her up and all at once she felt the deck of the ship beneath her feet.

"Welcome to the *Scarboro,* Miss. Here—you, young Rawlins, show this lady to her cabin."

"Aye, aye, sir. Come with me, Miss, if ye please."

The eerie fog drifted around them and only the slight creaking of the ship and the slap of water against the wharf kept her in touch with reality. She shivered and took a last look at the dock below where pale lights shone vaguely through the heavy shroud. She felt young Rawlins tugging at her sleeve.

"Are ye feelin' well, Miss?"

"This fog is a little frightening. But I'm all right otherwise," she said shakily.

He led her by the hand down a ladder to the deck below where the cabins for the passengers were located. He lit the lamp in her tiny cabin and she saw that he was a young lad of about fourteen with a mop of curly blonde hair and enormous grey eyes.

"Me name's Peter, Mum. If ye want anythin', Oi'll take care of ye."

"Thank you, Peter. You are very kind." She handed him a coin but he refused. "That's all right, Mum. 'Tis not often we get anyone as pretty as ye on this 'ere ship. Tis a pleasure to do fer ye, Mum. Oi do 'ope ye'll be comfortable. Good mornin', Mum."

Left alone once again, she stood still and surveyed the tiny, stuffy cabin that was to be her home for many months. She noticed that her bags were neatly stacked against one wall. She was overcome with a terrible feeling of depression and she found that she was trembling, more from apprehension than from cold. Then she remembered Harry's parting gift. She unwrapped the package and found a beautiful, leather-bound diary with a gold lock and key. He had enclosed a letter with it:

Dear little girl,

By now you must be feeling about as alone as one can possibly be. Perhaps even your courage is threatening to fail you. I bought this diary in hope that you might be able to fill the lonely hours by pouring out your joys and sorrows onto these pages. Who knows what adventures may befall you? These pages will be your friend, little one, a friend you can reveal your innermost thoughts to without fear of being judged or betrayed. In this diary you may write the story of Mademoiselle Eugénie Fabré and I very much doubt that it will be a dull one.

All my love,
Harry

She pressed his letter to her lips in a gesture of love and gratitude. Then taking her quill pen, she dipped it in the ink and wrote:

January 17, 1790—On board the Scarboro:

Harry, dearest, how well you understand me! We have known each other such a short time and yet we couldn't know each other any better if we had had a lifetime together. As I glance out of the porthole, I see heavy fog and dim pinpoints of lights. I do feel very much alone but I have no wish to go up on deck for I am sure they will be loading the convicts shortly. Oh, Harry, how I want to run down that gangplank and back to all of you—Marie, Mag, Moll and you, dear friend.

I wonder if Lord Gordon has come on board yet? Though I know he doesn't like me, still I am sure he would help me if I ever needed it. Heaven forbid that I should ever need that man's help! I also wonder if poor Nan Coward will be put on this ship. I shudder when I think how close I came to the same fate. My cabin is so tiny and smelly, I am sure the convicts' quarters will be much worse. Thank you, my friend, for giving me this diary. It helps to put my thoughts on paper. How wise you are! How wise you have always been—and, oh, Harry, I shall miss that wisdom so much in the days and perhaps the years to come! But I shall keep my chin up.

Having penned these few words, she closed the diary and lay down on her bunk. Before too long she had fallen into a restless sleep.

Meanwhile up on deck, the fog was lifting and Paul stood watching in anguish and rage the suffering of the poor wretches who were now being herded past him in chains. Old people who were too slow were butted and knocked down and there were many who seemed, to his trained eye, to be desperately ill. Now and then he heard someone shout, "Silence on deck! Quiet, ye scum!"

Paul walked up to the captain of the marines and gestured to the convicts. "Is all this brutality necessary, Captain?"

"Sir, it's Captain Dudley's orders, I'm afraid. He insists we show force from the outset so that they will not be tempted to mutiny. I don't like it anymore than you, but there is nothing I can do about it. As you are, I am sure, aware, on board his ship Captain Dudley's orders are law."

Paul was seething with disgust. "I ask you, Captain, how in the name of God could those poor wretches mutiny? Isn't there anything we can do for them?"

"Sorry. I've tried to tell Captain Dudley just that, but he won't listen. My job is to see they get on board."

He held out his hand to Paul. "By the way, my name is Crandell, Robert Crandell."

"Delighted to meet you, Crandell. Gorden is my name. Paul Gordon, physician."

They watched in silence as the convicts were packed 'tween decks and the hatches secured by cross-bars, bolts and locks. And as if that were not sufficient, the men were put in irons by order of Traill, the master of the *Neptune*, who commanded the fleet.

"Who is the surgeon attached to this ship?" Paul asked.

"I believe his name is Beyer."

"Well, perhaps he can lodge a protest. The captain should listen to him, surely?"

Robert Crandell didn't reply to this observation. After a few minutes, he excused himself and went to issue orders to his lieutenants.

Left to himself, Paul wondered if Eugénie had come on board. He had tried to keep an eye out for her, but with the fog and everything else it was an impossibility. He had a premonition that this journey was not going to be easy. Already he had seen things that certainly would not have been tolerated for an instant with the first fleet under Arthur Phillip's command.

When the last of the convicts had been put below, Captain Dudley came on board, a tall, thin man with a face branded by the pox. The marines formed an honor guard for him and he walked past them with a look of complete disdain. Shortly thereafter the order was given for departure. With a cry of "Heave-ho!" the anchor was pulled up and catted. Like a great panther released from its cage, the ship headed out to sea. The tears and curses of those poor souls left standing on the wharf watching the ships taking their loved ones and friends away, perhaps forever, filled the air.

Paul expected to see Eugénie that evening at dinner but she was not among the Captain's dinner guests. He found himself seated by Captain Crandell's pretty wife, Rachel. She was very obviously pregnant but tried to conceal the little bulge with her shawl. He enjoyed chatting with the young Mrs. Crandell but found he wasn't terribly impressed with the *Scarboro's* captain, though that gentleman did make an effort to impress the few passengers around the table.

He ran across young Rawlins on his way out of the dining-room. "Here, lad. Do you happen to know if a young French girl has come on board?" he asked.

"Aye, m'lord. Early this morning when the fog was as thick as a wall. She's a right pretty lady."

"Is she ill?"

"No, sir. Perhaps a mite down in the dumps, but Oi took 'er a bite to eat not long ago. 'Tis a pleasure to look after 'er, sir."

"Thank you . . ."

"Rawlins, sir," the boy supplied.

"Thank you, Rawlins."

When Eugénie didn't appear for breakfast the following morning, Paul decided to ask Rachel Crandell for her help.

"Mrs. Crandell . . ." he began.

"Please, don't you think we could call each other by our first names?" She was a cheerful little person and smiled at him encouragingly. "Is there something I can do for you?"

"As a matter of fact there is. A young lady for whom I feel responsible, is on board and I can't for the life of me understand why she hasn't come to take her meals with the rest of us. The cabin boy assures me she is not ill, but nevertheless, I am worried. Rachel, I'd be deeply indebted to you if you would call on her and see if she needs help. Her name is Eugénie Fabré."

"I'll go to her right away. She's probably just very lonely," said Rachel kindly.

When Eugénie heard the knock on her cabin door, she was startled. She certainly wasn't expecting anyone. Young Peter Rawlins had already brought her something to eat. She opened the door and there stood a dainty little woman with dark hair framing her olive face and the longest black lashes, which made a perfect frame for the dark, soft eyes that were looking at her so kindly.

"Hello, Mademoiselle Fabré. My name is Rachel Crandell. Lord Gordon asked me to call on you. He was worried when you didn't appear for breakfast. Is there anything I can do for you?" She smiled in such a lovely, gentle way that Eugénie's lonely heart warmed to her at once.

"Please come in, Madame. I am afraid I was feeling too lonely and shy to be very good company so I just stayed here."

"Now, Eugénie—may I call you Eugénie?"

"Oh, please do, Madame."

"Then you must call me Rachel. Now that we are on a first name basis, why don't you join me on deck? It's rather stuffy in here and we have a long, tedious journey ahead of us. Quite frankly, Eugénie, I am badly in need of some female companionship. There are only two

227

other women on board and they are, I'm afraid, not exactly my cup of tea.''

''Rachel, thank you for caring. I too need a friend,'' said Eugénie fervently.

''Good! Now I want you to meet my husband. I dare say we shall find him on deck.''

Rachel led the way, followed by Eugénie, and sure enough Robert Crandell and Paul were leaning against the rail of the main deck, chatting and, judging from their expressions, Eugénie thought, quite enjoying their conversation.

''Darling, this is Eugénie Fabré. Eugénie, my husband Robert. Of course you already know Paul.''

Robert bowed. ''A please, Mademoiselle.''

Paul said nothing for a moment. He simply stared at her with those intense yellow eyes. It was difficult to ascertain just what he was thinking. Eugénie found herself blushing under his disconcerting gaze. Finally he spoke and his voice held a trace of sarcasm which was not lost on either Eugénie or the Crandells.

''Well, Mademoiselle, I am delighted Rachel was able to persuade you to join our humble company. I was beginning to think you were going to stay hidden away for the duration of the journey.''

Eugénie glared at him. The Crandells could feel sparks flying between them and they looked at each other in wonder.

''Lord Gordon, I would never 'hide away,' as you so put it, for a journey of this length. Contrary to what you may believe, I *do* have more sense than to risk my health by locking myself up in my cabin.''

Paul didn't answer, only smiled in a most infuriating manner.

Eugénie and Rachel discovered in the course of the day that they really liked each other. Eugénie had never had a close friend of her own age other than Marie, and it warmed her heart to share some of her thoughts and dreams with Rachel. Rachel in turn talked about the coming baby and her hopes and plans for the future. By that night they were more than friends. Each felt that they had discovered a sister.

After dinner that evening, the four of them strolled on deck, Rachel and Robert walking a little ahead of Eugénie and Paul. Seeing the obvious love and tenderness that the Crandells felt for each other made Eugénie feel a little envious, and when Robert gently turned his wife towards him and gave her a long, lingering kiss she turned to Paul, saying, "They are very much in love, aren't they?"

"I should say so. But you surprise me, Mademoiselle! Don't tell me you believe in love!"

"Perhaps for others." She sighed. "But . . ."

"Go on. But what?"

"If you don't mind, I'd rather not discuss it. It's too painful a memory. I shall never love again—that I know."

Young Peter Rawlins broke the tension by bringing them all a hot toddy and they stood gazing out over the ocean while they sipped it.

"It's very beautiful, isn't it?" said Eugénie at last.

Paul's face lit up. "Yes, the ocean truly reflects the magnificence of almighty God. Do you know, if I hadn't succeeded in becoming a physician I would have followed the sea. It offers a challenge to a man and challenge is what I thrive on. That is why I chose medicine. Death is the ultimate challenge. When I cheat him, my reward couldn't be greater."

The four young people stood side by side in silence for a long time, drinking their toddies and filling their eyes and souls with the beauty of the night. The *Scar-*

boro followed her sister ships with sails full. Though it was quite cold, the air was filled with a salty tang and Eugénie smiled and couldn't help exclaiming, "It's so exhilarating! It makes me feel so alive and free."

Out of the darkness suddenly she heard a yawn. Poor Rachel, embarrassed, said, "Oh, do forgive me, but I'm afraid I really must get to bed. I don't seem to be able to keep my eyes open."

"I'll walk with you, Rachel. I'm feeling somewhat tired myself," said Eugénie. "It's been a long day and I haven't had this much fresh air since I left France." They said goodnight to Robert and Paul and arm in arm made their way to their cabins.

Eugénie undressed, turned down the lamp that swung from the crossbeam and with a sigh stretched out on her bunk. The soothing motion of the ship began to lull her to sleep. She listened to the cracking of the planks and the musical sounds of the rigging and felt quite happy in the knowledge that she had found friends like the Crandells at the start of her new life.

Chapter 18

Though it was winter, the travelers were blessed with amazingly good weather at first. For four days the sky was blue, but on the fifth day it suddenly clouded over and the sea turned to iron grey. A storm raged and battered the ships for four frightful days. The *Scarboro* was tossed by the raging waves, and to Rachel and Eugénie, huddled together in the Crandells' cabin, it seemed that the ship screamed in agony. Sails tore, lines parted and were mended in frantic haste. Three of the crew were swept overboard and were carried away by the surging sea.

The girls stayed together throughout the storm, terrified that at any moment they would see water filling the cabin. Young Peter Rawlins managed to bring them a cup of hot soup or tea every once in a while. The lad tried to assure them that there was nothing to be afraid of by telling them that the *Scarboro* had seen worse storms in her time.

At last the angry winds ceased. Patches of blue sky appeared and the sea became gentle once more. An exhausted Robert Crandell came to his cabin and slumped onto his bunk. Between them, the girls tugged off his boots and then Rachel lovingly covered him with a blanket.

"Let's get some air, Eugénie," she suggested. "If I stay here a minute longer, I know I shall faint."

With great relief they climbed the ladder to the deck above and stood side by side at the rail, giving themselves up to the sheer pleasure of feeling the salt spray on their faces once more and filling their lungs with the fresh, crisp air.

On February 8, 1790, Eugénie wrote in her diary for the second time. Since it was Harry who had given it to her, she wrote as though she were writing to him, though she never for one moment intended that anyone should ever read a word written between the leather bound covers.

February 8, 1790—On Board the Scarboro
Dear Harry,

The Crandells, Paul Gordon and I have become inseparable though Lord Gordon still irritates me with his condescending manner. He treats me like a child and I resent it.

Inevitably our thoughts are centered on New South Wales and since Paul has already been there, I'm afraid we are driving him quite mad with our incessant questions.

Oh, how I would have loved to have sailed with Captain Cook! Just imagine sharing in the discovery of Tahiti. Why, even the name "Tahiti" has a magic ring to it. Paul says that at that time the Far East was like a closed book. Africa was a mere outline and as for the Pacific, it seemed like a great, mysterious, dark cavern. The suspense must have been terrific! What lay behond the dark cavern? Monsters? Or could there possibly be a beautiful kingdom? Well, dear Harry, I am sure you know they found a land filled with happy, beautiful and healthy people. Someday I shall go there. Wouldn't it have been wonderful to have sailed on with Cook and on April 28, 1770 (I wasn't even born then) to sight the land of New South Wales?

Paul says it is nothing like Tahiti and it is going to take years and years of back-breaking work to make something of the country. What a pity such a land has been turned into a prison without bars! If only the American colonies hadn't decided to fight for independence—but then the land wouldn't have been put to use, at all, perhaps.

They bombarded Paul day and night with questions about New South Wales and he tried to be patient. In a way it helped to pass the time. It became a habit with them to find a cozy corner in the passengers' lounge every afternoon when most of the other passengers were resting. Eugénie recorded their conversations in her diary:

February 18, 1790:
We have continued to question Paul and I must say he is patient. We are curious as to why he first undertook such a journey and he told us that all his life he had been dogged by a restless spirit and when he heard that the First Fleet would sail under the leadership of Captain Arthur Phillip, he couldn't resist the call of adventure. I must say he isn't the only Gordon with a sense of adventure. His old Aunt Aggie who had raised him insisted on going with him. From what Paul has told us about her, she must be quite a woman.

They made their preparations and sailed from England on May 13th, 1787. There were eleven ships in all—H.M.S. Sirius, the sloop Supply, the nine transport and storeships. Apart from the crews there were four companies of marines and wives and families of some of the officers. There were also about four hundred and forty-three sailors and the ships carried eight hundred prisoners, one third of whom were women, poor souls. Thanks to Captain Phillip, their journey was uneventful and they sailed into the harbor of New South Wales on January 18th. Arthur Phillip didn't like the looks of Botany Bay and so he sent the Supply to investigate Port

Jackson which was the harbor Captain Cook had spotted eighteen years before but hadn't entered.

Paul said they were all anxious to set foot on land after eight months at sea. We were shocked when he casually mentioned that they had only lost twenty-three convicts. But we understood when he told us how dreadful conditions were on most convict ships and that those who had died had been ill before leaving England anyway.

They waited for the return of the Supply with great impatience and when she finally returned a day or so later with a favorable report of Port Jackson, the whole fleet sailed there without delay. Port Jackson has the most magnificent harbor. The cove is about a quarter of a mile wide at its entrance and a good half mile in length. Everyone who was able, convicts included, stood on the decks watching the densely wooded shore, some anxiously, some with delight and anticipation. Arthur Phillip renamed the place Sydney and the flag was raised. Paul said at that moment he felt a surge of pride that he was going to take part in the making of that land into something great, for he shares Captain Phillip's dream that one day New South Wales will be a great and productive country.

He didn't have much time to dream, however. The enormous task of disembarking began. First, those strong enough were given the task of clearing some of the land. Tents were pitched and little by little the camp took shape. A boundary was drawn around it which was patrolled day and night by marines to prevent escapes. Life was extremely hard and Arthur Phillip could well be forgiven for getting a little discouraged at the thought of the task ahead. He knew, as did Paul, that crops would have to be raised within the next eighteen months in order for the Colony to survive alone.

Paul said that at the time it all seemed impossible. They needed farmers and skilled workers and among the convicts there were few with talents that could be useful. He laughed when he told us that if one wanted a pocket picked or a throat skillfully slit, there were plenty who could do a more than adequate job.

They planted seeds but the sun was so hot that it

destroyed anything that took root. It was incredibly hot that summer, so hot that the earth was strewn with the bodies of dead parakeets and bats. Four of their cows and the only two bulls they had ran off and couldn't be found. It was certainly a devastating beginning to the venture.

Arthur Phillip rallied everyone and, undaunted, planned for a new town with a main street two hundred feet wide, but when Paul left three months later for England, most of the colony were still living in tents or huts made of branches and clay. They had only managed to build two small brick and stone houses, an observatory and a wooden hospital.

The person who intrigues me the most is Paul's Aunt Aggie Gordon. Just think, a woman of sixty-five undertaking a journey like that! What courage, what a spirit of adventure, what love! Paul left her and her maid Bella in the care of some convicts whom he says are reliable and strong, capable of taking care of his aunt. We weren't so sure—although when I thought of dear Nan Coward, I felt a little guilty for having my doubts. At any rate, Aunt Aggie Gordon sounds as though she is very capable of taking care of herself. In fact, Paul expects to find his aunt, Bella and the convicts safely ensconced in the house he had planned outside Sydney in a place called Parramatta.

We asked him about the Aborigines and he assured us that they seemed to be quite friendly and compassionate, though not particularly handsome. He felt that they would respond to kindness as much as anyone does.

The more I hear about Captain Arthur Phillip, the more I admire and wish to meet him. Paul thinks very highly of him and says he is a man who is kind, yet firm, competent and not power-hungry. He has since been made Governor of New South Wales and we all feel that he will prove worthy of his position.

Paul was afraid that he had painted too gloomy a picture for us and was quick to tell us that it wasn't all that bad. In fact, he said, there was much that was very beautiful in that land and he felt very sure that one day we would all be proud to belong to it. He refused then to discuss New South Wales with us anymore. I for one felt

*even more sure that I was destined to go there. Robert
was full of enthusiasm but poor Rachel, though she
didn't say much, I feel is worried about bringing her
baby to such a wilderness.*

Eugénie had listened to Paul with intense interest and
now she felt all her former enthusiasm for the journey
surging through her and her confidence renewed itself.
She was, indeed, more than ever convinced that she was
meant to go there and that everything would turn out
well.

On February 20, 1790 they docked at Teneriffe, the
largest of the Canary Islands. The *Scarboro* dropped
anchor just long enough to replenish supplies and then
set sail for Cape Town. Though Rachel and Eugénie
hadn't gone ashore, the sight of land lifted their spirits.
Eugénie had longed to go ashore and explore but Rachel
was big and uncomfortable with her child and not
feeling at all well so she just didn't have the heart to
leave her. Robert, busy as he was, realized Eugénie's
sacrifice and thanked her. Poor Robert—with each day
that brought the birth of his baby closer, his anxiety
grew. What he had seen of Surgeon Beyer had filled him
with dread. The fellow reeked of rum most of the time
and Robert very much doubted if he had once made a
check on the convicts' condition since the voyage began.
He became more and more convinced that he couldn't
possibly trust that man to deliver his child. He made up
his mind to ask Paul's help at the first opportunity.

A few days after they had sailed from Teneriffe, he
found Paul standing by the rail on the top deck. His
thoughts seemed to be very far away.

"Paul, sorry to interrupt your thoughts, but I've got
an enormous favor to ask of you," Robert began.

Paul could see that his friend was extremely agitated

236

and he said in a calm voice, "Of course, Rob, ask away."

"I'm frightfully worried about Rachel. You know the baby is due soon and I just can't bear the thought of that drunken Beyer taking care of her. Paul, I beg of you, as a friend, will you see to the delivery?"

Paul laughed. "Don't look so worried, Rob. It will be my pleasure. Before we reach the Cape, old boy, I guarantee there will be a new little Crandell on board."

Robert clasped his friend's hand in gratitude. "How can I thank you enough? You've certainly taken a load off my mind. I've felt guilty enough, dragging Rachel in her condition on this voyage, and I'd never forgive myself if anything happened to her or the baby. How that man Beyer ever succeeded in becoming a surgeon is a mystery to me."

While this conversation was taken place, Eugénie and Rachel were in the Crandells' cabin sewing clothes for the baby. Rachel looked so tired, Eugénie thought. Suddenly she had a marvellous idea—Nan Coward! She smiled mischievously at her friend and Rachel looked at her inquiringly.

"Rachel, how would you like to have a maid?" Eugénie asked.

"Oh, Eugénie, you dreamer! But I must say it would be heavenly. Only where in the world does one find a maid in the middle of the ocean?"

"Do you remember my telling you about Nan Coward, the woman I met in Newgate? I know she's with this fleet, perhaps even on this ship. Now, Rachel, she doesn't look like much but she is strong and good-hearted. Why, if it hadn't been for Nan, life would have been completely unbearable in that terrible place."

Rachel looked doubtful but Eugénie continued to persuade her. "Rachel, you must admit you are exhausted. When the baby comes, you're going to need all the help you can get. This journey has been tiring enough and in your condition it must be a thousand times worse."

"Dear, it sounds like a wonderful idea, but I'm not sure Robert will like the thought of a convict taking care of his child. But let's go ask him. The worst that can happen is that he'll say no."

"Displeased" was a mild description for Robert's reaction. He was astounded. Rachel tried hard to persuade him.

"But darling, a convict caring for our baby! Just think what you're saying, Rachel!" he pleaded.

Paul, surprisingly, came to the rescue. "It might not be such a bad idea, Rob. Rachel will need help when the baby comes and you'll find none other than convict help around here. If Eugénie vouches for this woman, your fears should be put to rest."

"Robert, do you honestly feel that I would suggest someone who would be a danger to your child?" Eugénie added.

Robert blushed and became apologetic. "Oh, heavens, Eugénie, you know better than that! Of course I trust your judgment in this matter. In fact I'll check on the whereabouts of your Nan Coward right away."

True to his word, Robert went immediately to Captain Dudley and got his permission to search for Nan Coward. If she wasn't on the *Scarboro* they would have to wait until they reached the Cape to find her. Up to now, his contact with the prisoners had been very slight. As Captain, he saw to it that his men were put on guard duty and his other orders were passed on to the men by his lieutenants. The convicts didn't particulary interest him. Once in a while he did see a group being taken on deck for air, but he had had no desire to make closer contact with them.

Robert climbed down the ladder deep into the bowels of the ship where the convicts were lodged. It was dark down there and the light from the lantern he carried was very feeble. The air was unbelievably foul. He passed the men's quarters and all seemed quiet there. Finally, he came to the section which housed the women prisoners. The sounds of cursing and snarling hit his ears loud and shrill. He looked at the guard questioningly, who simply shrugged and unlocked the door. Robert braced himself and went in. Immediately there was an hilarious furor.

"Well, well, well! Wot 'ave we got 'ere then?"

"It's a flippen merman, that's wot!"

"That's no merman, Gert, it's a real live 'uman man person."

Gert, he could see in the feeble candle light, was a dirty, scrawny, snaggle-toothed creature. She was grinning from ear to ear.

"Aye, yer right, Flossie, and wot a looker 'e is! Come 'ere ducks, give old Gert a little kiss," she cackled.

Robert was stunned. The gun ports were closed and the stench of unwashed bodies and bad food was overwhelming. My God, he thought, animals are treated better than this! He heard children crying and in the feeble light cast by his lantern he saw pale, hungry faces looking at him and their eyes seemed to plead for help. He was furious. Why hadn't he been informed about these conditions?

"Wot do ye want then, ducks?" the toothless harridan yelled at him.

"I'm looking for a woman by the name of Nan Coward," he managed to say.

A tall, thin shape stood out and came forward. "Oi'm Nan Coward. Wot do ye want wi' me?"

Robert barely glanced at her, so much in a hurry was he to escape that stench-filled pit. "Follow me," he said curtly.

" 'Ave a good time, dearie," yelled some of the women. "Charge 'im plenty!"

Eugénie was waiting for them when they climbed up to the top deck. Her face lit up when she saw Nan but changed to one of horror when she saw how debilitated Nan looked.

"Nan! Oh Nan, are you all right?" she cried. She ran towards her to hug her but Nan stopped her.

"Don't touch me Eugénie child, Oi'm crawlin' with vermin. Blimey, it's good to see ye! But Oi 'ave to go with his 'onor 'ere, though wot 'e wants with the likes o' me is more than Oi can say."

Eugénie laughed until the tears ran down her face. "Oh, Nan, it isn't what you think!" Robert's face was as red as a beet and a delight to Eugénie. He was staring in disbelief at Nan who was standing very close to him. She looked much worse than usual. Her hair was a mass of tangles. Her eyes were bright and hollow and her clothes were hanging in shreds. To make matters worse, she smelled like a dozen rotten eggs.

"Nan, this is Captain Crandell and he wishes to hire you to be his wife's maid. I have vouched for your character," Eugénie said.

"Ye mean Oi don't 'ave to go back in that 'ole? If Oi was a cryin' person Oi do believe Oi'd cry right now," gasped Nan.

Robert looked as if he were just about to send her right back to the hold so Eugénie quickly said, "Come with me, Nan, and meet Mrs. Crandell. We shall have to get you cleaned up a bit."

They went to Rachel's cabin. Poor Rachel was just as horrified as her husband at the sight of Nan. Eugénie could just imagine the thoughts that were scampering through Rachel's head but Rachel, ever polite, recovered herself quickly, as Eugénie said, "Rachel, this is Nan Coward. Nan, this is Mrs. Crandell and she is going to need you very much in the near future."

Rachel cautiously extended her hand and said in a somewhat feeble voice, "Yes, Mrs. Coward, I certainly shall need you very much and so will my baby."

"Thank ye, Ma'am," Nan muttered.

"Come on, Rachel, let's get her cleaned up," said Eugénie brightly.

Eugénie went in search of young Peter Rawlins, the cabin boy, and for the next hour he was kept busy running back and forth from the galley with hot water.

They stripped poor Nan and scrubbed her from head to toe. By the time they were finished with her, her skin was pink and didn't blend too well with her vivid red hair. They trimmed her red locks and cut her nails and at last she stood before them clean and shining. Eugénie couldn't believe how thin Nan had got in the few months since she had last seen her at Newgate. Nan's clothes had to be burned and she sat in Rachel's cabin wrapped in a blanket as Rachel and Eugénie tried frantically to find something for her to wear. They decided to give her some of Eugénie's clothes, since she was taller than Rachel. Even so, the skirt barely covered Nan's knees. But at least she was presentable and ready for inspection. They took the well-scrubbed Nan up to deck where Robert was making Paul roar with laughter at his description of the would-be nursemaid. Robert felt a bit peeved. "I don't think it's one bit funny, Paul! Just wait and see for yourself. If Eugénie hadn't whisked her away so quickly, I would have sent her right back down to the hold.''

Nan looked a great deal better than when Robert had seen her last. He was quite surprised, as he could hardly imagine how one so dirty could ever look clean. He saw that Rachel had made up her mind to keep Nan so he said nothing.

"Nan, you have already met Captain Crandell. This other gentleman is Lord Gordon,'' said Eugénie, indicating Paul.

"Blimey, a bloomin' Lord!'' Nan made a great effort to curtsy. It was comical to watch. Much to Eugénie's surprise, Paul took Nan's hand and bent over it as he would any great lady.

"Mrs. Coward, a pleasure to meet you. Please call me Dr. Gordon. I think of myself more as a doctor than a lord.''

Nan blushed as red as her hair. From that moment on, she worshipped him.

"I know you will take good care of Mrs. Crandell and her baby, when the time comes," Paul continued. "Eugénie has spoken very highly of you, Mrs. Coward.''

"Oh, Oi will, sir, Oi will!'' From then on Nan stuck by Rachel's side like glue. Poor Rachel, in order to get time to be by herself, had to wait until Nan fell asleep, when she would sneak out of the cabin.

Now that the matter of Nan was settled, Robert turned his attention to the plight of the convicts.

"Paul, you have no idea what a mess it is below. Those poor devils are filthy and do you know that several babies have been born since we left England?''

"My God! Are you telling me that *babies* are down there with all that filth and foul air? Surely Beyer has been attending them—he can't be as bad as all that.

242

After all, he was appointed by His Majesty's Government to this position. Even so, we must look into it."

But in the hustle and bustle of the ship, Paul was unable to pin down either Beyer or Captain Dudley. Every time he tried to speak to either one, an excuse was made for avoiding the conversation.

They were about a week out of Cape Town when Rachel's baby decided it was time to join the world. Paul stayed with her while Eugénie tried to keep Robert from going into a complete panic. He paced up and down like a caged tiger. His face was as white as a sheet and nothing Eugénie said helped to calm him.

"Robert, I'm surprised at you! You are a soldier and here you are trembling like a child. You know very well that Paul will take the very best care of Rachel. Why, here's Nan now!" Eugénie cried.

Nan was running towards him and Robert's face turned ashen. "Is something wrong, Nan? Tell me the truth!"

"Lor' luv ye, sir, ye 'ave a foine boy and Mrs. Rachel is fit as a fiddle. Why, she popped that child out like she'd been doin' it all 'er life!" chortled Nan.

"Eugénie, did you hear? It's a boy! Eugénie, I have a son!" He was so deleriously happy that he even hugged Nan.

"Robert, it's marvellous. Congratulations," said Eugénie happily.

He stood murmuring in sheer happiness, "I have a son, a son!"

"Sir, why don't ye go 'ave a peek at 'im instead of just standin' there mutterin'?" Nan suggested.

"Yes, Robert, whatever are you waiting for? Go see them," urged Eugénie.

He gave Eugénie a hug, went to his cabin and timidly

knocked. Paul opened the door. He grinned when he saw Robert's dishevelled state. "Well, well, if it isn't the proud father."

"How is Rachel?"

"Rachel's fine. I'm not so sure about you. She's sleeping now but come, hold your son." He placed a blanket in Robert's arms with a small, warm bundle wrapped in it. Robert gazed at the little face with its crown of dark hair and he held one of the little fingers.

"Welcome to the world, Andrew Gordon Crandell," he whispered. "Paul, how can I ever thank you?"

"It was a pleasure to welcome my godson to this great, marvellous world of ours. I am sure between us we can make him as good a man as his father," said Paul, clapping Robert on the back.

Little Andrew Gordon Crandell let out a loud wail and Paul smiled. "Run along now, Robert, and send Nan back to me, there's a good chap."

As Paul returned the baby to Rachel's arms, he murmured, "Someday, little Andrew, God willing I may have a son like you."

Chapter 19

They arrived at Cape Town, the last stop before their final destination, on June 13th. The passengers were relieved to get their feet on firm land once more and were excited at the prospect of staying in the bustling town. Rachel, Nan, and Eugénie were filled with a wonderful sense of security the solid earth seemed to give them, but it was hours before they ceased to imagine the rolling motion of the ship under their feet.

They were entranced with Cape Town, which seemed like a little bit of Holland. The pulsing city was filled with more variety of races than any other city in the world. Its wide, clean streets were laid out in orderly fashion, and each whitewashed house had its own well-kept garden. The public houses, Paul and Robert were quick to report, were crowded with sailors from all over the world, enjoying to the full the good Cape wine.

While Paul and Robert were busy during the day buying livestock and other provisions needed for their life in New South Wales, Eugénie, Rachel and their landlady, who had taken them under her wing, strolled in the open countryside, filling their souls with blessed peace and wishing that their stay in this clean, friendly city could be prolonged.

In the evenings, Paul and Robert escorted the ladies

around the town. It was a delight to watch the towns-people contentedly sitting in their gardens, the women busy with their needlework and the men watching the world go about its business, at the same time sending up great rings of smoke from their pipes. Small wonder they were loathe to continue their journey—if they had but known what lay ahead of them, their reluctance would have turned to fear.

They left Cape Town on the 14th day of July, well rested. Nan had gained weight, much to Eugénie's and the Crandells' satisfaction, and they had managed to buy some clothes to fit her so she looked a bit more presentable. Before them the sea stretched calm and seemingly endless. When they had sailed several miles from the Cape, the convicts were brought up in small groups for air. The men were in irons, and to Eugénie and Rachel, seeing this for the first time, it was pitiful indeed. They looked so dejected it was difficult not to feel compassion for them and to remember that they were convicted felons. They had been kept in the hold the entire month and now they could scarcely bear to open their eyes under the bright, glaring sunlight.

"My God, Robert, look at those poor devils! What's been going on?" asked Paul in distress. "I just found out this morning that this is the first time they have been allowed up for air since we docked at Cape Town. God help them! Most of them look half dead or starving," sighed Robert.

"That does it! Robert, I should have insisted on seeing Captain Dudley long ago. At this rate, they are liable to lose the whole bunch of them. Now I'm going to have a word with Beyer. Something will have to be done."

Without warning, the weather changed and a storm broke in full fury. Perhaps the heavens were matching the rage felt by both men. The ship pitched and tossed as though the sea were alive with a million unseen devils. The poor, wretched convicts were now soaked to the skin to add to their other miseries, and were herded below once more. The animals were terrified, but no more so than the wretched human cargo the ships carried. But the storm passed, as eventually all storms must do, and once more the sea was tranquil.

Paul went directly in search of the ship's surgeon. He found him in his cabin with his mug of rum. Paul tried to make the man see just how serious the plight of the convicts was, but Beyer laughed at him. Paul had an overwhelming urge to punch that fat, repulsive face. Beyer looked at him with his heavy eyes. His voice sounded slurred. "Why should I waste my time on the like of that scum?" he asked thickly.

"May I remind you, Dr. Beyer, that you are a physician and as such, sworn to help the sick and relieve their suffering to the best of your ability. My, God, man have you no feelings?"

Beyer laughed, "Aye, I have a feeling right now I'd like a warm body to curl up to and another jug of good rum."

"You are contemptible, Beyer, and I promise you, you won't hear the last of this. I shall inform Captain Dudley of your attitude."

"Aye, do that, you interfering young whippersnapper! Just you do that." Beyer's bloated face broke into a wide, leering grin. Paul felt his control snapping and walked out of the cabin before he smashed the face to a pulp.

With every step he took in the direction of Captain Dudley's cabin, his rage increased, so by the time he knocked on the door he was out for blood. He knocked impatiently.

"Come in."

"Captain Dudley . . . " Paul began.

"Oh, it's you, Gordon." The captain was less than delighted to see his passenger, but Paul wouldn't be put down.

"Captain, something must be done for those convicts of yours. Are you aware that most of them are ill? I informed your surgeon of this fact and he refuses to be bothered. That man is a complete nincompoop! I appeal to you, sir, do something before it's too late."

"Are you serious? We have done too much already for those dregs of humanity. The more that die before we reach New South Wales, the fewer mouths there will be to feed," said the captain coldly.

Paul couldn't believe that those words were coming from the mouth of a captain of His Majesty's Fleet. "Captain Dudley, mark me well, I shall see that a full report is made to Governor Phillip."

This threat didn't seem to make any impression on Dudley, but he made one concession. "Lord Gordon, if you wish to take care of those filthy wretches, you have my permission to do so, but only in so far as their medical care is concerned. I warn you, Gordon, stay out of my business. Now get out!"

Paul would have dearly loved to have called him out, but the thought that he wouldn't be much good to anyone if he were killed or confined to his quarters helped him to remain under control. On the sea, the captain of the ship was the law. But he swore to himself, "I shall make him pay for this. Someday I shall see that he pays for every bit of suffering he has allowed to happen on this ship."

None of the passengers had paid any attention to the deaths that had occurred among the convicts since leaving England. Many of them had been ill anyway, and a death here and there was to be expected on a voyage of this nature. However, since leaving Cape Town, the funerals had become more and more frequent. The bodies wrapped in sailcloth were becoming more numerous and the sight of the flag-draped sailcloth stretched on a plank and the drone of the captain's voice chanting the burial service was becoming a daily ritual. This was the situation when Paul obtained permission to tend to the convicts.

His first visit into the hell-hole of the holds was enough to make the strongest man cringe. Many were lying in their own filth which was crawling with rats. The odor of urine, feces and vomit filled the air. He immediately gave orders through Robert that water and scrub brushes should be brought down and pitched in himself, along with any convicts that had the strength, to clean the place up. Robert and several volunteers from among the marines joined him. The gun ports were opened and at last, with fresh air filtering in and the place cleaned up, he was able to give his full attention to the sick. It was as he had feared—scurvy! As yet, the disease hadn't broken out among the crew of the *Scarboro*. Paul wondered just what kind of conditions prevailed on the other convict ships. He did his utmost for the convicts stricken with the disease but it seemed to be a fruitless battle.

The next three months were a living hell. Surgeon Beyer was so drunk most of the time that he was all but useless. Paul hoped that he could contain the disease among the convicts, but it was a vain hope. When the first five cases among the crew had been diagnosed, Paul ordered the passengers and especially Rachel, little Andrew, Eugénie and Nan to remain in their cabins and to take their meals there. At this time Eugénie wrote in her diary:

*August 10, 1790—*Scarboro

My admiration for Lord Gordon couldn't be greater. This is a death ship and Robert tells us that he is working night and day to save the lives of the sick. He has no help, medically speaking. The ship's surgeon is usually too drunk to be of any assistance, even if he would. Robert and his marines are doing their best to give Paul assistance. We passengers have been ordered to remain in our cabins and I am going quietly crazy. I could be of help to that insufferable man, but he refuses to let me. What good will he be to anyone if he drops from fatigue, or worse yet, catches the disease? Oh, but I forgot—no disease would dare invade the body of the mighty Lord Gordon! Oh, I know that wasn't very nice, but why is he so stubborn?

Eugénie obeyed orders unwillingly and remained within the confines of either her own or the Crandells' cabin until one day Robert stopped by and spoke to them from outside the door. He wouldn't risk coming in. He admitted that conditions had grown considerably worse and that half his men were now down with the disease.

"That settles it, Robert!" said Eugénie grimly. "I can't stay in my cabin one minute longer. There are sick people on board and I'm going to help!"

"Eugénie, don't be mad. Paul is adamant about you remaining below in your quarters," said Robert.

"He can't stop me, Robert Crandell, and neither can you!"

With that last word she opened the door and flounced past him and up the ladder to the deck above.

Robert stared after her and then turned helplessly to the startled faces of his wife and Nan. Nan spoke up. "Sir, Miss Rachel is stronger now and Oi'd like to 'elp, too. Oi do think Oi'm needed more up there than down 'ere."

Robert frowned. "Nan, it's bad enough that Eugénie is flaunting Paul's authority, let alone you. Besides, your place is with the baby."

Then Rachel unexpectedly spoke. She seldom crossed Robert in anything, but this time she looked at him with a steady, serious gaze. "Darling, this is an emergency. Don't you think that everyone who *can* help, should? The lives of the sailors are especially important. If all of them fall sick, who will sail this ship?"

"Oh, my love, you amaze me sometimes. Of course you are absolutely right. But *you* aren't thinking about coming up, surely?"

"No, darling. I know I must stay with the baby, but if I could I would. Nan, go on up, dear and my prayers are with you." She blew a kiss to her husband and gave him such a look of longing that he wanted to throw caution to the wind and clasp her in his arms. Instead, he closed the door and followed Nan to the deck above.

Eugénie, momentarily shocked by the bodies lying all over the deck in various stages of the illness, soon rolled up her sleeves and set to work. She was kneeling by a marine washing his fevered body when Paul spotted her. His face went scarlet with rage.

"What the devil are you doing up here? I told you to stay below! Get down to your quarters, Mademoiselle. That is an order!"

Eugénie was prepared to do battle with him and he noticed the glint of anger in her eyes.

"Dr. Gordon, will you please stop yelling at me? I'm not one of your lackeys. You don't own me. It's *my* life and I shall do as I please with it!" she snapped.

"I insist that you go back to your cabin. You've jeopardized the lives of Rachel and the baby, not to mention Nan. Now you'll have to remain in your own cabin. Are you satisfied now, Mademoiselle?" he raged.

"I'm not going! You need me here, I don't care what you say. If you carry me down to the cabin I shall come back up!"

"You little ninny! Have you no sense at all? I'm telling you for the last time—*go back to your cabin!*"

Eugénie looked him steadily in the eye and loudly and clearly spelled out, "N-O!"

"You are damnably mule-headed, Eugénie Fabré," he sighed, too exhausted to argue further, and Eugénie turned her back on him and continued administering to the sick marine. Just then Nan arrived and Paul snapped at her. "Well, I suppose it's useless to argue with *you,* Nan Coward. I see you are every bit as foolish."

Nan stood up to his withering looks and said, "Aye, sir, and Mrs. Rachel would be here too, if it weren't for the wee one."

The three of them, with the help of Robert and his marines, labored night and day. The unfortunate part of the dread scurvy was that the symptoms came on gradually and so the disease had already gotten a good foothold before it was discovered. The dead were thrown overboard by the dozens. Captain Dudley, his face impassive and his voice matter-of-fact, rushed through the burial services. " 'I am the resurrection of the life,' saith the Lord. 'He that believeth in me, though he were dead' etc." Captain Dudley didn't even both to finish saying the words and that "etc." somehow made the whole thing a mockery and gave a sense of meaningless to the lives of those unfortunates whose bodies were committed to the deep. Paul's anger was festering like an ucler deep within his body.

A makeshift hospital had been set up on deck and shelter had been rigged to protect the patients from the elements. They made the poor wretches as comfortable as they could. Everywhere lay the sick and dying—men, women and babies with sallow complexions and sunken eyes, their every muscle in pain. For some, there was no hope. They were in the final stages of the disease. Their teeth had fallen out and they were hemorrhaging, had diarrea and their kidneys and lungs were damaged beyond repair.

Eugénie worked without ceasing. Sometimes she thought she couldn't go on any longer, but always she found the strength. She watched Paul with eyes full of wonder. It was clear that he was a man who did not flinch at the prospect of doing the impossible, and even then, he didn't give up. Clearly human life was precious to him and he fought for every life, however mean, on board ship. She was full of admiration for him but yet she thought him the most irritating, domineering individual she had ever met.

It was three in the morning, just eighteen hours away from New South Wales. Paul was checking on his patients when he saw Eugénie kneeling beside one of the young sailors. The poor wretch stared at her with eyes filled with fear. He clung to Eugénie's hand in desperation, as though by clinging to her he could hold onto his life which was relentlessly slipping away. This was a scene Eugénie had participated in countless times. As she spoke to him softly, Paul couldn't help noticing how weary she was. She hadn't complained once during the past three horrifying months. Then he saw terror in the eyes of the young sailor, and with a deep sigh he breathed his last. Paul walked to them and, bending over, closed the poor devil's eyes. Then gently pulling Eugénie to her feet, he murmured, "Eugénie, come with me."

Wearily she slipped her arm through his and they

walked along the deck until they came to a reasonably secluded spot. He pulled a small flask of wine from his pocket and handed it to her. "Here—drink some of this. It will do you good," he said gruffly. They sat side by side with their backs against the rail. She drank and sighed wearily. She could feel the wine trickling down her parched throat and it relaxed her somewhat. She turned to hand Paul the flask, and suddenly his face was very close to hers. She felt his warm breath on her cheek and a shiver went through her as she closed her eyes. His lips touched hers softly, making her body tremble. She felt a sensation of weakness steal over her and swayed towards him. He held her close to his heart, which he now realized was filled with love for her and admiration for her spirit and pluck. He loved her chestnut hair and twinkling eyes, her compassion, and yes, even her prickly pride. She fell asleep in his arms and it was close to five when at last he reluctantly woke her.

"Eugénie, it's amost morning. We shall be in New South Wales today," Paul whispered. But she didn't want to move. She felt so content and she had been having the most marvellous dreams . . . She murmured André's name. In her dreams, she had joined André and it was in his arms she was now resting. Paul heard the name and his heart grew heavy. Nan Coward had told him something about Eugénie's life and of her love for André de Varney. He thought to himself as he stroked her tangled hair, "Someday you will love me, my precious. Someday you will want me as I want you."

Chapter 20

The breeze was blowing from the north as the ships sailed steadily in towards shore. Those who were able to stand were on deck, watching the approaching coast of New South Wales. All were ecstatic that the dreadful journey was over at last. Though it was eight o'clock at night, there was a crowd thronging the waterfront. Eugénie stood beside Nan at the rail and strained to see the people who were just blurs in the distance. They were making good progress for a while, but then suddenly the breeze died down and they were forced to wait until morning before making it to Sydney. It was a great disappointment, as everyone was longing to set foot on land and anxious to get on with their lives.

As on the previous night, the waterfront was filled with people. They appeared to be half-starved scarecrows. Robert came to stand beside Eugénie at the rail, and she cried, "Oh, Robert, look at those poor people waiting for us! How horrified they will be when they see what's on board these ships!"

A cry suddenly went up from the shore, and the passengers watched in dread as they saw that those bodies which had been thrown overboard during the night were now being washed ashore. The cries of horror and consternation that arose from those on shore tore at the heartstrings.

Governor Phillip had been rowed out to the ships, and after inspecting the *Neptune* and meeting with the Fleet's Commander Traill, came on board the *Scarboro*. Paul went forward to meet him. The governor's face was ashen and careworn and his eyes held a look of shock and utter disbelief. He came on board the *Scarboro* in a daze, but when he recognized Paul, he came forward and shook his hand warmly. There was such depth of sadness in his eyes that Paul's heart ached in sympathy. Arthur Phillip's voice shook with emotion. "Paul, what devil stirred up this tragedy? The *Neptune* is a floating charnel house. God help us all!"

The governor inspected the *Scarboro* and then returned to shore, where he had organized the convicts into stretcher parties. The old tents they had used when they had first come to New South Wales had been dragged out and set up to be used for shelters. He felt thoroughly helpless and prayed fervently for aid and guidance.

The soldiers of the New South Wales Corps under Robert Crandell's command were the first to go ashore, closely followed by the other passengers. The beach was covered with a conglomeration of ragged tents and equally ragged convicts who were scurrying back and forth in their efforts to prepare for the arrival of the sick. Other convicts were dragging the dead bodies that had floated onto the beach and laying them out so that they could be buried.

Eugénie was in her cabin packing the last of her things when Rachel, Nan and the baby came to get her. "It's time to go ashore, Eugénie. Are you ready?" asked Rachel.

Eugénie hesitated. "Well, actually, I was thinking

that I should stay on board. I'm sure there is much that needs to be done."

Rachel shook her head and spoke firmly. "No, Eugénie. Paul said we must go. They're going to bring the sick ashore in the next few hours and besides, Dr. White from Sydney is here now to help. I understand he's a good man and a fine doctor. Come, we must go. Robert has already gone ashore with the Corps and their families. We stayed behind to wait for you."

They left the cabin and young Peter escorted them to the longboat which was to take them to shore. He had managed to avoid falling ill, thanks to the efforts of Rachel and Eugénie who saw to it that he ate well and had his share of fruit. That was something that puzzled even Paul Gordon—why had scurvy broken out when there had been plenty of fruit brought on board at Cape Town? Certainly the passengers didn't lack for any, but there was none to be found for the sick. Captain Dudly insisted that most of it had been rotten and he had managed to salvage some for himself and the passenger's use. At any rate, young Peter had survived and he was extremely grateful. Eugénie touched his face gently. "What will you do now, Peter?"

"Why, Oi'll 'ead back to London, Miss, as soon as this ship sails. Oi love the sea and Oi'm goin' to stick with it. Oi got a lot to learn yet. Someday Oi'll captain me own ship."

"I hope you will, Peter. You'll make a wonderful captain. If ever you come back this way again, please come and see us. You took good care of us—like another young boy I once knew back in France." Eugénie kissed him on the cheek, making him blush. "Take care of yourself, Peter, and thank you for being so good to us," she said.

"'Tis Oi should thank *you*, Miss. Oi wish all of you

257

luck, too, and young Master Andrew there. Goodbye, now."

They were rowed to shore, and what a sight awaited them! Though Paul had attempted to prepare them somewhat for Sydney and the hardships they might find there, it was still a shock to see the miserable rows of mud-plastered huts and the crowds of emaciated men and women with their starving children. Robert was watching for their party and he made haste in escorting them to one of the huts that served as a pub. Matthew Skinner, the owner, came forward to meet them. He was a tall, skinny, middle-aged man with one leg and close-set eyes. His skin was like leather and his face more than half hidden by his whiskers and mustache which gave him a certain daredevil appearance. Robert's blue eyes looked grave and his curly hair was rumpled from the habit he had of running his fingers through it when exasperated or worried. He was worried sick about his wife and child. He strongly regretted permitting Rachel to come out with him, especially since she was about to have the baby. But it was too late now for fruitless regrets. "Ladies, I am afraid I must leave you here. Mr. Skinner will take good care of you," he told them.

"Aye, laddie, that Oi will. Run along now and don't ye worrit none," said the jovial Skinner.

Robert kissed Rachel and hurried back to the wharf. There was much awaiting his attention.

"Mr. Skinner," Rachel said, "do you have a room where we might be able to lie down for a while?"

"Aye, lass, everything is ready fer ye upstairs. Yer luggage is already there. The captain 'ad it brought 'ere when 'e came ashore this morning." He led the way up a narrow flight of stairs to a little room with two cots, a table and a few chairs. It was clean and neat—and it didn't smell. Rachel and Eugénie looked at one another, and it seemed that they could read each other's thoughts, for they were both wondering if they would ever get the stench of the ship out of their nostrils.

"Are ye 'ungry, then?" Mr. Skinner asked.

They realized that they were. Perhaps it was the relief of being finally on solid land that made their appetites return. They nodded.

"Well, Oi'll see if Oi can get ye summat."

"Thank you, Mr. Skinner, that would be marvellous," sighed Rachel.

They took off their cloaks and bonnets and Nan sank gratefully into a chair while Rachel changed the baby. Matthew Skinner was back in a few minutes with some salt pork, biscuits and goat's milk. "Oi'm afraid there isn't much, but it's the best Oi could muster up," he said by way of apology.

"Thank you, Mr. Skinner. We appreciate it."

"Well, ladies if there is anythin' else Oi can do fer ye, just yell." Mr. Skinner departed, closing the door behind him.

They ate their salt pork and drank the goat's milk with relish and then Rachel fed little Andrew. She was thankful that she had plenty of milk of her own; otherwise the baby would never have survived. While Rachel tenderly fed her son, Nan took up some mending, but before long she was snoring loudly. Rachel and Eugénie looked at one another and burst out laughing.

"Poor dear, she must be exhausted," said Rachel.

"Yes," said Eugénie. "How I wish I had her aptitude for falling asleep at the drop of a hat! Even in Newgate, Nan was never so troubled that she couldn't sleep."

Eugénie couldn't sit still. She paced up and down, her thoughts constantly on the plight of the sick convicts. Finally she could bear the inactivity no longer. "Rachel,

I'm going to talk to Mr. Skinner. Try and get some sleep.''

Matthew Skinner was dusting the tables in the tap-room for want of anything better to do, though the place was already spotless. He looked up when he heard Eugénie coming down the stairs.

"Oi 'ear tis a fearful sight on yon ships, Miss," he said.

"Mr. Skinner, I shall never forget the horror of that voyage. It was like a nightmare. But from what I saw down at the wharf, the people here don't seem to be too well off, either."

"Aye, lass, we were left without supplies for a long time. The *Justinian* took eleven months to get here, and 'er supply ship 'it an iceberg, they say. We were counting on supplies coming out with this second fleet, not more sick folk. 'Tis a terrible state of affairs. Wot 'appened to the supplies ye were supposed to be bringin' 'ere?"

"I don't know," said Eugénie. "All I know is that the ships were provisioned at Cape Town."

"The captain tells me that ye are all goin' out to Paramatta to stay with Miss Gordon. If ye don't mind me sayin' so, the sooner yet get out to Miss Gordon's the better off ye'll be," Mr. Skinner advised.

"Mr. Skinner, I'm not going. I want to stay in Sydney and I'd like to rent that room of yours upstairs. I came out here determined to make my own way, and I'm not going to start out by being dependent on my friends. Perhaps when things improve, you'll need help here. I have worked in taverns in France as well as in England," she told him.

Skinner looked at her in horror. "Oi don't believe it, Miss! Not you! This 'ere place is not fer the likes of ye.

Ye don't look like any bar wench Oi've ever seen."

"Please, Mr. Skinner. My mind is made up. Will you rent me that room or not? I'll pay you a year's rent in advance."

"Wot will the captain say—or more to the point, Dr. Gordon?"

Eugénie's eyes flashed. "What Dr. Gordon thinks is no concern of mine! He has no authority to tell me what I can or can not do!"

"Very well, Miss, if yer mind is made up—but wot d'ye think yer friends will say? They aren't goin' to be too 'appy about it," Skinner conjectured.

"I'm sure you're right, but let me worry about that. Now I'm going to see if there's anything I can do for those poor convicts."

Skinner watched her leave and shook his head. "Yon is one stubborn lass, but Oi think she'll do," he muttered to himself.

It was bitterly cold, and since the settlement hospital was already crowded, the sick convicts from the ships were put in the threadbare tents that had been erected earlier. The settlement convicts were rallying around, helping where they could and sharing their meagre belongings. They did their best to feed and clothe the poor miserable creatures. The tents were crowded and in some cases, one worn blanket had to cover four people. Many were unable to move. They lay shivering and filthy from their own excrement. Their bodies crawled with lice. Groans and cries of pain filled the air. Everyone who was able among the settlement convicts worked like beings possessed in spite of their own weakened condition. They had but one thought and one purpose among them—to help the poor souls who were so much worse off than they. Some saw to it that fires were kept lit between the tents, but on this bitterly cold winter's night the fires' warmth barely penetrated those shivering, sick bodies. Other convicts spent the night digging graves and burying the many who had died.

Eugénie worked alongside them, bathing dirty bodies, changing the grass that had been placed under the sick for want of mattresses. She had been working without ceasing since she had left the pub that afternoon, and it was far into the night when Paul spotted her in one of the tents, bathing a poor woman's head. He had been so busy himself that he hadn't been aware that Eugénie wasn't safely resting with Rachel, Nan and little Andrew at the tavern. He watched her for a minute, his eyes filled with a glow of tenderness and longing. Then he chided himself and, pushing his loving thoughts aside, he shouted, "Mademoiselle, are you insane? Get back up to the tavern at once!"

"Sir, are you presuming to give me orders? I must remind you I am a free woman," Eugénie said coldly.

Paul could see that she was bone weary. From the stiff way she moved, her back seemed to be hurting. He longed to soothe her and ease her burden rather than upset her as he always managed to do. But Eugénie was so furious that she stood up quickly, ready to give him a piece of her mind. A wave of dizziness washed over her and Eugénie swayed, then fell in a heap at his feet. He lifted her into his strong arms and carried her back to "The Pig & Goat," as the tavern was called. Her eyes were circled by dark shadows, a result of long nights without sleep, and her hair hung damp and matted about her pale face.

Matthew Skinner bounded awkwardly from behind the counter when Paul walked in with his precious burden.

"Don't worry, Matthew. She's just fainted. The girl is exhausted and is too damn stubborn to admit it," Paul told him. He carried Eugénie up the rickety stairs to the room were Nan and Rachel flew into a panic.

"My God! Wot's wrong with 'er? Is she 'urt? Aow, me poor little dear!" wailed Nan.

"She'll be quite all right after a good night's rest. Why in the name of heaven did you allow her to go down to those tents, Rachel?" Paul snapped.

"Just how do you think we could have stopped her? Besides we didn't know she was going to do anything of the kind. We thought she was downstairs with Mr. Skinner."

Rachel and Nan were sitting by the bed watching her anxiously when consciousness returned to Eugénie. She looked pale and wan. "What happened? How did I get here?" she asked weakly.

"Paul found you in one of the tents. Apparently you fainted from sheer exhaustion. Are you feeling better, dear?" asked Rachel.

She nodded. "Where is Paul? I remember that he was furious with me and I'm afraid I wasn't very polite to him."

"He was worried sick about you," said Rachel. "Do you know something? I have a feeling he cares a great deal about you. Anyway, he went back to the tents."

Eugénie closed her eyes and her mind wandered back over the horrors of the past months. After a while she drifted into a restless, nightmare-filled sleep.

Meanwhile, Paul had gone back to his patients. There wasn't much that could be done, but his presence seemed to raise the convicts' morale. His rounds were interrupted by a Marine bringing a message from Governor Phillip. "Sir, Governor Phillip would like to speak to you as soon as possible, at his house."

Paul nodded and walked back with the Marine towards the Governor's house. Arthur Phillip was the very epitome of dejection and paced up and down until he saw Paul approach. His face was drawn from strain.

"Paul, in the name of God, tell me I am dreaming! Tell me all that I've seen these past twenty-four hours hasn't happened. Tell me I have just had a dreadful nightmare," he pleaded. Paul could see his friend was heartsick and furious. He wouldn't have thought it possible for Arthur Phillip to get quite that angry.

"I wish to heaven I could, Arthur," he said sadly.

"Wasn't there anything you could do? Surely you had some influence."

"I tried, Arthur. I really tried, but it was useless. It was already too late for the poor devils when I realized something was terribly wrong. I shan't forget what that bastard Dudly has done. Someday I swear he will pay for it!"

"The *Neptune* was worse. Nothing had been done for those poor wretches. One in three of the prisoners died. As long as I live, I shan't forget the horror of that ship. If I were not the Governor, I would have killed Traill with my bare hands. God willing, I shall see to it that he never gets another position as master of a ship."

"I know how you feel," Paul agreed, "but I blame those devils in Whitehall. If they would take the responsibility of seeing that the convicts are treated humanely, none of this would have happened. But what could one expect? Our prisons are in terrible condition, too. Doesn't anyone in authority care? I certainly hope we can make this new country of ours an improvement over the old, a country where all will be treated fairly and where consideration for human life and dignity is a way of life."

"I see we share a dream," said the governor. "Will you do me the honor of dining with me tomorrow night? I am forced by protocol to give a dinner for those scoundrels. Damn protocol! As Governor, I must comply, regardless of my personal feelings. If you are there, I might just be able to get through the evening."

"Sorry my friend, but that would be too much to endure. I would do a great deal for you, but I'm afraid that I shall be in Parramatta tomorrow night. I am taking the Crandells and Mademoiselle Fabré out to my place. But I certainly wish you luck."

Just then Dr. White came hurrying over to them, bloody and dishevelled. "Paul I need your help. It seems to be reaching a crisis point." He sank down on the steps and buried his head in his hands. The good doctor was worn out.

"Farewell, Arthur," said Paul, shaking his friend's hand. "I expect I shan't see you until I get back from Parramatta. Keep your temper—you have too much to lose."

"I'll try very hard, Paul," the governor replied.

Paul grinned at him then turned to the exhausted Dr. White. "Come on, old boy, let's go back to our patients."

As they walked back to the tents, Dr. White shook his head sadly. "Paul, in all my days as a physician I have never been through anything quite like th is. There was no need for this to happen. The captains had sufficient funds to replenish their supplies at Cape Town. There couldn't have been a shortage of fresh fruit, so what in God's name went wrong?"

"That's a major mystery. I know those supplies were put on board. We passengers had our fill of fruit and when the scurvy broke out, I questioned Captain Dudly and was told that the fruit spoiled and had to be thrown overboard. He had only been able to salvage enough for his passengers and certain of his crew, or so he said.''

Then their conversation was terminated as both dedicated men involved themselves in the task of keeping people alive and easing the pain of those they couldn't save.

Chapter 21

It had been a long, busy night for both Rachel and Nan. Eugénie had a fever and they took turns putting cold cloths on her head, trying to make her comfortable and soothing her as she tossed fretfully and cried out in panic. Their efforts were rewarded, however. By morning the fever had broken, but all three were exhausted. Skinner brought them more goat's milk and cheese for breakfast, which renewed their strength somewhat. When they had eaten, Nan took the dishes downstairs and was just going back up when Paul arrived with Bill Larsen, his Aunt Aggie's overseer.

"Nan, are you about ready to leave?" he asked. Then anxiously, "Is Eugénie feeling better, do you think?"

"Aye, sir, she had a little fever but she's feelin' better now. But Oi don't think she'll want to go with us to yer aunt's."

"Well, Nan, we shall just see about that!" said Paul, frowning.

"Sir, let me run up and see if they're dressed. Oi'll come down and let ye know when 'tis safe to come up." About ten minutes later she yelled down at them to come upstairs.

Paul immediately went over to little Andrew and picked him up. "How is my godson this fine morning?"

he asked, smiling. Suddenly he remembered Larsen.
"Ladies, this is Bill Larsen, our very capable overseer.
Bill, may I present Mrs. Rachel Crandell and Mademoiselle Eugénie Fabré. Nan Coward you met downstairs."

Rachel smiled. "I can see why you weren't worried
about your aunt, Paul. Mr. Larsen looks extremely
capable." Her little hand was completely lost in
Larsen's big one as they shook hands. He was just about
the biggest man they had ever seen. He was like a tall
oak tree, and looked as though he could crush a man
with his bare hands—as indeed he had done on more
than one occasion, though only in self-defense.

"Are you ready to go to Paramatta?" Paul asked.

Rachel and Nan exclaimed at the same time, "Oh,
yes! We can't wait to leave here."

Paul looked at Eugénie. His yellow eyes bored right
through her but she met his gaze with a stern one of her
own. "Paul, I really don't want to go. If I'm going to
make my home here in Sydney, I might as well stay on
and get settled.

Paul's eyes flashed with annoyance. "What
nonsense! You aren't well. I insist you come with us if
only for a week. By then you will at least have regained
your strength."

Eugénie was too weary to argue with him. With a
defeated sigh, she said, "I suppose you're right. I *do*
feel rather weak and it would be so very nice just to
relax and not worry about sick people for a while."

"Then it's settled. You will come with us?"

"I'll come—but mind you, only for one week,"
Eugénie reminded him.

They gathered up their belongings and Bill Larsen
lifted four of their bags as though they were filled with
feathers, carrying them downstairs to the waiting cart.

Rachel carried little Andrew and Nan followed with the rest of the bags. Paul picked Eugénie up in his arms despite her protests.

"Put me down! I can walk—I'm not an invalid. *Put me down,* I say," she cried.

He laughed. "I'll put you down, you little wretch!"

And indeed he did. He put her down when he placed her in the cart.

Robert rode up, leading Paul's horse, and the two men rode behind the cart while Bill Larsen expertly guided the old mare over the rough trail.

The road to Paramatta had not been travelled much and so the journey was quite uncomfortable. Their bodies were jarred by every bump and rut in the road. But they soon forgot their aches and pains, so entranced were they by the many signs of wildlife and the exotic birds that flew overhead and hopped from branch to branch. It was a land unlike any they had ever seen before. When Eugénie spied a kangaroo with a baby in its pouch, she knew without a doubt that this was the land to which she truly belonged. She felt a wonderful feeling of oneness with the life around her, and her heart gave a great surge of pride and love. Rachel and Nan, though they were also entranced, were still a little apprehensive and jumped every time a strange sound emanated from the bush. Rachel didn't like the dusty roads and began to wonder why she had ever left England. But she knew she would keep up a brave front for Robert's sake.

At last Aggie Gordon's house came into view. It was made of wood and a veranda encircled it. There were a few outbuildings scattered around, including the overseer's house and a bunkhouse where the other men would stay. There were pens for the animals and a big barn, though Aunt Aggie didn't have much livestock as yet. Paul had bought animals in Cape Town but had decided to leave them in Sydney for a few days. To the eyes of the weary women, the house and its barren surroundings seemed depressing after the beauty of England, but to Paul it was home. He was pleased to see how much land had been cleared in his absence.

"Larsen, you have done a good job. I appreciate it," he told the overseer.

"T'weren't nothin', Guv. That Miss Aggie drove us every bit of the way. Yon is one tough-minded lady."

Paul laughed. "You're right, Larsen, but you deserve my thanks just the same."

The cart pulled up in front of the house and an elderly woman came striding out to meet them. The first thing they noticed was that she was tiny and looked quite fragile. Her stride certainly didn't match her figure. Her skirt was hoisted up and beneath it they saw well-worn, scuffed leather boots. It amazed Rachel and Nan to see her attire, for they had heard that Aggie Gordon had been used to every luxury. But she was indeed tough-minded as Bill Larsen had said, and she had adapted quickly to her new environment. New South Wales was no place for silks, laces and bows. She had brought good, serviceable clothes and several pairs of riding boots with her. Her once beautiful hands were now coarsened by hard work. Unlike many people who are content to leave the work to others, Aggie Gordon pitched right in with her convicts and did her part in clearing the wilderness that she and Paul had chosen for their land. She carried herself with dignity and her snow-white hair was piled high. Her face glowed with good humor. Little wrinkles fanned around her eyes, which led her visitors to believe that laughter was no stranger to her.

Paul jumped down off his horse, picked her up, and

kissed her warmly. She had tears of joy in her eyes, but she protested laughingly, "Paul, you scamp, put your old aunt down at once! I'm too old for that sort of nonsense. Now let me look at you!"

She had such a look of loving pride on her face that it was clear to Rachel and Nan that Aunt Aggie Gordon thought that the sun, moon and stars rose and set on Paul.

"Aunt Aggie, allow me to introduce Captain Robert Crandell and his lovely wife, Rachel. This little imp is Andrew Gordon Crandell, my godson, and this good lady is Nan Coward."

Aunt Aggie looked at Nan Coward with some surprise. She had never seen such a woman before, such hair—but the woman apparently had strength and that was what was needed out here. She welcomed them warmly and then spotted Eugénie asleep in the cart. "And who have we here, pray?" she asked.

"That is Eugénie Fabré, and the poor girl is exhausted. She has been working tirelessly, helping those unfortunate convicts ever since the scurvy broke out. She worked most of last night, and finally collapsed," Paul told her.

"I am sure you are all tired. We must get that poor child to bed at once."

She ushered Rachel and Robert into the house and Nan followed with the baby. Paul once again picked Eugénie up and this time she didn't resist. He carried her into the house and Aunt Aggie led the way to a small bedroom. As he laid her on the bed, that shrewd old lady saw something in his face as he looked at Eugénie that she had never seen there before, a tenderness that softened his craggy features. She returned to the others and was most gracious.

"Mrs. Crandell, I think you had better share the

room with Mademoiselle Fabré and the baby if you don't mind. I'm afraid we are rather lacking in bedrooms at the moment. Captain Crandell, perhaps you wouldn't mind sharing Paul's room; and Mrs. Coward, if you don't mind, I'll put up a cot for you in my good Bella's room. Bella had been with me for years. In England she was my housekeeper but I'm afraid since coming out here she has had to turn her head to cooking and cleaning and other uncongenial chores. I must say, I couldn't have got over the rough spots without her. Now do make yourselves at home.''

Nan went in to attend to Eugénie, undressing her and tucking her into bed, while Rachel bathed little Andrew and freshened up. They were all dusty and tired from the journey. Robert went out to help Bill Larsen with the bags and Aunt Aggie went into the kitchen where Bella was fixing something to eat. They still had a few chickens left and for this special occasion Bella had killed one, which was roasting on a spit over the fire when Paul walked in.

"Bella, my love, you are as pretty as ever," he teased affectionately.

"Now, Master Paul, I'll have none of yer drivel— but I must say ye are a sight for my poor sore eyes!'' Those grey eyes twinkled up at him with pride. Ever since Paul's mother and father had been killed, Bella had taken the two orphans under her wing. It was she who had nursed them when they were ill and comforted them when they had come under Aunt Aggie's stern admonishments. Paul had been a sturdy lad of ten and young Anne just a wee bit of a babe.

Bella and Aunt Aggie went on with their work and Paul sat down at the kitchen table. "Aunt Aggie, I do hope you don't mind me bringing all these people out here. It was impossible to leave them in Sydney under the circumstances. The Crandells are looking for land and a place to build a home. They've decided to stay out here. Rob intends to resign his commission when his tour of duty is finished," he explained.

"They seem like fine young people and the little one is precious. What about Mademoiselle Fabré?" she said, with a sharp look at her nephew.

"She has had a very difficult time these past two years. She fled from France with her sister Marie and then was unlawfully imprisoned for theft. Uncle Charles happened to see the incident and tried to find her, but I'm afraid it was quite some time before we finally located her in Newgate. She endured the horrors of that place and came out as sweet and loving as she went in. I only know this because of what Nan Coward told me, who, incidentally, is a convict. She's a good soul, though. Eugénie has never spoken of her ordeal to me. Both her parents were murdered by the very people they had helped so much. Eugénie saw their mutilated bodies. Can you imagine how much that child has had to bear?"

"Heavens, how much tragedy can one person withstand! But why did she come out here to this desolate land?" his aunt asked.

"Nan had told her something about New South Wales, and I suppose it intrigued her. She got the notion that here she could make the kind of life she wanted for herself."

"But what on earth will she do? Has she any money?"

"I don't really know what she has in mind, and I am the last person she would take into her confidence. The girl has spunk. In fact, my dear, she reminds me of you in many ways—the same stubborn streak."

"Well now, Paul Gordon, when it comes to stubborness, look to yourself for first place!'' said Aunt Aggie fondly.

''Why don't you let Bella take care of dinner and come and sit down with me on the verandah so we can talk?'' Paul suggested.

When they were seated outside on the verandah, Paul gave his Aunt Aggie a searching look. ''I must say you don't look much the worse for wear. Bill Larsen tells me you pitched right in with the laborers and gave them hell when they slacked off. But then, you always were a trooper.''

''Bill Larsen talks too much for his own good! Now tell me about Anne. Did you see her before you left England? I miss that girl so much, but I know she must finish her education before she can even think of coming out here. Does she look well? Has she grown?''

''Aunt Aggie, please! One question at a time. My sister has grown into a very beautiful young lady. She's quite tall, you know, and she looks very much like Mother, dark as night and those big, brown eyes of hers, like a gentle doe. She sends you her love and I must say I shall be happy when she leaves school and can join us here,'' said Paul.

''Oh, my dear, so shall I! I missed you too, you rascal. Most of the time, thank God, we were so busy I scarcely had time to be lonely, but there were moments when the loneliness was overwhelming. I'm really pleased that such a fine young couple as the Crandells have decided to make their home out here.''

They were just about to leave the verandah when Nan walked out. ''Miss Eugénie is sleepin' peacefully now. Is there anythin' Oi can do to 'elp?''

''Thank you, no, Mrs. Coward. Why don't you lie down for a while? I'm sure you must be quite tired yourself. I shall call you when it is time for supper.''

"Yer very kind, Ma'am, but Oi'd just like to sit out 'ere, if it's all the same to you," said Nan. "Oi'd like to feast me eyes on all that nice dry land!"

"Of course, Nan, do as you like. Aunt Aggie, I'm going to look for Robert and show him around," said Paul, kissing his aunt on the cheek.

Aunt Aggie returned to the kitchen to help Bella, and Paul went in search of Robert. He found him chatting to Bill Larsen in the barn.

"Would you like to look around a bit?" he suggested. "Dinner will be ready in about an hour. Bill, by the way, I'm afraid I'm going to have to depend on you again for a while. I'm going to have to return to Sydney and give Dr. White a hand. I shouldn't have left him and I'm anxious to get back."

"Ye can depend on me, Guv," Larsen said, touching his cap.

Paul showed Robert around and explained the laborious problems of farming this uncultivated land. They returned to the house in time for dinner, hungry as bears. Aunt Aggie was delighted to have such a gathering at her table. It had been so long since she had seen Paul that she felt in quite a festive mood. Eugénie slept on and it was decided to leave her alone. They had just finished eating when there was a knock on the door, and a pleasant voice bellowed, "Aggie Gordon, are you going to let me in?"

"Well, John McCallum, how marvellous of you to pay us a visit! Allow me to introduce Captain and Mrs. Crandell."

John McCallum extended a massive hand in greeting. "Welcome to New South Wales—and you Paul, it's good to see you again!"

"It's good to see you, John. Things have been pretty bad out here, I understand. I must say I feel sorry for

275

Arthur, with such a burden on his shoulders."

"Arthur Phillip has been like a rock. He lives as most of the people out here have to live—meagerly. God help him! If those fools in London would get off their duffs we wouldn't be in such a plight. We are in a sorry state right now but I'm quite sure that someday this country of ours will be glorious, one that we can all be proud of," said McCallum.

"Speaking of land, Mr. McCallum, I wonder—could you advise me about claiming some? We plan to make our home out here and I'm really anxious to get started," Robert said.

"Well, as a matter of fact, Tom Campbell is giving up his place and returning to Scotland. His health is failing and I'm afraid the struggle out here is just too much for him. His house isn't much, but I'm sure you could fix it up."

"Robert, Rachel and the baby are welcome to stay here as long as they want," put in Aunt Aggie. "So don't rush into anything."

"Thank you, ma'am, but Campbell's place sounds just right. I'd as soon pay for what he has since I won't have too much time for the next few years to do a lot of work. Since his land is already cleared, I should think it will be a good start for us."

"Would you like to ride over and see him tomorrow? I could arrange to be there," said McCallum.

"Thank you, Mr. McCallum, but Paul and I are going back to Sydney. Perhaps we could stop off there on our way there. Where is the Campbell place?"

"It's the closest property to Sydney. Campbell was one of the first to lay a claim. He's a good man, but he wasn't strong when he arrived and he's much worse now."

"I'm sorry to hear that, but it's certainly a windfall for me," Robert said.

Bella wheeled in the tea cart laden with fine china cups and saucers, a silver cream jug and silver teapot and sugar bowl. Aunt Aggie insisted on observing the niceties even in this wild country.

Rachel sighed at the sight, all at once very homesick. The conversation turned to England. John McCallum asked a thousand questions. Though as he had said, he belonged body and soul to this new land, there was a piece of his heart that would always belong to the mother country. It was late when he finally took his leave of them.

"That's a very nice gentleman," said Rachel after he had gone.

"Yes, Rachel, a gentleman he is in the best sense of the word, and a good friend and neighbor."

"Doesn't he have a family? I didn't hear him mention a wife."

"His wife died before he left England. He has a daughter, Kathleen, and I must say old John is a loving father. Poor Kathleen is very delicate and I know she misses a mother's touch," Aunt Aggie said, shaking her head sadly.

"He's not a young man. Just how old is Kathleen?" asked Rachel.

"She must be about twenty now. John and his wife had just about given up hope of having any children when along came Kathleen. His wife's health began to deteriorate after that. John, I'm happy to say, is a strong man for his age, or indeed any age."

They sat in silence after that, each one absorbed in his own thoughts and enjoying the warmth of the fire. Paul was the first to break the silence. "I hate to end this happy evening, but I do think we'd better say goodnight. I'll take a look at Eugénie first, though I don't think there's anything wrong with her that rest won't cure. Goodnight, Aunt Aggie. Goodnight, you two. Sleep well."

Eugénie awoke early. The house was very quiet. She lay back contentedly, enjoying the stillness of the morning and thrilling to the occasional call of a bird. She felt wonderfully rested and ready for anything. As she lay there she made up her mind to go back to Sydney as soon as possible. She had to get on with her life and stand on her own two feet. Then her thoughts turned toward England and Marie, Mag, Moll and Harry and she felt a great longing to be with them. She thought about her little sister, Joséphine, so far away in revolution-torn France and prayed that she was well. She prayed that Matthew would need her help, as at this point in time she desperately needed to be useful to someone. She finally decided to get up and, dressing quietly so as not to disturb Rachel and little Andrew who were peacefully sleeping, she went outside and sat on the verandah.

Aunt Aggie found her there an hour or so later and was quite surprised to see the young girl looking so well.

"My, I didn't expect to find you up and about, Mademoiselle. How are you feeling?"

"Oh, you must be Paul's Aunt Aggie Gordon. It was really kind of you to take us in like this. You are exactly as he described you."

"Well, I'm not sure if that's a compliment or not, young lady." She smiled at Eugénie. "I do think you shouldn't overdo things too much today. Take it easy and I am sure you will be back to full strength in a week or so. I am delighted to have all of you here."

"Madame, you are too kind, but I don't intend to stay quite that long. In fact, I intend returning to Sydney as soon as possible."

"Goodness gracious, child! Where will you live? What on earth will you do? Sydney is no fit place for a young girl like you, especially at the present time."

"Please don't worry. I have everything arranged. I persuaded Mr. Skinner to rent me a room at 'The Pig & Goat,' " Eugénie said briskly.

Aunt Aggie's eyes blazed. "My dear young lady, that is the most outrageous suggestion I have ever heard! You cannot possibly do that. Live in a tavern? What utter nonsense. I cannot allow it!"

Eugénie began to feel irritated. She realized that Miss Gordon had her best interests at heart but she was tired of being told what to do.

"I am sorry if it offends your sense of propriety, Madame, and I mean no offense but that is what I shall do. I know you mean well and I am grateful for your concern, but there is nothing more to say."

"Very well, I shan't say another word. But young lady, you will regret it, mark my words!"

Aunt Aggie turned on her heel and went storming into the house. She glared at Paul as he came into the living room. "See if you can talk some sense into that stubborn young woman's head," she snapped, then stormed off, leaving him staring after her in bewilderment.

"What in the world was that all about?" he muttered to himself.

Just then Eugénie walked in and Paul put two and two together. "What did you say to Aunt Aggie to put her in such a tizzy? I haven't seen her this put out for an age."

"I'm truly sorry, Paul, but I'm afraid I shocked her terribly. I told her I was going back to Sydney as soon as it can be arranged and that I had rented Matthew Skinner's room upstairs at 'The Pig & Goat'.''

It was his turn to be aghast. "Eugénie!''

"Don't, Paul. Please don't say *one word*. My mind is made up and I'm just not feeling up to a lot of arguments.''

He saw that familiar spark of anger in her eyes and knew it would be useless to protest.

"Very well,'' he sighed. "You may ride back with Robert and me this morning. But I insist that you eat a good breakfast before we set out. Will you do that, at least?''

Two hours later they were on their way. Robert rode alongside and Paul drove the wagon since he was going to bring back supplies and didn't feel that Eugénie was up to riding that far. They made a stop at the Campbell farm and Robert successfully clinched the deal, to his satisfaction and that of Tom Campbell. It was close to evening by the time they reached Sydney. Robert joined his men immediately and Paul dropped Eugénie off at "The Pig & Goat.''

"Well, Lor' bless me! Oi didn't expect to see ye back 'ere, Miss, so soon,'' said Matthew Skinner.

"Mr. Skinner, we had an agreement,'' Eugénie reminded him.

"Aye, and so we did lass. The room is ready for ye and welcome.''

"Skinner, take care of her,'' Paul ordered.

"Don't ye worry none, Sir. Oi'll take care of 'er like she wuz me own.'' Paul turned his steady gaze on Eugénie and it was full of concern.

"Eugénie, I'll try and come back later tonight. I have something for you from Uncle Charles. If by chance I can't get back tonight, may I call on you tomorrow?''

"Of course, but I shall probably be down at the tents tomorrow," she replied. Paul exploded—his yellow eyes flashed fire. Eugénie found herself shrinking from him.

"For God's sake, girl, promise me you will rest for at least two more days. You won't be any good to anyone if you don't get back your strength. The sick will still be there two days from now, unfortunately." He grabbed her by the shoulders. "Promise me, Eugénie."

She saw the look of anger give way to concern and his eyes seemed even more yellow and intense. At last she said reluctantly, "I promise. I'll rest for two whole days. Now goodnight, and thank you." Overcome by a sudden impulse, she stood on tiptoe and shyly kissed his cheek.

Paul lovingly watched her as she climbed the rickety stairs to the room above. He sighed, then went directly to the Governor's house.

"Paul I'm so glad you are back," the Governor said, clasping Paul's hand.

"Arthur, how has it been going here? Is Dr. White worn out?"

"Yes, poor man, he hasn't spared himself. By the way, the mystery has been cleared up about the food supplies."

"Well, Arthur, go on."

"Those damned thieves had the effrontery to hoard it all, and this morning they set up their stalls, selling everything at high prices. I'm afraid they had us right where they wanted us."

Paul stayed with Arthur Phillip for several hours helping him draft a report to London. Then he went in search of Dr. White and checked on the condition of the convicts. Dr. White was delighted to see him. "Paul, I'm glad you're back. I'm exhausted, but I'm happy to say we have no fresh cases."

"Sorry old boy—I got back as soon as I could. I'll be on call now, so go get some rest. You've certainly earned it."

"I have a few things to see to first, so why don't you go get a drink and a bite to eat?"

"Perhaps I'll just go up to 'The Pig & Goat.' I have something to give to Mademoiselle Fabré. I won't be long," said Paul.

It was quite late when he returned to the tavern, but there were still a few people swilling rum, rum which Matthew had had to pay dearly for. The captains had doubled the price.

" 'Ello there, Sir, ye want to see Miss Eugénie? Oi 'eard 'er movin' around a minute ago so Oi think ye might go on up."

"Thanks, Matthew."

Paul climbed the stairs, grinning at the thought of Eugénie's surprise when she saw what he had brought her. He was whistling as he reached the top of the stairs. Eugénie heard him and rushed to the door. "Paul, I didn't think you were coming. How are things progressing?"

"Not too well, though I doubt if too many more will die. It is so tragic that this vast empty land should have so many graves so soon. But enough of this gloom. Uncle Charles gave me a present for you before we left England. His words were, 'Give this to that lovely child whom I respect so very much. Give it to her at an appropriate moment.' I think you have won my esteemed uncle's heart, Mademoiselle."

"Oh Paul, what is it? Give it to me! He is just too

wonderful—he has done so much for me without giving me presents too. I think I shall cry.''

Paul threw up his hands in mock horror. ''Spare me your tears, Eugénie. Here, open this.'' He handed her the parcel and a purse. ''That is the money you gave him for your passage. He felt that you could use it more than he.''

Eugénie turned quite pale. ''Oh that dear, dear man! I really don't deserve this.''

''All right—before you become too maudlin, open the parcel. I believe you will find it to your liking.''

She opened the package with all the excited anticipation of a child. There, wrapped in soft paper, was an exquisite white lace dress with a satin petticoat. The dress was covered with tiny seed pearls. It was even more beautiful than any dress she had imagined so long ago when she lay dreaming by the stream in Poissy. She held it up and her cheeks were flushed with delight.

''I must try it on! Paul, would you mind just going outside for a moment? Don't go away, though.''

''Your wish is my command, Mademoiselle.'' He gave a bow that would have put Beau Brumell to shame. ''I can hardly wait to see it on you.''

He wasn't kept waiting long before he heard her soft voice calling him.

''Paul, come in now but close your eyes. Don't peek. I want to surprise you.''

She guided him through the doorway. ''You may open them now.''

He was stunned. She stood before him like a fairy princess. The dress fit perfectly. She looked proud and breathtakingly radiant.

''Say something, Paul. Please say something,'' she whispered, wondering if perhaps he felt the dress did not suit her.

"Mademoiselle Fabré, your beauty at this moment is beyond words," said Paul. His heart had jumped into his throat. He wanted to take her in his arms and speak to her of his love, but he knew that was impossible. It was just as well that he would be occupied with the sick and after that with his farm at Parramatta because it would be too much for him to endure being so close to her and yet unable to express his feelings. He became aware that Eugénie was speaking.

"Paul, aren't you listening to me?"

"Sorry! My mind wandered. You were saying?"

"I said that it is amazing how your uncle knew my exact size and—oh, Paul, he has such exquisite taste!"

"I grant him the exquisite taste, but I rather suspect it was Giles whose mathematical genius was responsible for the exact fit. Did you know he was once a professor at Oxford?"

"Oxford? What is this Oxford, Paul?"

"It's a great English university, my dear."

"How did he come to be working for your Uncle if he was a professor?" Eugénie asked.

"Unfortunately, Giles had a passion for gambling, and on a professor's salary and without much luck, it wasn't long before he found himself deep in debt. He and Uncle Charles had attended the university as students together, and so when he found himself in trouble he rather reluctantly turned to Uncle Charles for help. The upshot of the whole thing was that he and Uncle Charles grew quite attached to each other and finally Giles gave up teaching and moved in with the Earl. He is trying to write a book, I believe, in his spare time."

"How very interesting! It seems that both Giles and I have a lot to thank your uncle for," said Eugénie.

"Eugénie, I must leave now. Do remember your promise to rest for a few days. I shall be returning to Parramatta as soon as things settle down here. I don't imagine we shall see too much of each other for a while. Be careful, my dear. I know Matthew will watch over you and Robert will be around from time to time. I shan't presume to tell you what to do with your money —I doubt if you would listen—but if you ever need me, don't hesitate to send word."

"Goodbye, Paul. Thank you for being such a good friend. I know I exasperate you terribly, and yet you still put up with me."

"My dear girl, a friend is one who cares regardless of our faults. Besides, I know I can count on you, too, even though I make you seethe with rage at times."

He held her away from him and looked deep into her eyes; then very gently he kissed her forehead and left.

Chapter 22 ───────────────

The months passed and life had resumed some form of normality for the colony. Eugénie's entries in her diary at this time were full of a mixture of enthusiasm and at that same time tinged with much that was sad and forlorn:

November 2, 1790 (My first entry since arriving at New South Wales)

The terrible scourge of the scurvy has passed and everyone is busy trying to make ends meet. Matthew finally consented to let me help him and now we have become partners. We are planning our new tavern—"The Black Bear" in memory of that other "Black Bear" which meant so very much to me. It will have a house attached where I plan to live, and Matthew is going to make his home here. We are very excited about the whole project and every morning we go down to the site and pester the builders. We must seem a very odd couple to be partners—Matthew with his wooden leg and bewhiskered face and I, a young French girl who barely reaches to his shoulder.

Rachel and Robert have settled down on the Campbell farm and little Andrew is putting on weight. I think Rachel is happy now. Poor Robert has to spend most of his time with the Corps here in Sydney and he stops by to see me at least every other day. He has finally admitted to me what a Godsend Nan has turned out to be.

She still exasperates him but he laughingly told me the other day, and I quote, "That woman rules our house with an iron hand, Eugénie. But though I hate to admit it, we'd be lost without her."

I never thought I'd say this, but I miss Paul Gordon. He left Sydney as soon as the disease was well under control and I haven't seen him since. It's been at least six weeks. Bill Larsen has driven Aunt Aggie in to town several times and stopped by to see how I was getting along. But Miss Gordon, on the few occasions I have bumped into her, shows her disapproval of me—oh, not by what she says (she's too well mannered for that) but she can't conceal the expression on her face. I'd like her to like me for Paul's sake and because I do admire her tremendously. But I cannot change what I am.

"The Pig & Goat" is doing a thriving business, but it is just too small. "The Black Bear" has really become a necessity. We are now able to get supplies directly from Cape Town and I have a notion one day I'd like to own my own ship.

Sydney is growing and I hear that more and more free settlers are planning on coming out here to New South Wales. That is just what this colony needs—people with skills and money.

My days are full and I'm deeply grateful because it means I have fewer hours in which to feel lonely. Oh, how I miss Marie, Mag, Moll and my dear Harry! I have written to them but I doubt very much if they have received my letters yet. I have also written to my little sister Joséphine, but I have very little hope that she will ever read it. Oh, my dear little sister, I hope that someday you will forgive me for leaving you behind, but I thought it was best for you. Someday I shall try and find you. Someday when France has recovered from the madness that has taken possession of it.

What a treasure I have found in Matthew, and how I do enjoy our customers! Aunt Aggie Gordon's friend and neighbor John McCallum comes in at least once a week with his friend John McArthur. Mr. McArthur talks about nothing but sheep. He maintains that New South Wales is ideally suited to the raising of those wooly beasts. I'm inclined to agree with him but Mr.

McCallum disagrees. When they come in I'm afraid I get
very little work done for I am completely enthralled by
their talk about farming and their friendly arguments
about the merits of sheep.

So often I think of the little verse that Paul's Uncle
Charles, the Earl of St. Swithin's, quoted for me (it
seems like a lifetime ago)—

> I hear a voice you cannot hear,
> Which says you must not stay.
> I see a hand you cannot see,
> Which beckons me away.

It seems I was right after all. New South Wales did
beckon me away and I know now I belong here in this
wild land.

Suddenly it dawned on me, with a great jolt of pain,
I'm afraid, that two of my birthdays have passed by un-
noticed by even myself. My sixteenth birthday was over-
shadowed by the horrors of the Bastille, and the dis-
covery of the horrible conditions the convicts were
enduring overshadowed my seventeenth birthday. I
shudder still when I think of what Paul saw in those
dreadful holds that day on board the Scarboro.

November 17, 1790—New South Wales
John McCallum is coming in more and more fre-
quently. I do hope he is not heavily troubled. Drink is
not an answer for anyone. I asked Matthew what he
thought and he gave me a rather peculiar answer.

"Lassie, that man is troubled but it's not wot ye
think. Don't ye ken lass, 'e's taken a fancy to ye."

I laughed and teased him about having an incredible
imagination and he just said very seriously, "Lass, laugh
all ye want. Oi ken 'e's old enough to be yer father, but
mark my words, Eugénie Fabré, 'e's taken with ye."

I think Matthew Skinner needs his head examined!
Perhaps he's had a bit too much sun lately. It's been
very hot here.

But Matthew's words were proven to be all too true.
A few nights later John McCallum came into the "Pig &
Goat" early. He looked a little embarrassed and talked

for a few minutes with Matthew about trivial matters but it was obvious his mind was far from his conversation. When Eugénie came downstairs she greeted him warmly and he, seeming to take his courage in his hands, smiled back.

"Mademoiselle Eugénie, would you do me the honor of taking a walk with me? It's a beautiful evening and you aren't really busy right now."

Eugénie was so taken aback by his request that she agreed before she knew what she had said. They strolled along the waterfront, in silence for the most part, and it wasn't until they came to a stop and were gazing out beyond the horizon that John McCallum finally spoke. "Eugénie, I am an old man, yet I feel that you like me and are not bored by my company. I certainly have the greatest respect and admiration for you. My wife died before we came out here and you have heard that my daughter Kathleen is a very delicate young woman. I worry about her future a great deal. I'm sure you realize that a man of my years has not too much longer to live and I have become more conscious of that fact of late. In truth, I have become consumed with anxiety for Kathleen's future. Mademoiselle Eugénie, after a great deal of thought I am now, with all humility and great admiration for you, begging you to be my wife. Kathleen and I need you."

Eugénie was stunned. She had not expected this and it must have showed on her face, because John continued, "I don't expect an answer right away. I know that you feel no love for me, but I also feel that you are not involved with anyone else. Am I right?"

"Yes, Mr. McCallum you are. There is someone I love, but he's far, far away and nothing can ever come of that love. He belongs to another. But I'm afraid I still love him and always will," Eugénie confessed.

"Eugénie, please be assured that if you consent to our marriage, it will be one in name only. I will take care of you as though you were my second daughter. All I ask is that you prepare yourself to take care of Kathleen for the rest of her life and see to the disposal of my property after I'm gone."

Eugénie looking at the rather portly, moustached gentleman with his gentle grey eyes and knew that he meant every word he said. He was a gentleman in every sense of the word. He looked so vulnerable for such a large man, and she felt her heart overflow with sympathy for him.

"Mr. McCallum, I'm afraid I don't quite know what to say. You honor me, sir. Surely you would not be getting much of a bargain! I shall never love you the way a wife should love a husband, but I too have the utmost admiration and respect for you and you are certainly *not* boring. But please, I must think more about this before giving you my answer."

"My dear girl, do you really mean that you will consider my offer? Oh, Eugénie, I promise you, you won't have a worry in the world," he said eagerly.

He walked back with her to the tavern and left. Eugénie became so busy then that she didn't have much time to think about John's proposal. But when at last they closed the door for the night, she took Matthew's hand.

"Matthew, I need to talk to you."

"Of course, lass. Can it wait until we clean up? Ye know Oi'm always glad to lend an ear."

They worked quickly and in silence and when at last the place looked spic and span, Matthew poured Eugénie a glass of wine and a generous mug of rum for himself.

"All right, Eugénie, let's 'ave it," he said.

"You were right, Matthew," Eugénie told him. "John McCallum has just asked me to be his wife. He knows I don't love him but that doesn't seem to matter to him. He said that I would be like a daughter to him. Matthew, he says he needs me and I really believe him. I believe that with all my heart."

"Well, lass, Oi can't tell ye wot to do, but Oi think ye could do much worse. If ye marry 'im, ye'll 'ave a position in this community and ye'll never 'ave to worrit again. Besides, Oi think yer right. They *do* need ye. A man like Mr. McCallum must 'ave thought this over for quite a long time. Oi don't think 'e's one to rush into things—and marriage is certainly something that should never be rushed into at the best of times."

"He's a good man, and I'm not in love with anyone— at least . . ." Eugénie paused thinking of André. "I could make him a good wife and I'm sure I'd enjoy Kathleen's company. We wouldn't be living that far from Sydney, so I can come in on weekends. You know that's your busy time of the week and you'll still need my help. So, Matthew Skinner, don't you dare rent my room to anyone!"

"Oi wouldn't dream of it. And since Oi see ye 'ave made up yer mind, me 'eartiest congratulations. Oi don't think ye'll regret it, lass," said Matthew with a smile.

The following evening, John McCallum came back to see Eugénie, eager for an answer but not daring to hope that she would say yes.

"Mr. McCallum, I didn't expect to see you so soon."

"I know, but I couldn't help hoping you'd have an answer for me one way or the other. I couldn't bear to wait," he admitted.

He looked so anxious that Eugénie spoke quickly. "I humbly accept your offer and I only hope that I shall prove worthy of your trust."

"I understand, but I hope that this will not prevent us from being friends," said John with a sigh. He looked so crestfallen that Eugénie laughed.

"Didn't you hear me? I said I will be your wife."

His face broke into a wide, wonderful smile and he clasped her hand in his. "My dear, how can I ever thank you? Can we be married soon?"

"I'd rather like to meet Kathleen first. If she likes me and approves of our marriage, then we can decide."

"Bless you for your thoughtfulness! I completely forgot that my daughter has never met you. When could you come out to the farm?" he asked.

"Perhaps Matthew could ride out with me on Monday. By then Kathleen will have had time to adjust to the idea of meeting me and the possibility of our marriage. If she approves, perhaps we could arrange to be married a week from then. Matthew can be one witness and if you like, I suppose your friend Mr. McArthur could be the other. What do you think?"

John grinned like a schoolboy. "My dear, it's the best news I've had in years! But you are so young—wouldn't you like to have a big, exciting wedding?"

"No, John," Eugénie said firmly. "I'd just like it to be as quiet as possible. Will you please make the arrangements if Kathleen gives us her blessing? And I'll see you on Monday then."

"Don't look so worried, Eugénie. I'm quite sure Kathleen will love you and accept you. How could she help herself?"

Eugénie stood looking after him until he was out of sight, thinking to herself how strange life was—rather like a card game, in fact. Some hands were fantastic, some terrible, and some very, very strange and confusing. Eugénie had her share of the fantastic and the terrible. Perhaps this was the strange and confusing one. But she was never one to turn back from anything once having come to a decision. If it all worked out and Kathleen accepted her, she was quite sure her life wouldn't be too terrible at all. Even if there wasn't a great, consuming passion-filled love between them, she and John McCallum respected and admired each other, and that was a great deal going for any alliance.

November 23, 1790—New South Wales

Today Matthew and I rode out to the McCallum farm. We arrived in time for lunch. I'm afraid I was feeling quite nervous about meeting Kathleen. John's house is like Paul's in structure. When we arrived, John came out to meet us. One of his men took our horses and we followed him inside. He took us immediately to a cozy room in the front. It had a large window which John had brought specially for Kathleen from Cape Town because it was here that she spent most of her time. The window gave her a grand view of the country-side.

Kathleen was lying on a chaise longue. She looks much younger than her years. Her skin has an almost transparent look and is drawn so finely across her high cheekbones. Her face is heart-shaped and she looks so pathetically thin and delicate, yet there is an odd dignity in her manner and her large brown eyes are deep and unusually bright. John spoke gently to her. "Kathleen, my pet, this is Eugénie Fabré whom I have spoken of, and my worthy old friend Matthew Skinner, whom I have also told you about."

Kathleen looked at me for what seemed an interminable length of time but at last she smiled sweetly and held out her hand to me.

"Welcome to our home," she said. "My father has told me a great deal about you. I must say he was right about one thing."

"What was that?" I asked with an answering smile.

"You are very pretty."

At her words I felt such relief! I told her that she was just as pretty as everyone had said. John beamed with satisfaction and I could hear Matthew breathing a sigh of relief. He was nervous, too, and we were a little relieved when a little roly-poly woman walked in, grumbling, *"Now, Master John, do ye think that lunch is going to wait all day for ye? A body slaves to fix something tasty and everyone ignores 'er. It's really too bad!"*

"Eugénie, this is Cassie, and I must admit, she's the one who really rules this household. But don't let her fool you. Her bark is really worse than her bite."

"Someone 'as to keep things runnin' right. Yer welcome, Miss, and Oi do 'ope you enjoy yer lunch," she said as she bustled out.

We went in to lunch, and when we had eaten as much as we could Cassie started dropping hints that we were sitting a bit too long at table. So John took Matthew off on a tour of the farm and that left Kathleen and me alone. We discovered that we really liked each other, and Kathleen gave her wholehearted approval of the marriage. Her words were very reassuring.

"My father needs someone. He has been alone for too long. We love each other dearly, but I'm afraid I cannot be the companion to him that he would like me to be. I too, Eugénie, will be very happy to have someone young and gay to talk to. Cassie means well, but she is not exactly the most frivolous, gay person in the world!"

I told her how much I thought of her father and that I would try to be a good companion to him. She knew that our marriage would be in name only but asked no questions and seemed content about the whole arrangement. The men came back about three o'clock and it was obvious from the expressions on our faces that all was well. Matthew and I left shortly after that.

I must say I am now looking forward to our marriage. I'm sure that I shall feel very much at home with the McCallums. I'll have a family again, and what's more important, two people who need me.

Before I came to bed tonight Matthew patted my

hand. *"Aye, lass, ye'll be all right. Oi feel 'tis all meant to be."*

I too feel perhaps it is all meant to be. Perhaps our destiny is laid out for us after all.

Chapter 23 ———————————

Eugénie Fabré and John McCallum were married a week later in the presence of the Rev. Johnson, Matthew, and John MacArthur in Sydney. They went immediately to John's home where Kathleen welcomed them with loving arms.

Since it was so close to Christmas, Eugénie's first few weeks as Mrs. John McCallum flew by in the bustle of preparations. The Crandells, the Gordons, Doctor White and Matthew were to spend Christmas day with them. The McCallum household hadn't been so cheerful in years. Eugénie longed to see and feel snow again, but in New South Wales it was the hot time of the year. Nevertheless, peace filled all hearts here as much as it had in France or in England. But she couldn't help thinking of the Christmas she had spent in England with her sister and her friends . . .

In the weeks and months that followed, their life took on an aura of blessed tranquility. Darling Kathleen, so gentle and patient, became very attached to Eugénie and she in turn loved her step-daughter. The McCallum household was a happy and cheerful one. Even Cassie was forced to smile once in a while, although she felt this detracted somewhat from her dignity. Eugénie was quite happy. It was marvellous to wake up in the morning without a care in the world. For the first time since she had left Poissy, she was really at peace.

She enjoyed life to the fullest, stretching in bed when she awoke like a pampered cat, and then waiting for Cassie to bring her breakfast tray. John got up so early he didn't expect her to eat breakfast with him and Kathleen always ate in her room. After she had eaten, she would sit at her dressing table and leisurely brush her hair. The face in the mirror was now beginning to blossom again. Her eyes were bright and sparkling as they used to be so long ago in her beloved France. Yes, her life was very good now. John had kept his word and she had never doubted him for an instant. They had connecting bedrooms, but the door remained locked and he had given Eugénie the key.

The next few hours were spent helping Cassie with the household chores and at about ten o'clock she joined Kathleen in the front room where they chatted and shared confidences and read books. As time passed, Eugénie talked about her family and her childhood in France, about her escape and her life in England with Marie, Mag, Moll and Harry. But she didn't share with Kathleen the horrors of the weeks spent in Newgate prison, nor the pain of her deep love for André de Varney.

At noon, John and his overseer Patrick Curran would join them for lunch, after which Kathleen would take a nap. John then spent the next few hours teaching Eugénie something about the running of the farm. He also taught her to shoot and, as she had done with fencing, she practiced diligently until at last she was able to hit what she aimed at. John seemed so anxious for Eugénie to learn to run the farm and she couldn't understand why. But to please him, she did her very best and learned as rapidly as she could.

Some evenings Rachel would come over for a visit, and less often, Paul and Aunt Aggie. Each of them had reacted to the news of the marriage in his or her distinctive way. The Crandells were happy for her; Aunt Aggie thought John was an old fool, and said so in so many words, though not in his hearing. For her old friend's sake, she held her tongue in his presence and continued to visit the McCallums as she had done in the past. Paul had congratulated them and tried to pretend he was happy about it. No one, except perhaps Aunt Aggie, had an inkling of his true feelings. He threw himself into his work with renewed vigour and avoided Eugénie as much as possible.

However, six weeks after they had been married, John took Paul into his confidence, telling him that the marriage was one of companionship and need. Paul felt ashamed but he couldn't help feeling much happier about the whole thing—though it didn't bring Eugénie any closer to him. He cursed André de Varney for what he had done to her. She wouldn't have allowed herself to be persuaded into a loveless marriage if it had not been for that cad. With his next breath, he cursed himself for being such a fool as to waste so much time mooning over a chit of a girl.

On Friday mornings, true to her promise to Matthew, Eugénie rode into Sydney to help him through the weekend. They had finally moved to "The Black Bear" and their business was better than ever. John wasn't so happy about his wife working, but they had discussed all this before the wedding and he had given his word not to stand in her way. However, he had taken it upon himself to write to Harry Boggs in England begging him to come out to New South Wales. He had also sent a letter of instructions to his bank in London, authorizing it to pay for the expenses incurred. He was praying that Harry would come. He had also extended an invitation to Marie, Mag and Moll, though he knew it was a great deal to ask of people, to uproot themselves and give up the old familiar places and come half way across the world to a strange, wild land.

The McCallums' routine remained unbroken for six months or so. Then one day, when John came home for lunch as usual, he asked Cassie to pack some food for an overnight trip.

"Where are you going, Father?" Kathleen asked.

"I'm going to take Eugénie out to the Hawkesbury. I think it's about time she saw our land out there. Somehow, my dear, I have a strange compulsion to take her there now."

"Oh, marvellous! I have heard you speak of it so much I already feel that I know it. What a wonderful surprise," cried Eugénie happily.

"Talking about it can never do it justice. You will see for yourself."

A few hours later, they said goodbye to Kathleen and Cassie and rode off towards the Hawkesbury river. They rode until dark and then made camp for the night. They sat by the fire and John told Eugénie of his dreams for the country. Since she had married John, she had had time to really look at this wild, beautiful country. Everything was so very different from Europe—the trees, the birds, the colors of the earth, even the smells of nature. Reading her thoughts, John spoke seriously. "Land, Eugénie, is worth working for, worth fighting for. It endures long after everything else is gone. It can get in one's blood if one will allow it."

"You know, John, I'm simply overwhelmed by the brooding austerity of this crazy country. I knew before I left England that I belonged here and I was right."

They sat in silence then, the silence of two dear

friends who understand each other completely.

The following day they sat in their saddles looking at the Hawkesbury river, so named by Governor Phillip. It rolled deep and wide between sloping green banks. From where their horses stood, it still had a hundred miles or more to journey before it reached the sea. It was breathtakingly beautiful.

"Eugénie, I own over one hundred acres here, and I have my bid in for more. I've dreamed of building a magnificent home over there on that hill so that when we wake up in the morning, the first thing we shall see is the river, calm and serene. I see this country covered by grazing cattle and," he smiled, "Yes, even sheep, if you and John MacArthur have your way."

They dismounted and, standing by his side, Eugénie looked up at John's earnest face. Then with a voice filled with glowing determination, she said, "John, that dream will come true. I know it will!"

They spent hours mapping out the house in the earth with sticks, like two young children. It was one of those wonderfully happy moments in her life that would be stored in Eugénie's heart forever, a warm memory that she would share one day with her loved ones.

But while these two happy people were planning a dream, her friends in England were in a state of shock.

It was about eleven o'clock at night. Marie had just gone upstairs to bed and Mag and Moll were having a last cup of tea. It was quiet and they sipped their tea in peace. However, their peace and quiet were unexpectedly shattered by Harry banging loudly on the door.

"Wot's the blinkin' row then? Who is it?" shouted Mag.

"Open up, Mag. It's me, Harry. Open up!"

" 'Arry, for the Lord's sake! Where's the bloomin' fire? Oi'm openin' it as fast as Oi can."

He thrust a letter in her hand. "Here, read this. Read it out loud! Where's Marie?"

"'Arry Boggs, ye know good and well Oi can't read a whit in this light, and fer yer information, Marie's upstairs, in bed where any decent body belongs at this hour."

"Call her down. Call her down! Quickly Mag, don't stand there looking at me as though I have taken leave of my senses!"

Mag was about to retort that she thought he had, but something in his eyes made her do as he said. She yelled at the top of her lungs and Marie came racing downstairs as fast as she could.

"Mag, what's wrong? Harry? What are you doing here so late?"

"Nothing's wrong, lass," Harry assured her. "Sit down. I've had news from New South Wales."

"Oh, at last! It's been months since we heard from Eugénie," Marie cried.

"Lass, this is not from our girl. It's from her husband."

They were struck dumb. Mag was the first to find her voice.

" 'Usband, ye say? Are ye gone daft 'Arry Boggs?"

"Whisht, woman! Listen to this."

January 28, 1791—Sydney, New South Wales
Dear Friends,
  I take the liberty of calling you friends because my dear Eugénie speaks of you so often and with such love that I feel as though I have known you a long time. We were married in December and though I know that Eugénie is content, it would indeed bring her great joy if you could all be here with her in New South Wales.

Before we married, Eugénie had bought a partnership in a tavern called "The Pig & Goat." Since then, she and her partner, Matthew Skinner, have built a much larger one called "The Black Bear." Yes, Mr. Boggs, it was named after your "Black Bear." Though we live some distance from Sydney, Eugénie insists on going there every weekend to help Matthew. I don't approve of her working, but I do understand her commitment.

If you were to consider coming out here, Mr. Boggs, you could run Eugénie's half of the business. Believe me, business is blooming. Matthew cannot handle it alone. There are fine living quarters attached to the tavern which would be yours. Mr. Skinner lives in the old place they owned and which he now calls his "mansion." As for you, dear sister-in-law, and you, Miss Boles, and you, Miss Finn, I assure you, you would be well taken care of if you decided to come out here.

I realize that it's a tremendously big step to leave the security of your home and country to come out to a wilderness and so if you decline my invitation, I shall certainly understand. Eugénie has no idea I am sending this letter nor shall I tell her until you arrive if indeed you do. Think about it carefully. In the event that you decide to come out here, I have written to my bank manager with instructions to take care of all your expenses.

> *Your friend,*
> *John E. McCallum*

The three woman sat in stunned silence for a moment. It was all so completely unexpected. Finally Mag gasped, "Wot do ye know about that! Did Oi 'ear right? Were me ears deceivin' me?"

"Well, if your ears were, then mine were too," said Mag, flabbergasted.

"No, ladies, you all heard right. What do you think about it? It's a big step. From what Eugénie tells us and what I have heard, it's a rough land to live in."

"Wot, go out and live with the 'eathen savages? Oi

must be losin' me mind to even consider such a notion!'' squawked Moll.

Mag looked at her friend aghast. "Moll, yer never considerin' it! 'Ave ye gone daft?''

"Well, wot 'ave we got to lose 'ere that's so bloomin' great?'' Moll reasoned.

"A lot! Oi'd rather 'ave the devil Oi knows than the devil Oi don't.''

"Well, girls, it' won't do any good to argue about it. Let us just sleep on it for a few nights and then we'll decide. But we'll all go or none of us will. Agreed?'' suggested Harry.

"Wot do you think, Marie love? Ye 'aven't opened yer mouth.''

"Well, it would be wonderful to be with Eugénie, but I do think Harry is right—we should think about it, and then as he suggested, we'll all go or we'll all stay,'' said Marie at last.

Mag and Moll nodded in agreement.

Several nights later they met at Mag's and Harry called for a vote. "Are we going?''

Moll spoke up. "Aye 'Arry, we're all willin' to take the chance. 'Ow about you?''

"I made my mind up to go that very night. I was hoping you would all agree as well. There is so much we have to do, but I think the first thing we should do is go and see the bank manager and have him arrange for our transportation out to New South Wales. We shall have to sell our places here and then make preparations for the journey. I'll write to Mr. McCallum tonight, though it's likely the letter will arrive no sooner than we do. Now, ladies, why don't we drink a toast to John McCallum for giving us the opportunity of being with our Eugénie again?''

"To John McCallum!" they chorused, raising their glasses.

"Mag, yer 'eart don't seem to be in yer toast," said Moll.

"Well, Moll, Oi know Oi said Oi'd go but Oi can't 'elp bein' nervous about the whole thing. 'Ere Oi am— Mag Boles, who was always the rock of sense, plannin' on leavin' me own safe country to go out to God only knows where, maybe to be murdered in me bed by a pack of 'eathens! Oi must 'ave gone stark, ravin' bonkers!"

"Chin up, old girl, we'll take care of you," said Harry with a grin. "And love, just think, you could have lived your whole life out in such a prosaic manner. Now just think of the adventure and excitement! Very few people get the chance of being murdered in their beds."

"Oh, 'Arry, don't tease 'er, she's liable to change 'er mind," groaned Moll.

"If it weren't fer the chance of seein' our girl again, Oi wouldn't dream of goin'. But ye needn't worry, Oi said Oi'd go and Oi won't change my mind fer anythin'."

"Good for you, Margaret my dear."

" 'Arry Boggs, Oi *told* ye me name is Mag and don't ye ferget it!" Mag snapped.

"I know love, just teasing you. Just teasing."

" 'Arry Oi think we'd better go 'ome now before Mag 'its ye with somethin'," said Moll, getting to her feet.

"Besides, we all got a lot to do tomorrow."

"You are absolutely right, Moll, and I shall call for all of you first thing in the morning."

"We'll be ready, 'Arry Boggs, and Oi suppose ye

might just as well eat breakfast with us," sighed Mag.

"Why, Miss Boles, you are too kind."

"Get out! Get out before Oi lose me mind!" she grumbled.

Chapter 24

July 15, 1791—New South Wales

Today is my eighteenth birthday and everyone has been marvellous. Cassie fixed me a very special breakfast and John came to my room with his present, a beautiful pair of sapphire earrings. Kathleen gave me a lovely red dressing-robe. I spent most of the day with Manaka, though. Oh—I forgot—I haven't written about my new friend and he is so important to me.

A few days after our return from the Hawkesbury property, I was picking vegetables for Cassie in the back garden when I heard a scuffling sound close by the bordering hedge. When I saw it was an aborigine, I was a little scared. I had heard that they could be dangerous but until now I had only seen them hovering in the distance. To me it seemed that they did not wish to have any close contact with us. As I said, I was scared but then I noticed that he was hurt and he looked at me in such mute appeal I knew I had to help him. I was just about to go to him when two marines rode up.

"Beggin' yer pardon, Ma'am, we're searchin' the area for a dirty thievin' black. Have ye seen 'im around here by any chance?" one of them asked.

I moved so that my skirts hid the poor soul from their view and stood as tall and dignified as I knew how. I looked the fellow who had spoken straight in the eyes and answered, "Now, sir, I ask you, if I saw a wild, dirty aborigine, would I be standing here calmly picking vegetables?"

The fellow grinned. "Sorry to 'ave bothered ye, Ma'am, but keep yer eyes peeled."

I waited until they had ridden out of sight and then stooped to examine the man on the ground. I found that he had lost consciousness so I ran for help.

I ordered two of our men to carry the black to one of the laborers' huts.

"Beggin' yer pardon, Mrs. McCallum, but yer not thinkin' of puttin' 'im in 'ere?" said one.

"Il va sans dire!"

They looked at me blank-faced and I realized that I had spoken in French. "Why ever not?" I snapped impatiently.

"Ye'll 'ave a mutiny on yer 'ands, that's wot. The men won't stand fer it."

"Such rot! Oh, very well then, carry him up to the house."

"To the house, Ma'am?"

"You heard me. To—the—house."

"We'll not be responsible when Mr. John 'ears about it," mumbled one of the men with a scowl.

"Don't worry. I shall take full blame," I assured him grandly.

Reluctantly they carried the poor fellow up to the house and Cassie, though quite upset at the thought of having an aborigine in the house, prepared a cot for him in the little storeroom at the back of the kitchen. I know Cassie only consented to help because of her grudging regard for me. She helped me clean his wound and make him comfortable. Gently I cleaned the ugly gash in his side and bandaged it, and soon he was sleeping peacefully.

"Eugénie McCallum, Oi just don't know wot Mr. John is going to say! He'll 'ave a fit," said Cassie.

When John came home that evening, the two men rushed to tell him what had happened and he came storming into the house. Since I had never even heard him raise his voice before, I was quite alarmed, but I went to meet him and simply ignored his outburst.

"Why, John, what has upset you so?" I asked sweetly.

"You know very well! I want that native out of here at once. At once, do you hear? You are upsetting all my men!"

My first reaction was one of anger, but I thought better of it and answered in a placating tone, "I'm truly sorry to have upset you, John. He's hurt and needs care. He is, after all, one of God's children just as we are. He had a heart and feelings like us and he deserves care and consideration. Are you so insensitive, John? I can scarce believe it. Why, I have seen you lavish such tender care on your animals. Can you do less for a man? Another human being?"

John's anger was completely obliterated. He is such a good man, so loving. "How can I refuse you when you put it like that?" said John. "You are right. It was cruel and contemptible for me to have spoken as I did."

"Thank you, dear." I hugged him. Dear John, how lucky I am to have you!

"Eugénie, love, you'll have to keep him close to the house until the men get used to having him around," John warned me.

The aborigine had a fever but with our good care he recovered quickly. But he was still too weak to travel. During the weeks he spent in our house, I tried to communicate with him. He was obviously quite intelligent, for it didn't take long for him to pick up a few English words here and there, simple words like, table, bed, chair. I discovered that his name was Manaka. He found it quite impossible to pronounce my name and so he called me Madami. We invented a sort of sign language and were soon able to understand one another quite well.

When he got his strength back, he stayed with us for several weeks doing odd chores around the house and then, quite without warning, he returned to the Bush. I miss him. I should have liked to have found out more about his people and his way of life.

Strangely enough, he was missed by everyone. Even the men had got used to him.

"Well, I expect that's the last we shall see of him," said John after Manaka had disappeared.

"Oh, I hope not. He is a dear, sweet man and he was really learning a lot of English. He didn't even say goodbye."

"That's probably their way, love."

"Do you know much about the aborigines, John?" Eugénie asked.

"Not a great deal from personal experience. I haven't had time to go exploring among them and I'm not sure it would be safe. When we first came out here, they appeared to be quite friendly and sympathetic, but unfortunately there were men among us who turned on them and so they in turn showed hostility towards us. For the most part, they tend to stay away from the white man."

"John, do tell me as much as you can about them," Eugénie urged. "Since Manaka came into our lives, I have really become interested in his people."

"Well, my dear, most of them look like Manaka, with large, ridged brows, sloping foreheads, strong jaws, wide, flat noses, and curly black hair. Their skin color ranges from deep bronze to occasionally a light tan or black. They all seem to be a lean and tough people and quite tall. The men, I would say, stand within the five-foot-six range. Did you notice how beautiful Manaka's teeth were?"

"Yes. Is that a characteristic of his race?"

"As far as I know, yes. Shall I go on?"

"Oh, please, John. It's all so fascinating!"

"They are a food gathering people and are absolutely dependent on whatever nature chooses to give them. There are many tribes around New South Wales and I suspect many, many more throughout this uncharted land. From what I've heard each tribe has its own moral code, sacred totems and religious faith as well as its own laws and punishments, spiritual chants and the inevitable superstitions. Each tribe has its own special territory, although they do not stay put for very long but roam freely about within that territory. The size of their territory varies with the richness of the food supply. Near the coast they don't wander very far because they have plenty of fish to eat, but in the more arid places the territory, of necessity, must be larger. Just how large I have no way of knowing. That, my dear, is the extent of my knowledge. Has it satisfied your curiosity?" John asked with an indulgent smile.

"Thank you for trying, dear, but I'm afraid you sould like a scientist writing a dreary book. What you have told me hasn't painted any pictures for me or brought me any closer to really knowing Manaka's people. If he comes back to us, I shall attempt to find out more about them. Perhaps one day we can all learn to live together in peace."

"I hope for your sake he does come back to see you, but I wouldn't count on it too much. Now I really must go back to work."

Contrary to what John believed, Manaka returned about five weeks later. Kathleen was sleeping and Eugénie had just come back to the house after a short learning session with John. When she opened the door to his knock, she was overjoyed to see him.

"Manaka, I'm so glad you came back! We missed you so much," she cried.

"Madami, come with me. I wish show you to my family."

Eugénie felt a little shiver of excitement course through her body. What an opportunity to see at first hand the aborigines in their natural environment! She was quite sure from what John had said that few white men had ever done so. She wrote a quick note to John and, dressed in her work skirt and boots, she set off on foot with Manaka.

They walked for about an hour until they were far into the Bush. She was awestruck by its vast emptiness and its eerie silence. As though for the first time, her nostrils were assailed by the smells of grass, bark and above all the perfume of the aromatic oils exuded by the trees. There was little sign of life and she was beginning to wonder just how long they would have to walk. Manaka took long strides and Eugénie found it difficult to keep up with him. Just as she was about to protest and give up for a while, they came within sight of the camp which was really nothing more than a place sheltered from the wind by a few broken hedges.

The sun gleamed on the naked bodies of the inhabitants. Most of them were busy with their hunting weapons, some making spears, others shaping spearheads out of stone by chipping away with another piece of stone. A woman was suckling her child and Eugénie was surprised to see that the child looked to be about three years old. In spite of the activity, there was a quiet, relaxed atmosphere about the place. Manaka signaled Eugénie to wait and he went towards the group of men. Almost immediately wild chatter broke out accompanied by gestures. Eugénie wondered if they were perhaps angry with Manaka for bringing her here. But Manaka came back for Eugénie and brought her towards the group, where they made it clear that she was welcome.

In her honor, the hunters decided to go on a kangaroo hunt. While they were gone, fires were lit and the women prepared the less substantial food of small snakes, lizards, kookaburras and crows, cooking them in hot ashes. Manaka's mother and sister took her under their wing and pointed out how things were done.

Eugénie was fascinated by the whole scene. When the men came back with the kangaroo, Manaka explained that it was now the men's job to cook this larger item on the menu. While the men prepared and cooked the large animal, the women passed around the food that had already been prepared. Eugénie's stomach revolted at the thought of eating those snakes and lizards. She was terribly afraid that she might be sick and thus offend her hosts. She forced a small piece of lizard into her mouth and surprisingly it wasn't bad, but the ashes which clung to it weren't very appetizing. She chewed and smiled and the aborigines, who had not taken their eyes off her during the whole process, smiled, chatted and gestured in a friendly manner. It was obvious that she had been unanimously accepted. Manaka grinned from ear to ear.

"Madami, you one of us now," he said haltingly.

Finally the tough, sinewy kangaroo flesh was passed around and everyone chewed in silence.

When the food had been eaten and everyone seemed satisfied, one of the men brought out an instrument called a didgeridoo. Manaka explained by words and gestures that it was made by hollowing out the bough of a gum tree. The sound it produced was as forlorn as the deepest notes of a great bassoon. Then everyone broke into song. The fires burned slowly and to Eugénie everything looked mysterious yet somehow beautiful. Manaka tried to explain that the songs were stories that had been handed down through the ages. It was, thought Eugénie, a fascinating and unforgettable experience watching these people, their naked bodies gleaming in the firelight, and listening to their chant. Time ceased to exist, or so it seemed to her. Gradually the singing ceased and the camp settled down for the night.

As soon as the sun came up the next morning, Eugénie and Manaka took their leave of the group and the headman presented her with a boomerang, a fighting type to strike down her enemies. It had been quite an honor, she felt, to have been allowed to share one evening with these unique people.

They walked at an easy pace this time and when they reached home it was close to noon. They came in through the kitchen and Cassie, when she saw who it was, raised her hands to heaven and exclaimed, "Thank God ye be safe, child! The place has been turned upside down. Captain Crandell has even had a company of his marines out searchin' for ye. As fer the master, why he is goin' around lookin' like a ghost!"

"I don't understand, Cassie!" said Eugénie, puzzled. "I left a note explaining everything. I put it on the hall table so that someone would be sure to see it. Manaka came while Kathleen was sleeping and you were snoozing in your chair. I just didn't want to disturb you."

Cassie went bustling out into the hall and sure enough, there was the note under the table where a draught from the door had blown it.

"Well, Oi never!" Cassie gasped.

"Cassie, I am so tired. I didn't get much sleep last night. I was too excited. I think I shall go and lie down for an hour or two. Manaka, will you stay?"

"Yes, Madami, I stay," said the aborigine.

Several hours later, John and Robert walked into the house, dusty and dejected. Cassie met them at the door.

"She's back! She's well! 'Er note that she left us blew down under the 'all table." She handed John the note and his hand shook as he took it from her.

"Where is she?" he asked.

"Why, she's sleepin'. The poor dear was so tired.

Manaka took 'er to visit 'is family.''

When Eugénie awoke, John was sitting beside her bed fast asleep. A lump came into her throat and she swallowed tears when she saw how careworn he looked. How could she have been so thoughtless as to give in to her impulse? She could have waited and gone the following day. She gave him a gentle, loving kiss on his rough, strong hand and he opened his eyes.

"Oh, Eugénie, what a fright you gave us all!" he sighed.

"John, can you forgive me? I just didn't think."

"Forgive you! I am only so very happy that you are safe, my precious. Do you feel well enough to see Kathleen? The poor girl has finally cried herself to sleep. She wouldn't go to bed last night. She just watched at the window and cried and prayed."

Hand-in hand they went to Kathleen's room where she lay with her lovely face stained by tears. Eugénie took her hand and at her touch Kathleen opened her gorgeous brown eyes. When she saw who it was she broke into a smile that was brighter than the sun. They hugged each other wordlessly and John smiled to see how much they cared for each other. He then carried his daughter into her favorite room where Robert was waiting.

"Eugénie, you gave us quite a fright. Why, the whole colony is searching for you! What ever possessed you to run off like that without a word?" asked Robert.

"Robert, I can't tell you how sorry I am, but I *did* leave a note. I realize now that I shouldn't have gone like that without a word to anyone."

"Well, as long as you're safe now, all's well that ends well. I'll be off now, John, and spread the word that our wanderer has returned."

He left and Cassie brought in a tray piled high with sandwiches. Eugénie all at once felt very hungry and she made short work of them. With the simple gesture of bringing in lunch, Cassie had restored the household to normal.

Chapter 25——————————

October 1791—New South Wales

Manaka stays with us most of the time now. His English is improving and he is quite devoted to me. John has been spending more time with me. I can't understand why there is so much urgency about knowing all there is to know about running the farm. He wants me to know as much about farming as he does, which is a complete impossibility. Still, I'm interested and I'm a willing pupil.

Paul stopped by the other day with some very disturbing news. Arthur Phillip is returning to England. It will be a sad day for New South Wales when he goes. I don't understand why Paul avoids me so much. He wouldn't have come in to see me but I happened to find out that he was down at the barn talking to John and so I went to see him. *Surely I haven't offended him.*

I had a letter from Harry and one from Marie last week. Their lives seem to be just as serenely uneventful as always. Oh, how I miss them! I'm afraid, much as I love hearing from them, their letters are like deep wounds in my heart, deep wounds of loneliness. How selfish I am. I have so much, yet I want more.

November 1791—New South Wales

All over the colony, preparations are under way for the big party which is to be our farewell to Governor Phillip. The ladies are bringing their fine clothes out of storage and the air is filled with a touch of excitement, albeit tinged with sadness, for no one wants to see Arthur Phillip leave.

Rachel has changed her mind a dozen times about what to wear, and Kathleen—yes, John has decided she shall go, too—is so excited I'm afraid she'll use up all her energy. I shall wear my white lace dress. John has bought me some beautiful clothes but none will ever compare with my white lace. It is my treasure.

John and his little brood went into Sydney two days before the party and stayed at "The Black Bear." Kathleen was radiantly happy. It wasn't often that her father would let her tax her strength like this. But she had to put up with Cassie, Eugénie and her father hovering over her like hens with one newborn chick. When they arrived at "The Black Bear" with their best clothes carefully packed and their faces glowing with anticipation, Matthew grinned in delight.

"Well, bless my soul, ye are a sight for sore eyes! Why, Miss Kathleen, ye look fair excited enough to burst."

"Oh, Mr. Skinner, I am! I really am. Do you know I've never been to a party before?"

"Why, ye'll be the belle of the ball," said Matthew with a broad grin.

They waited impatiently for the night of the party.

"Eugénie, why does it seem that time just crawls when we are eager to do something and when we are dreading something, time just *flies?*" asked Kathleen plaintively.

"*Chérie,* that's just life, I'm afraid," Eugénie answered.

At last the longed-for night arrived. Kathleen had chosen a deep pink silk dress which gave her a little color and made her eyes sparkle. The Crandells, Miss Gordon and Paul had arrived about noon that day and their company added to the excitement. Paul had gone

317

directly to Government House to spend as much time with his friend as possible. The girls shared a room, and amid much laughter they bathed and dressed. Rachel was the first to get ready and she joined Aunt Aggie downstairs. Eugénie looked radiant, and when she joined Rachel and Aunt Aggie that good lady had to admit, albeit grudgingly, that she looked exquisite. Aunt Aggie was quite elegant herself, dressed in regal purple. Robert looked handsome in his dress uniform. They were all in the parlor chatting to Matthew when John walked in. He went up to Eugénie and took her hand, gazing at her in open admiration.

"You look beautiful, my dear, just beautiful. Would you mind going up to Kathleen? She asked me to send you to her."

Eugénie hurried upstairs to Kathleen. Cassie was just putting the finishing touches to Kathleen's hair when Eugénie walked into the bedroom.

"Eugénie, I have something for you and I would be honored if you would wear them for me," Kathleen said softly.

She handed Eugénie a velvet-covered tray upon which nestled a necklace, earrings and a spray for her hair—the most exquisite rubies Eugénie had ever seen.

"They were my mother's," Kathleen told her. "I know she would have wanted you to wear them. Will you wear them, Eugénie?"

"Oh, Kathleen, they are so beautiful! Are you very sure you want me to wear them?"

"Very sure," said Kathleen firmly.

"In that case, I shall indeed be honored."

Eugénie put the jewels on and they glowed in the candlelight. The girls embraced, and just then John walked in.

"What's this? What's this? Come on, girls, you are

keeping everyone waiting. Paul has just arrived to help escort you ladies, so let's go."

Dinner was served at eight o'clock. The guests seated at the table to do honor to Arthur Phillip were arrayed in all the splendor that was available to the people of New South Wales. It was surprisingly lavish. One would have expected this in London but in New South Wales!

The ball began at ten o'clock and was held in the large meeting room. It was decorated with beautiful flowers which had been picked by the servants from every nearby bush that bore a blossom. The room was lit by hundreds of candles which shone on the jewels of the dancers and on the instruments of the orchestra which had been put together with whatever talent could be found among the convicts, marines and the free settlers.

The ball opened with a lively country dance. John, of course, had the first dance with Eugénie, but it was too much for him and he couldn't finish. Laughingly he said to his wife, "My dear, I must be getting old, but I simply don't have the energy to continue. I hate to admit it, but I'm just not a young man anymore."

"Nonsense, John! It's just that you're not used to dancing, and I must say this particular dance is particularly energetic," Eugénie soothed.

The next dance was a beautiful Hayden minuet and John turned to Paul. "Paul, would you mind taking my place for this dance? I'll just sit here with Kathleen and Aggie."

"I'd be delighted." His words were warm but his tone was strangely cool. Eugénie was astonished at how beautifully he danced. Paul had a wonderful sense of rhythm. She smiled at him and then was carried away into another world by the wonderful, romantic music. Paul couldn't take his eyes off her. Eugénie felt wonderful. Her eyes shone as though every candle in the room were reflected in them. For a wonderful moment in time it was as if they were alone in the room. But the dance came to an end all too soon. Paul escorted her to John's side and then politely talked to Kathleen, who was seated in a comfortable chaise where she had a splendid view of the dancers.

Eugénie danced every dance. She was so happy. This was, in a small way, what she had dreamt of so many times. If only André were here to share in her happiness!

All too soon it was time for the last dance. Eugénie had promised this to John, but when she went to claim her dance he looked tired and turned once more to Paul.

"Paul, could I ask you once more to take my place?"

Paul took Eugénie's hand and this time he whispered, "It will indeed be my pleasure."

The dance was a graceful ländler. Paul gazed into Eugénie's eyes and she felt very aware of him all of a sudden. She felt strangely shy and drawn to him, but she shrugged it off. It must be the music and the wine, she thought. Her fingers tingled as they touched his. When the final chords of the dance were struck, she glanced up at him and blushed when she saw how intently he was looking at her. The dance ended and Paul returned her to John. He bowed politely and she told herself that she had imagined the look he had given her. His face was now expressionless and since she didn't really want to acknowledge what she had seen—what she suddenly suspected, she put Paul out of her mind.

It had been a wonderfully successful evening. Kathleen had managed to stay up throughout the whole evening and her face glowed. It had been such a delight for her to watch all the beautifully dressed figures dancing around the room to the strains of the glorious music of Hayden and Mozart.

But the joy of the party was forgotten when a few days later they said goodbye to Arthur Phillip with heavy hearts. New South Wales was now in the rather dubious hands of Major Francis Crose and the New South Wales Corps. Crose had been appointed Lieutenant Governor and was to remain in charge of the colony until John Hunter was appointed Governor in 1795. So ended an era in the history of New South Wales.

Chapter 26 ———————————

Governor Phillip had sailed for England and in New South Wales preparations for Christmas were underway. It still seemed strange to Eugénie and to the other newcomers to the colony to see the sun shining and feel the tremendous heat of summer at this special holy time. It didn't seem quite right that there shouldn't be snow and cold, crisp air. Eugénie and Cassie were busy decorating the house and trying to make it especially festive looking. They tried to explain to Manaka what Christmas was all about.

"You see, Manaka, our God so loved us that he allowed his only son to take the form of man," Eugénie explained. "His son Jesus loved us so much that he suffered terrible agonies for us and then gave his life so that we could be allowed to enter Heaven and enjoy God's love. He was God, all-powerful, yet he chose to suffer and die for love of us. It is Jesus' birthday we celebrate at Christmas."

"Madami, that is wonderful thing. I must tell this story to my family. They will enjoy it. We not so different after all, your people and mine. We too have legends," said Manaka.

"But the story of Jesus is not a legend, it really happened," Eugénie told him.

"Why didn't he just strike down his enemies, Madam?"

"What would that have proved? That he was strong and fearless? No. What greater gift can a man give than to lay down his life for another? That's what Jesus did and his sacrifice was all the greater because he didn't have to. But it is not as sad as you may think, because three days after he died he came back to life in all his power and glory."

Manaka's eyes grew large with wonder and Eugénie could see that he was deep in thought.

Rachel had celebrated Hannukah, and now for Robert's sake was preparing for Christmas. Everyone was gay and visited back and forth much more than usual, exchanging recipes and decorations. Eugénie longed to be in England, though she never for one moment let John suspect. Her last Christmas there had been truly unforgetable.

It was December 19th. Eugénie and Kathleen were waiting for John and Patrick Curran to join them for lunch. They were later than usual and Eugénie was getting anxious. Then Patrick rushed in and his face was chalk white.

"What's the matter, Patrick?" Eugénie asked with a sinking heart, dreading to hear the answer.

"It's your husband, Mrs. McCallum! I think he has had a heart attack. I sent someone for Dr. Gordon."

Kathleen fainted and Eugénie rang for Cassie. Her thoughts were racing. "Where is he? Take me to him," she cried.

"Ma'am, I think you should stay with Miss Kathleen. We'll bring him in as soon as the doctor has taken a look at him. We were afraid to move him," Patrick said.

Thirty minutes later the men came in carrying John.

Paul was with them and Eugénie followed them to John's room where Paul tended to his friend for about twenty minutes. Then with a sigh he turned to Eugénie. "It doesn't look good. I would say this isn't the first attack he has had. To be honest, Eugénie, I don't have too much hope that he will pull out of this."

Eugénie's legs weakened under her and she felt a dreadful panic.

"My God, no! Not John. He's too strong and too good to die!" she cried.

"Pull yourself together, girl, at least for Kathleen's sake," Paul snapped. "I'm going to give her something to calm her. The shock might be too much for her. Now are you going to be brave?"

She nodded numbly.

Night came, and darkness. The lamps were lit. Eugénie and Paul sat by John's bedside. Towards midnight he regained consciousness and spoke faintly to Eugénie.

"My little one, don't grieve for me. You have given me so much happiness and peace of mind. You precious girl, God has been so good to me to allow you to come into our lives. I know that I leave Kathleen in good hands."

"John dear, please don't speak. Save your strength," she begged tearfully.

"Don't cry, dearest." He wearily closed his eyes for a moment then continued. "I have known for some time now that I had a bad heart. Perhaps I should have told you, but I didn't want to worry you. I am ready to go now, knowing that you will take care of my girl and that you love each other. Thank you."

He lost consciousness again. About two o'clock he died.

Two days later John McCallum's friends and neighbors gathered with his family by the banks of the Hawksbury river where Eugénie insisted he be buried. The Rev. Johnson came out from Sydney and delivered the eulogy. The coffin was lowered and the beautiful words of the twenty-third Psalm echoed over the land he loved so well, comforting all who gathered there:

The Lord is my Shepherd; I shall not want
He leadeth me beside the still waters;
He restoreth my soul.
He leads me in paths of righteousness for His name's sake.
Though I walk through the valley of the shadow of death,
* I fear no evil;*
for Thou art with me;
Thy rod and Thy staff, they comfort me. . .

Eugénie stayed by the graveside for a few minutes after the others had walked back to the wagons and the horses. With tears in her eyes, but with a steady voice, she said solemnly, "John, I promise you I'll see that your dreams for this place come true. It will be a place you can be proud of, a monument to your memory." Then she arose and walked with dignity towards the carriages.

After a few last words of sympathy to Eugénie, the mourners returned to their homes, with the exception of John MacArthur, the Gordons, the Crandells and the Rev. Johnson. These dear friends went back with Eugénie and Patrick Curran to the McCallums' house to pay their respects to Kathleen and be there when the will was read.

Cassie had prepared a meal, though no one had much of an appetite. Kathleen was very quiet but seemed to be bearing her father's death with comparative equanimity. They ate in silence for the most part and after the table had been cleared, the Rev. Johnson coughed and stood up. "Six weeks ago John came to see me and asked me to read this letter after his death. It is his last will and testament and was witnessed by me and Dr. White." He cleared his throat once more and proceeded:

> *To my friends, I give my thanks for your friendship these past years. Kathleen, my beloved, don't grieve for me, for your father will join your dearest mother and I know I leave you in good, loving hands. To you, my darling, I leave our home at Parramatta and £15,000 which is in safekeeping in my bank in London.*
>
> *To you, Patrick Curran, my faithful helper, I leave the sum of £1,000 a year, and to dear Cassie, who has held our home together for so many years, the sum of £2,000 a year. I hope that both of you will stay on with my family and help them as much as you have helped me in the past.*
>
> *To you, Eugénie, my dear wife, with a heart filled with thanks for your friendship and warm companionship, I leave the property at the Hawkesbury. Someday, if you see fit, I should like my body to be moved out there. Also, to you my dear, I leave the sum of £50,000 per year, which must be used for the benefit of both the Parramatta and the Hawkesbury property. For your own personal use, to do with whatever you wish, I leave you the sum of £15,000 per year. The profits from the Hawkesbury property will be yours and the profits from the Parramatta property will be Kathleen's.*
>
> *Eugénie, you have given me great joy, and now that my end is drawing near I am at peace with the knowledge that my little Kathleen will be loved and cherished by you.*
>
> *Goodbye and God bless all of you,*
>
> > *John E. McCallum, father, husband and friend*

There was a sorrowful silence in the room and Eugénie, overcome by uncontrollable emotion, excused herself and rushed into the garden. Paul followed her.

His heart was torn by watching her suffering and he prayed that he would find the words to comfort her.

Lost in her sorrow, she didn't turn when he came into the garden. He walked up behind her and slipped his arms around her waist. She turned then and buried her face in the warmth of his shoulder. He took her hands and raised them to his lips, covering them with tender kisses.

"Paul, I can't help feeling I cheated him," she sobbed. "I was never really his wife in the true sense of the word."

"Yes, I know."

She looked at him startled. "You know?"

"John told me several months ago. Don't worry—I am the only one who knows the truth. Eugénie, you made him happy. Those were his terms because he knew you did not love him in that way. You were honest with him every step of the way. You loved him like a daughter and when he saw that you and Kathleen had become friends, that was all he wanted.

"Yes, I loved him. He was so very, very good—how could I fail to love him? Oh, Paul, I *did* try to be the companion he wanted. I tried to learn everything he was teaching me, but little did I know—how could I even guess that he was teaching me to run the farm because he knew his days were numbered? Why is it we always feel that we could have done more for those we loved after it is too late?"

"My dear, I'm afraid that's just the way life is. We all mean well enough, I suppose, but we just don't take the time to say the things we should or do the things we want to do for others. Have you thought about the future, Eugénie? I suppose you'll sell out and move into Sydney."

"Absolutely not!" she said firmly. "I wouldn't dream of it. This is Kathleen's home and Patrick has already told me that he is willing to stay on and run the place. As for me, I intend to build John's dream house out at the Hawkesbury and have the best farm in the country. I intend the Hawkesbury property to be a monument to John's memory. I'm so glad I had him buried out there. I felt sure it's where he would want to be. Do you know, Paul, I think John was able to see into the future. So often he would tell me he could see wheat lands and cattle lands and even sheep lands, timber camps and perhaps even mines. He could see large towns and great cities all over this vast continent. I seem to have caught something of his dreams. Dreams make a person go on, for without them we would remain stagnant. Without dreams we would live in the same little groove to the end of our days. Safe it might be, but is it living? It's not the way *I* want to live!"

Her eyes glowed with the fervor of her feelings and Paul looked at her with pride and admiration and his heart ached for her.

"My love, you will have your work cut out for you. It won't be an easy task fulfilling your dreams. Remember this, Eugénie, if you need help or advice, don't ever hesitate to ask me."

She kissed his hand then, and his long, gentle fingers caressed her face. "Thank you, Paul. You're the best friend a person could possibly ever hope to have."

They stood there quietly for a few minutes, Eugénie lost in her thoughts of John and his dreams, Paul aching with his longing for her love. She was the first to break the silence.

"I think we'd better go in. Aunt Aggie must be tired and just about ready to go home."

Reluctantly he agreed and they walked into the house hand in hand.

December 22, 1791—New South Wales

Everyone left at last. Now we are alone with our grief, Kathleen, Cassie, Patrick and I. The house seems so empty. John was so vigorous. He filled our lives with his strength and his love and now he is gone. But I know I must be strong for Kathleen's sake. She has no one now but Cassie and me. Aunt Aggie was kind enough to ask us to spend Christmas with her, but none of us felt like it. We won't feel much like merrymaking this Christmas and we certainly don't want to put a damper on anyone else's festivities. They feel badly enough losing a friend —our presence would only add to their sorrow.

December 26, 1791

Our Christmas passed and we are glad. It was the most desolate one I have ever spent. We exchanged gifts only because we had already prepared them. Kathleen gave me her mother's rubies, the ones I wore to the Governor's ball, and I gave her a lace shawl. Poor Cassie did her best to make the day a little festive. She prepared some very special treats, hoping to tempt our appetites. The only bright moment of the day was when Robert and Rachel brought little Andrew to see us. His childish laughter filled our hearts with a few precious minutes of joy.

Oh, how I long to be with my sister Marie and my friends! I have written again to France and I pray that my little sister is safe. Will France never be at peace? Paul tells me that the guillotine is being used to exterminate every aristocrat in France. Thank God André is safe! What I fear most is that Joséphine will have become tainted by the horror. She was such a sweet little girl, a bundle of joy. God give me strength to carry on. I made a promise to John and I intend to carry it out.

As soon as the New Year had passed, Eugénie started work out at the Hawkesbury. She had plans drawn up for the house she and John had sketched out on the brown earth. Then she hired a crew of skilled convicts to build it for her. She transferred Vinnie McDonald, Patrick's assistant, out to the Hawkesbury to supervise the clearing of the land and she herself worked along with the men. Even Aunt Aggie was forced to admire her, though she never said so to Eugénie. Eugénie sought to drown her sorrows in work and drove herself to the point of exhaustion, the best therapy in the world for an aching heart.

Throngs of people crowded the wharf, their eyes agog with curiosity as they watched the passengers disembark from the ship that had just arrived from England. It was April 16th, 1792. Among the passengers was a rather distinguished, portly man, two older women and a young girl. They were obviously together. The watching eyes beheld one of the women who threw up her hands and covered her eyes. Then, recovering her dignity, those close by heard her exclaim, " 'E's naked! Aow, Oi knew we shouldn't 'ave come out 'ere. We're among the savages!"

The gentleman patted her hand and, as one coaxing a child to good humor, answered gently, "Now Mag, dearest, take it easy. He looks friendly enough and he's not exactly naked. Besides, we are here now so let's make the best of it. It can't be all that bad."

The object of their attention, a curious Aborigine, wandered away, oblivious to the upheavel he had caused. The portly man stopped one of the curious who was on his way home, having satisifed himself that no one of great importance had been on board.

"My good fellow, could you direct us to "The Black Bear" tavern?" he asked.

"Thirsty already, are ye? Well, just go along yonder

wharf and ye can't miss it. But it's not open yet and Old Skinner won't let ye in before it's time, no, not even if yer tongue were 'angin' out.''

Harry Boggs, for it was indeed he, led his little brood along the wharf and to "The Black Bear" where they found Matthew setting up the tankards and tables for the day's business. He was surprised to see them and was about to show them the door when they introduced themselves and gave him John McCallum's letter. When he read it his face broke into a huge grin.

"So ye be Eugénie's friends from England and 'er sister Marie! Welcome, welcome! Ye say she don't know ye are comin'? Oi'll bet she'll be the surprised little lassie. But sit down—ye must be tired after that journey. Make yerselves at 'ome. Oi'll certainly be glad of the 'elp. Eugénie 'as no business comin' out 'ere every weekend. She 'as enough to do. Oi don't suppose ye know, but McCallum died last December.''

"Heavens! He sounded like he was a fine man," said Harry. "I'm sorry to hear it. What happened?''

'' 'Is 'eart, Oi dare say. Yon lass 'as been workin' out at 'er property like a convict and then comes in 'ere on weekends. She'll kill 'erself. But now that yer 'ere, maybe ye can talk some sense into 'er.''

"We'll do our best," Harry promised. "It sounds as though Eugénie needs us.''

"Aye, she does—but ye ladies look tired. Oi'll show ye to yer rooms.''

After he had seen the ladies comfortably settled in the rooms upstairs, Matthew joined Harry for a drink and a chat.

"Oi'll send word out to Eugénie, though she'll be in 'ere tomorrow anyway," Matthew said.

"In that case, don't bother, Mr. Skinner. We are

anxious to see her, but it'll be more of a surprise for her to find us here."

"Oi'd be obliged if ye'd call me Matthew. We'd better think about accommodations for ye and the ladies. Are they 'appy about comin' out 'ere? That one lady, the skinny one, didn't look too thrilled."

"That, Matthew, was my dear wife, Mag. She is rather upset, but she's a good lass and she'll get used to it. She saw one of your natives down by the dock and I'm afraid his clothing—or should I say the lack of it—rather distressed her."

"Oi didn't realize ye were married. Eugénie never mentioned that," said Matthew.

"She doesn't know. Mag and I were married just before we left England. That will be another surprise Eugénie will like."

"Well, 'Arry, that changes things a bit. Ye and the missus can stay 'ere. Eugénie usually does when she comes to town. Ye can 'ave 'er room. Oi knows she won't mind since it's bigger. The other two ladies can stay at my 'ouse. If ye want to get cleaned up a bit, 'Arry, ye can, and then perhaps ye wouldn't mind comin' with me to find a bed fer the other room. Oi expect yer missis will enjoy fixin' things up 'ere fer ye."

Matthew carried a big pot of warm water upstairs for the ladies and after they had bathed and changed, he took Marie and Moll over to his house. Then he and Harry went in search of a bed.

By nightfall they were well settled in. Mag had taken over the kitchen at the "Black Bear," cleaned it up and had a meal ready when the men closed the tavern for the night. Moll and Marie had come back that afternoon and so when they had eaten, Matthew walked the two ladies home. He was quite taken with Moll, who was all too aware of the fact and teased him unmercifully.

Left to themselves, Harry and Mag settled down by the fire, Harry with his pipe and Mag with her cup of tea.

"Well, ducks, 'ow do ye like this 'Black Bear?' Do ye miss yer old place?'' Mag asked.

"It's not quite as grand as my old place, but people are people no matter where you are. I just hope that you can be happy here, love,'' replied Harry.

"Don't worry about me, dearie. Now that Oi got a roof over me 'ead again things don't seem so bad. We'll 'ave a nice 'ome 'ere, 'Arry, and we'll all be together again, which is wot's really important.''

The next day, Eugénie arrived in town with Manaka, who had scarcely left her side since John's death. He went everywhere with her. He didn't like coming into town but wouldn't let her go alone. She walked into "The Black Bear"—and stood still in a state of shock and disbelief. There was her dear Harry sweeping the floor while Matthew was sitting smoking his pipe and talking nineteen to the dozen with his wooden leg propped up on a table!

"I don't believe it! Am I seeing things?'' Eugénie gasped. She almost fainted, so great was her surprise.

They both looked up at Eugénie's startled exclamation.

"Harry! Am I dreaming? Is it really you?'' she cried.

With tears in his eyes, Harry held out his arms to Eugénie and she ran into them. She too was crying.

"There, there, lass, it's really me. The girls are here, too.''

Mag came running downstairs. "Luv, it's me, it's me! Let me look at ye!'' Then she also burst into tears as she hugged and kissed Eugénie.

Matthew looked at Harry. "Oi'll never understand

females! They cry when they're 'appy. Can ye beat that?" But Harry noticed that Matthew was slyly wiping away a tear or two from his own eyes.

"Oi'll go right over and fetch Miss Finn and yer sister, Eugénie, lass," he said at last.

"Oh, Matthew, thank you! I can scarce believe it's all true," Eugénie cried, her face wreathed in smiles.

She turned to embrace Mag once more. "Dear, dear Mag, you haven't changed a bit!"

"Well, luv, Oi 'ave changed a bit. Oi changed me name from Boles to Boggs." Then suddenly she spotted Manaka and screamed, "Get that 'eathen out of 'ere!" She ran behind Harry's back, peering out around his solid bulk.

"Mag, it's alright. This is my friend Manaka. He doesn't speak English too well, but he is learning. Please try and like him, for my sake. He has watched over me like a hawk since my husband died."

Mag softened immediately. "Ye poor child! Matthew told us about that kind man's death. Ye didn't know 'e sent fer us to come out 'ere fer yer sake."

"That's just the kind of thoughtful person he was— he never even hinted that he had written to you," said Eugénie softly.

"Oi expect 'e didn't want ye to be disappointed if we 'adn't come."

"Mag, did I hear you say you were now Mag *Boggs?*" Eugénie asked, suddenly harking back to what Mag had said earlier. Mag's face turned crimson.

"Aye, lass, that she is," Harry confirmed with pride.

"Well, I think it's marvellous and I must say it's about time you two came to your senses!"

"Oi'm not sure if it were sense or not," said Mag with a helpless shrug. "Oi don't know wot came over me. Oi don't know if Oi were foolish or not. Look where it's landed me." She cast a weary glance towards Manaka, who grinned at her.

"I hope you two will be comfortable living here. Moll and Marie can come and live with me at Parramatta," Eugénie suggested.

"Speaking of Marie and Moll, I do believe I hear them," said Harry, turning to the door.

Sure enough, the two ladies rushed in and there was more embracing and hugging and tears. Marie was ecstatic to see her beloved sister once again, and they sat up far into the night, talking about old times, after which Marie questioned Eugénie about her life in the colony.

When Eugénie returned to Parramatta on Monday, she took Moll and Marie with her, much to Kathleen's and Cassie's joy. After that she spent more and more time out at the Hawkesbury property and before too long, the house was standing in all its glory. She had furniture and curtains shipped out from Capetown and before long it looked like a small palace. No expense was spared. Then she moved Marie, Kathleen and Cassie out to the new house she had named "Bannion." Moll had agreed to stay at Parramatta to take care of Patrick Curran and the workers there (and also to be closer to Sydney and Matthew Skinner). Of course, she told Eugénie that she wanted to be closer to Mag and Harry, but she was determined not to let Matthew get away. She fancied him and had high hopes that one day she would become Mrs. Matthew Skinner.

Everyone had settled down in their new homes and everything seemed peaceful in New South Wales. The colony was growing and more new settlers were arriving every month or so.

One bright morning early in July Eugénie mentioned

at breakfast that she felt it was time to check on Parramatta. Marie immediately perked up. "Oh, Eugénie, I'd love to come with you! It's been so long since I had a really good chat with Moll. I can keep her company while you and Patrick attend to business."

"Why not? I think it's a splendid idea. Why don't you plan on staying with her for a bit? I'm sure she could use some female company."

Moll was chasing the chickens out of her flower garden when they rode up.

"Land sakes, 'tis good to see ye both," she cried. "Come on in the house—ye just in time fer lunch. Patrick ought to be 'ere in 'alf a mo'."

Scarcely were the words out of her mouth when Patrick Curran walked in, hat in hand.

"Mrs. McCallum, it's good to see ye. Everything's in fine fettle around here. In fact, I think we're just about ready to clear some more land and put it to use."

"Enough chit-chat now. Eat yer lunch," Moll ordered. "Ye can talk business all ye want later."

After they had eaten enough to satisfy Moll, Patrick and Eugénie rode around the farm. Her sharp eyes didn't miss a thing and she was pleased with the progress.

"Patrick, you take better care of this place than I could myself. John would have been grateful to you and proud of what you have done. Thank you."

"Thanks, Mrs. McCallum . . . What the devil!" He broke off as a company of marines rode up at a gallop.

"Ma'am, Mr. Curran, there's trouble. Bad trouble," said the captain. "Six of the most vicious convicts escaped from the stockade this morning. The last report we had on them was that they were headed in the direction of the Hawkesbury."

Eugénie felt her blood run cold. "No! Are you sure?

337

We didn't see any sign of them when we rode out here early this morning.''

"I'm afraid so, Ma'am. They broke out about three so it's possible they are holed up somewhere resting. You're very lucky you didn't run into them. They're a bad lot.''

"I'm coming with you,'' Eugénie stated flatly. "Patrick, you'd better stay here with Marie and Moll just in case they back-track.''

She jumped on her horse before anyone could stop her and galloped after the marines towards the Hawkesbury. On the way, they stopped to warn Paul and Aggie Gordon. Paul insisted on accompanying them. Eugénie's heart was pounding and she felt the same sinking sensation that had come over her when her mother and father had been murdered. They were just a few miles for "Bannion" when the acrid smell of smoke assailed their nostrils. Eugénie was filled with self-reproach. "Oh, why did I move everyone out here so far away from any kind of help?'' she moaned.

The smell of smoke grew more pungent and now they could smell burnt flesh and hear the screaming of terrified animals. The barns and other buildings were on fire and there was no sign of life.

The marines dismounted and searched among the rubble and the outlying areas while Eugénie and Paul headed for the house at a run. Eugénie almost stumbled over the figure of a woman lying in the doorway.

"My God, it's Cassie!'' she gasped. "Is she dead, Paul? I don't see any blood.''

"No, thank God. She's just out cold. I'll take care of her.'' Paul knelt beside the unconscious woman as Eugénie ran through the house, calling Kathleen. There was no response. Then she found her, lying in a pool of blood on the floor by Cassie's bed. A hysterical scream soared from Eugénie's throat. She was still screaming when Paul ran into the room.

"Eugénie, for the love of God be still," he shouted, taking hold of her trembling arms. His voice brought her to a certain level of calm.

"Paul, tell me she isn't dead. Say she isn't dead!" Eugénie begged.

"It's all right. She's alive, but heaven only knows how," said Paul as he quickly examined Kathleen. "The poor girl has been through the devil of a time! She's been raped—not once, but many times. What an ordeal for that innocent girl to go through!"

Eugénie burst into tears. "I'll kill them, I swear I'll kill them!" she sobbed.

"She'll be fine," Paul assured her. "I've managed to get the bleeding under control."

He lifted Kathleen gently on to the bed and covered her up. "She'll be all right now. We'd better see to Cassie and the others, God help them."

They had just come into the kitchen when two of the marines came to the house with Ben Dixon, one of Eugénie's convict helpers who had been wounded. He was bleeding profusely from the shoulder.

"It looks like they've gone, Ma'am, so we're going to head out after them. We'll check back with you later. They shouldn't be too hard to find—they've left a pretty good trail behind them," the captain told Eugénie.

Paul bandaged Ben Dixon's shoulder and Eugénie attended to Cassie, who soon regained consciousness. She was terrified and furious all at the same time.

" 'Ave they gone? Oh, me poor wee lassie! Where's me poor wee lassie?" she wailed.

"There now Cassie, it's all right. They've gone and the marines are pursing them. Go on upstairs, there's a good girl, and take care of Miss Kathleen. That poor child has been through a hell of a time and she's going to need all the love and attention she can get to bring her out of this," said Paul.

Cassie did as Paul had asked. She sat by Kathleen with tears streaming down her face and twisting her apron into knots. She kept murmuring, "Me poor wee lass. Me poor wee lass!"

Eugénie looked anxiously at Paul. *"Will* she be all right?"

"We can only hope and pray," he said grimly. Then they walked outside to look around.

Ben Dixon came after them, looking very shame-faced.

"Oi'm sorry Oi didn't try to go up to the 'ouse. But t'weren't no good. They surprised us and when Oi felt me own blood runnin' Oi just took to me heels and ran. Oi didn't know where Oi wuz goin'."

"I understand, Ben," said Eugénie wearily. "It's just as well you did. Have you seen any signs of Vinnie?"

"Aye, Miss, but Oi wouldn't look if I was you. They cut orf 'is 'ead. 'E's not a pretty sight. Oi don't rightly know if there's anyone left alive."

"Eugénie, go back to the house," Paul commanded. "Ben and I will look around some more."

In a daze, she did as he suggested and took Cassie's place while that poor soul fixed a pot of tea, the life-saver of the British in times of crisis.

After thirty minutes of searching Paul and Ben had only found two men alive, both in bad shape. They dragged cots into the kitchen and laid the wounded men on them. Ben and Paul had decided it would be better to barricade themselves in one room in case the convicts decided to return. Then Paul went upstairs to get Kathleen and carried her to a sofa he had dragged in from the parlor.

340

Now that everything seemed to be under control, Eugénie suddenly felt very ill. She staggered outside and sank to her knees in the dirt. Everything was slipping away into a terrible blackness. She forced herself to cling to consciousness. At last the spell of faintness passed and she looked around at the smouldering barns. She felt a great sadness now. All her anger seemed to have disappeared. She knew those convicts had suffered and that their every instinct was to escape—but why murder and torture innocent people in the process? All the terrible memories of seeing her parents' bodies butchered almost beyond recognition seared her heart and mind. She had fled France because of bloodshed and cruelty. Was this new land to be just like it, built on hatred, fear and bitter resentment? It couldn't be allowed to happen! With that firm resolve, she went back into the house and drew up a chair close to Kathleen while Paul did his best to make the two wounded men comfortable for the long night ahead.

Hours passed, hours in which every minute seemed like an eternity to Eugénie. Her muscles were tense and every one of her nerves was on edge. Her ears were alert to every sound. Cassie sat in her rocking chair by the fire and snored loudly. Kathleen, wrapped in blankets, seemed to be sleeping more peacefully. Paul was fighting for the two men's lives. Eugénie tried to help, but in spite of their efforts, one of them died about two-thirty that morning. By then Eugénie's nerves were in very bad shape. Every noise made her jump. She was filled with fear that the convicts would come back. Her eyes tried to find the source of every sound, wide open in terror.

After a while she found it impossible to stay in the kitchen any longer with that dread feeling in the pit of her stomach that something even more awful was going to happen. Without a word to Paul, she got John's gun out of the cupboard in the hall and went slowly through the house, checking all the windows and doors. But her ragged nerves overcame her and she was forced to flee back to the companionship of the others in the kitchen. By now, every noise sounded like a cannon shot to her. She put her hands over her ears to drown out Cassie's snores and the groans of the wounded man. Paul, sensing her distress, came over and put his arms around her.

"Eugénie, love, sleep. Ben is keeping watch outside and I'm quite sure the convicts won't dare to come back," he told her gently.

Sleep would have been most welcome, and for a moment she let her weary body rest against his. He thought he had succeeded in calming her, but then she pulled away.

"Paul, I can't sleep. I have a strange foreboding. I can't quite explain it. I must keep watch. I must! Oh, of only it were morning! If only the marines would come back!" she moaned.

Somehow Eugénie managed to get through the next few hours. It was close to dawn when she decided to take Ben a cup of tea and then walk through the house again.

Ben gratefully accepted the tea, warming his hands at the same time on the hot cup. He took a swig of it and sighed. "Thanks, Ma'am, Oi wuz jest about ready fer somethin'. There's nought stirrin' out there. 'Tis *too* quiet, if ye arsks me."

She left him and, taking her gun from the kitchen table, once more made her way from room to room. On the way back to the kitchen she heard a slight noise, which to her nervously listening ears, seemed like a clap of thunder. The noise seemed to come from the direction of the storage room in the back of the house. She crept towards the door softly, like a cat, pausing now and then to listen. Her heart seemed to be beating like a thousand drums. Surely it must be heard by whomever was hiding in there. She opened the door cautiously. All seemed quiet and she was about to turn away when a big, hairy hand shot out of the darkness and clamped around her mouth. Her heart seemed to stop and her blood to freeze inside her body, but with the superhuman strength born of sheer desperation she bit the fingers that were across her mouth, and broke away. The hairy hand was quickly removed, accompanied by a cry of pain.

Her eyes having now become accustomed to the dim light, she now beheld a filthy, hairy beast of a man, reeking of rum and sweat. She levelled the gun at him but he was too quick for her. With a kick he sent the gun flying across the room. Then he grabbed her in a vice-like grip. "Don't make a sound of Oi'll break yer bloody neck," he growled.

His hands circled her throat and she could feel his thumbs pressing against her windpipe. She couldn't have screamed even if she had wanted to. He turned her roughly around and his hands jerked forward, ripping her bodice from neck to waist. "Miss 'Igh and Mighty, we'll 'ave some action now!"

He pulled her down to the floor. Then his great, bulky, sweaty body came down upon her. She felt his swollen manhood pressing against her and at last she had the will to struggle. But he hit her hard and she lay there helpless, stunned, thinking, "Is this how it is all going to end?"

She closed her eyes in revulsion as he pressed his slobbering lips to her bruised mouth. In a state of semi-consciousness she seemed to drift away from her attacker. She was running through the woods at Poissy, listening to the birds and feeling the sunshine on her face, running towards the stables and her beloved father. Then she heard a muffled scream. She opened her eyes and in the moonlight saw a face with a terrible look of surprise and pain on it. It was an evil face and she closed her eyes once more, trying to recapture the beauty of the woods and reach her father's protective arms. She heard a voice which seemed to be calling from a great distance. The voice was calling her name. In her delirious state she imagined that she heard the voice of her dear Papa. There was that special sound of love in the voice, though the words sounded a little strange. Her father hadn't known how to speak English!

"Eugénie, dearest love, speak to me."

"Oui, Papa, Je ne me sens pas bien, mais ne vous inquiétez pas."

She sighed and smiled contentedly. Everything would be all right, now that her dear Papa was here to take care of things . . .

Paul picked her up in his arms. There were tears of anxiety and rage in his eyes.

"Oh, my lovely girl! What has that brute done to you?" he moaned.

Eugénie murmured sleepily, "Hold me close, Papa. Hold me close. I had such a dreadful dream. It scared me so . . ."

Paul knew terror at that moment. He feared that Eugénie's mind had become unhinged. He held her in his arms, praying that she would recover. He was completely absorbed in his anguished prayers when Eugénie opened her eyes.

"Paul, what on earth are you doing?" she asked in her normal voice.

"Oh my love, you're all right! Thank God! Oh, Thank God!"

Eugénie looked down at her torn dress. Then she saw the body of her attacker and the horror came rushing back to her. Trembling she asked, "Is . . . is he . . . dead?"

Paul answered grimly. "He'll never bother anyone ever again."

She began to tremble all over. Suddenly she felt very cold. Paul put his arms around her shivering body and now she felt warm and secure. He held her so tightly that every feeling of chill and fright was expelled. He kissed her eyelids and whispered soothing words. When her body had relaxed somewhat, he took her face between his beautiful, strong hands and smiled gently. She was puzzled, for she saw something in his eyes that she had never seen before. Surely not controlled passion —no, Paul loved her as he would love a sister or a very dear friend. Or so she told herself, though there was a disturbing flutter in the pit of her stomach that she refused to acknowledge.

He lifted her up in his strong arms and carried her back to the kitchen where Cassie stood with her eyes full of fright. "My Lord! What's happened to me little lady?" she cried.

"She's all right now, Cassie. See if you can find some brandy," Paul ordered.

Cassie knew Moll had hidden a jug somewhere in the kitchen the last time she had visited, but it took her a good ten minutes to find it. She poured some in a mug and held it out with trembling hands to Eugénie. The poor woman was shocked and horrified at seeing her mistress in a dirty, torn, bloodstained dress. There were purple shadows under Eugénie's eyes and the flickering light of the oil lamp only made her look much more haggard.

Paul was looking at Eugénie with such love in his eyes when she happened to look up at him that she felt quite light-headed. She turned her eyes away. She couldn't look at him. He made her feel very strange.

"Paul, I thought you were my father back there when you rescued me," she said.

"I know. You called me 'Papa.' I was afraid that you had lost your mind."

She looked up at his strong, loving face and thought how much her father would have liked this man. They were two of a kind, although perhaps Paul would be a lot harder to handle. She nestled in his sheltering arms, her eyelids drooping with exhaustion.

She was completely unaware of the effect she was having on Paul. He was devastated. His need for her wracked his mind and body with an agony of frustration. The fragrance of her body sent his senses reeling. He could no longer control himself, and whispered, "I love you, Eugénie. God, how I love you! No man will ever love you as much as I do now. I doubt if any man could."

But she gave no reply. She had fallen asleep in his arms. He sighed as he held her. What a blow fate had dealt him! In all his life he had not met a woman he could really love and now that he finally had, her heart belonged to another. At that moment he hated André and was consumed with jealousy. He had forgotten Cassie's presence and that sweet old lady was sitting in her rocking chair with a very puzzled look on her face.

The remainder of the night he spent in a fight for the life of his remaining patient. About ten o'clock the next morning, the marines finally returned. The convicts had all been accounted for. Three were dead, one had been captured alive and unhurt, one was alive but wounded so badly that he wasn't expected to live and the one Paul had shot lay dead in the yard. The long, terror-filled nightmare was over—or was it?

Chapter 28

Dr. White washed his hands in the basin and looked over his glasses at Eugénie. "I'm sorry to say this, but that poor girl is pregnant. No doubt about it."

Eugénie turned pale. "Not Kathleen! How could God allow this to happen? It just isn't fair!" she cried, distraught.

"Lass, don't blame God for what man did," the doctor said sternly.

"How am I ever going to tell her? Will you, Dr. White? Please?"

"No, lass, I fear it is up to you. Perhaps you should ask Aggie Gordon to help. She might supply the mother image better than you, and I think poor Kathleen needs a mother desperately right now. That girl has never been strong, and I'm very much afraid this pregnancy might prove to be too much for her. God only knows what the shock will do to her when she finds out!"

"Don't worry, Dr. White," Eugénie sighed. "I'll take care of her."

He looked at her kindly. "I know you will, lass. I know. Now be off. Go fetch Miss Gordon. I'll stay with Kathleen until you get back."

Eugénie saddled her horse and took the sad news to Aggie Gordon. Paul wasn't at home. That good lady wasted no time in ordering her carriage, and they returned quickly to "Bannion." Dr. White met them at the door.

"Ah, Aggie, I'm glad to see you. Young Kathleen is going to need your strong common sense. She's such a frail little thing, poor lass."

Aggie Gordon nodded without a word and went in to Kathleen.

Kathleen's eyes lit up with pleasure when she saw Aggie. "Oh, how marvellous to see you, dear Miss Gordon," she said softly.

"How are you, child?" Aunt Aggie asked.

"I have been so sick lately. I can't imagine what's wrong. Perhaps it's just nerves after . . ." She blushed and lowered her eyes.

"Yes, child, I know," Aunt Aggie took a deep breath. "Kathleen, your father was one of the bravest men I ever knew, and I know his daughter must be, too."

Kathleen grew pale and her eyes widened. "Miss Gordon, what are you trying to tell me? Am I going to die? What did Dr. White tell you?"

"Child, it's not nerves. And you are not going to die. You are going to have a baby," said Aunt Aggie calmly.

Kathleen let out a wild cry. "No! No!"

Aunt Aggie's heart was wrenched with pity for the girl, and in the hall Eugénie held back her tears when she heard that cry. She wanted to rush into the room but Dr. White held her back. Aunt Aggie pulled herself together, sat down on the bed and gripped Kathleen's hands hard.

"Now listen to me, young woman. Just stop pitying yourself for a moment and think of the mite you are carrying. That poor little thing did nothing to deserve this, no more than you. It's going to need all the love you can give it."

"But . . . a . . . but a convict for a father! Those horrible men! I . . . I don't even know which of them it might be." Kathleen shuddered and broke down in hysterical sobs.

Aunt Aggie spoke sternly. "Now listen, girl. Yes, it's true a convict fathered the child, but don't forget you are its mother. The seed of John McCallum will be in it too. It's up to you to produce a son or a daughter that will carry on the name of McCallum with pride. That child, young Kathleen, will walk in his grandfather's footsteps, I'm sure. Now are you going to be your father's daughter, Kathleen McCallum?"

There was a long silence as Kathleen's sobs gradually subsided. Finally she nodded and tried bravely to smile through her tears. Aunt Aggie brushed the tears away and opened the door.

"You can come in now," she said quietly.

Dr. White felt Kathleen's pulse and nodded in satisfaction. Then Eugénie rushed over and took the girl in her arms. "It's going to be a wonderful baby, you'll see," she promised. "And it will have more people to love than any other baby in the colony!"

After that the McCallum household looked forward to the birth of the baby. Even Manaka was excited. He now spent his time hovering between Eugénie and Kathleen. The baby was expected around May.

Meanwhile, Sydney was growing by leaps and bounds. More free settlers drifted to the shores of New South Wales, adding to its prosperity. Harry and Matthew were thriving. Business was booming and they were now able to afford to hire a young man to help take care of things during the day.

Matthew wandered out to Parramatta quite

frequently. He was really enamored of Moll but couldn't quite pluck up his courage to speak to her of his feelings. Moll knew how he felt but kept up the pretense of being completely unaware. She had settled down very well. Harry and Marie were also very happy, but Mag still was not quite ready to acknowledge Sydney as her home.

As for Eugénie, as long as her herds increased and the crops grew she seemed content. Only Harry was aware that underneath her seeming contentment was an aching emptiness which she tried to fill by concentrating on achieving more material wealth. She had worked hard repairing the damage done at the Hawkesbury property, but had moved the household back to Parramatta because of Kathleen's pregnancy. She had bought more land to add to the acreage at the Hawkesbury and had bought property in Sydney. On Paul's advice, she invested in several hundred acres adjoining her own land at the Hawkesbury so that Kathleen's baby would have an inheritance other than money.

Harry was greatly disturbed by Eugénie's drive for wealth. He guessed that her desire was to become wealthy enough so that she could return to England and somehow win André de Varney back. He worried about her until he couldn't keep silent any longer. One weekend when she had made an unexpected trip to Sydney, he broached the subject.

"Are you ever going to be satisfied, Eugénie?"

She knew exactly what he meant. Her face was like stone when she answered, "Yes, Harry. I'll be satisfied when I have great wealth, so much wealth that even London society will have to acknowledge me."

"London or André, lass?" asked her old friend shrewdly. She didn't answer, but Harry knew the answer and he was saddened.

As things turned out, Eugénie did not have to go to England to see André de Varney again. One stifling hot day, she rode into Sydney and arrived at "The Black Bear" exhausted and thirsty.

"Mag, love, would you bring me a lemonade? I'm dying of thirst," she said.

"Eugénie, it's just too 'ot fer ye to go traipsin' through the country like a wild thing. Ye'll kill yerself," Mag reprimanded.

She caught Harry's eye and motioned for him to follow her. He ignored her deliberately until Mag said in a peeved voice, " 'Arry Boggs, ye great big lug, come with me and hand me down the box of lemons."

When she got him in the pantry, she whispered, " 'Arry, are ye goin' to tell 'er?"

"Tell her? Tell her what?" asked Harry uncomfortably.

"Men! Are ye all dense? Tell 'er about André de whatever his name is—about 'im 'avin' come out 'ere."

"Yes, I suppose I had better. She'll find out sooner or later, and it would be better if I told her first."

That night, after Matthew had left for home and "The Black Bear" had closed for the night, Harry took the opportunity to talk to Eugénie. She was about to go up to bed when he called out to her.

"Eugénie, love, sit down a few minutes with me while I smoke my pipe."

Eugénie grinned at him. "Now Harry, what is it? You have something on your mind, I can tell. I know you too well."

It was too late to pull back now. Harry said, "Lass, I have to tell you that André and Lady Angela arrived in Sydney two days ago. I believe they are staying at the Governor's house."

Eugénie couldn't believe her ears. Her heart pounded wildly with excitement. "Harry, are you telling me that André is here? *Here* in New South Wales?"

"Aye, lass, I'm sorry to say. I *also* said that his wife was with him. His *wife*, Eugénie. So whatever ideas you may have flitting through your head right now, get rid of them. He never was for you and he never will be."

Eugénie was silent. Harry knew her so well. It was uncanny how he could read her most secret thoughts. She looked at him and his face was etched with lines of worry.

"Harry, don't look so glum," she said, forcing herself to sound calm. "I probably shan't see him very much, if at all. You know I'll be out at 'Bannion' a great deal for the next few months or so. I'm glad you reminded me of Angela, though. If he's happy, I wouldn't dream of interfering."

"And if he's not? Never mind—don't answer that. I'm glad you'll be busy. If he wants to get in touch with you, I'm quite sure he'll find you. Promise me, Eugénie, you won't go looking for him."

She kissed his cheek lovingly and said, "I promise."

October 7, 1792—"Bannion"
I'm a nervous wreck. Every time I see a rider in the distance I think it might be André, but as yet he hasn't come. I'm working night and day in an effort to keep him out of my mind, but it's impossible. If only I hadn't promised Harry, I'd go and find him. My pride doesn't seem to exist where André is concerned. All I can think of is his touch and the feel of his lips and his warm, strong body next to mine. God forgive me for my thoughts! I'm trying. I really am.

October 19, 1792
I was painting one of the barns today when Paul rode up. He was in a very good mood.

*"Can you come down here, Eugénie?" he asked. "I
don't wish to strain my neck looking up at you."*

*We sat on the veranda drinking Cassie's refreshing
lemonade. I knew he had come for a purpose—Paul
seldom visits just to pass the time of day. Finally I asked
him—"What's on your mind, Paul?"*

*"If you must know, I've had an invitation to dinner at
Government House. Since Aunt Aggie doesn't feel up to
going, I was wondering if you'd want to accompany me.
Since Crose and I don't exactly see eye to eye, I hope
you'll say yes. In your company I might be able to enjoy
the evening."*

*My thoughts raced pell-mell. Here was the perfect
opportunity to see André. Surely he would be there. I
wouldn't really be breaking my promise since I hadn't
sought this invitation. It was almost as if fate had
decreed that we should meet again. I didn't hesitate.*

*"Paul, I'd love to go. I need a bit of excitement.
When is the dinner to be given?"*

*"Next Saturday. Shall I pick you up here on Friday?"
he asked.*

*"No. I'll go to Parramatta tomorrow and then ride
into Sydney. We can meet at 'The Black Bear,' " I told
him.*

*Paul left and my heart pounded with excitement. Oh,
God, I can't wait to see André!*

Eugénie did go back to Parramatta the next day and
soon drove Kathleen and Marie ragged by constantly
asking their advice about what they thought she should
wear. Then just as they thought she had made up her
mind, she'd change it again. At last she settled on a blue
silk that matched her eyes. Then for hours she fussed
with her toilette and brushed her hair until it shone. She
despaired of her work-worn hands, and rubbed them
with endless creams and lotions. Kathleen, Marie and
even Moll were glad when Thursday came and they saw
Eugénie on her way with Manaka by her side. Her
precious dress was wrapped carefully and placed in the
back of the wagon.

When she arrived at "The Black Bear" Mag and Harry, as usual, were overjoyed to see her. But their job quickly turned to apprehension when they learned why she had come to Sydney.

"No good can come of this, Mag," Harry said darkly to his wife when they were alone that night.

"It was all Oi could do to keep me mouth shut from givin' 'er a piece of me mind," Mag agreed morosely.

Saturday evening came at last and Eugénie spent three hours getting ready. Looking in the mirror, she could hardly believe her eyes. The reflection that looked back at her was of a breathtakingly exquisite woman. Was it really she, that lovely lady in her low-cut gown? It made her waist look so tiny, and her breasts so full. That lady with the sapphires sparkling in her ears and around her neck—was it possible it was she—Eugénie Fabré McCallum? Surely it must be a mirage! Her wondering was put to flight by Mag's shout.

"Are ye goin' to tear yerself away from yon mirror long enough to go to dinner? Paul's down 'ere waitin' fer ye."

Eugénie sailed down the stairs, feeling like a queen. Her face was aglow and incredibly lovely. She was vibrating with the exciting anticipation of seeing her deerest love once more. She gave Paul a gloriously radiant smile but she wasn't seeing him. He took her arm and hoped she wouldn't hear the pounding of his heart.

"Well, be orf ye two and 'ave a marvellous old time. Don't stuff yerself, Eugénie. That dress would never stand fer it," Mag admonished.

Eugénie laughed and Paul led her to the waiting carriage and helped her into it. Then he took the reins in his capable hands. Soon they were at Government House, where Lieutenant Governor Crose greeted them with surprising warmth.

A servant took their cloaks and the lieutenant governor escorted them to the drawing-room where the other guests were gathered. Eugénie knew she looked her best, and with that knowledge her whole personality took on added vivaciousness and sparkle. She felt herself tremble inwardly when the Lieutenant Governor presented herself and Paul to André and Angela. Her eyes met André's for a breathless moment; then André bowed low over Eugénie's hand and whispered how marvellous she looked. Eugénie blushed. That blush was not lost on Paul, who cursed himself for bringing her here. If he had known they would meet André de Varney he would never have asked Eugénie to come. Then the terrible, incredibly painful thought tormented his mind. Had she known he would be here? Damn her if she had!

Angela spoke to Eugénie with a great deal of warmth and showed absolutely no sign that she was aware of the former relationship between her husband and Eugénie. As for the dazzling Mrs. McCallum, she gave not a thought of Lady Angela. Though she chatted politely to her, Eugénie's entire awareness was centered on André.

When dinner was announced and they proceeded to the dining-room, André and Eugénie found themselves at opposite ends of the long table. Nevertheless each was in full view of the other. Eugénie's eyes were drawn to his like a piece of metal to a powerful magnet. In spite of this attraction, she managed to play the part of the sparkling society belle, dazzling everyone with her wit and vivacity and all the time very much aware that André's grey eyes were watching her every move and his ears straining to hear every word that fell from her lips.

Dinner came to an end at last and everyone returned to the drawing-room. André without a word to his wife came immediately to Eugénie's side. Paul, watching them, was tortured by the demon jealousy. Eugénie was standing so close to André that her soft hair brushed against his cheek. Her eyes, glowing with happiness and adoration, maddened Paul and at the same time sent fire coursing through his veins and he wanted her more than ever. When he heard her melodious voice raised in laughter he could stand it no longer. He strode across the room and stood before her like an avenging angel. She knew he was upset, but chose to ignore it, never dreaming that she was the cause.

"Eugénie, I'm afraid it's time for us to leave," he grated between clenched teeth.

"Oh Paul, surely not! It's far too early," Eugénie pouted. "The fun is just beginning."

His voice cut like a knife as he replied, "I said it was time to leave, Eugénie. Good evening, sir." He bowed briefly to André and took Eugénie's arm in a vise-like grip. She flinched in pain but, not wanting to cause a scene, had no choice but to go with him. They said their farewells to Crose and the other guests and Paul escorted her to their carriage in silence as Eugénie fumed.

Once outside, Eugénie's temper erupted. "I have never—*never,* do you hear—been to humiliated in all my life! How dare you treat me like that! What right have you to drag me away like a naughty child?" she hissed.

"Madame, your behavior tonight was outrageous. How dare you flaunt yourself at that boor with his poor wife looking on? How dare you, Madame, make such a spectacle of yourself and embarrass that poor woman? And lastly, Madame, how dare you use me for your own devious purposes?" Paul's voice was icy cold, yet trembling with burning anger.

Eugénie was so taken aback by his rage that she could

only retort in a feeble voice, "Paul, I . . . didn't . . ."

"Madame, you most certainly did! Is it possible you weren't even aware of it? Are you still so besotted by that foolish fop?"

All at once she too was filled with rage and lashed out at him. The slap she dealt him seemed to signal the heavens to open, for rain descended on them with such violence that they were soaked to the skin in moments. The downpour did nothing to cool them tempers, however.

"Get in the carriage, Eugénie," Paul ordered.

Ignoring him, she ran in the opposite direction with her skirts held high.

"Damn that girl!" His temper completely out of control now he jumped into the carriage, whipped up the horses and followed her. When he caught up with her, he pulled the horses to a halt, leaped down from the carriage, grabbed her and practically hurled her inside. She noticed that his face was like granite and his eyes ice-cold and unreadable. Not one bit unnerved by his temper, she wickedly needled him.

"Sir, surely it can't be that you are jealous? Not you, who has ice-water in your veins instead of blood." She tossed back her head and laughed at him.

"Damn you, Eugénie! Yes I'm jealous! I'm jealous of any man who stands beside you, of any man who touches you, while I must stifle the slightest evidence of my yearning for you. Tormenter! You must have known what you were doing to me. I must have shown it quite plainly, like a bloody fool. One doesn't feel such anger, such tenderness, such need for a person without showing it. One emotion could perhaps be hidden but three such powerful ones? Impossible!"

Before she had time to collect her startled wits they pulled up in front of "The Black Bear." Eugénie felt a

358

desperate need to get away from him and jumped down from the carriage. But before she could reach the door, Paul had caught up with her and, pulling her roughly to him, he pressed his mouth urgently to hers. She struggled to keep her control as his lips, warm and moist, rained kisses on her face, her neck, her bare shoulders. She was conscious of the racing and thudding of his heart and very much aware to her astonishment that her own was throbbing outrageously. She felt light-headed and wanted to kiss him back. But just as she was about to surrender to passion, he suddenly pushed her away, climbed into the carriage and soon was swallowed up in the darkness of the rainy night.

For a long time after he had gone, Eugénie stood in the rain, trying to regain her composure. She told herself that he must have been drunk and she chided herself for allowing herself to respond to him. She should have realized his condition and not needled him so.

"I'll apologize the next time I see him," she told herself. "We'll be the best of friends again." With these comforting thoughts, she went inside. But after she had gotten out of her wet clothes and was snug and dry in bed, sleep would not come. She lay awake for many hours, still feeling the touch of his lips on hers . . .

Chapter 29

André wasted no time in riding out to "Bannion." Eugénie saw him coming and ran to meet him. As André came towards her, his hair glowed like a golden halo in the sunlight. He whispered her name and she rushed to him, her heart beating with a passion long suppressed and eager to be released. He showered kisses on her forehead, stroked her soft hair, and then her arms reached around his neck and she drew his lips to hers. Ripples of excitement flowed from one to the other. How long she had waited for this moment! She moaned with desire and they clung to each other fiercely, reluctant to break the magic of their embrace.

André was the first to speak. "God, Eugénie, it's been so long! Too long. I want you so much."

"And I you, *mon amour,*" she moaned.

"I have to leave you soon but I'll be back, Eugénie. I can't do without you."

"Why did you come to New South Wales? I still can't quite believe you're here," she said breathlessly.

"Why, for the adventure of it, my love. I got so damned tired of Lady Jerningham's hovering and Angela's parents always dropping in unexpectedly, never leaving me alone. I'll make my own decisions out here."

"You're wonderful, André," Eugénie sighed. "New South Wales is a hard land, but I know you will prove yourself equal to the task of making your own way. I certainly haven't regretted coming out here. Life is so very different, André! Here everyone is expected to work hard, regardless of whether they are titled or not. We all mix quite freely. Here land and money count, not the family one was born into. Why, even the convicts will get their chance. When they regain their freedom, they'll be able to get land and direct their efforts to the good of the country. It may not seem so now, André, but someday this will be a country we can all be proud of!"

During the next three months, Eugénie spent most of her time at "Bannion." André became a frequent visitor and they went for long walks or sometimes enjoyed a ride together. Her life was sheer heaven. She had eyes and thoughts for no one but André and her ears were deaf to the admonishments of her sister and her friends. Kathleen was the only one who did not seem to judge her, and for this Eugénie was grateful. Harry spoke his mind in no uncertain terms, but it did not do one bit of good.

"I love him Harry. I can't help myself," she said.

"Lass, you're in love with a dream that you won't let go of," Harry told her.

"No, Harry, I really do love him with all my heart!"

"Aye, Eugénie, but does *he* love *you?*"

She didn't answer him. Of course André loved her. Hadn't he told her so over and over? Yes, she was walking on clouds. She gave no thought to Angela or to the fact that she hadn't seen Paul since the ill-fated night of the dinner.

The months passed and it was May. The anticipation of the new baby at the McCallum house was at its peak. Eugénie stayed at Parramatta and didn't go too far from the house. The women were busy making baby clothes and coaxing Kathleen to choose a name. She finally decided, after careful thought, that if it was a boy he should be given the name David John McCallum. If it was a girl, it was to be named Catherine Ann McCallum after her mother. So far, in spite of her delicate health, she had been doing quite well. She hadn't suffered from morning sickness for a long time and had been quite well mentally throughout her pregnancy, thanks to Aunt Aggie.

Eugénie was down at the stable currying Sultan, her favorite horse, and talking to him fondly, when Marie came running and shouting breathlessly, "Kathleen's in labor! Come quickly, Eugénie! It doesn't look good. She seems to be in a great deal of pain."

The cold hand of fear clutched at Eugénie's heart. "Ride over and fetch Paul. He'll know what to do. Hurry, Marie—we've no time to lose!"

Marie rode off to the Gordons' and Eugénie quickly washed up and ran to Kathleen's room. Cassie was hovering over the suffering girl.

"Well, my love," Eugénie said cheerfully, "It won't be long now before you hold your baby in your arms."

Kathleen smiled weakly but then her sweet face was wracked with a spasm of pain.

They waited for Paul impatiently for an hour or more, an hour of sheer torment for Eugénie and Cassie watching Kathleen suffering and not being able to help. But at last Paul came. After he had examined Kathleen, his face looked grim, but he spoke words of encouragement.

"Kathleen, it's difficult right now, but I assure you,

when you see your baby, all the pain will be forgotten."

Eugénie sponged her pain-wracked body and tried to comfort her. At times the pain was so intense Kathleen screamed. Her screams reached the kitchen where Marie, Moll and Manaka waited. Tears trickled from their eyes and Manaka covered his ears to shut out the awful cries.

Eugénie cried out, "Oh, why doesn't that baby come? *Mon Dieu,* it is taking an eternity!" Her heart was rent in two watching the tortured face of this girl who was so dear to her heart. Paul knotted two ropes to the head of the bed and put the ends in Kathleen's hands.

"Pull on these when the pains come, there's a good girl. It will help a little."

"Can't you give her something to ease the pain? Anything?" Eugénie pleaded.

Paul shook his head.

The hours of pain dragged on but, at long last, on a final wave of terrible agony, a little red, shrieking baby boy came into the world. Cassie took the baby, cleaned him and wrapped him in a soft blanket, while Paul took care of Kathleen. The poor girl had fallen into merciful unconsciousness. Her face was drawn in pain and her eyes in their dark sockets were sunken. When she regained consciousness, her voice was terrified and terribly weak.

"Eugénie! Eugénie!"

"I'm here, love," Eugénie whispered.

"My baby, Eugénie?"

"*Chérie,* it's a boy. A perfect beauty, just like his mother. Now rest, please, darling."

Kathleen's eyes filled with tears. "Please—let me hold him."

Eugénie looked at Paul. He nodded and she placed the tiny bundle in Kathleen's arms. Her pale face lit up with a wonderful smile. Then she sighed and was still. Eugénie screamed, "Kathleen! Oh dear God, *no!*"

Paul gently pulled her away and Cassie took the baby from his poor dead mother's arms. Paul held Eugénie and murmured, "Eugénie, I'm so sorry. There's nothing more we can do."

They buried Kathleen beside her father near the banks of the Hawkesbury river. It rained and a sombre yet peaceful gloom pervaded all things. Even the trees were dark in color, and seemed mournful. The wind and rain wreathed the branches into strange, spectral shapes that seemed to share in the sadness of untimely death and joined with the mourners in their sorrow.

The baby was christened a few days later and given the name David John McCallum. It would indeed have been a sad household but for the presence of that "bonnie wee laddie," as his "Uncle" Matthew fondly called him. Yes, there was no doubt, the child was deeply loved. Little Andrew Crandell was fascinated by the tiny creature. Rachel was pregnant again and hoped for a girl. Yes, Eugénie thought, life has a way of going on, regardless of our grief, and somehow we are compelled to endure in spite of ourselves.

The weeks that followed were sad ones for Eugénie. Every part of the house reminded her of Kathleen until it became so unbearable that she moved Cassie, Marie and the baby back to "Bannion." André resumed his visits there and helped her to forget her sorrow. She was proud of "Bannion." It had become one of the most resplendent properties in the colony. A long, winding driveway led up to the two-storied house with its wide balconies looking down over lawns that were just now beginning to take shape, fringed by giant eucalyptus trees, and looking towards the Hawkesbury river in the distance. As John had wished, the house had been built on a hill away from the river, yet one could see the shimmering waters from every front window of the house.

André was impressed as she had meant him to be. Ben Dixon, who had more or less taken over Vinnie McDonald's duties as overseer under Patrick Curran's supervision, wasn't at all charmed by André. In fact he showed his contempt of him in many ways, though he was very careful not to let Eugénie see. One thing he tried to do was to see that André was seldom left alone with Eugénie.

It now struck André that Eugénie was a very wealthy woman and it made him see her in a different light. After their first delirious meeting at "Bannion" they had kept their relationship gay and frivolous, but now he was beginning to think a future with her just might be possible.

They were down by the river one day, walking and chatting about the old days in France. Without warning, he reached for her hand and they stopped and looked into each other's eyes.

"You are enchanting, *chérie,*" he murmured. "When I saw you at the Governor's house that night, I thought I was dreaming. But if I was, I didn't want to wake up. I realized then how much I had missed you. Is there a chance you might still love me, Eugénie? Say you do!"

Eugénie had been waiting to hear him say something like this for so long. Tears came to her beautiful eyes, but strangely the feeling of elation that she should have felt was missing.

"Oh, my dearest Eugénie!"

Before she could speak, his lips were upon her, touching first her mouth then her eyes and then, more demanding and hungrily, her lips once move. But she didn't feel the same passion that she had felt just a few months ago. Perhaps she was numb. She had waited for André's love for so long. He didn't seem to notice her lack of passion but continued to murmur endearments and shower her with kisses.

"What about Angela?" she managed to say at last.

"Angela? Don't worry about her, *chérie*. I can only think of you and how very much I love you."

Before any more could be said, they were interrupted by Manaka.

"Madami, Missy Rachel at house," he said.

"Manaka, tell her I'll be right there."

"Darling, I suppose I must leave you now—but remember I love you, Eugénie. I love you so much. We must find a way to be together!"

He looked so handsome and boyish. His golden hair gleamed in the sunlight. For a moment she felt some of the old stirrings she had felt so long ago. Tenderly she pushed away a lock of his hair and gave him a long, lingering kiss. "Goodbye, *mon chér.*"

On the ride back to the house, Eugénie wondered why it was that she didn't feel radiantly happy. Hadn't she wanted André's love all these miserable, long, painful years? But one niggling question gnawed at her—how could he dismiss Angela so easily, as if she were a rag doll of no consequence? She remembered how very pleasant Angela had been at Lieutenant Governor Crose's dinner, not one bit snobbish, and it bothered her that André could treat her so shabbily.

She brushed these thoughts aside and spent the next few hours enjoying Rachel's visit. But before Rachel left she had decided she must see André as soon as possible, and so she returned to Parramatta with her friend. The following day she went into Sydney. She was so disturbed by her lack of response to André's lovemaking and his declaration of love that she had to see him.

"Perhaps," she told herself, "I have been working too hard. When I see him again, everything will be wonderful."

Harry and Mag were, as always, happy to see her. Mag fixed a big pot of tea and they chatted for hours after Mag and Harry had set up the tavern for the evening rush of business. Then Eugénie began to yawn.

"I'm so sleepy all of a sudden. Would you mind if I lie down for a while?"

"Aye, do that luv. Oi'll wake ye in time fer supper," Mag said.

Eugénie lay down on her bed but she really wasn't tired enough to sleep. Her mind was in a turmoil. How was she going to get a message to André? She had been mulling this problem over in her mind for about an hour when there was a knock at the door.

"Eugénie, let me in." Eugénie opened the door in amazement. Why in the world was Mag climbing the stairs? She always made good use of her lungs.

"What's wrong?" she asked.

"Sssh!" Mag came in quietly and closed the door. "She's 'ere."

"Who's here?"

"It's 'er ladyship, that's who. She's 'ere in me parlor!"

Eugénie gasped. "What in the world is Angela doing here? How on earth did she know I was here? Surely she doesn't suspect."

"Aow! Oi told ye, but ye wouldn't listen to me," said Mag righteously.

"Mag, we've done nothing wrong, really."

"Humph!"

"Now Mag Boggs, just what do you mean by that 'humph'?"

"If the cap fits, wear it, that's wot Oi say."

Eugénie was feeling very nervous. Her conscience was bothering her for the first time. How could she have put Angela so completely out of her mind? Why, she was just as bad as André! How could she face her now? But face her she had to. She went down to the parlor where she found Angela sipping a glass of sherry. She looked so small, sitting in Harry's big chair. Her pale face was framed in a cloud of smoky dark hair. Her large, brown eyes looked sad but when she saw Eugénie, she smiled sweetly.

"Mrs. McCallum, it's good of you to see me. I took a chance that you might be here."

"How do you do, your ladyship? Is there anything I can do for you?" Eugénie asked nervously.

Angela smiled at her, a sad little smile. "Please, may I call you Eugénie?"

"Of course—please do." Eugénie was not prepared for what came next.

"Eugénie, I know my husband is in love with you," said Angela.

Eugénie gripped the arms of her chair and was about to protest, but Angela continued. "I think he was in love with you even on the day we got married. I didn't know, of course, it was you, but I did know that he didn't love me. But I loved him so much that I convinced myself that in time he would return my love. I really think he was beginning to care for me—and then we came out here and, of course, seeing you again brought it all back. I know now who you are."

"But . . . but how did you guess?" stammered Eugénie, too stunned even to attempt to dissemble.

"From the moment you walked into the drawing-room at the Governor's house that night, he thought only of you. I love him, Eugénie. God, how I love him! I know he is just a spoiled child, and perhaps my father and Lady Jerningham were right to cut him off and send him out here. They thought doing so might make a man of him. But I would have been content to live with that spoiled child, if only he loved me. I wouldn't let him come out here alone. I wanted to share everything with him, the good and the bad." She sighed. "Perhaps if we had a child, things might have been different. I don't really know. I only know that he is my life. But because his happiness means more to me than anything else in the world, I have decided to return to England and leave him here with you."

Eugénie was speechless. What unselfish love this woman was capable of! How sweet and gentle she was and oh, how she must have suffered being married to André, loving him and yet knowing her love was not returned! Eugénie felt so ashamed. Words came tumbling from her lips unbidden, but they came from the heart.

"Angela, you're wrong. Don't give him up. I don't think he knows what love is. Oh yes, I have loved him since I was a little girl, but I know now you are what he needs. I have no doubt about it. Harry told me once that I was in love with a dream, and perhaps he was right. I think deep down I knew we weren't right for each other, but I just wouldn't let go of my romantic delusions."

"Do you really mean that, Eugénie? You aren't just saying it to make me feel better or because you feel guilty?" Angela whispered, trembling.

When she answered, Eugénie knew that she meant every word she uttered. "Yes, Angela. I promise you I do. Someday I hope you will find it in your heart to forgive me. And I pray that God will forgive me for lusting for another woman's husband."

Angela stood up gracefully and walked over to Eugénie and embraced her with tears in her lovely eyes.

"Eugénie, there is nothing to forgive."

They talked for about an hour. Mag had her ear to the parlor door but couldn't hear a thing, much to her chagrin. Harry found her there.

"Mag, shame on you! Come away from that door at once!"

"Oi can't 'ear a bloomin' thing, so Oi might as well," said Mag sadly.

Their eyes were filled with curiosity when Eugénie and Angela finally came out arm in arm. They were even more flabbergasted when they saw them embrace as Angela was leaving. They said nothing, even though they were bursting to know what had gone on. Harry's warning look shut Mag up before she got a chance to question Eugénie. They were deeply worried about her, though, and when she left for home the next day, Mag spoke up.

"Eugénie, luv, ye know 'Arry and me are 'ere if ye need to talk . . ."

Eugénie hugged her. "Yes, I know and I love you dearly. I don't know what I would do without you both. Don't worry about me, Mag, I feel wonderful!"

And she left them with their curiosity unsatisfied.

Chapter 30

Eugénie returned to "Bannion." A few days later she was sitting on the veranda enjoying the peace and quiet. Marie and Cassie had taken little David to Sydney to do some shopping. But her peace was broken by thoughts of André and what she would say to him when she saw him again. Suddenly she heard a shout and saw Manaka running frantically towards her, gesturing wildly.

"Come quick, Madami! Come quick! Doctor Paul, he is fighting with long, flashing knives down by Dingo Swamp!"

Eugénie felt sick with fear. "My God! Get my horse, Manaka. Don't bother with a saddle—please follow with the wagon."

He brought Sultan to her and she jumped on his back. Her face was drained of color. If anything happened to Paul! Sultan went like the wind, a great black streak against the skyline.

At Dingo Swamp, the trees grew so close together they cast an eerie gloom across the place. It was said the area was haunted, and indeed it seemed so. Not a breeze blew nor a bird twittered. The silence was broken only by the harsh voice of Captain Dudley as he glared at Paul and snared, "To the death, you son of a whore!"

He plunged into immediate attack, viciously and with

murder in his heart. Paul stayed cool and parried each of Dudley's thrusts with ease. Then he too began to attack. Dudley was no novice at fencing, but lacked finesse. They matched blow for blow until Paul, seeing an opening, thrust. Blood oozed from Dudley's shoulder. He bellowed in rage and then swung his heavy cutlass with both hands. Their swords locked above their heads and for a moment they stared into each other's eyes, every muscle strained. Then they were free of each other. Though both were weary, hatred spurred them on. Dudley thrust and Paul parried. Suddenly Paul thrust and his sword found flesh in the stomach of Captain Dudley. Dudley fell back and Paul, seeing he was mortally wounded, threw down his sword in disgust and walked away. He was disgusted at himself, a doctor, who had sworn to preserve life.

His anger had cooled and he was about to go back and care for Dudley when he heard a maniacal scream, and the next moment felt the cold touch of steel penetrating his chest. He collapsed in agony and through the swirling blackness of oncoming unconsciousness he waited for Dudley to finish the deed. He did not know that Dudley had used his last ounce of life to deliver that blow and was at that very moment a dying man.

It was thus that Eugénie found Paul. She ran to him with fear in her heart. His face was grey under his tan and blood flowed from an ugly wound close to his heart. Fearfully she felt for his pulse. It was very feeble but at least he was still alive. She looked around for Manaka. "Where is he? Where is he?" She was frantic. She knew she had to get Paul home quickly.

She tore his shirt and tried to staunch the blood. Her tears flowed so fast that they mixed with the blood from that beloved body.

Manaka arrived at last with the wagon, and gently he lifted Paul and placed him on a pile of blankets in the wagon. Eugénie cradled his head in her lap.

"Oh Paul, please don't die," she cried. Then she pointed to Dudley's body. "Manaka, you'd better check on him."

Manaka shook his head. "Ugly one dead, Madami."

"Then for God's sake let's go! Quickly, Manaka!"

When they finally reached "Bannion," Manaka carried Paul into Eugénie's bedroom. She bathed the ugly wound and bandaged it. Then she turned to Manaka.

"Manaka, would you fetch Missy Gordon? I'm so afraid . . ."

She yelled frantically for Ben Dixon and he came running.

"Oh Ben, Dr. Gordon has been wounded. Please hurry—ride into Sydney and fetch Dr. White. Tell him Lord Gordon's life depends on him!"

She ordered two of the men to bring Dudley's body back to the farm. She'd have to think of something to do with the corpse when Manaka got back. Paul could be in serious trouble, for duelling was frowned upon even in New South Wales.

Eugénie hurried back to the bedroom. Paul was sweating and muttering feverishly. She went to the kitchen and put some of her special herbs on to boil. When the concoction had boiled down enough, she made a poultice of the herbs and poured the water in a mug. She was placing the third poultice on the wound when Aunt Aggie hobbled in on Manaka's arm. The poor old lady had fallen from a ladder several weeks ago and had fractured her leg. Under protest, Manaka carried her up the steps to the house. Eugénie heard her demanding voice shouting, "Take me to Paul at once!"

Eugénie came to the head of the stairs. "Manaka, bring Missy Gordon up here."

Manaka carried Aggie Gordon up the stairs and placed her on a chaise in the bedroom. Eugénie's heart went out to her when she saw how tenderly and how anxiously she looked at her beloved nephew.

"What happened?" Aunt Aggie asked tersely.

"He met with Captain Dudley. There was a duel— Manaka saw them and came to tell me, but I was too late."

Aunt Aggie saw tears in the girl's eyes and noticed how pale she looked, so she said in her brusque fashion, "There, there, girl, tears aren't going to help. You are going to save him, I know you are. I'll just sit here and be quiet for once."

Eugénie checked the poultice. The bleeding had stopped but Paul was still delirious. She wrung a cloth out in cold water and laid it across his forehead. Just then she heard the men coming back with Dudley's body. "Miss Gordon, I must see to Captain Dudley's body. I'll be back soon. Call if you need me."

She went out to the men and glanced at their burden. She couldn't make up her mind what to do. Finally she ordered, "Take the body to the far barn. It's getting dark . . ."

Suddenly she heard Aunt Aggie screaming. "Eugénie! Eugénie, girl! Come quickly!"

Her heart jumped. *"Mon Dieu!* He mustn't be dead. It can't happen!"

She ran to the bedroom to find Paul sitting up in bed and vomiting on the floor. He looked at her for a second with a look of deep humiliation, tried to speak, but sank back exhausted onto the bed. Aunt Aggie was crying quietly, tears trickling down her loving face.

"Oh, if only I could help you, child." For the first time she spoke gently to Eugénie.

"Miss Gordon, I'm just so glad you're here. Your presence is comfort and help enough to me," Eugénie responded.

She knelt and cleaned up the mess. The smell was nauseating. Then she put a basin near the bed in case he might vomit again and once more wiped the sweat from his body.

All through the night she stayed by his side. Once or twice he had to vomit and she was there with the basin, helping him sit up, speaking softly to him, encouraging him to live. She made another poultice and this time forced him to drink some of the liquid. The night passed slowly and agonizingly. He was retching with such violence that she was afraid he would reopen the wound. She was exhausted and her eyes ached.

The mists of a second night gathered around them. Eugénie hadn't left Paul's side for more than a minute or two, and then only to fetch fresh water or fresh linen. Manaka tended to her needs and Miss Gordon's, though they ate little. Towards morning of the second night he seemed better and slept quietly. Eugénie sat motionless and looked at his dear face. By now she knew every line and furrow. She felt such an overpowering tenderness for this man as she thought of all they had been through together. It was so strange how she could always talk so easily to Paul and even more strange how he listened so patiently and somehow understood. Then why did they always seem to irritate each other so? She had missed him these past months. She hadn't even had the chance to apologize to him after the Lieutenant Governor's dinner. Overcome with emotion, she sank to her knees and prayed, "Oh, dear Holy Mother, take Paul under your protection and give him back his strength. He has done so much for others—oh, please, I beg of you, restore him to health! I cannot bear to see him suffer!''

Aunt Aggie, who had dozed fitfully throughout the night, heard the girl's prayer. She called Eugénie to come to her and then held out her arms. Eugénie ran to her and Aunt Aggie held her. Eugénie cried great tears of pain until she had no more left to shed.

"There, there child. He will be all right, I know it. You must care a great deal for him, my dear.''

"Oh, Miss Gordon, he is so good, and even though he makes me dreadfully angry at times, there is no one I respect more,'' Eugénie sobbed.

Aunt Aggie felt like telling Eugénie how much Paul loved her, but saw that it would do no good. She was convinced that Eugénie loved Paul, but the child didn't know it, so obsessed was she with that spoiled André de Varney. No, she wouldn't interfere—it might only make things worse.

Morning came and Eugénie was fixing Paul's bed-clothes when she became aware that he was watching her. She looked at him concernedly but her concern rapidly turned to joy. His eyes were clear. The fever was gone. He smiled warmly at her. "Bless you, my love.''

She clasped his hands and hot tears splashed on to them.

"Oh, Paul!''

They stayed like that for several moments; then he drifted back to sleep.

"Aunt Aggie!'' she cried, hurrying to where the old lady had been dozing fitfully in her chair.

"What is it, child? Is something wrong?''

"He's going to be well! He's going to live! The fever is gone!''

"Thank God! Now, child, you must get some rest," Aunt Aggie said firmly.

"Later. He might wake up and need me. Perhaps this afternoon—Now let me fix some breakfast for us both, and I shall make soup for Paul."

That afternoon as Eugénie was sitting by the bed she fell asleep in spite of herself. Aunt Aggie was pleased. The poor girl needed rest. Paul awoke and gazed lovingly at Eugénie. He was startled by Aunt Aggie saying, "You love that girl, don't you?"

"Aunt Aggie, you surprised me! What did you say?"

"You heard me, young man. You might be wounded, but there's nothing wrong with your hearing," she snapped.

"I always suspected you were a witch. Yes, God help me, I love her more than my life."

"Then what are you going to do about it? I am convinced she loves you, but the foolish child just doesn't realize it."

"Aunt Aggie, she has been in love with André de Varney since she was a mere child. How can you possibly think that she could love me?" Paul sighed.

"Humph! Are you afraid of trying? I never thought you were lacking in courage Paul, but now it seems you are."

Their conversation was cut short when Eugénie awoke.

"Oh, Paul, you're awake! Are you feeling better?" she asked anxiously.

"Yes, much better, thanks to you."

They heard excited voices and with a rush Marie, Moll and the baby, along with Dr. White, came into the bedroom.

"Wot's the matter, luv?" exclaimed Moll.

"Well, well, it looks like I made this trip for nothing, Paul," joked Dr. White. "You look as though you've been well taken care of."

"Sorry, old chap," said Paul with a weak smile.

"I'm sorry too, Dr. White, but we despaired of his life at first," Eugénie added.

"What happened, Paul?" the doctor asked.

"I went into Sydney on business. While I was there, I spotted that devil Dudley sauntering around. The very sight of him enraged me, and when he took his whip and started lashing one of the convicts, I'm afraid I lost control. I called him out. You know the rest."

"You called him out without any provocation?"

"I had all the provocation I needed on that trip out from England. That fiend deserved to die. By the way, where is he?"

They all looked at Eugénie questioningly.

"He's in the barn. I'm afraid I quite forgot about him," Eugénie admitted.

"This is very serious, Paul," said Dr. White frowning. "Crose isn't going to like this. I'd advise you to have Manaka take him into the bush and leave him there. By the time he's found, there'll be no way to prove how he died. He was a bad lot and I'm sure no one will shed any tears over his demise."

Paul shook his head. "I can't do that. Would you mind taking his body back with you? Tell Crose I'll come in as soon as I'm able. How long would you say it will take before I'm fit to travel?"

"About six weeks. You ought to be well on your feet by then. You are not to attempt to get out of bed for at least a week. If Mrs. McCallum doesn't mind, you should stay here for at least two weeks until that wound is on the mend," the doctor said. "Now then Moll, give me a drop of rum and I'll be on my way. Can Manaka come back with me?"

"Oh, Dr. White, can't you spend the night? That is a lot of travelling for one day and it will be getting dark in a few hours," said Eugénie.

"I'd like to, dear, but Mrs. Danvers is due any minute and I'm afraid she's not going to have an easy labor. I have a strong suspicion she might have twins."

It wasn't until Dr. White had swilled down his rum and was on his way back to Sydney that Eugénie turned to Moll.

"What are you doing here, Moll? Where's Cassie?"

"When Oi 'eard wot was goin' on out 'ere Oi says to Cassie, 'Cassie, stay out 'ere at Parramatta and let me go back in yer place." Cassie wasn't too agreeable, but Oi convinced 'er. And now, ducks, ye are goin' to 'ave a wash and get into bed." She turned her steely eyes on Miss Aggie Gordon. "And so are ye, Miss Gordon."

Eugénie and Aunt Aggie were too tired to protest. Paul had fallen asleep again and they knew Marie and Moll could take care of him now.

A week passed and Paul was at last able to get out of bed. Rachel, Robert and little Andrew Gordon Crandell came to visit. Close behind them came Mag and Harry. Little Andrew begged to have a party, and so after dinner Harry got out his pipe and made himself comfortable and Marie sat at the piano. They sang songs and tapped their feet. Little Andrew went up to Eugénie and bowed gracefully.

"Aunt Eugénie, I would be honored if you would give me the pleasure of this dance," he said solemnly.

" 'Ere—listen to the child, Mag!" cried Moll with a laugh.

" 'E's not a child—'e's a little man cut short," Mag said, and everyone laughed.

Eugénie curtsied. "Sir, it is my pleasure."

Marie played a minuet and Paul and the others watched fondly. Eugénie was so happy to have all her dear friends around her. They played with baby David and listened patiently to little Andrew's happy chatter.

The Crandells and the Boggs stayed a few days and then returned to their own homes. After they had said their goodbyes, Eugénie left the house and took a walk by the river. She wanted to be alone for a while. Paul saw her leave and followed her. Aunt Aggie was dozing and the others were busy so no one noticed his departure.

It was an unusually beautiful day for that time of year, perhaps a little chilly, but the sky was dotted with soft white clouds. Eugénie was lying in the grass chewing on a blade and watching the clouds chase each other across the sky. She didn't hear Paul approach and wasn't aware of his presence until his shadow fell across her. Her heart fluttered strangely. She could smell the manly scent of him and the marvellous smell of leather from his boots. She held up her hand to him and he sat down beside her. She felt slightly dizzy and a nameless longing took possession of her. Abruptly she stood up and walked towards the river. Paul followed her. His heart was pounding in unison with every emotion that was running through his body and mind. She turned to him and they gazed at one another for what seemed an eternity. Then she swayed towards him. He reached out to her and drew her close. She could feel his powerful muscles against her body. Her mouth parted to receive his kiss and for a few minutes she was lost to time as she felt herself responding to him. Both were filled with a wonderful, aching need for each other.

Then she pulled away from him, stunned and confused. How could she feel like this? Was she not in love with André? Her legs felt weak and she was trembling. Paul, who had deliberately avoided Eugénie ever since the Lieutenant Governor's dinner, now felt his self-control slipping away. He gave in to the violent, savage, totally selfish emotions that now possessed him, drawing her to him in a frenzy of passion, fondling her breasts, kissing her neck, her lips and her eyelids. Then through the mist that enveloped him he heard her cry out, "Paul! Paul! Stop, oh please, stop!"

It was like a cold splash of water. Grimly he walked away, leaving Eugénie shaken to the very depths of her soul. She watched him depart and marvelled at how he had filled her with such an extraordinary, irrational sense of delirium. Why did she feel like this? Could it be possible that she loved Paul? She knew the answer at once and her heart was filled with a joy she had never known before in her entire life. She wanted to rush after him, hold him and shower him with kisses, but she had to see André again. She had to be sure that she really did not love him, because all at once she was afraid that she had denied her love for him out of pity for Angela. Perhaps what she now felt for Paul was mere physical passion. She had loved André long before they had even shared a kiss. All at once she couldn't face Paul. She stayed by the river for several hours, trying to get her emotions sorted out. But she need not have worried, for by the time she got home, Paul and Aunt Aggie had left for their own home.

Late the following afternoon, André rode out to "Bannion." Eugénie heard his horse before he had a chance to dismount and she ran to meet him.

"André, wait. I'll get Sultan and ride with you for a while. I must talk to you," she said breathlessly.

They rode side by side for a few miles in silence and then dismounted. André rushed to Eugénie and took her in his arms. He kissed her but she felt absolutely nothing. She knew then, with a total certainty, that it was Paul she really loved and probably always had. She felt like singing, so deliriously happy she was.

André was puzzled when he felt no response from Eugénie. "What's the matter? Eugénie, darling, why are you so cold to me? Oh, *chérie,* I love you madly! I always have. I know now that we were always meant for each other."

"Stop it, André! Stop it right now. You don't even know the meaning of love."

"Darling, I don't understand."

"I have finally come to my senses after all these years. We were never meant for each other. You, André, have a wife—one, I think, who is far too good for you. You are a weak creature, André. First you leaned on me, then on Angela's money. Your father would not have been proud of you. Perhaps you are not fully to blame, though. You were spoiled by your family and I too spoiled you. You could do no wrong in my eyes. I was too blinded by my love to see you as you really were. But Angela loves you in spite of what you are and it is much more than you deserve. I think the time has come, André de Varney, for you to grow up! If you can't be a man for your own sake, then do it for Angela and for your father's memory. He was an honorable, brave man and he deserves a son who will make his name one to be proud of."

André listened in amazement, completely stunned and baffled by Eugénie's tirade.

"Eugénie, you can't mean it," he faltered.

"Oh, yes I do. You disgust me, André, and I have no longer any desire to pursue our friendship. If I were you, I'd take your darling wife and go back to England to the life you are best suited for. If you don't gamble and try very hard to make yourself useful, I am sure Angela's family and Lady Jerningham will be only too glad to welcome you back to the fold."

"Eugénie!" André groaned, reaching for her once again.

"Say no more, André. It's best we say goodbye now. I wish you well."

Her eyes softened as she looked at him, for he looked so helpless. He was a child in so many ways, but it was high time for him to leave the nest. It was getting dark and she had but one thought—to find Paul and tell him how much she loved him and needed him.

Without another word she climbed into the saddle and rode at a gallop for the Gordon farm. Aunt Aggie was surprised to see her, but happy.

"Come in, child. What brings you here at this late hour?" she asked.

"Aunt Aggie, where is Paul? I must see him!"

"He's not here," the old lady said. "He left this morning for Sydney."

"But he's not well enough," Eugénie cried.

"Nevertheless, he wanted to go and I couldn't stop him."

Eugénie's heart sank. "When will he be back?" she asked. "I must see him. Oh, Aunt Aggie, I love him! I love him so much. I never dreamt life could be like this."

Aunt Aggie was considerably surprised, and quite upset for Paul's sake. The day they left "Bannion" in such a hurry, Paul had told her there was no hope for him with Eugénie and he was determined to put her out of his mind.

"Eugénie, he's going to England, to stand trial for

the death of Captain Dudley. His ship sails on the morning tide. Oh, child, you've got to try and reach him. If he sails thinking there is no chance of your ever loving him, it might be too late. His last words to me, bitterly spoken, were that he might look for a wife in England since he needs an heir.''

"I must get there in time! I must!" cried Eugénie. This was certainly not what she had expected to hear.

"I'll ask Bill Larsen to go with you."

"Oh, please do. I must say I'm a little nervous about riding by myself at night. And could you send a message to 'Bannion'? I don't want to worry them."

Bella prepared some food for them to eat on the way. When everything was ready for their departure, Aunt Aggie took Eugénie in her arms. "God speed, my dear. I shall pray that you get there in time."

Eugénie and Bill Larsen rode as fast as they could, but since it was dangerous to go too fast at night they made little progress. Eugénie was filled with anxiety. Had she forfeited Paul's love because of her obsession with André? If she had lost Paul, life would have very little meaning for her. If it wasn't for Kathleen's baby, she was sure she wouldn't want to live.

The sun had already risen high in the sky when they reached Sydney. They rushed to the wharf and got there just in time to see the ship sailing out of the harbor. Eugénie watched with tears in her eyes until it disappeared over the horizon.

The months that followed Paul's departure for England were empty ones for Eugénie. Life seemed pointless and empty. She missed his steady gaze and reassuring strength. She even missed his stern admonitions when she had done something he disapproved of. She was all too aware that she missed him in a thousand different ways. She longed for the months to pass and at the same time feared that he would marry someone else. It was fortunate that she didn't realize it would be two long years before Paul would set foot in New South Wales again.

Eugénie was haunted by nightmares that he might not come back at all or, even worse, that he would bring back a wife. She tried to fill the endless days with work or occupied herself with little David. But the long nights were another matter. Unable to sleep, she often wandered down to the bank of the river. She ached with loneliness. A painful, desperate longing for him consumed her. She remembered all too well those hypnotic, strange yellow eyes of his, his strong jaw, his tanned skin and above all his wonderful voice. She felt herself grow weak when she remembered his fingers touching her breasts—those long, gentle fingers. She remembered vividly the taste of his mouth when they kissed. Oh, why hadn't she realized all this when he was here? What a fool she had been! She tortured herself with her thoughts but found it was even more painful not to think of him, not to remember. Without Paul, she realized, she was incomplete.

December 27, 1792—"Bannion," New South Wales
Another Christmas has gone by. We had a big party at "Bannion" for all our friends. It was little David's first Christmas and everyone showered gifts upon him, though he's a bit young yet to appreciate them. I should have been happy surrounded by so much love, but . . .
I can't believe I've been such a fool. I had a gem of love right in the palm of my hand and I allowed myself to be dazzled by a pale imitation. So much time has been wasted, and now my love is far across the sea.
I am scourged by the thought that he might never know how much I love him. It torments me night and day. I could write and let him know, but my pride stands

in the way. I lie in bed at night and will my love to speed
across the miles and compel him to realize that I long for
him every moment of the day and night.

   Dear Father in Heaven, I know I'm not worthy, but
please have pity on me and send Paul back to my arms.

   Only one bright spot occurred in those long months to
make Eugénie feel that perhaps all hope was not dead.
Angela and André had left for England. Before she left,
Angela had ridden out to "Bannion" to say goodbye
and her face was a joy to behold. Apparently Eugénie's
words had made a difference to André, and he had
promised Angela to do his best to make his marriage a
success.

Chapter 31

Fourteen long, miserable months went by and at last Aunt Aggie received a letter from Paul, saying that he had been pardoned for the death of Captain Dudley and that he would be sailing soon for home. He had to buy medical supplies and equipment and was bringing Aunt Aggie a very special surprise. He asked her to tell Eugénie that Uncle Charles sent his best wishes. That was all. Aunt Aggie folded the letter and looked at Eugénie with pity.

"That's it, my dear. Not much of a letter, I'm afraid."

"Oh, but Aunt Aggie, he's coming home at last! I can't wait—and yet I'm so afraid that it might be too late for us," sighed Eugénie.

"I pray that it won't be my dear," Aunt Aggie said. "You two are perfect for each other."

Feeling very woebegone and afraid to hope, Eugénie needed to confide in Mag and Harry. Now that Paul was definitely coming back to New South Wales, she was in need of support from those two dear people who had taken the place of her parents, so without further delay she rode to town.

They were relaxing after a good meal when Eugénie brought up the subject of Paul.

"Aunt Aggie Gordon had a letter from Paul. He's coming home."

Harry looked at her sharply.

"Is he now girl? How do you feel about that?"

"I love him. I know that now. In fact, I've known it for many, many months," she said.

"Oh, luv! Oi'm so 'appy fer ye! Oi thought ye'd never get over that André!"

Mag jumped up and gave Eugénie a loving kiss.

Harry puffed on his pipe calmly and admonished his wife, "Sit down, Mag. I think there's more to this."

"Unfortunately Harry, I'm afraid you're right. The last time we were together things didn't go at all well. I'm so afraid that whatever love he might have felt for me was permanently quenched that day. Still, I continue to hope. Oh, Harry, promise me you will watch for the ship from England and send me word at once. Will you do that for me? He's probably more than halfway home already, and I must be there to meet him the very minute he steps off the ship. Will you help me?"

"Of course I will, my dear. I'd like nothing better than to see you married to a good man like Paul Gordon. He's right for you, Eugénie. I only wish you had come to realize it sooner," Harry added with a sigh.

Eugénie stayed with her two dear friends for a week and then returned to "Bannion." She counted each day anxiously and wished they would pass more swiftly. The days would have been unbearably slow if it were not for the fact that it was spring. Eugénie was frantically busy with the sheep shearing from dawn to dusk and the problem of feeding the extra men she had hired. She spent her time running between Parramatta and "Bannion" helping where she could and keeping records. On November 27th while she was at "Bannion" absorbed in the task of preparing lunch for her hungry workers, Cassie rushed in with a letter from Harry. Feverishly Eugénie broke the seal and read:

> *Eugénie love,*
> *Come quickly. The ship has been sighted outside the cove. Due to the low tide it will not be able to sail into the harbor until morning. If you hurry you'll be here when it docks.*
>
>
>
> *Good luck,*
> *Harry.*
>
>

Eugénie turned to the older woman, her face glowing with excitement.

"Cassie, please take over here for me. I've got to go into Sydney at once! You'll just have to manage without me. Have one of the men saddle Sultan for me while I change and please tell the messenger to come in and wait. I'll ride back with him to Sydney."

They reached Sydney long after dark. It had been a long, hard ride so Eugénie went straight to bed. She slept badly, however, and her nerves were on edge when she awoke early the next morning. Mag had breakfast on the table when she came downstairs but every bite seemed to stick in her throat.

"Harry, can't we please go now?" she begged. "I'm too restless to sit here one moment longer."

Harry nodded and they walked to the wharf where they stood among the throngs of curious people watching the big ship sail in. Eugénie's heart quickened and she thought it would burst with joy when, after searching frantically for Paul, she at last saw his tall figure silhouetted against the morning sky. Then her heart seemed to stop beating, for she noticed that he was not alone. A young, dark-haired woman was standing by his side, gazing adoringly into Paul's face. When Paul put his arm around the girl, Eugénie was torn by such an assault of jealousy and longing that she almost fainted where she stood. She ran back to the tavern and sank down on her bed, sunk in utter misery and despair.

Harry watched Eugénie's departure in total astonishment, but when he saw Paul with the girl, he understood.

"Poor wee lamb," he whispered to himself.

He waited for the ship to dock and then went forward to meet Paul. Paul smiled with pleasure when he saw Harry and clasped his hand in friendship.

"Harry, how wonderful it is to be back! You are a sight for sore eyes. And now, allow me to present my sister, Ann Gordon. Ann dear, this is Harry Boggs, my good, dear friend."

Harry smiled at Ann Gordon, a wave of relief washing over him. "Your *sister,* you say. I'm certainly glad to hear that! Eugénie bolted like a wild colt when she saw her. Miss Gordon, may I say how very pleased I am to meet you. You're a bonnie lass."

Paul had turned quite pale. He grabbed Harry's arm.

"Harry, did you say Eugénie was here? Here to meet me?"

"Aye. She loves you, Paul. She's come to her senses at long last."

Paul gripped Harry by the shoulders. "Is this true? Are you sure?"

"Aye, lad, I'm sure. She told us herself, and her heart was shining from her eyes."

Ann turned to her brother. "Go to her, Paul. I'll walk with Mr. Boggs. Don't waste another minute. I am so anxious to meet your Eugénie."

"Where do you think she might be, Harry?" Paul asked frantically.

"Probably back at 'The Black Bear,' Harry told him.

Paul kissed his sister and ran all the way to the tavern. When he burst in the door, Mag was so carried away by her happiness at seeing him that she kissed him soundly. "She's upstairs in 'er room," she said, beaming from ear to ear.

He bounded up the stairs and found Eugénie lying on the bed, crying. He came slowly towards her.

"Go away, Harry, please," she moaned. "I want to be alone. He's married and I deserve it. I hope he'll be happy—but oh, I am so miserable! Please, please leave me alone!"

Paul smiled and his eyes were full of love. He whispered, "Eugénie."

She couldn't believe her ears. Then she turned her head and saw him. They looked at each other searchingly for a long, breathless moment, and then they were in each other's arms. Their lips meeting in a rapturous kiss.

"Oh, Eugénie, my dearest love, to think I had almost given up hope!" Paul sighed.

"Paul, I love you. I love you with all my heart. I want to go on saying it forever! But—" Eugénie pulled away, remembering. "But you're married! Why have you come to me? Where is your wife?"

Her lashes were wet, her eyes brimming with tears. She pulled away from Paul's embrace, but he held her firmly.

"I have no wife, my dearest. You and only you have filled my heart. Come with me and meet my sister, Ann."

They heard Harry calling to them. "Come down here you two!"

And so they did, their eyes shining with love. Paul immediately led Eugénie to where Ann was standing.

"Darling, this is my little sister, Ann. Ann, this is my

wonderful Eugénie," he said proudly.

Ann put her arms around Eugénie and kissed her sweetly. "I'm so happy for you. I'm sure you will both be very, very happy."

"Well, Oi 'ate to break this up but yer Aunt Aggie will be waitin', and ye'd best be on yer way, Paul Gordon," said Mag. "Ye'll 'ave a lifetime to be together. We're ridin' with ye. There'll be plans to make, and Oi'll not be left out. 'Arry, go see if Matthew can take over 'ere for a week or two," she ordered.

On the way, they picked up Moll at Parramatta, and when they reached the Gordon place, Paul had a quiet word with Eugénie.

"Darling, will you meet me tonight after dinner down by the river?"

"Oh, yes! It's the only place where we can be alone. Oh my dearest, how I do love you!"

"Until tonight, my darling."

Eugénie, Harry, Mag and Moll rode on towards "Bannion." They made very good time and Eugénie was in seventh heaven. Cassie and Marie were overjoyed to see them all ride in and had cooked a huge dinner. There was an air of contained excitement about the place. They ate and they laughed and even Cassie lost her habitually dour look. After dinner, when the baby was tucked up in bed and everyone had calmed down, Eugénie slipped away.

She saddled Sultan and led him out of the barn. Then quietly she mounted and walked him out of range of the house. The moon was shining and millions of stars above seemed to be twinkling their delight at her joy. Paul was waiting by the river when she arrived. He pulled her down off Sultan's back and held her close to him. The excitement in his blood grew. He touched her lips tenderly, intoxicated by their soft warmth. He stroked her hair and murmured endearments in her ear. The fire of passion spread through them both as he pressed his body to hers. She put her arms around his neck and drew him closer still. She could feel his heart pounding. She clasped him tighter and they kissed with all the passion that had been held in check for far too long.

Plans were made immediately for the wedding. Only families and closest friends were to be invited. The Rev. Johnson agreed to come out to "Bannion" to perform the ceremony. Harry was overjoyed when Eugénie asked him to give her away and Marie and Paul's sister Ann were to be bridesmaids. Paul and Eugénie felt that time had stopped. They longed for their wedding day, the day on which they would be one at last.

> *December 15, 1793—"Bannion"*
> *Today is my wedding day and it's a glorious one. The sky is cloudless and the sun is shining brightly. Everyone has arrived except for the Rev. Johnson and John MacArthur, but I expect they'll be here soon. I'm not nervous, but I am anxious. I'm so afraid that I won't make Paul happy. He is my life.*
> *I hear Mag coming now, so this will be the last time I write as Eugénie Fabré McCallum. My next entry will be sighed Eugénie Gordon—or perhaps I might keep Fabré. I don't feel guilty about dropping the name of McCallum, because we have little David to carry it on.*

Mag bounded into the room with her usual exuberance, followed by Marie carrying Eugénie's bouquet. They helped Eugénie dress in her white lace gown, and finally Mag put the finishing touches to her veil.

"There luv, ye never looked more beautiful!" She sniffed and happy tears started rolling down her cheeks.

"Mag, why in the world are you crying? Aren't you

393

happy for me?'' Eugénie asked affectionately.

Mag dabbed at her eyes. "Oh luv, Oi'm happy, but Oi feel like Oi'm losin' me own child!"

Eugénie's laughter pealed throughout the house. "Mag you're priceless, simply priceless! I'm not going anywhere. Things won't change very much. Besides, someday you might even have 'grandchildren' to worry about. You know dear, you're like a mother to me and nothing can ever change that."

Harry knocked at the door interrupting the tears and laughter. "Mag, will you get out here? Everyone's waiting," he called impatiently.

He paused when he saw Eugénie. "Oh, my dear, you couldn't look more lovely!" Eugénie took his arm and her feet seemed to glide across the floor and down the stairs.

A grotto of flowers had been erected on the front lawn and the Rev. Johnson clad in a white lawn surplus and white wig, waited there with a nervous Paul and an amused Robert, who was Paul's best man. All eyes were turned towards the house, waiting for the first sight of the bride.

At last Eugénie appeared, looking radiantly beautiful in her white lace dress and gauzy veil. A tiara of diamonds held her veil in place, a wedding gift from Aunt Aggie. Harry led Eugénie proudly towards Paul and he saw such a look of love and longing pass between them that he averted his eyes. No one should intrude on a tender moment like that. Marie and little Andrew, who was ring-bearer, took their places and a short time later, Paul and Eugénie were man and wife.

Shy but deliriously happy, they greeted their guests. Rachel and little Andrew hugged and kissed them both. Rachel had put on a little weight since the birth of Robert Jr., two months before, but looked the picture of contentment. Big Nan, dear, wonderful Nan, was almost in tears. She was holding little Bobby, as he was called, and that poor little mite squawked in protest as she squeezed him, so great was Nan's emotion.

"Aow, me precious girl! Ye've garn and done it. Oi dare say ye could 'ave done a lot worse," Nan told Eugénie with a grin.

"Why, thank you very much Mrs. Coward! And to think I thought you liked me!" Paul teased.

While Paul chatted with Nan, Eugénie looked around her at all the dear faces—Mag and Harry, Matthew Skinner and Moll; Marie and Patrick Curran. She wondered for the first time if there was an understanding between those two. Marie had been spending a lot of time at Parramatta lately . . . Then there was dear Aunt Aggie Gordon with Anna and Bella, Cassie and Ben Larsen, Dr. White and John MacArthur, and little David snuggled fast asleep in Robert's arms.

"How very lucky I am," she thought then with a pang, "If only Joséphine and Aunt and Uncle Brogard could be here too!"

"What are you thinking of, darling, to make you look so sad?" Paul asked anxiously.

Eugénie forced a smile. "I'm afraid I was thinking about my little sister Joséphine and my aunt and uncle. I wonder how they are—and the wonderful Dupons family who helped us to escape from France."

"Precious love, as soon as possible, I promise you we shall go and find them all. I want you to be happy, my darling. I love you so much, my beautiful Mrs. Gordon —or should I call you Lady Gordon?"

"Do you know Paul, I quite forgot about your being a lord," Eugénie confessed. "Somehow, in this country, a title doesn't mean very much, I've discovered."

For the next four hours the wedding party danced and sang, feasted and drank to the health of the bride and groom. It was well after dark when finally Paul seized Eugénie's hand.

"Come, love, come with me," he whispered. "They'll never miss us now."

Hand in hand, they stole away towards the river. There, lying in the grass under the starry sky, they kissed deeply and passionately. This time there was no restraint on either side. Eugénie felt her body responding to Paul's. Her mind and limbs were ablaze. Their bodies burned, sought and found each other, and in the sweet, silent dark, they became one flesh at last.

Later they lay in each other's arms, ecstatic in their love and filled with a wondrous peace. Under that star-sprinkled sky they planned for their future as lovers have always done, and as lovers will do until the end of time . . .